The McTavisl

Simon Alisby

Alisby Publishing

www.alisbypublishing.com

The McTavish Betrayal
An Alisby Publishing Book: ISBN 978-0-9573260-7-1

First Published in Great Britain by Alisby Publishing

Copyright © Simon Alisby 2024

Simon Alisby has asserted his right under the
Copyright, Designs and Patents Act 1988 to be
identified as the author of this work

This book is a work of fiction and, except in the case of
historical fact, any resemblance to actual persons, living or
dead, is purely coincidental.

All rights reserved.
This book is sold subject to the condition that it shall not,
by way of trade or otherwise, be lent, resold, hired out,
or otherwise circulated without the publisher's prior
consent in any form of binding or cover other than that
in which it is published and without a similar condition,
including this condition, being imposed on the
subsequent purchaser.

Alisby Publishing
PO Box 1323
Maidstone
ME15 9EE

Printed by
KDP

My thanks to Jo

Prologue

Lily stood at the edge of the loch watching the slow-moving ripples glide lethargically towards the shore. Little else was visible with fog shrouding the trees and obscuring the pathway to either side. There was no way of telling how she had come to be there, not without help and who was there to help her?

She raised her arms and studied them closely as the sleeves of her blouse rolled back. Her pale-white skin was transparent ... everything was transparent – her hands, her ground-hugging skirt, her body ... And it should have been cold, yet she could feel neither the crispness of the air nor the dampness of its moisture. It was all very odd. Nothing made any sense, nothing at all.

She listened: it was as quiet as the dead of night. There was no sound nor sign of movement: the shoreline flora was listless, the trees breathless, the air still. A spell had been cast that nothing seemed able to break and yet, as she continued to wait in that unworldly atmosphere, she could feel a presence, something on the water that was biding its time. And then, as if the presence had sensed its discovery, a slow, distant noise broke the spell.

Gradually the noise grew closer and louder until, as ethereal as everything else, a rowing boat eased through the fog into view. A cloaked figure glanced around, observed the woman standing on the shoreline, then turned the boat to point back the way it had come. With a gesture, Lily was invited to climb aboard.

Lily was uncertain what to do and did not move.

The figure pulled back the cloak's hood to reveal the face of a young woman. There was sorrow in her eyes as she stared in sullen silence. She forced a smile and beckoned Lily into the boat once again.

Lily relented, viewing the invitation as predestined – what other reason could there be for her sudden appearance on that pathway or for the manner in which she had been found? She stepped into the water feeling its resistance but not the bite of its cold. Once in the boat, she sat down opposite the young woman who, without a word, began to row back into the fog.

The unerring journey involved no conversation and lasted no more than ten minutes. They arrived at a small island where the boat was manoeuvred as before and its passenger allowed to step out. To Lily's surprise, the young woman did not follow. Instead, she stroked once, then twice, back into the fog and stopped.

Lily stepped from the water onto the shore and turned to face the boat. Her new acquaintance was aging quickly, no longer the young woman that had ferried her across, but someone already well into middle age. The smile had gone. Only the sadness remained in a fast-withering face.

'What are you doing?' Lily asked.

The woman did not reply. She remained morose, her brooding eyes fixed on her prisoner.

Lily took a couple of paces into the water. The shore fell sharply away. Without the boat, there was no escape.

'What are you doing?' Lily repeated more earnestly, once she had returned to dry land.

The woman, who now looked old, did not respond.

Lily sat down, crossed her legs and stared back. As the woman had brought her to the island for a reason, there seemed little choice but to be patient. One thing was certain though: this must be the afterlife. She was not dreaming, just plain dead, and if this was the spirit world, so be it. But why here? And why had this woman sought her out only to hold her captive? Lily had questions she needed answers to. Her harsh life had apparently ended in an early demise and the cruel separation from her only daughter. Maybe getting to know her fellow spirit could help safeguard her child's future, perhaps that was the purpose of her being there. And if, in the process, it helped to avenge herself against Death for his untimely intervention, so much the better. Vengeance, in one shape or form, for what life had thrown at her was well overdue.

Chapter 1

Jualth

(pron. Jewel-ff)

1894
'Och! At last, Daniel, I've never known a journey to take so long.' The jaded young woman slipped from her horse onto the hardened mud track, relieved that the discomforts of a wearisome day's ride were at last over. 'I wasn't born with enough padding in my backside to be stuck in the saddle for such a length of time.'

Daniel remained seated on the cart, loosely gripping the reins of two sturdy, but compliant, shire horses. He cast his eyes upon the contorting figure of the petite redhead as she proceeded to engineer life and feeling back into her body.

Bending to touch her toes, her long fine hair glided over her white blouse to all but embrace the dirt of her Scottish homeland. The ecstasy of taut muscles stretching and blood freely flowing once again, induced a satisfying groan. Straightening, she thrust her hips forward and growled as the tired, protesting stiffness surrendered its grip. Finally, she stretched skywards, her face first twisted in agony, then serene with pleasure.

'Daniel, *Daniel*. That is *so* much better.'

Daniel grunted in bemused agreement. 'Aye, did a lot for me as well, young lady. It's a rare delight to be accompanied by you or your sister on one of these trips – you're both shameless.'

The woman's youthful smile grew; such comments were taken as compliments. 'The delight will be for me alone for the rest of the summer. Lily, as you well know, will be grappling with the terrifying ordeals of motherhood.'

The discordant tones of a demanding infant would soon announce the emergence of a new generation within the McTavish clan. Lily's own cries, borne from days of frustrated inactivity, had already blessed the Highlands with a tirade of advance warning.

'How soon?' Daniel asked.

'Very. A week is probably pushing it. No time to hang around on this trip. I'll be straight back tomorrow.'

Daniel inhaled sharply, his features gripped by a generous show of concern for his fellow villagers. 'And what about all those admirers, the ones that seem barely able to survive during your long periods of absence?'

The thought ushered forth a muted but wicked laugh. 'Oh to be missed, Daniel. Think of the edge it will add to future visits.'

The genial cartman pushed up the peak of his cloth cap and scratched his forehead, ruminating like an old sage who had seen trouble before and felt its like brewing again: 'More than an edge – usually a brawl to receive whatever attention you care to mete out.'

'As I said, Daniel, I like to be missed.'

'Perhaps for the sake of peace in our community, you should take a leaf out of Lily's book and settle down.'

Jualth offered no such reassurance – where was the fun to be found in a peaceful, slumbering community? Instead, she led her mare around to the back of the cart and secured the reins to the wooden rail. The scent of a very special cargo rode a light, transitory breeze. It was lovingly inhaled as possessive fingers stretched out to gently stroke one of the darkened oak casks. The moment of parting had arrived, a loss that provided no warmth to the vendor. Sadly, fiscal needs governed the rights of ownership. Her eyes flicked up to the first-floor window of a cottage that stood as a sentry post to the main gate. Spying eyes had undoubtedly noted her arrival, but she saw no shape or shadow inside, only the reflection of the blue evening sky.

Jualth strolled back to the cartman's footrest. '"Peace in our community", Daniel?' She shook her head. 'No chance. I have a well-earned reputation to consider. My hand will not be given away meekly.'

Daniel grunted. He almost regretted making the suggestion, almost enough to leave it at that, but not quite. 'Are you sure there isn't one particular young man?'

'Not one, Daniel, *fifteen*, and all, at present, equally unworthy.'

'Then how will you decide between them or are you intending to marry the lot?'

It was a thought that evoked a mischievous smile from his companion. But Daniel would not be allowed to pry.

'My bones are telling me that trouble looms not far ahead,' the old sage declared.

'Those creaking bones of yours never stop talking. Their premonitions match the number of drams you've consumed to soothe their groans.'

'When *your* body starts complaining, you'll take all the sympathy *and* all the whisky you can get.'

For Daniel, youth was now as distant as the Ice Age and the crisis that was middle age embraced and dealt with. He had lived in Brethna and been a cartman and long-term employee of its distillery all his life. Casks of pure malt whisky nestled in the back of his cart, a product of a small, near-inaccessible distillery hidden in the hills to the east. Even with an early start and only the briefest of stops, a hot and sunny day had resulted in their late afternoon arrival.

Jualth opened the gates and bade him enter. 'I'll catch up with you later,' she called out.

Daniel tipped his cap as the cart trundled forward along the gentle pitch of a track that led to the bonded warehouse. Jualth secured the gates and stood momentarily to watch her precious whisky wheeled away. The cart caught the attention of a large black cat that, in its role as distillery protector, cautiously shadowed the new arrival from the side.

Jualth took a few short paces to the left and skipped up a couple of steps to the door of an inauspicious-looking wooden hut that lay on the opposite side of the entrance to the main office. A fleeting play of knuckles upon the door was enough to announce her presence. Pushing her way in, she stood radiating warmth towards a person that demanded both respect and, as far as Jualth and her sister were concerned, much love too. Sitting in the hut's solitary room at its sole desk, mulling over important figures, was Arthur Whibley – the Excise officer.

'Arthur, fancy finding you in your little hut,' Jualth said cheekily. The door closed with encouragement from the well-sprung heel of her boot. She walked round the desk, kissed him fondly on each rosy cheek, then pulled up a chair to his side. 'Missed me?' she asked.

One moment of Jualth's company in the colourless, sedentary workplace was enough to transform Arthur Whibley's officious world into an agreeable heaven. Maintaining a semblance of authority when he could all but feel the warmth emanating from his young admirer was not easy. 'And if I were to say no?'

Jualth gasped. 'Arthur! You know how much that would hurt.'

Arthur's cheeks began to glow even brighter. 'In which case, I will not lie. Having one of my two favourite young ladies sitting in such close proximity is not a custom someone in my position can normally expect.'

'Ah, but you're no ordinary *someone*, otherwise neither Lily nor myself would possess such great affection for you.'

Arthur raised an eyebrow that very nearly touched the panelled ceiling. 'And if I'm not mistaken, the reason for that *great affection* just rumbled past my front door.'

Jualth smiled endearingly. 'I did not come alone, I must admit, but if I had I would still be in the exact same position as I find myself now.' She reached up and kissed the top of Arthur's middle-aged hairless dome, another unmistakeable sign of affection. 'If only my mother were still alive. You two would have made a perfect match.'

The Excise officer emitted a pained sigh of distant loss: 'She used to declare undying affection as well.'

'I know she did and if you did choose to come and visit us one day, you know how welcome you'd be.'

Arthur felt touched by an offer frequently made but regretted that circumstances made it an impossible invitation to accept. He heard himself uttering the usual excuse, 'You know how it is, having time off with so much to take care of …'

Jualth admired his resolve. 'I understand, work comes first, an admirable quality that I shall raise a glass to at the Whisky Makers' Arms tonight.'

Mention of the establishment that would provide the stage for Jualth's evening entertainment jolted Arthur's memory. He had worrisome news to impart: 'We have a visitor at the inn, have you heard?'

Jualth leant back, her eyes interrogating his concerned countenance. For the first time since her arrival, the smile disappeared. Visitors in Brethna were not uncommon, so what merited the need to mention this one?

'A tall, dark-haired man with a southern accent,' Arthur told her.

'England?'

'London, so I'm led to believe.'

'That's quite a long way to come. How old?'

'Thirty. Maybe a bit more.'

'A spy?'

'Hard to say. He listened attentively on his guided tour, by all accounts, and asked what questions he had a mind to, but he has one of those guarded demeanours, the type that gives little away.'

'Aloof?'

'No. I'd say respectful and educated. He seems knowledgeable about his whisky.'

Jualth paused to think: a traveller taking his time to pass through who appeared to be a long way from home. That was the bit she did not like, the *long way from home* bit. 'Sure he's not one of your lot, Arthur?'

Arthur seemed reluctant to commit. 'Not that he's disclosed. He should have done so straightaway if it was an official visit.'

'Should have?' She found the uncertainty in his voice disquieting. It paid to be vigilant at all times. 'I shall have to seek him out this evening and discover what I can. And if I find out he's nothing to worry about, tall and dark doesn't sound at all disagreeable. It will aid my cause no end.'

Noticing Arthur's puzzled look, the smile returned to her face. 'Ask Daniel,' she said. 'He has a notion of what I'm up to.'

The name of the cartman stirred the Excise officer into belated action. 'And speaking of Daniel, I think we'd better get down to business.'

'Of course,' Jualth agreed. With her papers miraculously appearing from a hidden pocket concealed within her inner clothing, she moved the chair a respectable distance to the side and took the opportunity to despair Arthur's working conditions whilst she waited. The hut was confining, a government sentry post to all that left and entered the premises, plain but functional with cabinets and shelves full of books and folios that went with the job. Summer warmth made it reasonably habitable, but in the winter a small stove was all that kept the occupant from freezing.

Arthur carefully scrutinised the papers, allowing not even their warmth to distract him. The matter at hand was of the utmost importance, not least because it strayed beyond the permitted procedures he had sworn to uphold. If found out, ruinous consequences would befall all parties. So despite the presence of a twenty-year-old he was deeply fond of, Arthur kept his mind firmly on the delivery notes.

A key from his right-hand top drawer unlocked a cabinet to the side of the desk. It yielded a familiar folio. The Excise officer relocked the cabinet, pocketed the keys and returned to his desk to make light, graphite entries. His job was a simple one: to liaise with the distillery boss to make the Kvairen whisky Jualth brought with her look like a product of Brethna. In practical terms, this required a gap in the production process, the necessary ingredients from Brethna's in-house store secretively migrating to the Kvairen Distillery and a volume of water – equal to that shown in Arthur's folio – leaked into Brethna's adjacent stream. If done properly, any subsequent inspection would then be unable to detect the subterfuge.

When Arthur had finished, the delivery notes were locked away and a long measuring implement removed from its cover in the corner. 'To the bonded warehouse before nimble feet and quick minds are tempted to remove valuable cargo,' he declared.

Outside, they made their way along a slightly curved track towards the second of two bonded warehouses. Jualth sensed the searing glare of eyes emanating from the first floor of the main office. She did not turn to look; it was far too early to acknowledge the presence of authority. Jualth traditionally left her meeting with the distillery boss to the very end.

The Brethna Distillery was built on a far larger scale than her own as it distilled, blended and also stored part of the end product. Beyond its two sentry posts the track split: ahead towards the river and, to the right, up a shallow incline to outer stables and fields for grazing. An unkempt wooden fence that ringed the distillery marked its boundaries.

A workshop stood between the perimeter fence and the track, with a bonded warehouse to either side. Several whistles and greetings were shouted in the direction of Arthur's companion as they passed the open doors. All offenders were content to receive a wave in return for knowing that each had a date at the inn later that evening.

Beyond the workshop stood the single-floored stone building of the original bonded warehouse, with a small wooden fire hut between it and the river. They found Daniel watching the remainder of the casks being unloaded. It did not take long – the Kvairen Distillery output was not great.

The agreement between Brethna and Kvairen, to supply malt whisky in exchange for materials and sufficient cash on the side, suited both parties. The deal was clandestine and carefully guarded by the villagers. It did no recognisable harm, only considerable good to those lucky enough to sample its blend.

Once unloaded, each cask was branded and then Arthur got to work, dipping for quantity and alcohol content. Jualth had witnessed the official process many times; it never varied and neither did the results. She left Arthur in trust and, with her grey mare, accompanied Daniel and the empty cart up a wide cobbled track to the stables. The track was one of several that ran parallel to the stream and separated the main buildings, starting with the granary and drying house closest to the river and finishing with the blending rooms closest to the main gate.

'Arthur tells me we have company staying at the inn,' Jualth remarked. 'You didn't mention it.'

'I didn't expect him to still be here,' Daniel said, sounding surprised. The person in question had arrived a couple of days before the cartman had left. 'What did Arthur say?'

'That he's from London.'

'*London*. Then he has travelled a considerable distance.'

'That's what I said. He couldn't journey much farther on our wee island.'

Daniel noted the raised guard, the discovery of an unknown signature in the register. 'A traveller or something more?'

'Undecided. Arthur thinks he's okay but allows doubt to hang in the air. I shall interrogate him myself this evening.'

'Will you not be busy this evening?'

Jualth chuckled and attempted to make light of Daniel's concern: 'Even busier than I thought. Arthur has painted a picture of a tall, dark, mysterious stranger and I'm betting he's a handsome one at that.'

'Jualth, you have no time for this person,' Daniel warned. 'Arthur is a worrier and with good reason, the risks he takes on your behalf. If he's almost certain then we're in no danger, so make better use of your time.'

Jualth smiled endearingly at the anxious cartman. 'You know, Daniel, if I had a dad, I'd want him to be just like you, always looking out for me, always telling me off, but knowing full well I'll do as I please all the same.'

Daniel scoffed at the very thought. 'One daughter is enough for me. Now I have a granddaughter to worry about and that's another reason I'd like you to settle down. The men from hereabouts need to get their heads straight and to start looking for a less exciting future.'

Jualth laughed. 'Imagine, Daniel, me as a model wife and mother.' She shook her head. 'No, I couldn't settle for a drab life of endless dullness.'

'Lily's trying.'

'But she will not succeed; we're too much alike. If there's nothing happening, we will make it happen.'

They reached the stables. The cart was housed in its shed, and the horses fed and groomed. Daniel accompanied Jualth to the main gate and, with a promise to meet up later, departed for his cottage.

Jualth returned to the Excise hut and waited whilst Arthur made a record of his notes. One last duty lay ahead before she could follow Daniel into the picturesque village of Brethna. When Arthur had finished, his entries were checked and agreed. He was then lovingly hugged and left in peace. With her own record of the delivery, Jualth crossed the short distance between Excise hut and administration office and, gathering her resolve, entered the precinct of Brethna's all-ruling and all-important distillery boss. Jack Vardy was a very different proposition to the Excise officer and Jualth had to treat him with both respect and caution. The very existence of her own distillery and community depended upon it.

Chapter 2

The main office – a stone cottage on two floors – monitored all traffic in and out of the Brethna Distillery. Normally this meant immediate inspection upon arrival, but leniency was extended towards the provider of a very superior malt that, once blended with a variety of Brethna's grains, created Brethna Burn. She was invariably left to find her own way to the office.

Jualth popped her head round the door of each ground-floor room to bestow a friendly greeting as well as official notification of her arrival. Once upstairs, she headed straight for the end room, knocked and momentarily waited at the gold-plaque-embellished door. Nobody could ever have doubted the name of the person who ruled this tiny empire. Anticipating the command from the other side, she entered a room that overlooked both the distillery and the incoming lane. Gently leaning back to close the door, her eyes fixed upon the office incumbent. From behind a vast oak desk that stood at an angle to the window overlooking the distillery, the fierce countenance of Jack Vardy stared back.

'As ever, Miss McTavish, having acquainted yourself with every miscreant in my distillery, you deem it fit to make the laborious trek to my office and then enter before being instructed to do so.'

The distillery boss inhaled deeply, his expression a mirror of graven intensity. In his late forties, he was a touch overweight, clean shaven – except for bushy sideburns – with a greying, full head of brushed-back wavy hair. His eyes were close, nose prominent and voice deep, all adding up to a severe and intimidating appearance. Fortunately for Jualth, her fiery nature formed a natural defence to such intimidation. In their own very different ways, each had imposing characters.

The severity of the distillery boss slowly melted and turned into the accustomed welcoming smile. He rose, walked around the desk and, taking both her hands, bent down to kiss his visitor on each cheek. 'You had a good journey, Jualth?'

'Slow and tedious actually, Jack, but no hardship when in the company of our beautiful Scottish countryside.'

'Glad to hear it. And how is your sister?'

'Fit to burst and already spitting blood. Any time now the ordeal will commence and my presence is expected. First light tomorrow, I shall be on my way.'

Jack acknowledged the need for haste. He also knew that no one ever defied an order issued by the McTavish household. 'In which case, we should complete our business without delay and you can retire to the inn for an early night.'

Jualth grunted, unimpressed by the distillery boss's display of dry humour – she had said nothing about an early night. The flirtatious ways of her mother were well known; to expect the daughters' behaviour to withstand the call of their blood foundered in the face of past experience.

Jack held out the chair on the opposite side of his desk for Jualth to sit down. 'First though, permit me to offer you a wee taster.'

'Make sure it is the smallest of wee tasters. I want a clear head for business.'

The distillery boss opened the drinks cabinet and poured a couple of small measures from an unseen bottle. He handed one to his visitor. 'To many years of sustained and highly successful business.'

Jualth sipped the whisky and paused to assess its qualities. It was pleasant enough, but light – very light – and contrasted too greatly with the potent force of her own malt. 'Brethna Pure Blend,' she declared, 'the original whisky of Brethna, with the added malt of Glenoch.'

'Amongst other minor additions, and the result, our finest and most popular drink.'

'Alongside Brethna Burn,' Jualth corrected. Sales were admittedly smaller, but that was only due to the limited supply. Jack acknowledged the correction and returned to his seat. Jualth handed over Arthur's paperwork and allowed a period of scrutiny.

When satisfied, Jack reached into his breast pocket and produced a key. A brown folio from the bottom drawer soon appeared on the desk. With the point of a pen dipped into a well of black ink, the contents of the paperwork were carefully copied. When finished, he warily blotted the damp ink and turned the folio for Jualth's inspection, handing back the original paperwork at the same time.

Jualth took her time, allowing the distillery boss to watch whilst sipping one of the few Brethna blends he had not had a direct hand in creating. 'All seems to be in order,' she declared, closing the folio and pushing it back across the desk.

'I shall have the figures costed tomorrow. Your account will be forwarded with the next delivery. Is there anything else you need beyond the usual supplies?'

'Nothing apart from the obvious, Jack.'

The distillery boss smiled; the young woman rarely parted empty-handed. He once again reached down to the bottom drawer, this time producing his own paperwork and an envelope.

'The last account I sent you showed how much was due. You'll find it in the envelope.'

Jack handed it over. It had never been wrong but, to retain his respect in the world of business, Jualth opened and carefully checked the contents. She then picked up the pen and signed the account. All was agreed. And as quickly as the money had appeared, it disappeared, nestling somewhere within the inner sanctum of Jualth's clothing. Jack politely turned away, his attention caught by imaginary happenings outside.

'I have often wondered what mysteries lay concealed within a woman's clothing,' he said, once the act was complete and he had returned the account to the drawer and the key to his breast pocket.

'Are you asking?' Jualth enquired unashamedly.

'No, no, just commenting,' said Jack, politely but forcibly. 'Now, is there anything else?'

'No, that's it till I deliver the next batch.' Jualth finished her drink and stood up. 'Lily will no doubt be this way soon enough to show off her baby. She's never been one to hide when praise is due.'

'I shall look forward to her visit. Send me word once the birth has taken place.'

Their business complete, they parted company, Jualth returning to the Excise hut where she found Arthur hard at work.

'All done?' the Excise officer asked.

'All done, the vital and most important part of our work. Without it, and Arthur Whibley, where would my little community be? Now, what time are you off home? You can walk me into the village if you like.'

'Another time,' said Arthur, excusing himself. 'Word is about, Jualth. I expect company is waiting at the gate.'

'I didn't notice any just now. Come to the inn later, then. We'll have a drink together and I'll tell you all I've found out about our visitor.'

The Excise official was his usual noncommittal self. His job represented taxes, a leakage of funds that went south to a distant authority who returned little to favour the locals. He was not the most popular man in Brethna.

Jualth dispatched a parting kiss, then left the hut. Once through the gateway, she headed down the hill towards a village full of eager suitors and one mysterious stranger. The evening held both promise and uncertainty but, in one way or another, would be anything but quiet. She would make sure of it.

Chapter 3

1742

Jade stretched out her foot and tapped Ruth on the heel, causing her friend to stumble forward. In nothing but undergarments, both girls giggled and carried on – it was just part of the game. With Ruth close behind, Jade clambered up the side of the waterfall to a narrow ledge that marked the point where the steep gradient of the falls turned into a vertical drop. With careful footsteps, she inched her way along, the water smacking across the back of her legs. At the midpoint, she let out a huge scream and leapt forward, plunging into the small pool below. It was barely big enough to break her fall and, if judged incorrectly, could easily have resulted in a serious injury. But adrenaline was flowing fast and she quickly scrambled out just in time to avoid Ruth landing on top of her. The water was icy cold, but they loved it all the same – the colder the better. They would quickly dry out in the warm sun when they had finished.

The game went on, each fighting to be the first up the side and onto the ledge, the second barely giving the other enough time to get out of the way. Finally, when they were all but exhausted, Jade led Ruth up to the top and stopped a foot or two back from the edge of the waterfall's steep descent.

'Come on,' Jade panted, encouraging her friend to rise to the challenge of a far more hazardous leap.

Ruth looked down and the carefree delight in her face quickly vanished. She took a step back. 'We'd never make it. The slope and the ledge – it's too far to jump.'

'No it isn't. We just need to be brave, that's all.' Jade closed her eyes, playing the leap over in her mind and held her ground as Ruth tugged on her arm.

'Jade!'

Jade stayed firm until the tugs of her worried friend became too strong. Her eyes popped open and she was quick to smile. Although the youngest and the smallest of the two, she was the boldest by far. She enjoyed the daring, the thought of jumping out as far as she could go and then falling through the air into the water below. But she had never really intended to jump, no sane person would, not even a young child such as herself.

'Maybe another day when neither of us are so tired,' she teased.

With overgarments retrieved, a sunny spot was found above the falls to flop down. The giggling recommenced as, excited by their exertions, they relived their endeavours. Eventually, their nervous energy spent, they stared up through the trees with heavy eyelids. Soon both girls were peacefully snoozing.

The muted sound of a table and several chairs being overturned echoed in Jade's ears. She looked up from the splintered wreckage to a giant figure yelling and pointing. The man appeared so angry, yet she could barely hear him. She was small again, no more than a toddler.

A woman holding a heavy bag was pulling her towards the door. Fire shone in the woman's eyes as she stared defiantly upon the sweat-drenched, rasping giant.

'You will never see me again, Tapper. *Never!*' the woman yelled.

And then they were outside in the early morning sun, the light getting brighter and brighter until …

Jade opened her eyes. She sat up sharply, now wide awake. She was still at the falls, the sun peering through the trees and the stream gently flowing past. At her side, Ruth slept on undisturbed.

'Tapper,' she muttered. After all this time, why had the landlord of The Hidden Lodge suddenly chosen to reappear, large as life, as she had last seen him? Four years had passed since that acrimonious split and she now lived in a small cottage close to Lonistle where her mother administered potions to the local community. Her friend Ruth had a distant family bond with Tapper Joe, whom she regarded as an uncle, but neither girl ever had cause to speak about him. Her mother had kept her word and never returned, so why had he shown himself now? Ruth stirred and woke.

'Good dreams?' Jade asked.

Ruth nodded and sat up. It was getting late and a fair walk lay ahead. With thoughts of the past still lingering in Jade's mind, they dressed and departed, following the stream north.

Unnoticed, close to a nearby shaft of light, an ethereal figure stepped forward and wandered over to the place where the girls had slept. The spirit smiled, content with her day's work. It would serve as an introduction to one of her daughters that, in time, would provide Jade with a peep into the future as well as the past. Her daughter (a granddaughter by direct lineage) would learn more as she grew into a young woman and understood the kind of life she was destined to lead.

'Lily,' a disapproving voice grumbled urgently from behind.

The spirit looked around. Her contented expression changed in an instant. She did not like being disturbed, least of all by the spirit of this long-dead, pious priest. He was apt to frown on contact with the living, but it would change nothing. She would look after all her daughters, now and in the future, regardless of interference from the Cloth. They stared uncompromisingly at one another until Lily had had enough. She stepped past him and disappeared into the shaft of light. Their reckoning could wait until another day.

Chapter 4

1894

Brethna, like so many small villages, sat amidst the imposing Scottish hills, with a notable distillery amongst the open fields and woodlands half a mile to the east. Jualth could have ridden to the stables at the rear of the inn but had chosen otherwise – the walk along the lane into the village was favoured by all who knew it. Trees, tiled and thatched-topped roofs, and partially hidden stone cottages unfolded ahead, with swathes of barley and wild flowers in bordering fields. Once across the single-arched stone bridge at the edge of the village, she briefly followed the stream's ice-cold waters and the grassy, willow-covered banks before rejoining the lane that ran into the heart of Brethna.

She stopped at a large sign proudly depicting a traditional farming and whisky community that hung above the centrally placed door of a predominantly white building. It was the Whisky Makers' Arms, a thriving establishment that stood at the centre of village life.

Ascending two large stone steps, she opened the door into a lounge that, apart from a couple of retired locals immersed in a table game, presently lacked for customers. Propped up behind the bar, where he had probably stood for the last hundred years, was Gus, the stoic innkeeper.

'Where is everyone?' Jualth asked, leaning across the counter to bestow a greeting kiss on the landlord's cheek.

Gus shrugged. 'Missing your admirers, are you?'

'As they will me if I decide to head on straight home.'

The landlord offered a word of reassurance, just in case the young woman chose to act upon her threat: 'It's early yet. I expect news of your presence has yet to engulf the village. Those that do know are more than likely having their first wash in a week. They'll turn up soon enough.'

'Well, they'd better make sure they do. I won't be around tomorrow to greet the stragglers. I have orders to return and, if it weren't for the delivery, I wouldn't be here at all.'

'Must be close,' said Gus, aware as was everyone else of Lily's condition. 'She won't be pleased if you miss the birth.'

The gruff and down-to-earth landlord was telling Jualth nothing she did not already know. Now in his sixties and with many years of service behind him, he had witnessed the beginnings of the Brethna Distillery first-hand. He lived with his wife and was content to end his days where most had been spent.

'I hear we have a visitor: a tall, dark, mysterious man,' said Jualth.

'This past week. His name's William.'

'How very regal. How very English. A week is a long time to remain a mystery, Gus. I want his life story and the reason for his visit.'

Gus scratched his chin and leant forward, the act of discretion drawing Jualth closer. 'His name is William.'

'And …'

'He likes whisky.'

'I'm still listening.'

Gus displayed the bare palms of his hands. He had divulged the extent of his knowledge.

Jualth was incredulous. 'And that's it … in a *week*?'

'He's not particularly forthcoming.'

'You don't say. It sounds to me like he has something to hide. I asked Arthur if we had a spy in our midst – what do you think?'

'It doesn't necessarily follow. We all have a right to keep private matters to ourselves.'

'In Brethna maybe, but if they affect my community, I want to know. Where is he now?'

'In the garden, taking the evening air.'

Jualth stepped to the side of the bar and peered down its length to the open doorway and the large beer garden beyond.

Outside, cradling a pint of beer, the visitor sat alone, his back to the inn. Slowly, the hairs on the nape of his neck began to rise as he felt the intense burning charge of someone's stare boring holes through the airwaves. He turned to see the silhouette of a long-haired woman gazing intently from the distant end of the bar. The silhouette lingered, her apparent interest undaunted by its discovery. And then the figure moved away, the brief, initial moment of scrutiny over.

'I've seen worse, Gus,' said Jualth, returning from her inspection.

'He's pleasant enough, a touch proud but not vain or aloof. I'd say a boss of some kind, someone who is used to giving instruction rather than receiving it.'

'Has he said anything about his plans?'

'The first two days seemed to cover all his interests at the distillery. Ever since then, he's been biding his time.'

'Biding his time for what?'

Gus mulled over the question. He saw no reason to stray from his initial viewpoint. 'William does not appear the type to lack direction. If anything, I'd say he has a purpose, though what it might be …?'

The more Jualth heard, the more ill-at-ease she became. Someone with a purpose who did not care to share it with others was a reason for concern. 'Sounds dangerous to me. A name, a country and a place of origin are not enough. It's no way to be civil in another's home.'

Jualth glanced back around the corner. 'He's getting up. Looks like he's after a drink or maybe he's after something else.'

The landlord nodded. He had a feeling it was *something else*.

'I shall meet him later when I'm ready. First, I need to freshen up. Can I have some hot water, Gus?'

'I'll see to it now. You'll find your usual room ready. Do you want a meal brought up?'

'Aye, Gus. I think that would be best.' As the stranger entered the lounge, she moved swiftly towards the stairs.

The landlord called back to the kitchen behind the bar, 'Hot water for Jualth please, love,' then moved to the side to greet his guest.

'Same again, if you would, Gus,' said the stranger.

'Right you are, William.'

Gus reached above his head for a jug and then pulled on the hand pump, drawing up the ale from the cellar below.

'Jualth?' said William. 'Was that the name of the young woman?'

'That's her name all right, sir.'

'Is she local? I haven't seen her before.'

Gus warily noted the interest that with the minimum of effort she had sparked in the stranger. Although not an unusual response in men, he wisely opted for caution with his answer: 'Local, but not resident – lives to the east.'

'What's the name of her village?'

The stranger was direct in his curiosity if nothing else. If only he'd deign to be more forthcoming when it came to their interest in him. Gus obliged with a vague response. 'She doesn't exactly live in a village. The cottages from her part of the world are well scattered.' The stranger stared intently, waiting for something more definitive. 'South of Lonistle,' said Gus, surmising that, by pinpointing a place several miles to the north, he was giving little away.

William nodded, paid for his drink and turned away. The front door opened and in burst two young men, each barely past their teenage years. Their eyes darted from side to side, then strained to see into the garden. Frustration soon surfaced.

'Jualth, Gus! Is she here?'

Gus placed both hands on the edge of the bar and calmly looked at each youngster in turn. He did not wish to dispense with the well-established custom of pleasantries. Their more pressing needs could wait.

'Good evening, Craig. Good evening, Ted.'

Craig made a polite, if pained attempt to slow down: 'Yes, sorry. Good to see you, Gus. Now, where is she? We know she's around somewhere; Daniel's been spotted. She must have finished her business at the distillery by now.'

The landlord's manner did not change. He had a business to run and a living to make. 'Can I serve either of you two gentlemen a drink?' He glanced towards the garden as he asked. William was still by the door, watching and listening. The stranger caught Gus's eye, held it a moment, then continued into the evening sunlight.

'A pint for me,' said Craig. 'Ted?'

'Same for me and an answer to Craig's question. *Gus*, where is Jualth?'

The door opened and another youth hurriedly entered, performing the same ritual as his friends, and wanting the same question answered. Gus made them wait, pouring each a slow jug of beer and relieving them of their hard-earned money.

'Gus,' a voice rang out from the kitchen. 'Ready.'

Gus disappeared, leaving the young shepherdless flock without a reply. He re-emerged from the end of the bar, carrying a large bowl of steaming water for his guest upstairs. As he walked past, each of the three men had the answer they needed. Patience was now the sole requirement, a tall order all the same.

In the garden, the stranger sat down and looked to the east, following the line of the road through the rooftops and between the trees, until he caught sight of smoke drifting slowly and lazily into the sky. He lifted his beer, his thoughts on plans he had painstakingly laid out before his departure from London. At last he felt he had something to show for his efforts.

Chapter 5

Jualth's visits to the Whisky Makers' Arms never failed to enliven proceedings or attract a gallery eager to witness an impending drama. Regulars, such as Daniel, sat in their accustomed positions at the side, whilst those passing through (drawn in by the spectacle) did likewise – the stranger had found a seat in the corner that afforded an unconcealed vantage point.

Jualth allowed Gus sufficient time to extract a suitable profit from a thrifty crowd before emerging from her room. By then at least a dozen potential suitors would have gathered, drunk sociably and had time to size up the opposition. With her red hair having benefitted from a long brush, the soft tread of her footsteps on the stairs heralded the appearance of the young woman freshly attired in white blouse and ground-hugging skirt. As the lounge hushed into nothing more than a gentle murmur, she stood radiant, the focal point for every pair of eyes. Satisfied that her spell had been cast, she smiled warmly.

'Evening, boys. Anyone here to see me?'

Craig spoke up for all, 'Aye, well we're not here to see Gus, that's for sure.'

As nervous laughter followed, Jualth took up a stool by the bar where Craig and the sharpest of rivals gathered around. The less forceful had to wait, but no one would be overlooked; Jualth would not permit it. She made out she was interested in what they had to say, which was not much and differed only slightly from what they had told her on previous visits. Life to these youngsters did not vary greatly, but they were men and, apart from the odd man in her own community, the only men on offer. So, to make it an interesting evening for herself, she played one against the other, a game which had inevitable consequences. When one suitor did not wish to be pushed aside, he pushed back, and then another joined in and another until Gus had ordered half the youngsters out of his inn and told them to go on home.

'That's better; room to breathe,' said Jualth, settling back onto her stool ready for a further stint of attention. Three young men had managed to avoid the eviction by being out the back when the commotion started. Craig and Ted were joined by Frazer. It was Frazer's second sighting of Jualth that day, having first seen her from the workshop as she passed by with Arthur on her way to the warehouse. He was the tallest of the three and the oldest, but also the least talkative.

Jualth spent a few minutes in pleasant enough dialogue with at least two of her admirers, until her antenna turned towards the figure content to sit apart in a hospitable environment. 'Boys,' she whispered quietly, 'what can you tell me about our visitor over there?'

'Not a lot,' Craig answered. 'We tried speaking to him, didn't we, Ted? But his answers were guarded and vague, and our interest in him turned into an interest in us.'

A traveller who had no desire to share his business; so Gus was right. 'Have you noticed the stranger, Frazer?'

'Yep.'

'And have you spoken to him?'

'Nope. Didn't see much point.'

Jualth sighed. She had considered the question worthwhile, even if there had been little hope of gaining any useful insight. Although Frazer lacked basic communication skills, he was no one's fool. It was a pity he had not made the effort. 'Okay, Craig, back to you. What did you find out?'

'He's about thirty, comes from somewhere in London and is travelling in Scotland.'

Jualth's exasperation quickly grew. 'That must have been some deep conversation you had with him.'

Craig nodded, not quite catching her sardonic drift.

'I think a woman's touch is needed.' She called over her shoulder, 'Two Burns please, Gus,' then locked eyes with the visitor. When she had arrived at the inn, she had made no secret of her interest in him. He was now doing the same with her and had been all evening. The drinks appeared on the bar.

'Thanks, Gus. Now, if you men will excuse me. Let's see if I can extract those tiny missing snippets of information without the need to tell my own life story.'

She picked up the drinks and wandered over. Without a word, she took a seat opposite the stranger and placed a glass under his nose. 'I thought you might welcome a refill.'

The essence of an unmistakable vapour rose from the glass.

'You know *this* to be my whisky?' the stranger queried.

'Gus could have told me.'

'But he didn't, you just ordered.'

Jualth fixed her gaze upon the stranger, his dark eyes staring defiantly back. 'I was told you like your whisky, so I bought you the best in the house.'

A barely discernible nod was the only sign that the visitor appreciated the gesture. 'Your health,' he said, raising the glass.

'And yours, whoever *you* may be,' Jualth responded, providing a clue as to the likely direction of their conversation.

The mutual gaze remained unbroken as each sipped Brethna's finest blend. Jualth lowered her glass and tapped it on the table; she had little patience for drawn-out games. She began with what she knew: 'So, I have been told your name is William, you come from London and, as previously mentioned, you like whisky; a sparingly small amount of information to have divulged for your time in Brethna. Folks are wondering if they've offended you in some way or could it be that you've just been waiting for the right person to speak to?'

William raised his glass, sipped and placed it back on the table, his eyes still fixed upon his inquisitor. 'Jualth …' he began.

'Aye, that's me.'

'An unusual name. Where does it come from?'

Jualth tutted and shook her head – this was not the way she intended to play the game. 'There you go, wanting answers without feeling the need to provide any yourself. But this is my soil and my land, William, and that gives me certain rights. So, I'm going to try once again and you can either answer, remain silent or lie, but if you turn my questions into questions of your own, you will receive no answer. Understood?'

'And if I do not wish to proceed according to your rules?'

'You will return to London none the wiser.'

'And by *none the wiser* you mean …?'

'You know what I mean, William. You are here for a reason and I want to know what it is.'

The glass hovered above the table as the stranger weighed up the young woman's proposal. He felt under no obligation to answer, but there was something about this bold redhead that made him want to do just that. Refusing to be rushed, he once again sipped his whisky.

Jualth tapped her fingers on the table; she was getting nowhere. 'Are you married, William?' It was a question she had absolutely no right to ask but, if it helped to unsettle the annoyingly high level of poise demonstrated by the stranger, it would serve its purpose. Contentedly noting the surprise in his eyes, she put his mind at rest. 'Don't feel threatened, William. You would only complicate my life.'

The stranger put his glass back on the table, prevaricated sufficiently to further annoy his inquisitor and then, after what appeared to be much soul searching, yielded to her rules. 'No wife, no attachment,' he answered.

The minimal expression attached to his answer was difficult to interpret. If his bachelor status carried a genuine sadness, he concealed it well.

'So, you are able to do as you please without family commitment or responsibility, though I reckon a way around such obstacles could be achieved if the need arose.'

The point was acknowledged with a small nod, but there was no unnecessary comment. It was not a question, merely an observation.

'What do you do, William?' She watched him closely. His dark features and tight muscular skin chose not to react. He was handsome yet thin. He needed flesh to balance the prominent bones in his face.

'I work in London, in one of its boroughs.'

'Doing what?'

'It varies.'

'In what way?' Jualth asked.

'Many.'

Jualth sighed and glanced over to the bar where Gus and her remaining admirers were in muted conversation whilst they bided their time waiting for her return. She could see why they had struggled. 'Gus over there, he thinks you're some kind of boss. Is he right?'

'In some respects.'

'And what would they be?'

'I oversee projects.'

'What sort of projects?'

'The sort that need materials.'

Jualth breathed out in further exasperation, her fingers all the time tapping an involuntary beat on the table. 'Be careful how you play this game, William. It doesn't always pay to be so secretive. People may start to believe you're some kind of threat.'

Again, a small nod but no comment – the point had been acknowledged.

'You dress casually, William. You are neither aristocratic, nor working class: something in between. Yet your work involves materials – a builder or an architect, maybe?'

A tilt of his head indicated both were possibilities.

'Why have you come here? Jualth asked again. 'Why have you left the comfort and familiarity of your home for the distant wilds of our Scottish hills? Have you come to see me?'

The notion forced a half smile from the stranger. He already felt respect for his young inquisitor, but it would take much more than that before he confided in her or anyone else.

Jualth did not wait for an answer. 'So what is it, then?' she asked. 'If you haven't come to see me, why have you come?'

The stranger relented, but only a little: 'The answer is … I am in Scotland travelling. I have spent a few pleasant days in Brethna and tomorrow I shall move on.'

That minor revelation was at least informative, though also irritating if he planned to escape without first revealing his identity. 'Where to, William? Where are you going tomorrow?'

The stranger relapsed into his silent state.

'*Where?*' Jualth repeated. The urgency in her voice attracted a sideways glance from the locals feigning engagement in other business.

'I'm not sure,' the stranger answered unhelpfully. 'I just know it's somewhere south of Lonistle. I was hoping you might show me how to get there.'

Jualth did not take kindly to the stranger's presumption. Tension crept into her voice. 'You do not know where you're going, but you want *me* to show *you* how to get there.'

'I want to travel to your inn, wherever it is. That's where I want to go next.'

Jualth's fingers were now more than tapping the table, they were pounding it. 'What makes you think I have an inn?'

'Do you have an inn?'

'*William!*'

A bottle suddenly appeared on the table between them. 'I thought you might have need of a top-up,' Gus said, glancing around.

Jualth realised she had raised her voice a little too much and attracted unwanted attention. She sat back whilst the glasses were replenished and, as Gus retreated to the bar, waited for the inquisitive faces to turn away. She then lowered her voice. 'Well, William, you were about to say.'

William was not about to say anything, but the situation was becoming unnecessarily taut, something that would not help his cause. He started cagily. 'That by adding the parts ...' Noting the young woman's eyes narrow, he realised only a much fuller explanation would suffice. 'Okay,' he said eventually. 'Daniel, I have learnt, is a cartman who collects and delivers casks for the Brethna Distillery. Yesterday, he set out alone with an empty cart. Today, when he returned, he had a full load and company that had business at the distillery. That company was you and the load your property, and not only do you have an inn, but you also have a distillery, one that is not shown on any map or referred to in any guide but is somewhere south of Lonistle. So ...' William took a breath, 'Jualth, would you mind if I accompanied you to your home tomorrow? It will be much easier than finding the way by myself.'

Jualth felt an irritation at the ease in which the stranger had pieced together his little puzzle. His desire for an uninvited visit was equally irksome. But acting as his guide had its advantages. Firstly, there was control over a foreign body that would otherwise wander in of its own accord. Secondly, she could choose the route in and out, one that he could not possibly use unaided when alone. And finally, if he was an honourable man – something she was yet to make her mind up about – an act of good faith on her part should be matched by an equal act on his.

'But I still don't know who you are, William. I do not know if you are trouble and a problem that will do me and my community no good. You are here for a purpose and if you discover that purpose where I lead you, what then? What will you do? Will I regret agreeing to your request?'

William assumed a more serious tone. 'I intend no harm to you, your home or your community. I am just a traveller with no prescribed path or timetable other than to return to London in the autumn, where I will guard your privacy with the same care I guard my own.'

'If I knew you better, I might believe you. If you're not a builder or an architect, what are you? Who are you?'

William lifted his replenished glass, staring intently into Jualth's piercing blue eyes. He did not answer.

'Six a.m. Be ready then. I have good reason to travel early.'

The arrangement made, Jualth stood up and walked away. Her initial impression of the dark, mysterious and annoyingly good-looking man made her both worried and angry. She had meant what she said; he was a *complication* she could do without. Unfortunately, gut instinct told her that a complication was exactly what the stranger would be.

Chapter 6

1752

Jade sat precariously perched at the top of the falls. An inch or two farther or the slightest loss of balance and she was in the stream, tumbling down towards the ledge and the pool beneath. She was playing a dangerous game, one that pitted herself against nature to see who held the upper hand.

Through the years she had spent many hours at the falls, either in the company of her childhood friend, Ruth, or on her own. But she was never truly alone; she always had the company of that warm, soothing voice, the one that so often slipped in and out of her dreams. According to her mother, it belonged to a close ancestor, a spirit that was only for them to know about. If Ruth suspected, she had never said, though there were times when her dreams also seemed disturbed. Jade had listened to her friend's vague recall, then laughed them off. Neither had ever dwelt on the matter.

Jade edged back onto safer ground. Playtime was over. Childhood was over. There was one last thing to do before departing. She found a comfortable spot, lay down and closed her eyes. It did not take long to slip into the dream world where the familiar voice of her forebear always lingered.

Lily relaxed. Her daughter's aptitude for testing the strength of her character had, not for the first time, gone too far. Sadly the young woman was now at an age where she could be guided but not controlled. A lot rested on her shoulders and youthful invulnerability was a notion that she would have to grow out of quickly if she was to survive in the far darker world that lay ahead.

'I thought I would find you here,' said a gruff voice.

Lily looked around brusquely. Fellow spirits had the unfortunate ability to appear without warning. 'Go away, Devra. Your timing could not be worse.'

'Really,' the priest grunted, sounding a note of disapproval. There were not many that spoke to him in such a manner – most held respect for his venerable position. He took a step back, aggrieved but, for the moment, prepared to accede to his fellow spirit's wishes. He knew her mortal life had not been an easy one and its conclusion unsatisfactory, hence her inability to rest in the afterlife and a fondness to meddle where it was forbidden. If the spirit intended to use her daughter to fulfil plans that had been thwarted by an early demise, it was his duty to be on hand when least wanted. Then he might be able to do something to prevent her straying beyond permitted boundaries. He watched closely as she cast her net towards the young figure lying on the grass.

The meeting of minds did not last long. Lily smiled, satisfied that her daughter had understood the purpose of her upbringing. Her destiny would soon unfold.

Jade stood up, stared one last time at the waterfall, then started her journey home. Enough had been said. She knew what she had to do and why she had to do it.

'Well?' the priest demanded, hoping for an explanation.

Lily cast her eyes from the living to her spiritual companion; the smile quickly disappeared. She was neither impressed by the show of religious importance nor his insistence to always resemble his older, more intimidating self. As a spirit could be whatever age it wished at any given moment, most, unless they had good reason, chose a more flattering image.

The customary standoff between the priest and his troublesome transgressor ensued. For years Lily had chosen to ignore him, yet still he would not leave her alone.

'What do you want from me, Father?'

It was not a difficult question to answer. 'How about a confession?'

Lily shook her head. 'That will never happen. I have unfinished business, as you well know.'

'And that stops you from confessing?'

'I will not seek peace and meekly disappear into contented immortality for your convenience.'

'Confession could serve another purpose.'

'And what is that?'

'Your propensity to interfere. You know the lives of the living are off limits.'

'Not a rule I choose to recognise, Father. And as there is no one who wishes to stop me other than you, I shall make rules to suit myself.'

The priest grumbled, but a few harsh words and a display of angry posturing were the extent of what he could do. In the spirit world his powers stretched no farther.

'Why do you not like me speaking to my daughters, Devra?' Lily asked, fighting to control her frustration.

'Because I do not know what you are saying.'

'Is that any of your business?'

'If I knew what you were saying, I could tell you.'

'Then why not trust me? Is that too much to ask?'

The priest grunted the sentiment away.

Lily threw him the smallest of bones: 'My interest is to help the community, as it was yours all those years ago. There is no need for you to know more.'

'Is that so?' said the priest. He did not like being played with. 'And your interference in other areas, does the same apply?'

'What are you referring to?'

'You know very well. That young man and the wretched woman who resides on the loch.'

'Agnes?! Do not blame Agnes for what happened to that young man. It was unfortunate, but he had only himself to blame.'

'Which may or may not be true. If she would allow him to speak to me ...'

Agnes had a habit of intercepting tortured souls before the priest got to them. She held them on one of the tiny islands situated on the loch, where they were beyond his reach.

'You could venture into the mist and talk to Agnes.'

The priest shrunk at the idea. The loch, when covered by thick mist or heavy fog, was a forbidding place. Its small number of spiritual inhabitants harboured few remnants of goodwill.

Lily tutted, she knew what the priest was thinking: 'That guilty conscience of yours, Devra. You have nothing to fear from them, they do not know what part you played in their deaths. You must overcome your shame if you want to help that young man. He will not willingly come to you.'

'And what about his young wife?' the priest asked. 'She needs comfort, which she is unlikely to get whilst he remains with Agnes, imprisoned by her resentment.'

Ruth had recently lost her husband in unfortunate circumstances, leaving her with the burden of bringing up a child barely out of the womb. 'In respect of her comfort, you have no reason to fear, Father.'

'Lily?' The priest looked at his fellow spirit suspiciously. 'What do you mean by that?'

'Jade and Ruth's young brother-in-law, Jamie, will help her. Once the departed sees his wife is coping, he may be more inclined to seek you out.'

The priest nodded. 'As soon as he can then,' he said, trying to muster the authority his position normally held. It was a show that never worked with Lily. She had cared little for the controlling clergy in life and saw no reason to change her ways now. In her eyes, the priest and his institution owed her for the life she had suffered and, if she was to go on suffering, she would not suffer alone. They would repay their debt to her in full.

Chapter 7

1894

Just after dawn, Jualth found her uninvited companion not only ready but sitting patiently at the bar with his bags. 'Been waiting long?' she asked, sensing a lack of trust.

William was slightly less abrupt in his response, 'Good morning, Jualth.' With no greeting offered in return, he answered the question sparingly, 'Long enough.'

'Long enough to make sure I did not leave without you.'

The stranger was pointedly frank with his reply. 'I like to keep to pre-arranged plans and I can see no harm in being prepared for all eventualities.'

'You learnt that in the army, did you?'

'From my father at an early age.'

The morning had started as the evening had finished, with Jualth uptight and frustrated with the stranger's secretive nature and how he had contrived to accompany her home. She made no attempt to be polite. 'We need to leave straightway, William. If you haven't already eaten, bad luck. There will be no further chance until we arrive at the other end … wherever a certain "somewhere *south* of Lonistle" happens to be.'

'Will it take long?'

'Half a day, no more. There's nothing to delay us.'

Jualth waited at the front of the inn whilst William retrieved his horse from the stables at the rear. She then led him up the lane to the distillery.

'I take it I'm not aiding and abetting an early-morning runner, William?'

'I settled my affairs with Gus last night. I do not leave debts unpaid.'

'Very honourable, just what I would expect from an officer of the Crown. *When* did you settle, before or after our chat?'

William was not quite sure how he felt about being so openly challenged. The implication was that he had decided to accompany her whether she liked it or not. 'I have settled up and I would prefer to leave it at that,' he said firmly.

Jualth gritted her teeth and looked away. Not for the first time she was being told to mind her own business. It made her all the more determined to keep probing. The man could not hold out for ever.

Once she had saddled her horse, they mounted and briefly followed the lane to the east before turning into an open field to begin a long trek across country. After an hour of tackling fields, valley inclines, streams and rocky woodland, Jualth broke a long silence. They were approaching an area of many more trees than glades, where the land rose and fell with startling regularity.

'Why do you keep looking up to the sun, William? Are you trying to remember the way for when you have no guide?'

'We're heading east, aren't we?'

'Oh, well done. Did you not know that before we started? I bet you look at the stars as well, but always with a purpose and never a dream.'

William ducked beneath a branch without commenting as they crossed a tree-lined perimeter.

Jualth had intentionally waited for the undulating woodlands to continue questioning her companion. She began ominously, 'A man with a purpose, a man who lives far away, and the only thing preventing him from getting lost in the untamed, Scottish wilderness is a wee lass he has known barely half a day. Oh, and quite possibly the sun, though I question how much use that will be to a city dweller. Are you worried, William?'

He did not answer, but acknowledged the threat. With the forest floor showing no sign of a pathway, he stuck as close as he could to the young woman's side.

'Tell me what you do, William,' said Jualth, returning to a familiar topic.

'The clues I gave were insufficient?'

'Enough to arrive at the wrong conclusion and nothing more. I need help or, better still, a straight answer.'

She veered away to avoid a cluster of trees and, having provided a moment of anxiety for her companion, manoeuvred her grey mare back alongside. 'Is your work secret? Do you have a sinister reason for concealing your trade?'

'It is no secret.'

'And nothing that would shame you if identified?'

'Far from it.'

'Then why not tell me?'

Jualth watched closely as the stranger struggled with the simplest of requests. If the man was not a threat, why was it so difficult to answer? Another tree enabled William to turn away, giving Jualth the chance to react as she had always intended. If her companion wished to continue playing this ridiculous game, then she had one of her own where the odds were heavily stacked in her favour. Smacking her hand sharply across her grey's rear, she leant forward and galloped swiftly into the forest. With the experience of many a meaningless life-and-death race against an equally determined and cavalier opponent, Jualth's mare required little encouragement as it sped away.

William and a wary horse were no match in such a fruitless chase. Ascending a mound from another ditch, he swung around a tree on his rise and accidently dislodged one of his bags. A desperate lunge could not stop its impending thud on the forest floor. William pulled on the reins and glanced back in irritation. Ahead, a glimpse of white was quickly disappearing into the trees. As he retrieved his bag, the sound of hoofs did not return. He had been abandoned. Where, was anyone's guess.

'East,' he muttered, looking up through the trees to the flickering sun. That was the course they had set and the course he intended to follow. It might require a diversion to Lonistle, but wherever south of that place happened to be, he would find it. He remounted and followed the only guide he had left.

His slow progress from then on provided the opportunity to assess the character of his redheaded deserter. In a very short space of time she had created quite an impression, though not necessarily a good one. Somebody who stubbornly thought they had the right to pry into another's business before a bond of trust had been formed was not behaviour he warmed to. On the other hand, with a mind of her own and few inhibitions in showing it, she was the type of person he could properly get to know given the chance. He liked that, the lack of pretence and, if and when their paths crossed again, working towards an understanding (and seeing where it led) would not be the greatest hardship.

Suddenly, he felt the same burning sensation he had experienced when sitting in the garden the previous day. He pulled on the reins and without turning did something he had not done in a very long time – he laughed. He should have been angry and up until that moment he had been. However, when he turned to see the figure clad in white sitting astride a grey mare on a raised patch of land, his emotions were back in control. After an accustomed period of staring, Jualth slowly made her way to the side of her lost soul.

'Enjoying the scenery, William? I haven't been this way before. I've never been good at climbing rockfaces on a horse.'

Despite himself, William smiled, the first such sight Jualth had seen and a pleasant one to her eyes. Characteristically, she did not hide her feelings. 'How have you managed to stay single all this time, William? We're used to making big catches in these parts, so you be careful if you've a mind to return to London.'

'I do have such a mind. I have very little choice.'

'And why is that?'

His smile dimmed. Something deep lay within this mysterious man, suppressed, caged, shared with no one. Perhaps there was danger around him that spelt danger for all.

'Okay, how about telling me who you are instead. You will eventually, so why not now?'

'Perhaps another clue will help.'

'Make it a big one.'

William chose otherwise; trust was still a long way off. 'The materials I use need water. They serve no purpose without it.'

Jualth emitted a pained sigh; the clue meant nothing. The game that had delayed their journey home had yielded nothing but water.

'Thanks, William. Did I not sufficiently emphasise the word *big*? That could still leave you as a builder or an architect. Can you say no more?'

William held his tongue. The trickle of clues had hobbled into another dead end.

'Well, in that case, we'd better move on. We have time to make up and, as you have managed to wander way off course – *well done, sun worshipper* – a considerable distance too.'

Jualth turned her horse and set off. William quickly tucked in behind. Being lost in an unfamiliar and possibly hostile environment was not an experience he cared to repeat. He would not let his guide get away again.

Chapter 8

1752

Jade's memory of The Hidden Lodge, as she had glanced back on that fateful day of her departure, was of an imposing building with a haunting air. Now, standing in the front garden all these years later, it appeared far less impressive: a rather unremarkable, isolated cottage on a westerly incline with trees on all sides. Even the loch that stretched out behind did not possess the vast size of the huge ocean that she remembered. It was all so very different, all so very much smaller.

Through the windows, lanterns burned dimly, providing sufficient light to see a few shadowy figures within but little else. A sorry, bedraggled wisp of smoke rising from one of its chimneys was the only sign of warmth emanating from within. It was a cold-looking place and if the manner of the landlord mirrored its sombre, grey appearance, her return would be brief, even with the support of her closest friend. Ruth, who stood by her side, afforded her entrance but nothing more.

'The sign could do with a lick of paint and something to stop that irritating squeak,' Jade remarked.

'Tapper does little to look after the inn,' Ruth replied. 'If the roof isn't leaking, he's happy.'

'No better inside, then?'

Ruth shook her head. 'Best not say anything. Speak out of turn and the only invitation you'll receive is to shut the door on the way out.'

'Which is likely to happen anyway, if our history is anything to go by. Tapper has a problem with the truth, my mother has said so often enough. He is pig-headed, obstinate and solitary, and, as a result, has no one he can rely on. Inheriting a home and a trade has done him no favours. It takes a very stupid man to spite himself when his life has so much to offer.'

'Are you sure you want to go in?' Ruth asked. 'It doesn't sound like you or your mother have forgiven him for what happened.'

'We haven't and, between you and me, we never will. However, circumstances dictate my visit and after coming this far the answer is ... I still want to go in.'

Ruth doubted the wisdom of her friend's desire to delve back into the dark days of their past and felt even more ill at ease than usual when about to see her distant relative. Tapper was about to be rudely reminded of an acrimonious split he had never fully recovered from and, if the territory remained hostile to her friend's family, there was only one way he was going to react.

Once inside, Jade hung back, stealing a brief moment to look around. Even in the dim light, the inn was visibly dirty – her mother had probably provided its last serious clean. A small fire yielded minimum heat, jackets for the half-dozen locals remaining resolutely buttoned up. Warmth obviously came from a different source. Sitting side-on behind the bar with his back towards the front door, the landlord paid scant interest in the new arrivals. He was evidently neither house-proud nor particular who entered his inn.

A young man approached and spoke to Ruth: 'You took your time, didn't you? I'd almost lost hope on you two appearing.' Jamie was Ruth's brother-in-law and, despite the less than cheery greeting, was not unsympathetic to Ruth's present situation. Both had suffered the same loss.

Noticing his niece, the landlord grunted a greeting, which was more than he afforded to anyone else. The extent of his observations went no farther – he was used to her being nervous in his presence. He did not understand or care why.

'Jamie, would you mind?' Ruth asked, glancing towards the figure who had not moved more than a couple of feet beyond the doorstep.

Tapper followed their gaze, at last realising that Ruth had not arrived alone. If he had spied a ghost, he could not have looked more surprised. Unsteadily, he staggered to his feet, ashen and wide-eyed. Jade had not long been walking last time he had seen her and now here she was, a grown woman with an uncannily close resemblance to her mother.

'Jade,' said Jamie, taking it upon himself to break the impasse. He beckoned her towards the bar.

Jade edged forward, her long red hair gaining colour as she drew closer to a lamp that rested on the counter. 'Hello, Tapper,' she said as calmly as the pulsing beat in her chest would allow.

Tapper stood tall. Normally, the landlord's behaviour was as predictable as the fine taste of the whisky, but no one could second guess how he was going to act today.

'Well, Uncle, say something,' Ruth encouraged.

Tapper said nothing and did nothing. He seemed incapable of doing anything other than stare.

'Perhaps a drink,' Jamie suggested. 'Ruth, Jade, fancy a whisky?'

'If the landlord's willing,' Jade answered, leaving the decision to Tapper.

'Uncle?' Ruth encouraged again.

The request allowed the landlord breathing space. He bent down, placed a couple of mugs on the counter and poured two small measures. Jamie reached out to pick them up but decided to leave one where it stood. He tugged on Ruth's arm and they moved away to a table. Jade spied the one remaining mug and felt the unwanted grip of attentive eyes. Tapper felt them as well and provided one of his less- -than-appealing glares to indicate such scrutiny was unwelcome. The locals murmured, shuffled in their seats and looked away.

Jade approached the bar, her eyes fixed on the landlord. She picked up the mug and passed it under her nose. Tales that surrounded its taste and the effect it had on those who drank too much were plentiful. Following her mother's warning – *'Get used to its bite first and pay the whisky the respect it deserves, otherwise control will lie with the drink and not the drinker'* – she put the mug to her lips and took the smallest of sips. Her eyes slightly welled; it had all the heat needed to warm the coldest of days, even with the smallest of intakes. The mug returned to the bar, the tears held back and the young woman none the worse for her first experience of Kvairen whisky.

Eye contact with the landlord did not flinch. He looked much older than his years, with thinning grey hair, large bags under heavy-lidded eyes and gaunt hollows beneath his cheekbones. His nose was red and his hunched, narrow frame breathed with a hoarse rasp. The intervening years had not been kind to Tapper Joe, which Jade could only put down to the liquid companion that had replaced her mother.

'Do you remember me, Tapper?' she asked softly.

The landlord did not move, his countenance remaining fixed upon her. It was impossible to tell how he was going to react. Jade was not even sure he knew himself.

When his mouth eventually opened, a stumbling drawl followed, 'What are you ...?'

Tapper suddenly stepped back and bent double. To the locals, the coughing fit that followed was nothing out of the ordinary. Only Jade was alarmed. She looked around to Ruth, who shook her head and remained seated. No one was in any hurry to offer comfort. Perhaps the landlord did not respond well to pity or concern.

'You should get something to help you with your breathing,' said Jade, once Tapper had regained a semblance of self-control. A succession of large gulps followed as he struggled for air.

'And ... what ... would that be? One of your mother's *poisonous* potions?'

It had not taken Tapper long to air one of the grievances he held against Jade's mother. Her propensity to rule when nothing more than a live-in barmaid was another. Neither sat well with Tapper, whose family's ownership stretched back to the laying of the inn's foundation stone. Jade's mother had been a popular figure when resident at The Hidden Lodge, far too popular for Tapper's liking. So what should have been a beneficial union that favoured everyone – occupants and patrons alike – had turned into an irreconcilable split where all had suffered.

Choosing to ignore the landlord's comment, Jade noticed two, well-dressed men sitting in the corner away from everyone else. They could only be outsiders boarding at the inn. 'Still offering hospitality, Tapper?' she asked, indicating towards the two men. Her easy manner and innocent appearance did not readily translate her comment into criticism.

'I'm not forcing them to stay,' he mumbled. In truth, there was nothing hospitable about Tapper or his inn. Outsiders took him as they found him as did everyone else. They had no choice.

'You don't sound well, Tapper, and yes, you could do with one of my mother's *poisonous* potions for that cough.'

Tapper belligerently raised his mug and gulped down a large mouthful of whisky. He gasped and wiped his mouth with the stained sleeve of his shirt. 'This is all I need. It's kept me alive up to now.'

Jade smiled thinly: to her eyes the whisky was doing its utmost to achieve the complete opposite. A conciliatory offer was the least she could make. 'Still, if you have a need, I hope you'll ask. Would you care to hear how my mother is faring?'

The landlord stared at the girl, uncertain how to take the offer. It could have been the same person standing in front of him, they were so alike, but that did not mean he wished to reopen old wounds. 'Is she coming back?'

'If that were the case, she would have done so long ago.'

'Then why are you here?'

'It was always going to happen at some point, you know that, Tapper.'

Tapper did. The possibility had always existed. He had waited and longed for it but, as time drifted past, with fading expectation. 'What does your mother say about you being here?'

'I can make such decisions for myself. I'm grown up in case you hadn't noticed.'

It was the first thing he had noticed, along with everybody else in the inn who remembered her as a child and had not seen her since. From the locals' point of view she was welcome, but it was still unclear whether the person behind the bar felt the same way.

'Well, I hope you don't mind me being here, Tapper,' said Jade, picking up her drink. 'Now, if you'll excuse me, I'd think I'd better return to Ruth.' She left the landlord to deliberate over his dilemma.

Ruth had kept a chair for her friend next to the fire. Jade sat down carefully. One sip was enough to make her feel light-headed. Her mother had warned caution and she now understood why.

'So far ...' said Ruth, crossing her fingers.

Jade nodded, then cast her eyes around to the locals. Abbreviated nods and covert smiles indicated a swelling of support for her presence. That undoubtedly was down to her mother, proving memories of a distant time were not forgotten. The Hidden Lodge had been a very different place when she had trod its boards and served alongside Tapper Joe.

'Any ideas?' Jade asked, pointing towards the corner. Ruth looked away. She did not like strangers and wanted nothing to do with them.

Jamie answered, 'Not that anyone has said to me. We'll find out if they stick around. Hopefully they won't.'

Despite her long absence from the inn, Jade knew what he meant. They were to keep strangers at arm's length unless word was given to do otherwise.

'Would Tapper put more wood on the fire if someone asked him?' Jade asked.

'If Ruth asked, perhaps.'

'I can give it a try,' said Ruth, who was sitting with her shawl tightly wrapped around her shoulders. She stood up and returned to the bar.

'He seems to forget the rest of us don't drink as much as him,' said Jamie.

'He doesn't look well,' Jade responded.

'And never has done as far as I can remember. Most reckon he's lucky to still be alive.'

In such a cold place and without help, his luck was likely to run out sooner rather than later. Jade's memories were of a brighter place, where voices had been louder and more animated. Now, no one seemed to raise their voice above a murmur through fear of drawing the landlord's displeasure.

Ruth sat back down as Tapper raised the counter and then wandered over with a large piece of wood from the store he kept behind the bar. He placed it on the fire, drawing a few sparks from the embers. Straightening, he caught Jade's eye before issuing a departing word to his niece, 'Let me know if you need another.'

The rumbles in the room turned into a moment of silence before resonating back to their previous low level. Such a gesture was unheard of and there could only be one explanation – the landlord had decided to allow memories of the past back into his inn. Jade had received her answer – she was welcome inside The Hidden Lodge. The question, now, was how long would that welcome last?

Chapter 9

1894

The travellers arrived at the small stables soon after midday.

'This is as far as we can go with the horses,' said Jualth. 'We'll take care of them, then walk the remaining distance.'

William indicated towards the paddock and the mounts already grazed there. 'Yours?' he asked.

Jualth groaned. Stupid questions were commonplace amongst the local menfolk; she had hoped for something better from the stranger. 'Now what would we do with a dozen horses, William? We're innkeepers not horse breeders.'

'Your patrons, then?'

'Oh, well done; got there in the end. I told you the community was well scattered. The inn is a popular meeting place and a dependable ride an essential part of the journey home.'

With the horses left to feed, they commenced the short walk along a tree-lined lane to the inn. 'Think you'll be able to find your way out or will the services of a helpful and tolerant guide be required again?' Jualth asked.

William had a feeling that such a guide would indeed be helpful, but not necessarily tolerant. 'I am in no rush to move on. Let's wait and see.'

'But you will go, William?'

He nodded, reaffirming the lack of choice he had previously stated.

When they reached the end of the lane, they found the garden in front of the inn deserted.

'This is it,' said Jualth. 'Right, I need to warn those inside that we have a guest. Drop your things on one of the table tops and take a stroll around the end there. It will give you the opportunity to put substance to what your nose has probably already discovered. The locals will ignore you should you come across any. Try not to take it personally.'

After Jualth had disappeared through the front door, William dropped his bags and took a moment to study his new environment. The inn and garden were situated on a relatively flat outcrop of land on an otherwise steep incline. Several paths appeared through the trees, heading towards the two-floored stone building with a red, peg-tiled roof. Prominently situated on the centre of the front wall hung a large sign.

'Matilda's,' William read aloud. It seemed an odd name for a remote Scottish inn, about as odd as giving the woman portrayed on the board fair hair. If anything, he would have expected a redhead like Jualth.

He walked to the far end of the cottage and around the corner until he reached the inn's rear garden. The peaceful blue waters of a hidden loch stretched out ahead, framed on all sides by slopes covered in trees and glades. The air had a scent and purity unmatched by any previously experienced. William was left in no doubt that he was at last in the place he had set out to find all those months ago.

A small cough and his eyes moved from the serene calm of the unblemished loch towards a group of onlookers seated around a table. William nodded to acknowledge their presence but remained silent. As Jualth had forewarned, it was a silence that no one chose to break. As William retreated back the way he had come, an elderly man indicated to a couple of his troubled companions. They stood up and followed the stranger round to the front where they could keep a close eye on him.

When Jualth had entered the inn, she had been quick to wave away the welcomes. 'Where's Lily? Where's Grandma?'

Several helpful fingers pointed to the ceiling. Her body stiffened at the thought of having missed the birth. She sped through the archway at the side of the bar, scaled the stairs around to the central landing and pushed open the first door on the right.

'*Jualth*, where in hell and molten fireflies have you been?' Lily shouted.

The greeting and verbal assault was curtailed by a huge cry of pain as another contraction ripped its full anger through the rigid figure of a young body suffering the end throes of her first pregnancy.

'*Grandma!* When did it start?' Jualth asked Edith, a tired but resolute nursemaid. She sat down on the edge of her sister's bed and unwisely grabbed hold of her hand. Nails immediately sunk into her flesh.

'Lily … *Lily!* Let go for the love of … *argh!*' Jualth torn her hand away and agonisingly stared down at the bloodstains weeping from the freshly punctured wounds.

'The contractions started five hours ago,' said Edith, unceremoniously thrusting a piece of rag-covered hide into her granddaughter's mouth and pressing her shoulders firmly back against the pillow. 'The doctor's downstairs; would you kindly go and fetch him?'

'*Jualth!*' Lily yelled through the encumbrance. 'I want you here!'

Jualth quickly withdrew to the door. 'Keep that thing in her mouth, Grandma. I'll be back when I've found myself a pair of thick gloves.'

Jualth hurried down the stairs and turned into the kitchen, a large room that stretched to the end of the building. She grabbed a cloth, stuck it under the tap and, whilst directing unflattering thanks to the ceiling, wrapped it around her hand. Having attended to herself, she wrenched open the door to the bar, lifted up the hatch and located the missing medical man.

'*Hey!* … *Doctor!* What the *hell* do you think you're doing? There's a screaming woman upstairs dislodging roof tiles whilst you're sitting all snug down here supping my whisky.' With her hands on her hips, the fearsome and angry redhead stood ominously poised over a rather nervous-looking doctor. 'If you don't get your backside off that seat sharpish, not one drop of my whisky will ever pass your lips again. *Now SHIFT!*'

With his shirt tail singeing, the young, rotund and bespectacled doctor scurried off along the bar and disappeared around the corner, ignoring the tall, dark figure that, of its own accord, had decided to venture into the premises.

'And what the hell do you think you're doing?' Jualth yelled at the stranger, from the other end. 'I told you to wai—'

She stopped. Even in her temper she knew it was wrong to shout at this man. Whoever he was, he had authority and was used to the respect that went with it. Humiliating him in front of her patrons was ill-advised and might lead to regret. Hastily, she returned to the hatch and indicated to the corner of the lounge nearest to the door.

'Take a seat, William. Give me a moment to sort myself out, then I'll do likewise for you.'

With an eye trained on her guest, Jualth grabbed a bottle from beneath the bar and poured herself a large whisky. A loud cry rang out from above as the doctor was cursed and then cursed again, the barrage of words ending with a cry of, '*Jualth! Where are you?*'

'My sister seems to have removed the encumbrance from her mouth. Hopefully my grandmother will learn to push it in farther from now on.'

In two swigs the whisky was gone. She flexed her hand under the blood-soaked cloth, then rested both hands on the side of the bar, her ears alert for the next cry. None came. She glanced to the end where Ned, the barman who had dutifully served on in the absence of his three mistresses, stood staring in her direction. She looked around – everybody was staring. The bandaged hand rose and pointed upwards. 'Lily ... having contractions.'

'We know,' said Thomas, from one of the seats opposite. 'She's been calling your name most of the morning. I wouldn't put it past her to come and get you if you don't get up there quick.'

Jualth shook her head. 'It seems to have quietened down now.'

'A momentary respite,' said Ned, daring to approach from what he had considered a safe distance. 'Would you care for a top-up, Jualth?'

The offer was tempting, but the pain was sufficiently bearable. She resisted. 'Later, when we have good reason.'

Ned's eyes flicked towards the table close to the front door. 'And your friend?'

Jualth looked over to the attentive figure sitting in straight-backed silence. His status as friend had yet to be established but, whatever the call, his introduction to Kvairen whisky could wait. His introduction to everybody else, on the other hand, could not.

'William, everybody … this is William. I cannot tell you much about him apart from his intention to stay with us awhile before he either moves on or returns to his home in London. He is a welcome guest if, as yet, a mysterious one. So, I would appreciate a show of hospitality.'

Suspicious eyes fixed on the stranger – great care would be attached to their show of hospitality.

'Right, Ned, if you would continue to look after everybody's needs,' said Jualth.

'Yep, but what about—'

'And I shall look after our guest.' Closing the hatch behind her, she joined William in the seat opposite. 'Sorry. I shouldn't have spoken to you like that.'

William bowed his head, accepting the apology. 'Your sister?' he asked, referring to the bloodstained cloth.

'Indeed, that abhorrent *racket* bellowing venomous curses from her bed. I was with her barely a minute, yet plenty enough time for her to generously share her pain. I shall be better prepared for our next encounter.'

William stretched out and lifted the bandaged hand. 'I have some ointment if you need it.'

'If the doctor cannot help—'

She was interrupted by the sound of floorboards struggling under the heavy weight of descending footsteps. 'Speaking of which …' said Jualth, as the doctor appeared through the archway and sheepishly approached.

'False alarm. Lily's resting, but she still wants you up there. Your grandmother would like a rest as well.'

'Aye, I bet she would.' The medical man received a cold stare for his trouble. 'Tell me, doctor, how much of my whisky have you drunk whilst you've been supposedly attending to my sister?'

Shifting nervously with the question, he did not answer.

'Not a drop more till you have delivered a healthy baby and returned my sister to her normal, sweet, fiery self,' Jualth instructed. She lifted her hand. '*And* you have another patient to tend to. I shall be over in a minute.' She dismissed him with a flick of the head and the doctor edged meekly away.

'Are you sure he's up to treating your sister?' William asked.

'He'd better be. We have no one else. If he can't cope, it will be down to my grandmother and me.'

William nodded, casting a concerned eye up to the ceiling.

'You're not a doctor, are you, William? Don't tell me your bags are full of ointments and doctor's things.'

'No, Jualth, I am no doctor and you will find little of interest in my bags.'

'But …' said Jualth, realising there was something more.

'But … on one occasion, I found myself in a position to aid a delivery. So, if the need arises …'

'When and where did that happen?' Jualth asked in disbelief. 'Are you some kind of ship's captain?'

William shook his head.

'How about a church minister, then?'

'Neither of those things and, then again, maybe both in a way.'

'And a midwife on top. A few more clues that add up to what, William?'

As usual, there was no answer.

'Right then, your room. I'll show you where to drop your bags in a bit, but you'll have to remain down here until my sister delivers or you are needed. Roaming is off limits until we establish some rules.'

'More rules?'

'Aye, and if you break any of them you'll be left with no roof over your head. Something else for you to think about if you want to be friends with me.'

Jualth departed to tend to her sister, leaving the stranger to mull over his limited options.

Chapter 10

Jualth and Edith spent the afternoon on alternate shifts tending to an unrepentant nightmare. Pain with profanities were delivered to nursemaids, doctor and locals in equal measure. In calmer moments, the patient learnt about the mysterious guest and offered to hold his hand during a bout of contractions if it would help to elicit information. Jualth thought it an excellent idea, the doctor did not, and as he had done a worthy job of dressing her hand his opinion, on this one occasion, was allowed to prevail.

William found his way back to the garden where, according to the landlady's wishes, he was guardedly welcomed. By early evening he had returned to the same table as before where he sat with Jualth and two prominent members of the community: Thomas, who was the boss of the local distillery and in his mid-forties, and Father Donald, the parish priest, who was a decade older.

'This is taking for ever,' Jualth murmured. 'If I knew the baby was going to take umbrage for the privilege of being born, I would never have hurried back from Brethna.'

Jualth supped her Highland water, a product of the stream that fed the north-western corner of the loch. Those unaccustomed or unwilling to follow suit drank ale in limited quantities whilst the patient lay bedridden. Only one person chose to defy the landlady's wishes; unchallenged and sitting in the farthest reaches of the lounge, a young man served himself whisky from a private bottle.

An echoing scream dislodged a cloud of dust from the ceiling's rafters. The cry for an absent sister quickly followed.

'Och, here we go again,' said Jualth. 'If you'll excuse me … there's no hiding from a voice like that.'

Jualth left to join the doctor and her grandmother at the possessed young woman's bedside. The three men remained, by now feeling a degree of ease in one another's company.

'Well, I don't know about you, William,' said Thomas, 'but I for one am thankful I was born a man. I should not welcome the ordeal that wee lass is having to endure up there.'

'We'll never know the pain the fairer sex suffers,' Father Donald agreed.

William imparted what reassurance he could: 'We won't have long to wait now. The time between contractions is shortening, a good indication that the child is making its move.'

'Aye, suppose that's right,' said Thomas. 'Can I take it you have children of your own?'

William shook his head. 'One day I will hopefully enjoy an occasion such as this, but not as yet.'

'Having your own children can be a wonderful thing ... most of the time,' said Thomas, feeling the need to qualify his statement.

William indicated to the young man drinking whisky alone in the corner. 'Who is that?' he asked.

Thomas and Father Donald had no need to turn. There was only one person the stranger could be referring to.

'*That*,' said Thomas, with heartfelt disapproval, '*that* is the husband of the bonny wee lass who is about to give birth. He hasn't been up those stairs once to offer support.'

'More interested in drinking the house dry,' Father Donald added despondently.

'Is that normal or just today?' William asked.

'Normal,' Thomas answered. 'He seemed a sensible enough lad before he married Lily and it's no reflection on her the way he's turned out.'

'No one, not even Edith, has been able to do a thing about his drinking,' the priest lamented. 'For a young couple about to bring a new life into the world, it's hardly an ideal situation.'

A scream from above thundered through the fragile floorboards, a volley of expletives hanging onto its echo.

Father Donald sighed as he lowered his eyes. 'When you meet Lily for the first time, William, I reckon you will be surprised that she's capable of such ... such ...' He pointed up without looking.

Thomas agreed, 'Both girls can be the sweetest, prettiest blossoms from any spring tree you care to mention and yet at other times ...' He shook his head in abject despair.

'When they inherited from their parents, they inherited double: Matthew's fire and Matilda's temper,' said the priest. 'It takes little to set either off. You probably noticed earlier on.'

William looked curious. 'Matilda? You mean the woman on the sign outside?'

'That's the one.'

More words rang out cursing the doctor and demanding his immediate demise. Thomas sympathised. 'It takes a brave man to deliver a McTavish child.' He raised his mug, indicating to Ned the need for refills.

'Will you be staying with us for long, William?' Father Donald enquired.

'I have time on my hands, Father. I hope I'll be permitted a short stay.' Back in London, during difficult and upsetting times, he had set himself a task, a mission to keep himself sane. Sitting at that table in that Highland inn many months later, he felt sure its accomplishment was close at hand.

The priest smiled in his kindly disarming way, as intrigued as any to discover the reason for the Londoner's sudden appearance. 'I'm sure you will but, if you are a light sleeper, you've not chosen a good time to lodge here.'

'The baby?' said William, catching his drift.

'Aye, and as Matilda used to walk both of hers up and down the corridor, regardless of the hour or who was staying, you can expect Lily to do the same.'

Ned brought over fresh mugs of ale and picked up the empties. Lily yelled, a familiar cry that stopped him rigid.

'I didn't quite catch that,' said Thomas. 'Is the girl making up words of her own?'

'Adapted Gaelic,' said Ned, in his light Irish accent. 'She only uses those words when at the end of her tether; usually when I've done something that I shouldn't.'

'Care to translate?' Thomas asked.

'Best not. Suffice to say it's a curse that has thankfully yet to afflict me.'

Another scream reverberated; no words, just unadulterated agony. All eyes turned upwards, everybody knowing that the last noise was different from all those that had proceeded it. A sympathetic gritting of teeth added their effort to the final push.

And then, as all held their breath, the first cry of a new life born to the McTavish clan rang forth.

Spontaneous claps and cheers accompanied much backslapping for the vital contribution made at the critical moment. Thomas stood up and held out his mug: 'To Lily and daughter. May both be in good health and spirit.'

Mugs were raised and the health of the aforementioned consumed.

'Ah, never did an ale taste better,' Father Donald proclaimed.

'Perhaps we can move onto something stronger?' said Thomas, looking across to Ned.

'On the landlady's say-so and none other,' the barman answered. He had no intention of risking his fragile existence by overruling an express order.

'A daughter, Thomas?' William asked curiously. 'You seem very sure.'

'Mark my words. We've already had one miracle this century with Matthew.'

'Perhaps it will happen again in the next one,' said Father Donald, 'or more likely, the one after that.'

In time, the crying abated followed soon after by the sound of slow tired footsteps on the wooden stair boards. Jualth appeared through the archway, signs of the epic struggle clearly visible in the shredded arm of her blouse and the bedraggled loose strands of hair that had been gripped by a savage, grasping hand. She reached out to rest against the bar and held up her free hand to silence the warm greeting.

'Remind me to get my own back one day,' she declared, leaving no one in any doubt that she meant it.

'Come on, Jualth, tell us how they are,' a voice cried out.

Jualth put her hand up again and spoke above the chorus of impatient locals, 'All in order, all female and …' she added, putting her hand to her ear, '*all* blessedly silent.'

The jubilant reaction that followed quickly died away when the young man in the corner rose from his solitary vigil and began to stagger along the bar. He bumped against a stool, then a table, then several patrons unable to step aside from his random path.

Jualth moved back to avoid a similar fate, watching as the unsteady figure stumbled past.

At the end he stopped and, through a sea of haze and double vision, stared through the archway seemingly intent on completing his short journey. But he did not move, his fortified courage unable to carry him farther. With a gallery of disapproving faces watching on, he began to edge away, one small uneven step after another until he collided with the door frame and tumbled out of the inn.

Jualth barely managed to contain her anger. 'I suppose I'd better follow,' she seethed. 'Ned – whisky. It's about time we all had a taste of the real thing. Pour a glass for everyone and put a flame to the lanterns.'

Ned's eyes flicked towards the stranger, making sure that 'everyone' meant 'everyone'. Jualth followed his eyes to the corner and nodded; the guest was included. Without another word she headed for the exit and went in search of her drunken brother-in-law.

The lanterns quickly shone bright in the fading light, throwing moving and distorted images across the walls. Drinks were allowed free reign and little sign was shown of anybody wishing to leave before the inn's entire supply of whisky had been consumed. Jualth's lengthy period of absence had Thomas and Father Donald setting up their own search party. She was located at the edge of the garden, sitting amongst the perimeter trees where the newly crowned father had vomited, cried and eventually passed out.

'That's all I needed at this time,' said Jualth, rising to her feet. 'We'll leave him be in the grubby bed he has made for himself. He'll do no further harm to himself or our Lily if he sleeps where he has fallen.'

Thomas was more than happy to separate Jualth from her burden. 'Ned has a well-earned dram waiting inside for you, lass. He thought it best not to bring it out.'

'A wise move,' said Jualth, glancing over her shoulder at Nathan. 'And speaking of wise moves, tell me how our secretive guest has taken to his whisky.'

'Quietly, and he has politely accepted all offerings,' said Father Donald.

Jualth felt aggrieved that an unwelcome but necessary duty had prevented her from witnessing the stranger's first taste of their whisky. 'I should like a quiet word with him on my own when we're inside. Could you please make sure he has no company?'

The two men shared a mystified look. 'Yep, we can do that,' said Thomas. 'Any particular reason?'

'Yes. I can better get to know him that way.'

After a momentary delay, the penny dropped. 'Ah,' said Father Donald, 'you're thinking the whisky might have loosened his tongue.'

'I'm thinking that very thing, but we shall see. If you could pave the way, it will give me a chance to check on Lily. With any luck, her more loveable qualities will have re-emerged.'

When Jualth had performed her sisterly act and checked in on her grandmother who was resting in her room, she found William at his allotted table. He was alone, a prey waiting for its predator. Rescuing her drink from the bar, she sat down opposite looking anything but her best. Her blouse was torn and, along with her skirt, covered in blood and vomit stains. One hand was bandaged and strands of hair clung matted to her face. She took a large mouthful from her generously filled glass and sighed forlornly, 'I felt so beautiful yesterday, William.'

Her guest recollected the image in the lounge of the Whisky Maker's Arms and found it impossible to disagree. 'It seems a long time ago now. Much can happen in a short time.'

'So it can.'

'How is your sister? You've just been up to see her.'

'Cradling her baby and feeling very pleased with herself. Permission for an aunt to hold her niece was flatly refused. Apparently I've got to get one of my own. You'll meet her tomorrow and find out for yourself what a nightmare she can be.'

Jualth took another mouthful and braced herself, requiring all its fire and bite to take on the stranger. 'So, William,' she began, 'have you got what you came for?' Her gaze did not leave his and neither would her resolve until she had an answer.

William looked bemused by the abrupt change in her manner. Jualth leant on her elbows and raised her glass level with her cheek.

'You think I came here for your whisky?'

'I know that's why you came here, so quit the pretence and do me the courtesy of admitting it.' Flickers of colour from a nearby lantern danced across her face furnishing it with a temporary mask of war paint. Behind, the commotion and boisterous goings-on could have been mistaken for the pre-battle festivity of a Celtic warring party. It was no place for a lone Englishman to defend his ground unaided. After what seemed an age, he lowered his gaze and finally nodded. Jualth had her answer.

A couple of glasses broke in a distant part of the lounge, as careless hands lost their sureness of grip. Jualth called to her side without moving her eyes from her guest. 'Ned – deal with it.' She had the answer to the first question, but what about the others? 'Now I really do want to know who you are, William. I need to know you're a man of your word and that you mean us no harm.'

'I can assure you—'

'I need more than assurances, I need cooperation. I've brought you into the heart of my community and provided you with the very thing you sought. I've trusted you and I want to know that I was right to do so.'

'This is not the time—'

Jualth impatiently banged the palm of her hand on the table; being denied her own way never improved her temper. William remained defiant.

Jualth irritably stood up and walked over to the bar, leaning over to grab a bottle and two glasses from the shelf below. She poured, filling each glass with an equal measure, and returned to her seat.

'Okay, William,' she said sharply, 'what is it about *our* whisky that has brought you all this way?'

'You mean … *how* do I know about your whisky?'

'That might be my meaning. You live a long way away from its source and I can guarantee you not one drop has travelled south of our border.'

'But Brethna Burn has and your malt is a part of its blend. As I understand it, the only malt.'

'Brethna Burn is not sold in England.'

'But once bottled and made available to the public, it can travel where it likes.'

'And you're saying it's travelled all the way down to you and … and then what? It's a blend, it tastes nothing like the drink in front of you. How could a blend, however good, send you on an expedition to a place where you would have absolutely no idea how welcome your company would be?'

William again felt like a lone Englishman on a foreign field. He took the threat seriously. 'A challenge to myself, accompanied by a considerable amount of free time. I've tasted numerous whiskies in London; we have a renowned establishment nearby that boasts many varieties.'

'The Highland Fires, aye, I've heard of it.'

'But I've tasted nothing like Brethna Burn and before I came to Scotland, I had only tasted it once. Despite what you say there is something distinctive about every whisky blend and every malt and, having tasted Brethna's other blends, I knew this one to be exceptional. There had to be something in the malt that made the whisky different.'

'It could have been the grain that Brethna produces, or some other.'

'No, it couldn't. There is nothing special about low-alcohol grain whisky; if there was it would not be blended with malts.'

Jualth could not disagree. William obviously had more than a passing knowledge of his subject. 'So, you travelled north to Brethna to discover which malt went into Brethna Burn.'

'No, I travelled north to visit the distilleries that I knew produced malt whisky for the Brethna Distillery. I had no intention of visiting a grain distillery or going anywhere near Brethna.'

'But you did not find the malt you were seeking, so you had no option but to visit the source of the blend. And when you did, you found no one in Brethna to help you.'

'No one. I received a courteous tour of the distillation process but saw nothing that helped me.'

'Did you ask for names of the distillers that provide their malt?'

'I did. I had visited every one of them.'

'So why were you so certain that there was one distillery missing? Could you not have made an error in your original assessment?'

'I could have but I was sure that I had not.'

'Which meant the only thing to do was to hang around and wait for a delivery of malt.'

'And when I learnt where you came from—'

'You knew there was one distillery you had not visited, the missing distillery with the missing malt.' William inclined his head. 'And is that your only concern, finding the missing ingredient in a blend that captured your fancy? Once your free time no longer exists, will you return to your life in London and forget you ever came here?'

'I shall return to London and stay in London, but I can hardly forget about you or your whisky.'

'The whisky stays here, William. It travels nowhere except Brethna. You will take not one drop with you nor purchase a single dram from The Highland Fires.' Jualth's words were cold, matter-of-fact and threatening. 'Your word, William – no harm.'

'You have my word. I will do you *no* harm.'

'And you'll tell me who you are?'

William laid down a condition, though he was careful to make no guarantee. 'If you would permit me a tour of your distillery …'

Jualth growled and shook her head. 'No chance, not until you've answered my question.'

The request, in itself, came as no surprise; they could hardly keep the kilns burning and hide them from the stranger at the same time. But any such arrangement would be at the landlady's choosing not that of the stranger's.

Jualth cocked an ear to the side and listened. Their attention had been so fixed upon one another that neither had noticed the deathly silence that had engulfed the lounge. Jualth looked sharply round to Ned behind the bar and followed his gaze to the hallway. All inner colour and outer reflection drained from her face. '*Lily!* What in hellfire and damnation are you doing out of bed?'

Lily, as Jualth had correctly and belatedly realised, had surfaced, struggled unaided out of bed and down the stairs. She stood in front of the archway facing the bar: her feet bare, her hair freshly combed and her body bedecked in a glistening white gown. In her arms, quietly snoozing, lay the reason for her mad endeavour. Proudly, she smiled upon her infant: 'I wanted everyone to see my baby.'

Jualth jumped up and stopped anyone coming near till she had Lily seated opposite her guest. 'Stay there and do not think about moving unless I give the say-so.'

Frustrated and trying not to be angry, Jualth saw to her sister's wish. 'Right,' she announced urgently to all those that had gathered at their end of the lounge, 'you'll each take a turn to meet Lily's baby and every one of you will be brief about it.' Jualth turned on her sister. 'After which, Lily, you will return to your room to lie down and rest until I next allow you to get up.'

Lily looked across at William and shared a faint smile, before the first of an orderly queue of patrons advanced to pay their respects and give Lily and her baby every compliment a mother could wish to hear. Jualth sat beside, hurrying the well-wishers on whilst keeping their intoxicated fumes at a safe distance.

Ned was the last to come over. He peered at the baby closely as it peeped its tired eyes out of the hooded shawl. 'Oh well, looks like we've got another one,' he hummed, before obeying the landlady to the letter and returning to the bar, his briefest of inspections over.

'Another what?' Lily whispered to her sister, slightly aggrieved at the barman's frugal comment.

'Another one of us. I think Ned is disappointed.'

'Well, what else did he expect?'

'He should be grateful,' Jualth agreed, sharing her sister's annoyance. 'I will speak to him later. Now then, as Ned was the last, there's nothing to stop you going back to bed.'

'Not so quick,' said Lily, again smiling across the table. 'How about a proper introduction first.'

Jualth bowed her head, firstly, to groan an apology for her glaring omission, and secondly, for not having realised Lily's foolish exploit had an ulterior motive. She made the introductions: 'William, this is my sister – the sweet version. Lily, meet William.'

'My pleasure,' said William. Lily was no different to how he had imagined – very much like her sister in both appearance and manner.

'Sorry about the noise,' Lily responded. 'You've heard the worst of me. I'm really quite shy.'

'In which case so am I,' said Jualth, convincing absolutely no one at the table.

'Have you named your daughter yet?' William asked.

Lily shook her head. 'I thought about Matilda, after my mother, but I don't know, it's a big name to live up to. I shall think a while longer and consult the drunken creature presently sleeping in the forest. Do you think we can build a lair for him out there, Jualth?'

'You're not going to let *him* name your child, Lily?'

Lily's conciliatory shrug clearly indicated that the possibility existed. 'For the sake of harmony ...'

'You should give up on him.'

'*No*, Jualth. I'm the one that brought a boy with the taste for a man's drink to live here, remember? Many older and stronger-willed men have succumbed in the same way.'

'Nathan is more than a boy but, unless he sorts himself out, he will always act like one.' Jualth suddenly turned on their guest. 'Are you taking all this in, William? This is a private matter between my sister and me, but with a concern that you should be made well aware of. That malt you have travelled so far to find can be a terrible curse if you let its fire take a hold. As Lily has pointed out, there have been many Nathans at this inn and he will not be the last.'

William acknowledged the warning.

Lily flinched in her chair and inhaled a sharp breath. Jualth felt a tinge of anger resurface. 'Lily, are you all right?'

Lily required several more intakes before she felt comfortable. 'I think so. It's passed now.'

'You shouldn't be down here. You should have waited.'

Lily forced a smile. 'I knew that before I managed to get a foot out of bed, Jualth dear. I'm done now. I shall be a good girl and return to my room, only ...'

'Only *what*, Lily?'

'Only, it was a bit of a struggle to get down the stairs; I could never make it back up by myself.'

'*Oh, Lily*, you are a case,' Jualth despaired.

'If I could ...' William offered, rising from his chair.

'You could, William. Considering the state the rest are in, you're the only one I trust to carry her back to her bed.'

Jualth eyed Lily with a mixture of anger, disbelief and affection. She saw her mother all over and loved her dearly for it. 'Lily, at the risk of wrenching your arms off, you will *have* to let me hold that baby.'

Reluctantly, Lily relented. She kissed the baby's head, an apology for the briefest of separations, and carefully handed over her dearest possession. William bent down, picked her up and followed Jualth to the bedroom where he placed his fragile load gently onto the mattress. Jualth lowered the sleeping baby into a cot at Lily's side and left mother and daughter to get some well overdue rest. When back on the landing, she thanked the bearer.

'She'll be quiet from now on. There'll be no more surprises.'

'What about Nathan?' William asked.

'As things stand, I sleep with Lily. Nathan, when he doesn't choose to sleep under the moonlight, has been banished to the end room opposite you.' Jualth made a move towards the stairs but William hung back.

'I won't come down. I shall retire to my room.'

'Okay, as you wish. You'll find a lantern on the chest of drawers. Give me five minutes to arrange some hot water.'

Jualth dealt with the water and wished her guest a pleasant night's rest. She, however, had much to do before she could follow suit. She roused Edith from her bed and rounded up Ned, Thomas and Father Donald in, what was now, a more reflective lounge. With whisky served, the Elders were brought up to date on matters that concerned their community. As Jualth had expected, the guest would be left to her. She had brought him in and it was up to her to get rid of him.

Chapter 11

1752

'Drop it there,' said Jamie once they had reached the back door at the top of the steps. Jade heaped the chopped wood onto the pile. She mopped her brow and brushed herself down. Providing sufficient firewood to keep the inn warm was hard work with questionable reward. As Tapper did not underplay his precarious health when such chores were concerned, others were imposed upon to keep The Hidden Lodge in its barely habitable state.

'That should be enough,' said Jamie, wiping the dirt from his hands. They moved into the back garden with its view east and waited for the final member of their party to return. The loch was in hibernation with winter fog clinging stubbornly to its surface. Only the trees in the higher reaches of the surrounding slopes were in view.

After a short wait, Ruth appeared on the hill path that passed below the side of the garden. She had accompanied them down but had then walked off on her own. Tales that the dead could be heard within the loch's veil of mist and fog were doing nothing to aid her recovery. Calling out her late husband's name had only been met by silence and a feeling of rejection. Downcast, the presence of her friend and brother-in-law went unnoticed as she followed the path that lead around to the inn's front door.

'She's spending far too much time down there,' Jamie muttered. 'It's doing her no good.'

'No,' Jade quickly agreed, having not counted on her friend's presence every time she wished to visit the inn. She did not welcome the role of nursemaid for however long the period of bereavement lasted. Ruth was the means to get her back into The Hidden Lodge and she was now rather getting in the way.

Jade nudged Jamie in the back. 'We'd better follow her.'

Inside, they found Ruth sitting alone with three mugs of whisky. She was staring into the fire, her thoughts elsewhere. Jade rubbed her back as she and Jamie sat down either side. If Ruth did not snap out of her melancholy soon and turn her mind from the dead to the living, she would end up losing far more than just a husband. Her mother-in-law, despite ill-health, would step into the breach and lay claim to her eldest son's only child Isobel.

'They've gone,' Ruth said quietly.

'Who have?' Jade asked softly.

'The two strangers who sat in the corner.'

'They went weeks ago, sweetheart,' Jade said patiently. 'It's only us now and folks that you know. There's no one else to worry about.'

Ruth looked up at Jamie. 'He didn't answer. Why doesn't he answer me? Does he not want to speak to me?' Tears began to run down her cheeks as she stared back into emptiness.

'He isn't down there, Ruth,' Jamie sighed, trying not to show his frustration. 'No one's down there. We buried Gregor in the churchyard. That's the place to talk to him, not down there.'

Their conversation and all others were interrupted by a sudden gasp from the bar. Tapper was on his feet, gripping the counter with both hands and struggling to breathe. No one moved. It was not the first time the landlord had suffered such an attack.

Jade sprung to her feet. She was fed up with standing by when help was needed. At the bar, she lifted the hatch and entered a domain that no one apart from the landlord had stood in since her mother's departure. Her mere presence seemed to help. Tapper's gasps turned into longer breaths and his chest settled back into a semblance of normality. In some ways he had perked up since Jade's arrival, but in others it had only served to amplify his loneliness, causing him to deepen his affection with his one true friend: the liquor that made his life bearable.

'You need to rest, Tapper,' Jade said softly. 'Go upstairs. I'll look after everyone down here.'

Tapper cast his eyes around the locals – none of the staring faces showed the slightest sign of compassion. He did not care. There was only one person whose sympathy he would have accepted if offered, one person that, he now realised, had become two. He nodded and without a word retreated through the bar door into the kitchen. When he made it to the stairs, the whole lounge followed the sound of his footsteps until he reached his bedroom. Attention then turned to Jade. She was a welcome sight and an immediate reminder of the days when another redhead – one with a smile, a kind word and many a tale – stood behind the bar. It was as if a very long shadow had suddenly been lifted from the room. News would spread quickly if the situation became permanent.

Warmed by the fire, the whisky and now the change in bar tender, many stayed on longer than usual. Chat served up with ale or whisky was a novelty to some and a distant memory to others. Later in the evening, Jamie managed to get a quiet word with Jade.

'Ruth needs to go,' he said. 'You should come with us.'

'I'm too busy.'

'I know you are but it's too late in the evening to leave you without an escort.'

Jamie was being overprotective, and Jade was unsure how she felt about it. She knew the paths well enough and had never feared walking on her own, whatever the time. 'I can't leave the bar. Tapper trusts me and I do not want to give him reason to think otherwise. You two go on ahead.'

'But—'

'Take Ruth home. She should be looking after her baby not wallowing away her time here. I can look after myself.'

Jamie did not doubt it but that was not his main cause for concern. It was the attention Jade was receiving behind the bar and the easy manner in which she played along. He had no reason to resent it, but he did.

Jade, however, could not be swayed. Ruth was no longer her priority, especially when a diamond-encrusted opportunity to get her feet under the table at The Hidden Lodge had presented itself.

Once Jamie and Ruth had departed, Madoc – a sturdily built, rugged-looking man – was quick to join Jade at the bar. 'You planning on staying there, lass?' he asked.

Jade shrugged, indicating that it was not in her power to make such a decision. And as long as Madoc and the rest of the patrons believed that, they would not suspect anything underhand if she did stay. In truth, she was fairly confident of her persuasive powers over the landlord and that that evening would be the mere start of her residence.

Madoc was the gravedigger, a job handed down through the generations. He hunted and performed other tasks such as roof thatching and chopping firewood and, although The Hidden Lodge did not currently require his services, there were plenty that did. 'What about your mother, any chance of her returning?'

'In the unlikelihood of Tapper giving her a good reason, none at all.'

'What sort of reason would that be?'

'How does an apology sound?'

Madoc chuckled. He understood; Tapper had never apologised for anything in his life. 'Pity,' he said. 'The life and warmth in this place died when she left. It was almost as if The Hidden Lodge knew she had gone and started to mourn. It will rediscover its soul if you stay, mark my words.'

Jade could not have asked for a more generous compliment. With Madoc on her side, others would follow.

When all the locals had departed, Jade locked the front door. It was now just her, The Hidden Lodge and Tapper Joe. She collected the empties and took them into the kitchen. With no fire and a biting easterly wind it was bitterly cold. Looking around it was hard to believe the inn was not infested by rats. Plates were left unwashed in filth-stained sinks; food rotted on all surfaces and the floor was covered in layers of mud. A tin bath propped up against a peeling wall was caked in dirt. The kitchen was in a vile state and provided yet another reason for the landlord's ill health. She would light a fire in the morning, boil some water and not stop cleaning until the kitchen was as inviting to humans as it currently was to small bugs and mould-like growths.

The floorboards above groaned of their own accord. It had been very quiet up there since Tapper had departed the scene. Hopefully that meant he was asleep and not dead. It was time for her to find out. Holding onto a lantern, she made her way up the stairs and stopped on the landing. Tapper's room was the first on the right, but before tending to him she took a moment to inspect the others. Each was as cold and uninviting as the next with no wood or tinder to make a fire. The bedding was dirty, another job to add to the many before the next visitor arrived.

Returning to Tapper's room, she squeezed quietly in and closed the door behind her. The beneficial effect of sending Tapper to his room was not obvious. The atmosphere was oppressive, a heavy mix of whisky and smoke hanging in the air. On the bedside table stood a mug and a jug containing a sufficient supply of whisky to render half the valley unconscious. Tapper's wheezing chest indicated that he was still alive, but it was hard to tell if he was awake. Embers in the fire at the end of the bed were all but extinguished. Jade stoked them up and added a log.

'Lil,' Tapper grumbled hoarsely.

Jade turned to see an unsteady arm stretching out towards her. She grabbed his hand and sat on the bed. 'It's all right, Joe, I'm here now.'

'Where have you been? Why did you not come back?'

Tapper's eyes were glazed. He was dreaming, longing for the one person he had ever loved, the woman who, in a fit of rage, had walked out on him. 'Stay,' he implored hoarsely. 'Don't leave me again.'

Jade released his hand and laid it gently back on the bed. She reached out for the mug, took a large gulp and then another. She waited for the elixir to take effect, then quietly lifted the blanket and slid underneath. The landlord had not needed to ask; she had had every intention of staying and not just for a solitary night. In one form or another, Tapper would get his wish.

Chapter 12

Tapper lowered his unfit, ill-humoured frame onto a kitchen chair. Two small mugs containing foul-smelling liquids swiftly appeared in front of him. 'What's this?' he asked gruffly.

It was late on the morning after Jade's first night at The Hidden Lodge and, unlike the landlord, she had long since surfaced. Having departed for home whilst it was still dark, she had arrived back in daylight armed with her mother's blessing and everything needed for an immediate stay. With that in mind, she had made up a fire, boiled some water and scrubbed out the bath. Essential garments were then washed for Tapper to later crawl into, which now left the bath free for the object in greatest need. Willingly or not, the landlord was destined for an extensive scrub.

'What does it look like?' Jade answered belligerently. Although she had taken upon herself the menial chores, it did not mean she was about to behave in a subservient manner. She had been warned that the landlord did not respect anyone he could bully and as she was not the type to allow it, the chances that he would eventually cooperate were reasonably good.

'Poison: the type your mother used to serve up.'

'And would serve up now given the chance. It will help that raw, smoke-damaged throat of yours. Sadly, its healing powers will not extend to your lungs.'

Tapper's ailing state of health had undergone lengthy discussion with her mother as well as the best potion to provide a short period of remedy.

'Why two?' the landlord asked curtly.

'One is for you, the other for me. I thought I would allow you first choice.'

Jade hoped her gesture would alleviate any misgivings, however deeply held. After all, she was hardly likely to poison herself. 'You cannot survive on whisky and little else. Look at the state of you, it's a miracle you're still alive.'

Tapper spied both mugs suspiciously. His distrust was understandable; the potions looked and smelt like poison. 'I never trusted your mother, why should I trust you?'

'You did trust her until everything went sour. Then she left. Do you want me to do the same?'

There was no sway in the landlord's manner. His state of health was ailing, a fact he was not blind to, but that did not make him desperate for remedies he knew nothing about.

'How do I know I can trust you?' he grumbled again.

'You don't. This is your chance to find out. Decide for yourself if you want to accept the offer of someone who wishes to help you.'

Tapper grunted. Even through the haze of the previous evening, he could piece together the events that had taken place in his bedroom. She had slept with him and he had forgiven her for every sin and grievance suffered at her hand. Only his grievances were against her mother and when he awoke and realized how skewed his absolution had been, he did not know what to think. He picked up one of the mugs and indicated to the other: Jade was being made to keep to her word.

She raised it up and downed the medicine in one. The patient followed suit. Unlike Jade, he could not conceal his disgust.

'Whisky, I need whisky,' he croaked, banging the table with his fist. Jade was unceremoniously knocked aside in his haste to find a pewter jug.

'You shouldn't mix them,' Jade cautioned. 'I brought some bread back with me. Try that instead.'

Tapper shook his head vigorously. Only one thing would dispel the taste of that potion and most of the vessels in the room contained it. The whisky was all too easily available and, up to that point, had served no purpose other than to get him from one end of the day to the other as quickly and painlessly as possible. Tapper lifted a pot and drank directly from the spout.

'When did you last have a hot meal?' Jade asked as she watched the landlord overplaying his dislike.

Tapper gasped, inhaled deeply, then eventually shrugged; he could not remember. He could not remember a lot of things, mainly out of choice.

'Well, you'll get one today ... and tomorrow ... and the day after that.'

Tapper took another mouthful of whisky. He did not appear overly grateful but, as he showed no signs of rejecting the overture, it was enough for Jade to take heart. Tapper needed to be told, not asked. That was the way to handle him. He needed a cook, housekeeper, nurse and mother all rolled into one, all qualities she either possessed or could conjure up.

Jade left him to munch on his bread and to muddle through his feelings about his sudden change of fortune. In the bar, she mulled over the task ahead. The lounge presented its own challenge. Years of dust had accumulated on all surfaces and in every corner. Spills had turned into mould, and soot blackened the walls and floors. The task was daunting and it did not end there. Repairs were needed to just about everything – rotting timber frames, cracked floorboards and unsteady tables and chairs. It was a miracle Tapper still had stalwarts prepared to trudge through the hills in all types of weather to provide custom. The whisky had a powerful draw as, more than likely, did the morbid desire to be on hand when the landlord finally succumbed to his drinking and followed the path of his forebears.

Back in the kitchen, Jade embarked on the most delicate of her tasks – Tapper's need for a wash. He had as many layers of dirt on him as the mud-encrusted trail from the front door to the bar.

'I need your clothes,' she said to the immobile figure, slouched at the table.

'Eh!' Tapper murmured. 'What for?'

'To wash, what do you think?'

'Don't need washing.'

'In which case neither do you, but both you and your clothes along with the bedlinen are getting the same treatment today several times over. Now, how about some help with the hot water.'

Tapper did not move. It was a long time since anybody had ordered him about. 'You sound like your mother.'

'We're very much alike as I'm sure you've noticed.'

Tapper remained glued to his wooden chair. Giving in on one issue would mean giving in on many more. 'I ain't doing this every day,' he mumbled.

It was begrudging agreement but Jade judged his resistance as little more than show, after all, why would any man object to being looked after by a woman? 'The water,' she repeated, indicating towards the pot hanging over the fire.

Tapper grumbled and levered himself up. As he turned his back, a smile fleetingly crossed Jade's face – she had established the necessary foothold. Now all that was needed was to keep the landlord alive for as long as it would take, an assignment that might prove slightly harder than the onerous task of cleaning. Fortunately, she had no illusions how tough living under the same roof as Tapper was going to be. She knew all about that from her mother.

Chapter 13

1894

Lily spent the next few days confined to the first floor walking her baby back and forth along the landing. Being young she healed quickly and, after a week had passed, felt restless enough to regain her active role in the community.

'I think I'm about ready, Jualth.'

'No you're not and I don't care what you say, the answer's *no*.'

They were sitting in the garden overlooking the loch with the baby in a pram at Lily's side. The hood was raised providing shade from the warm morning sun.

'*Jualth!*'

'*Lily* – NO!'

'I have to start sometime.'

'And sometime isn't now.'

'Why?'

'For one, your body's not up to it – how could it be? – and for two, there's the wee problem of parting from that child of yours for more than five seconds. You *can* trust Grandma to look after her. She had to put up with the two of us *and* her own.'

'I know she did and I do trust her … or rather I will, but not just yet.'

'*Lily!*'

'She's mine, Jualth, my own baby. I want her all to myself.'

Jualth slumped in her seat, giving up all hope for her sister. 'Oh, I do hope I'm not like you when I have mine. Motherhood had better not do this to me.'

There had been several such conversations, with Lily nothing if not persistent in her desire to fulfil her duty as a McTavish girl in a tradition that their mother had started – an annual swim across the loch to beguile wild salmon into the mouth of a concealed net. With the event fast approaching, the timing of her pregnancy had been unfortunate.

'Isn't it about time you and that husband of yours thought of a name for the poor girl? It's not as if the birth of a daughter came as any great shock.'

'Oh, did I not mention, she's had one these past two days.'

Jualth's blood began to boil. '*Argh ... Lily!* Are you deliberately trying to infuriate me?'

Lily laughed, enjoying her fun. 'Jualth, calm down. Nathan left it to me and now I've got used to my decision, you'll be the first to hear it.' She rocked the pram, a wilful act designed to further aggravate her sister.

Jualth waited as patiently as she could. Two very long seconds elapsed. '*Go on, then. What is it?*'

Lily laughed again and then put her sister out of her misery. 'Harriet. I'm calling my baby Harriet McTavish.'

Jualth ran the name back and forth through her mind. It was a name that had never featured in their family before but … 'Aye, I like that. It makes her sound, I don't know … aristocratic … ladylike.'

'Oh, that's definitely us. We might not own everything we see before us, but we certainly act as if we do.'

'Aye and speaking of everything we see before us,' said Jualth, casting an eye down to a large outcrop on the northern shore. It looks like someone has put down roots on our mother's rock.'

'I've noticed,' said Lily. 'I've been watching him from upstairs. He likes that spot, doesn't he?'

'It's almost as if he knows. Anywhere else would be fine, but he has to choose the one place where he is in the way.'

'Who gave him that fishing rod?' Lily asked.

'Ned.'

Lily laughed out loud. 'Oh, Ned, that was very naughty of you.'

'He should have realised by now that there are no fish to speak of at the moment.'

'Maybe he has. Maybe he's just being a good boy and keeping in sight to show us he can be trusted.'

'Perhaps he can. Perhaps he's no more than a smart man who likes creating and solving mysteries. When he tells us who he is we might know better.'

'Make sure I'm around when he does.'

Jualth let out a loud sigh of exasperation: 'Och, I'm fed up with this; I've had enough of pussyfooting around that man. He is sitting on our rock and I want to go for a swim. He stopped me yesterday and the day before that – in fact every day he has been here – and I'm not letting him do the same today.'

Lily half-heartedly attempted to hold her sister back. 'Jualth, you can't …'

'Just watch me.' Jualth bent down and kissed the top of her sister's head. 'How long have we got to the swim – two, three weeks at the most?'

'Let's say two and a half.'

'If you're moving freely in a couple of days, I'll think about allowing you a wee paddle. Nothing strenuous to begin with, mind. Ma wouldn't want any harm coming to you just to keep her annual tradition alive.'

'I'm ready now, Jualth; you can push me as hard as you like. Now get going, I'm dying to watch this.'

It was not long before Jualth was down by the loch and heading along the southern shore towards Finlay Bay. There she dropped a garment on the ground and stared across to a bemused onlooker sitting across the water. The stranger's interest was rewarded with nothing more than a quick smile and a fleeting wave. Unhurried, and with no further eye contact, Jualth calmly made her way around the loch until she reached the large outcrop. There she stepped onto the beach and crouched down at the edge of the shallows to splash her face. Then, with the water dripping over her cheeks, she clambered up the side of the rock and settled next to the irritant.

'Isn't the water a bit …' William began.

'Cold?' Jualth shook her head. 'A little warm for my liking. I prefer it when there's a thin layer of ice on top.' She peered into the loch, making it obvious she was searching for the unseen. 'Have you caught them all, William?'

The stranger sighed, realising he was in for another dose of Highland humour. 'One would suffice.'

'Then where are they?'

'You tell me.'

'What, that you're no fisherman? Probably true. Have you thought about calling it a day and finding something else to do?'

William was not so easily put off, especially when being coaxed to do so. He dropped a pebble into the water allowing both to watch its untroubled decent. 'It's a peculiar aspect of your loch, Jualth, that there is a thriving plant life growing from the shallow water and the banks, and yet the one thing that should be taken for granted is missing.'

'Then give up,' Jualth said again. 'Find yourself a more rewarding pursuit.'

'Such as?'

'Walking, riding. You have a horse.'

'Which needs exercising and I intend to follow both suggestions in due course.'

'Why in due course?'

William ignored the question and instead looked across to the bay. 'What did you drop on the ground over there?'

Jualth groaned: they were back on familiar territory with the stranger more interested in asking questions than answering them. 'We're not communicating here, are we, William? You want to talk about one thing and me another. You know what, I think I'll just get on with what I came here to do. Don't mind me, you carry on with your fishing, if that's what you call it.'

She stood up and started to unbutton her blouse, looking up to the inn as she did so. Lily was in the garden managing to shake her head vigorously whilst smiling broadly at the same time. It was all the encouragement her sister needed.

'Jualth, *what* are you doing?' William asked, sensing an oncoming threat to the surrounding calm.

With her blouse removed the skirt and footwear swiftly followed.

Thoroughly unnerved, the startled fisherman quickly turned his back. '*Jualth*, you did not answer me.'

'That's because the answer is blindingly obvious; I'm going for a swim. You can join me if you like. You can swim, can't you?'

The stranger fought the pull to turn around. 'Oh heck!' he murmured. He had not expected his host's uninhibited behaviour to venture to this extreme.

The undergarments were discarded and Jualth stood naked upon the edge of the rock facing the bay.

'I shall assume you can swim, William, but you do not wish to join me on this occasion, in which case, I shall take my leave. If you would kindly gather up my clothes and bring them back to the inn for me, it would be much appreciated.'

Jualth took one last glance at her sister, who was watching through splayed fingers, then dived in.

William turned to stare at the wilful young woman as she swam away. The dignified control he had so far demonstrated on his visit was in disarray. He reached out to the heap of warm garments at his side strenuously trying to fathom out what kind of person he had met. No female he had ever encountered came close.

When Jualth reached the far side, in a little under fifteen minutes, he did not divert his eyes as she emerged from the water and waded out towards the garment she had dropped. A cheeky smile over her shoulder was followed by a finger wave, first to William and then to the inn. William looked up to see Lily applauding warmly. He turned back to Jualth and then the mystifyingly empty loch, and began to wonder about the place he had been so desperate to find. There was clearly much more to it than just the whisky.

Chapter 14

'Ned, a word please if you have a moment,' said William, perching himself on one of the stools.

Ned, who had just lit the lanterns and returned to his accustomed position behind the bar, wandered down. 'Er … yes, William, something I can help you with?' He was hesitant because his summoner still had a full glass of whisky before him.

'Ned, I have a problem.'

'Do you now.'

'I do and I was hoping that, with the assistance of someone with extensive local knowledge, I might be able to get to the bottom of it.'

Ned glanced around to Jualth, who was at the other end of the bar with a crop of young admirers. It was strange that he had been selected for assistance rather than her.

'On your advice,' William proceeded, 'and with equipment you have placed at my disposal, I have spent the last few days sitting at the edge of the loch endeavouring to entice one of its fish out of the water. Now, admittedly, I am not the greatest fisherman to have ever yielded a rod – living in the vicinity of the Thames there is little opportunity to practise. The water is a hostile place to all living creatures and has been for decades. However, your loch …'

William stopped in mid-flow. All lochs had a name, he supposed, yet he could not remember having heard one for this secluded stretch of water.

'Something wrong, William?' the barman asked.

'Ned, what is the loch called?'

Ned wavered and again glancing around to Jualth. Without interference from the far end, he felt permitted to answer. 'Velana.'

'*Vela … What?*' William was taken aback. He had expected something with a strong Gaelic influence.

The barman felt dutybound to explain, 'It's all to do with a sixteenth-century Italian priest called …'

'*Ned!*' The warning voice of his mistress sounded loud and clear. Ned flinched and strayed no further. 'Umm, you were saying, William.'

William cast an eye towards the landlady. She appeared engrossed in conversation, yet the first time Ned had drifted into unpermitted territory, she had jumped in. He momentarily spared the barman additional interrogation. 'I was interested in listening to what you were about to say, but … maybe another time.' He returned to his problem. 'That loch, Ned, should be brimming with fish just like any other. So why is it not the case? Where are they?'

The barman assumed an air of bafflement. He rubbed the stubble on his chin and had a good, long think. 'Now, not wishing to be rude, but are you not perhaps guilty of blaming that rod I lent you?'

'No, Ned, I am no more blaming the equipment you gave me than I am my limited ability to fish. Each is as unlikely to be the reason for the absence as the unconventional swimming habits of your landlady.'

'Oh, that's quite a common event, her and Lily. I wouldn't eliminate that from your reckoning.'

'*Ned*, you're wanted at the far end,' said Jualth sternly, having suddenly materialised by his side.

'But have you heard the news—'

'*Ned, shut up*. As far as I am concerned, the less you say to our guest on this matter, the better.'

Ned raised his eyebrows, muttered under his breath, then obediently swapped positions.

'There you go, William, you have dragged me away from a pleasant conversation with amiable company. Now, if you wanted my sole attention, you have it.'

William opened his mouth to speak.

'*But* no more talk of fish. You couldn't catch one if it was presented to you on a dinner plate. Let's leave it at that. What do you want?'

William dispensed with the sideshow, though he intended to return to the subject with or without permission. 'Your distillery, Jualth, that well-hidden building in the hills, I want a visit.'

'And you'll get one, the moment you tell me who you are.'

'And if I chose to make the visit alone?'

'We've been here before, William. If you want to keep a roof over your head and the respect of the landlady, you'll stay away.'

She rested on the bar and leant forward, assuming a more alluring pose. 'Why not discover the countryside whilst you're mulling over your problem? To have come all this way without exploring would be such a waste, so why not accept your inadequacies with a rod and do as I suggest?'

'Without a guide?' William asked.

'Tied to Lily, my niece and the inn. I don't have time to show you around.'

'But you do have time for swimming.'

'And in a couple of days, with Lily as well.'

'So soon after having a child? Is that sensible?'

'No, shouldn't think it is, but you try telling Lily that.'

'Then why—'

Jualth cut him off: 'You first, William. You tell me something about yourself and then we'll see what we can do to return the favour. But until then, and if you'll excuse me, as you can see, I have devoted followers in need of my attention.'

Jualth left William to ponder his dilemma. The game would continue with the landlady's rules the only ones in play.

Chapter 15

1752

'Bring back memories, Father?' Lily asked her unhappy companion. Surrounded by thick winter mist, they were standing at the edge of the loch.

'Many, few of them pleasant,' the despondent priest answered. He had needed much persuasion to return to hostile territory.

'You cannot hide from Agnes indefinitely. It is not in your interest or the poor suffering souls you keep going on about.'

'And how will engaging in pointless, ill-tempered arguments with an unreasonable, cantankerous old witch help matters?'

The insult was greeted with several loud, tetchy-sounding splashes somewhere in the mist. Agnes was listening.

Lily sighed. 'Did you need to say that, Father?'

The priest immediately regretted his outburst. He should have known his adversary would be hiding somewhere nearby. 'Well, why should things be any different than before?' he asked more tactfully.

'They won't be until you two start being civil to one another.'

'It is not me that is the cause of the argument between us. It is the actions of that wretched ...' The ill-disposed priest reined in his tongue before Agnes suffered a further unwelcome insult.

'Does it matter?' Lily asked. 'Blaming one another is no way to resolve an impasse.'

'Then what is?'

'By allowing a third party such as myself to help.'

'And how can you do that?'

'By treading where you forbid me to go, Father.'

It took the priest a few seconds to understand her meaning. 'I do not see how you interfering with the living will help,' he rebuked. 'And how will it get me closer to the poor lad she keeps from me?'

'Be patient and you will find out.'

The dubious priest grunted dismissively. 'Who are you really trying to help? Me, Agnes or *yourself*?'

'All of us and to do that you need to trust me, or you and Agnes will never see eye to eye. Now if you don't mind, I can only help if I know what is going on and as my daughter is too busy to come to the falls, I must go to her.'

'So you can interfere with the living,' said the priest, bludgeoning home his point.

Lily angrily turned on her righteous companion; he was starting to fray her nerves. 'If you really don't like being down here, I will not insist you stay. Either accept there is a good reason for your presence or go away.'

The priest grumbled but remained put.

'Right,' said Lily, satisfied that she had finally won the day, 'let's find out what is happening over there.' Her daughter was apparently collecting wood on the other side of the loch with a young man. She needed to observe them closely.

'Any luck?' Jamie called out as Jade's petite figure re-emerged through the heavy mist.

Jade shook her head. It was more than half an hour since Ruth had wandered off in search of her dead husband's spirit. The muffled cries of Gregor's name had long since stopped and both Jamie and Ruth had become concerned.

'Where do you think she is?' Jamie asked.

'Hopefully on her way back to the inn.'

'You reckon?'

'I expect we both missed her; it's the most obvious answer. We'd better head back and make sure.'

Jamie helped to strap a bundle of dead wood onto Jade's back and then shouldered the main load himself. 'Is this permanent?' he asked as they headed off.

'Is what permanent?'

'You staying at the inn.'

A couple of weeks had passed since Jade had taken up residence and, although the list of jobs to do remained a long one, the transformation in that time had proved remarkable. With years of dust, cobwebs and dirt scrubbed away, The Hidden Lodge once again provided a pleasant setting for the consumption of ales and spirits. As Jade had showed no sign of going home, rumours were circulating.

'You mind if I do?' Jade asked.

'No. Why should I? I see a lot more of you this way.'

The answer was a bit on the hasty side. Jade had a feeling he did mind but smiled all the same for the well-meaning remark. Since she had upped sticks and settled in her new nest, she had heard many such comments, but never in the earshot of Tapper lest the impression was given that her return was for anyone's benefit other than the landlord's.

'Ruth asked, that's all,' said Jamie, glancing over his shoulder in the vain hope she was following.

Ruth's interest was a mite worrying and Jade needed to know why she was asking. Sensing that Jamie had something more to say, she let him continue.

'You don't need me to tell you how things have been between her and Ma since Gregor died. Ma's just not herself any more, with her moods and her health, and she blames Ruth for what he got himself into.'

'That's hardly fair,' Jade said indignantly. 'Ruth had nothing to do with it. I think it's about time my mother paid her a visit. A few well-chosen words and a regular potion is what your mother needs.'

'It could help,' Jamie said gratefully, 'but Ruth was hoping for something slightly different. She was thinking that you might speak to Tapper on her behalf. As she is his next of kin and with you staying at The Hidden Lodge for the time being, she was looking to do the same.'

Jade did not need reminding of Ruth's lineage, not when she was working so hard to break it. The request could not have come at a worse time. 'The baby too?'

Jamie nodded.

Tapper would not like another baby at the inn but, one way or another, that was exactly what he was going to get. 'I'll have a quiet word with him when we get back.'

Jamie appeared satisfied with the answer. With no cause to doubt the young woman, what reason was there to feel otherwise?

Having dropped the wood by the back door, they were relieved to find Ruth in the lounge huddled up by the fire. Apart from the three of them it was empty. Jamie stoked the dying ashes and added a piece of wood. The bar and lounge were now purged of extraneous life forms, and all surfaces exposed from beneath layers of grime. Metallic squeaks had been lubricated and windows washed to allow natural light to filter through. The landlord had watched without comment or the urge to join in.

'Where's Tapper?' Jade asked. It was unusual for him not to be behind the bar.

Ruth stared into the fire, watching as it gathered strength. She did not appear overly interested. 'I thought it best to wait here,' she said quietly. She was half-listening at best.

'He's normally sitting on his stool,' said Jade, looking slightly puzzled. It was a vigil he liked to keep whether he had customers or not. So where had he got to? 'Give me a moment,' she said, indicating to Jamie to stay where his company was most needed.

At the bar, she lifted the hatch and entered the kitchen, closing the door behind her. Tapper was sitting at the table staring into the embers of a struggling fire. 'What's wrong?' she asked. 'Why aren't you out front?'

Tapper did not answer. With what seemed a considerable effort, he lifted his gaze and fixed it on his young helper. Up until very recently he had been living in a slum, waiting for the day when he no longer had to contemplate the pain of a life that could have been so very different. Now, with a morning wash and a decent breakfast, he had a daily reminder. He no longer lived in a cold forbidding hovel that would have shamed his parents, he had a proper home and the company of a woman he should have seen grow up. What had he done to deserve it? He had no idea. After so many years of living alone, why had fortune taken it upon itself to grant him something he had never dared to wish for?

Tapper cleared the bile from his throat: 'I want to see your mother,' he said hoarsely. Despite the lack of heat from the fire, he was sweating and the smell of whisky on his breath was potent even from the distance of several feet.

'You're not well, Tapper. You have a fever and should be in bed.'

The landlord grunted irritably. His request had been deflected. 'Why you? Why you and not her?'

'My mother isn't coming back. She doesn't want to see you.'

'Then why are you here?' He was not deserving of such kindness, he had shown none and received none in return. So why the sudden change?

'You saying you don't want me here no more?'

Tapper thumped the table. Throwing a question back at him was no answer. 'I should have kicked your hide through that door the moment you stepped back into my inn. And do you know what? I very nearly did. *Why* are you here?'

Jade glanced over her shoulder. The kitchen door was shut, but if Tapper raised his voice any louder, they would be overheard. 'I wanted to see where I was born,' Jade said quickly. 'I only have vague memories.'

'And how is your memory now?'

'I can remember the shouting and the anger.'

Tapper grunted. He remembered as well. 'Bad memories, the sort best forgotten and yet, it didn't stop you slipping into my bed, did it?' He stared at her accusingly.

'I'm not a child, Tapper, I can do what I want. And you didn't turn me away.'

Tapper almost choked on the answer. Turning her away was beyond the call of any man, let alone one in his state. He looked towards the door knowing his niece was on the other side. 'And you want it back, the home that you wanted to see again. Is that what this is all about?'

It was an uncomfortably direct question, one that Jade wished he had not asked. But as he had, there was only one way forward. 'Yes,' she answered.

To her surprise, the landlord took her confession calmly. There was no further anger, no shouting, no movement towards the bar door to tell Ruth. He was composed and thoughtful. For him, unusually so.

'Fix me a potion,' he said. 'Something to help the fever. Then I'll go to bed and think on it.'

Jade fetched a couple of mugs and put them on the table.

'Just the one,' said Tapper. 'You can put the other away.'

In two weeks, it was the first sign of trust shown by the landlord towards his unpaid helper. What did it mean? Jade knew she would not have long to find out.

Chapter 16

Jade slid the last rusty bolt into place. The Hidden Lodge was now closed, its patrons sent on their way, the landlord and the servant who aspired to be much more the only ones left. If all went well, the next time the inn opened for business her future could be very different. Earlier that evening, Jamie had again broached the subject of Ruth's wishes.

'He wants to think it over,' Jade had replied. Seeing the uncertainty in his eyes, she had then added, 'If Tapper doesn't say no straight away, then it's an idea he isn't totally against. Leave him to think it through.'

She had not spoken to Tapper about Ruth and never intended to. The landlord had enough to think about and the less he thought about his niece the better. Having her best friend under the same roof might happen but, if she had anything to do with it, it would not.

With the bar cleaned and the fire left to smoulder, Jade carried a lantern through to the kitchen and sat down. Apart from the familiar groans the floorboards made as the night air cooled, there was no sound. The inn appeared content, almost restful in its restored health. Normally her late-night chores were punctuated by guttural noises emanating from Tapper's room, but not tonight. It could only mean he was awake and, if that was the case, he was waiting for her. The urge to climb the stairs without delay was strong, but Jade knew a further gesture was needed before she answered the landlord's silent call.

The fire was still lit when she pushed open his bedroom door. Tapper was sitting up, red-faced and wheezing heavily. She walked around the bed and placed a potion in his hand. 'That should help the fever,' she said softly.

Tapper drank the potion without complaint. He either trusted her now or had given up caring. Jade added some wood to the fire, stoked it up and let it take hold. By the window, she glanced out into the clear night sky where the stars shone as bright specks. It was silent except for Tappers drawn-out breaths and a resurgent fire.

'I don't want you here,' said Tapper without preamble.

Jade turned slowly to meet his gaze. Even though he was struggling to breathe, and perspiration had started to drip from his forehead, his face bore the remnants of what in days gone past counted as a smile.

'Tell your mother her little scheme didn't work. Tell her she should have come herself if she wanted her home back.'

Tapper paused. Speaking even a few words at a time was a huge effort. The sweating was getting worse, but the smile remained – the satisfaction of his decision made the effort worthwhile. He had had all the time needed to think through the events of the past few weeks. He was not the fool he was being taken for. 'You're with child, aren't you?'

Jade did not answer. She let the silence hang. Whatever Tapper wanted to say he could say. If vengeance, however wrongly assigned, was a more powerful motivator than being looked after by the daughter of the woman he still loved, she needed to know.

'She left me, your mother, walked out of my inn with a kid that should have been mine. And now she thinks that youngster can be used to get the inn back. Well, she's wrong. You have no proof I'm the father of your child and without it neither of you can stake a claim to my inn.'

The meaning of his words was clear even if he could not vent them as he wished. The strength of his bitterness had prevailed, just as her mother had forewarned. Jade had her answer and understood there was no going back.

Tapper struggled on. 'My mother treated Lil like a daughter, even after she disgraced herself. You never knew your father, *did you?*'

He was starting to enjoy his cruelty and Jade was beginning to see why her mother had departed never to return. His desire to punish Jade's mother for her perceived transgression had never faded. When it came down to it, he was not a nice man. The need to share his suffering outweighed all other needs. Jade did, however, know about her father and from a closer and more reliable source than the landlord. The brief relationship had been a loving one and if either parent had known there was a child on the way, her wayfarer father might never have journeyed on to some distant, unknown destination.

Jade ignored the landlord's childish provocation. The room was heating up, but she wanted it warmer still. At the fireplace, she bent down and piled on more wood.

Tapper leant forward and croaked out an order, 'No more. It's hot enough as it …' He slouched back; the potion was having its desired effect, and the sick and whisky-fuelled landlord was in no position to intervene. His eyelids were heavy, the need for sleep compelling. He reached out towards the window, but his arm fell limp as his body refused to follow.

When Jade left the room, she wedged a thick cloth in the gap beneath the door. No smoke would escape. Back in the kitchen she poured herself a whisky and sat down. Its soothing warmth provided the only friendship on offer at The Hidden Lodge. Revenge was inherent in Tapper's blood and his actions predictable, even if she had wished otherwise. Her mother had been right all along: Tapper did not forgive. For all his show of being the big man, he was a weak, spineless coward who blamed others for his misfortunes. He had suffered and, through his own cussedness, would go on suffering to his final soot-filled breath.

Jade blew out the whisky's comforting embers. 'You should have let me make the potion for two, Tapper,' she tutted. Men were so stupid. If they were not digging their own graves, they were allowing the womenfolk to do it for them. And it was all so avoidable. All she had wanted was the inn. Now she would have to find another way. Ruth, who would inherit it, needed a strong forceful companion at her side. But what then? Would she forever be the hired help?

Jade cocked an ear to the room above. The sound of coughing had stopped. It would not be long now. She would look in in an hour or so: that was more than enough time. In the morning, she would fetch the doctor, then the priest and finally the gravedigger. After that, she would visit her mother. There was much to discuss; the small matter of an unborn child to a single woman and the failure of their plans. If there was another one in the offing, she would need to know without delay. Time was now of the essence.

Chapter 17

Jade woke to the sound of banging on the front door. She was still sitting at the kitchen table, her whisky mug empty, the lantern low and the fire all but extinguished. The view outside was one of darkness. How long she had been asleep was difficult to say.

More thumps resonated followed by a loud cry, 'Anyone up?'

Jade recognized the voice but not its agitated manner. It was Madoc, the gravedigger, making enough noise to wake both the living and the dead. Why he should choose to call at that time of night was hard to say, but there had to be more to his arrival than mere coincidence.

She pulled back the bolts to stem a third assault on the already weakened door frame. Madoc stumbled past. He was breathing heavily, the look on his face that of a fearful man. When he saw Jade in the dim light of the lantern, he appeared mightily relieved.

'Madoc, what on earth is wrong? Why are you here?'

The unexpected visitor took a couple steps towards the archway as Jade closed the door. He cast his eyes around the bar and lounge, and then up to the ceiling. 'Well, if it isn't you …?'

Without invitation, he strode through the archway and up the stairs – Jade had no chance to stop him. She moved over to the bar and listened as Madoc entered Tapper's room. 'Well, if it isn't you …?' she murmured. In the circumstances, it was a chilling comment to make. How could he know? She heard coughing. The bedroom door slammed, then footsteps pounded down the stairs. Madoc reappeared through the archway.

'I've opened the windows,' he said. 'You'll have to close them before the doctor and priest get here. Anyone else you need?'

'Madoc …?' Jade was unsure what to say. She did not understand. Why had the gravedigger suddenly turned up and why was he not asking awkward questions about the landlord? With the gap at the foot of the door covered over, he must have known Tapper had not suffocated by his own hand.

'What … what will you say?' she asked hesitantly.

'That the useless landlord is dead.'

Jade looked baffled. For some reason, someone she barely knew was intent on helping her. 'Madoc …?'

'I'll get your mother, as well,' said the gravedigger, halfway to the door.

'No,' Jade called out urgently. 'Not her. Jamie. Get Jamie first. Tell him I need him, but don't say why.'

Madoc nodded and was gone. Any further explanation would have to wait. Her mother had never mentioned Madoc and neither had the spirits. Something was amiss. In the days to come, she would endeavour to find out more about him, but not for the moment. There was another matter to deal with that stemmed from an idea she'd had whilst supping her whisky. How she played it was as crucial as her handling of the deceased landlord, probably more so considering what had happened. Hopefully it would have a better ending.

Jade made up the fire in the lounge and waited. The original plan had worked well up to a point but had ultimately failed due to her employer's deeply embedded loathing for himself and all others. Facilitating his path into the next world had come sooner than intended and suspicion aimed in her direction would be inevitable. Only Madoc could give her away, yet she had a feeling he was the one man she could trust. Why was anyone's guess.

After an uncomfortably long wait, she noticed Jamie's lantern flickering on one of the outside paths. With the door unbolted, she allowed him to find his own way in. When their eyes met, his look of relief matched that of the gravedigger's. Madoc had roused the young man before departing, making it clear that he was needed at The Hidden Lodge without delay. He had been no more forthcoming than that.

Jade indicated to the whisky waiting on the table. She was gratified to see his concern, but did not wish to overplay the need for his presence. A wary respect and a willing hand were what she needed, not a controlling force for a hapless woman.

'What's ... what's ...?' Jamie began once seated. Jade helped him out.

'It's Tapper. He's dead.'

Jamie had guessed something of the kind. He took a sip of whisky as he grappled with the implications of what he had just learnt. The landlord was dead. That was good news as far as he could see – for the community, himself and Ruth in particular.

'His lungs gave out,' Jade said softly. 'I checked in on him after you left. He was asleep, so I left him whilst I cleaned up. When it's quiet, just me and the fires crackling, I can normally hear Tapper snoring up there, but when I'd finished I heard nothing, not even a cough. I looked in again. He was alive but struggling to breathe. I shook him, shook him as hard as I could, but it made no difference. So, I sat at his bedside and held his hand till he eventually stopped breathing altogether. I hadn't expected him to die so quickly.'

Jamie nodded. He was uncertain what to do. If Jade needed comfort, it was not obvious. She seemed resigned to what had happened. Although he would have welcomed the chance to show how much he cared, he held back.

'Madoc?' said Jamie after a few moments of silence. 'How did he know?'

Jade shrugged. 'The lanterns, maybe. Perhaps he saw them glowing much later than normal. It could have worried him.' She was groping in the dark. There was no obvious explanation.

Jamie thought about asking Madoc later on, but he had a feeling it would be wiser to mind his own business. The gravedigger was not a person to upset with unwelcome questions. 'Where is he now?' he asked.

'Fetching the doctor. Then he'll fetch the priest. He thought it best I had company whilst I waited. I thought of you.'

It was an explanation designed to make Jamie feel needed, the one person above all, at such a difficult time, Jade had asked to be with. It was almost enough for him to reach out and put a comforting arm around the shoulders of the young redhead. But not quite. 'That's a fair distance he has to cover.'

'We won't be seeing them any time soon. If willing, I need your help to make Tapper decent before they get here.'

Jamie raised the mug and took a large mouthful – it was not the landlord's needs that he wished to look after. He nodded, concealing his reluctance.

Jade picked up the lantern and led him up the stairs. The cold hit them the moment they entered the room – Jade had forgotten to close the windows. If Tapper had not already choked to death, he would surely have frozen.

'His spirit,' Jade said quickly. 'We had to let it out.'

Such talk was common amongst the locals and Jamie suspected no malevolence in such a deed. The windows were swiftly closed and the fire built up.

'Can you move all the whisky down to the kitchen whilst I deal with Tapper?' Jade asked.

Jamie scratched his head. 'There's more up here than behind the bar.'

'Wait till you see the kitchen,' Jade cautioned.

The room was soon presentable and just warm enough to be respectful for Tapper's corpse. At the doorway they stared upon the deceased landlord.

'This is not a bad thing,' said Jade, mirroring Jamie's own thoughts. 'This inn is important and Tapper was not a good custodian. He let his parents down and all those who served before them. All that must change now. The inn must be restored to its rightful place at the centre of our community.'

Jamie agreed. 'Aye, but do you think our Ruth's up to it?' It was a tough assignment for a young widowed mother still in mourning.

'By herself, no, and this place will fare no better if left to the sole management of someone as inexperienced as her. Ruth has a big heart but she doesn't have the strength to shoulder the burden without help.'

'Then she needs you,' said Jamie without hesitation.

'She needs *us*,' said Jade, fixing her eyes on the young man. She took a step closer to a position where he could provide the sort of comfort he wished to give if so encouraged.

'Us?'

'Yes, *us*. We could both be here to help Ruth.'

'What about …?'

'Your mother? Forget about her. You need a life of your own, and you can have it here with Ruth *and* me.'

It was the first time Jade had intimated that there could be anything between them and the first time his hopes had been raised.

'She needs us, Jamie. We must speak to her straight away before anyone puts ideas into her head about selling up.'

The last thing Jade needed was a sympathetic, silver-tongued voice undermining her newly laid plans. The vultures would start to hover very quickly. She moved closer, raised her chin and allowed Jamie to gently kiss her on the lips. Speed was now of the essence and, however abrupt and inappropriate, this was her opportunity. She could not let it pass.

'My room's just along the passage,' she said softly. 'Nip downstairs and put a bolt across the door, then come back up.'

Jade moved into the corridor and smiled over her shoulder as she walked towards her room. Jamie closed the door on the dead body. When he returned, Jade was already lying in bed. The time for hesitation was over.

Chapter 18

1894

Inclement weather over the next five days limited William's opportunities to explore the countryside. It did not, however, stop Lily from returning to the water. Ned escorted the two sisters on each occasion to the outcrop where they disrobed. He was invited to stare at their naked bodies if he so wished but, as on all previous occasions, dutifully turned his back. Discarded garments were flung over his shoulders and into outstretched arms and, after a parting pat or an occasional kiss, the women waded through the shallows and into deeper water. Diving for Lily was not yet an option and the crossings slow and exhausting. Fortunately, the determination of a McTavish girl soon had her improving.

After a day of rest, the sisters invited William for a horse ride, a trek north towards the valley of Lonistle.

'How long will this take?' William asked. They had ridden along Velana's northern shore then cut up to tackle the successive peaks and troughs that lay beyond.

'Hard to say, William,' Jualth replied. 'It could be a couple of hours or it could be a lot more, it all depends. What do you think, Lily?'

'Oh, I think the latter. Much as I miss my screaming child, it would not surprise me if we were away for most of the day.'

'Grandma and Ned can cope,' Jualth assured her.

'Ned?' William questioned. They were painting a picture of a man with unexpected qualities.

'With the bar, William, not the baby.'

William grunted. The short-lived notion had, of course, been absurd. 'And when we get to Lonistle, you intend to swim across its loch?'

'We do, and we will be suitably costumed as we have already explained,' said Jualth. 'You will kindly assist us with the horses and, as you've been broken in, the clothing too.'

'I still don't fully understand why—'

'*William*,' Jualth interrupted. 'Have I not mentioned a dozen times … *you* first. You tell us about *yourself*, then we will tell you about *ourselves*.'

'We'll break you,' Lily vowed, sweetly. 'No hope of fending off the two of us.'

After an hour they stopped at the foot of a small falls. Water tumbled down steeply onto a ledge and then vertically into a pool. Leaving the horses to rest and graze at the bottom, they scaled the rocks at the side until they stood at the top, staring down. It was an impressive natural feature to have suddenly stumbled upon.

'If it weren't for that ledge, we could jump into the pool,' Jualth pointed out.

William took the remark to heart and stepped half a pace back from the edge. 'Why have we stopped?' he asked.

'We're resting. I've just had a baby and I'm very tired,' Lily answered flippantly.

'But making remarkable progress in your recovery, dear. I only hope when my turn comes I will do the same.'

The women turned away from the falls and settled on the soft grass in the shade. William remained rooted to the spot, listening to the sound of the stream flowing over the rocks and splashing into the pool below. He cocked his head as if straining to differentiate a discordant note above the noise of the flow. For a moment he thought he heard something but then it was gone, lost amidst the hum of the falling water.

Lily broke his concentration, deciding it was time to be more truthful. 'All right, we've stopped for a chat or to put it more accurately, we've stopped so *you* can chat to us.'

'We know you want to,' said Jualth, 'and as you can see, we've thoughtfully provided a secluded location where your privacy will not be compromised. Come and sit next to us.' She patted a spot to her side.

William looked around the unfamiliar surroundings, earning himself a few precious moments to think. Keeping everything bottled up was stressful and had been for a considerable period. He felt a need to trust someone and his companions had provided the perfect setting and opportunity to do so. He decided it was time to give ground.

'So, William, are you ready to *at last* tell us who you are?' Lily asked once he was seated next to them.

'We need reassurance' said Jualth. 'It's one thing to say no harm will come to us, it's quite another to actually know that it won't.'

William understood. His countenance turned into a more serious frown 'You have absolutely no idea do you, neither of you?'

Private discussions in hushed gatherings, in and around The Hidden Lodge, had provided no conclusion and no comfort. He could still be a government official for all they knew and an unwelcome presence as a result.

'Materials, water, ship's captain, priest, midwife …' Jualth listed. 'You are all these things and yet they add up to … what?'

'Put together they add up to a profession that has played an important part in the life of the capital for six centuries. I am the master of a bridge … the first bridge to span the Thames.'

'London Bridge?' Lily asked.

William nodded. 'The oldest and most abused bridge in the world.'

Jualth and Lily glanced at one another, both looking puzzled.

'I thought it had been knocked down,' said Jualth.

'It had, but it is now in the process of being rebuilt. I supervised the first few years to make sure its reconstruction proceeded according to agreed plans. A spell away was then arranged, but I must return in the autumn to oversee the completion of the buildings by next summer.'

Both Jualth and Lily remained puzzled; they had expected something more sinister, something worthy of concealment.

'I'm not quite with this, William,' said Jualth. 'Why the secrecy? It's an association most would be proud to put their name to.'

'Presiding over the demolition of a structure that has seen more of this country's history than practically any other construction that remains standing today is nothing to be proud about.'

'Is that your fault?' Lily asked. 'Why does it matter so much to you?'

'Because my father fought hard to keep the bridge standing, so hard that the struggle eventually killed him. With the support of many well-positioned people I took on the fight, but I could not achieve the goal he had set. There are many ruthless and powerful people who value modernity and profit above our nation's long-term heritage. The bridge has survived many battles but the most recent was the toughest and I must shoulder the blame for our defeat. What we gained in no way compensates for what we lost.'

'I'm sorry about your father,' said Jualth, raising a hand to gently touch his arm. The loss must have been painful and the time spent in battle enough to push all thoughts of a personal life to one side.

'But it *is* being rebuilt, William,' Lily said softly. 'You did achieve something.'

'In some respects, yes. By using materials from the old bridge and maintaining the design of its arches and buildings, even though the platform is now higher and wider, the character of the old bridge has been retained. We have also managed to reinstate its chapel, strengthen its foundations and reconstruct buildings that had previously needed extensive refurbishment.'

'How?' Lily asked. 'It sounds virtually impossible to me.'

'Me too, especially when the water is so deep,' Jualth agreed.

William recognised a rural innocence in his companions. His reluctance to engage with them turned into a desire to explain. 'London has changed greatly in the last fifty years. Many mass endeavours have been undertaken and completed, changing the whole appearance of the city and its landscape.'

'Such as?' Lily asked.

'Such as bridges not just for the roads but also the railways.'

'Och, I hate the dirty, smelly monsters that use them,' Jualth said distastefully. 'They're nothing but soot, smoke and infernal noise.'

'And they defile the countryside,' Lily concurred. Acceptance of modernisation was set for a tough battle in the Highlands.

'That aside, ladies, and the benefits that justify their construction, major buildings like music halls, museums and theatres have also been erected. Large and impressive projects have been undertaken, the embankments for one, to stop London from flooding, improve its transportation and provide a healthy sanitation system that will also clean the Thames.'

'Urgh ... imagine!' Lily said, screwing up her face at the thought of the filthy river.

'No, Lily, let's not. Go on, William.'

The list resumed: 'Tunnels under the river, an underground train system ...'

'Trains underground!' Jualth exclaimed in disgust. 'If those overground were not bad enough. Do you all breathe soot in that town?'

The observation was anything but far-fetched, though not something William wished to dwell on for a place he loved. 'We have glass palaces in Sydenham and Alexandria, parks, markets and ...' his face hardened, 'we also have the docks.'

'You sounded quite enthused up to that point,' Jualth observed. 'What's wrong with the docks?'

'Their ability to grow westwards at a time when the Port of London is in decline and when more than enough room exists to the east of London Bridge to accommodate their needs.'

'But you have saved your bridge, haven't you?' Lily said again. 'It will still be there, regardless of its new shape and form.'

'And you'll be there too,' said Jualth.

William could not disagree. The maintenance of the bridge and his continued role to look after it were aspects his father would have welcomed. 'A bridge will stand on the original site of the first stone bridge. It will retain some buildings and because of that will be recognised as London Bridge.'

'But ...?' said Jualth, sensing that the loss was far greater than the achievement.

'*But* ... it will not be *the* London Bridge. Its historic appearance will have been rearranged to suit modern times.'

'Will that matter in a hundred years or more? As long as a bridge remains with some of the character of the old, then a reminder of its history will always be there.'

'Maybe. I'd like to come back in a hundred years to find out what people think.'

'Explain that bit about that chapel, the one you had to reinstate,' said Lily, needing clarification.

'The chapel was transformed into an ordinary residence during the Reformation,' William explained.

'That evil king of yours, the one with all the wives,' said Lily. 'It's a strange sort of justice that allows a man to kill one wife so he can marry another.'

'We'd have sorted him out, Lily, and he'd have been only too happy to have a daughter as his heir.'

'That was something I was going to ask you,' said William, seizing the opportunity.

'The daughter question will be answered along with all the others when we're finished,' said Jualth. 'Now continue with your bridge. I had no idea you were so interesting.'

William was of the view that very few of his questions would ultimately be answered but, having found two eager listeners with whom he could chat and unburden much-accumulated stress, he was now surprisingly reluctant to stop.

'There's not a lot else to tell. When the reconstruction is complete, two small arches will sit on each side of a large central span, which will have the chapel standing on its northern pier and Nonesuch House on the southern. A small gap will follow both buildings and then a row of houses built to overhang the platform.

'The east- and west-facing buildings will be connected by gangways above the central walkway. The Great Stone Gateway and the Drawbridge will be retained at the southern end and a new gate erected leading into the city. As in the past, gargoyles will hang from the parapets to protect the bridge from evil. You can judge for yourselves how successfully they have served their purpose.'

The two women nodded thoughtfully, picturing the bridge as it was described. 'As compromises go, it doesn't sound too bad to me,' Jualth concluded. 'Do you not think when it's done you'll still have a bridge of equal importance?'

'We'll have a representation with the same importance, but it won't be the same bridge.'

'Will you remain its master?' Lily asked.

'I will and I shall endeavour to make sure there are no further changes.'

Both Jualth and Lily approved, recognising the conviction of a forceful protector.

'What exactly is a bridge master?' Lily asked. 'I'm not sure what it means and I'm dying to know where childbirth comes into it.'

'I told her straightaway,' Jualth admitted. 'I thought if she knew there was another qualified doctor ready to assist, it would calm her down. I was wrong.'

The description drew a smile from William. 'Qualified doctor I am not but, when there is a need, I must turn my hand to whatever is required. The bridge master is responsible for his bridge and for everybody upon it. I can turn none of them away and would not wish to do so. Maintaining the bridge and its buildings has been hard work up to now, needing the help of many highly skilled craftsmen. My call on these people will soon fall and the employment of many good men and women will no longer be necessary, another sad consequence of the present change.'

'That's the builder bit – that really threw me,' Jualth admitted.

'Will you live in one of those houses on the bridge?' Lily asked.

'No. My accommodation is in the Bridge House on the southern bank where I have living quarters, an office and a clear view of the river. At the rear, there are workshops and a yard.'

'And those locks you mentioned,' said Jualth, 'I didn't understand that bit. What are they and why are you getting rid of them?'

'Not all. They are the spaces under the arches and between the piers, twenty-one when the bridge was at its longest and all with a name. Unfortunately, with the need to strengthen the piers below water level, the locks narrowed and the bridge became a barrier to the flow of the river. At times the river to the west was six feet higher than the water to the east.'

'Sounds dangerous,' said Lily.

'And was. The narrow channels have claimed many lives.'

'Then it's a good thing they've gone,' Jualth stated bluntly.

'Changes had already been made in past agreements,' William countered. 'It is the scale of the present change that I have issue with. The problem of the piers had already been addressed.'

'And the reason you did not wish to tell us, William?' Jualth asked.

'It's not something I enjoy talking about. I was proud of the old bridge, as many others were, and proud of what my father and those before him had achieved. Its demolition was, and still is, very painful.'

'I can see that,' Jualth said softly. Losing such a famous landmark must have been *very* painful, especially when William felt the need to bear some of the responsibility. She understood his need not to talk about it and took a moment to reflect, so freeing her once mysterious guest from his interrogation. Caution had been necessary for the sake of her community, but deep down she had always known this man could be trusted. She consulted her co-interrogator. 'Do you think that's enough?'

Lily nodded. 'Well done, William. You told us *at last*.'

'Why did you keep us waiting so long?' Jualth quipped. She shared a secretive smile with her sister. 'Well, Lily, shall we see?'

'Of course. There was little point in bringing William to Jade's Fall otherwise.'

'Brought me to—' William looked sharply towards the falls.

Jualth held up her hand to demand silence. Both she and Lily raised their faces to the overhead canopy and shut their eyes. A gentle breeze brushed against their light clothing and long red hair. William gazed at each girl without fear of interruption or reproach. That moment alone was worth the long exploration north, a moment that would last eternally in his memory.

Quietly the girls listened until each seemed satisfied. They opened their eyes and smiled – both were in agreement.

William remained bemused. 'What were you listening to?' he asked.

'Old friends and wise spirits,' said Jualth.

'To what?'

Jualth smiled again. 'Let's just say that they like you and leave it at that.'

'It's about time we made a move,' said Lily.

'But—'

'Later, William. We will explain later,' Jualth asserted. 'First we have some horses to find and a journey to complete.'

William followed the women to the top of the waterfall, then down its side. He listened carefully to the sound of the stream, again straining to hear anything out of the ordinary. He heard nothing. Whatever those born to the countryside imagined they could hear, he could not. He reproached himself for even trying.

'Did we say we liked him?' the matriarch asked her fellow spirits.

'I did,' said Tily.

'And so did I,' said Jade in support.

'I reserved judgement, just like you, Mother,' said Lil.

'Why?' Father Devra asked. 'He seems a nice enough man to me.'

'He has a troubled mind, the type that comes with responsibility,' said the matriarch.

'Then he has much in common with your family, so why the reserved judgment?'

'Because he should be at the other end of the country. Have we ever run away when it suited?'

'Never,' said Lil.

'He explained why,' said Tily. 'He fought and won, but at great personal cost. It must have felt very lonely when all was said and done.'

'Strength without a family; I admire that,' said Jade. 'It shows great fortitude.'

'And it justifies his choice to travel in search of our whisky. He said he would return to London, so he can hardly be running away.'

'He may have travelled in search of our whisky, but he has found far more,' said the matriarch. 'So if he intends returning, how will he deal with the minor problem of falling for one of our own?'

'How will he indeed?' said Lil. 'As we do not know how he fights his battles, my judgement will have to wait.'

'Taking Jualth from us is a battle he could never win. He would be foolish to try,' said Jade.

'On the contrary, when the prize is so great, he would be foolish not to try,' the matriarch corrected.

'He is an honourable man, I am sure of it. He said he intended us no harm and I believe him,' Jade countered.

'He did say that, more than once, and the need to repeat it worries me. Who is he trying to convince? Us or himself?'

'What do you mean?' the priest asked.

'If he intends to take Jualth, by what means will he do it? When I know that, I will better be able to judge the character of the man.'

'Now you are making him sound like a villain,' said Jade. 'You can be too suspicious, Matriarch. Not everybody is against us.'

The matriarch smiled thinly. It was always wise to be suspicious first in her experience. Far better to be wrong that way than to suffer the consequences of misplaced trust. No battle was ever won that way.

Chapter 19

They arrived at Lonistle Loch in a shade over two hours and, after a few minutes' rest, the women prepared themselves for their swim.

'Why have we come all this way to do what could be done in under an hour at Velana?' William asked.

'It must seem very strange,' Jualth said playfully.

'And look how much farther we have to swim to get across,' Lily pointed out.

'That had occurred to me, as well.'

'Trust us, William, we have our reason and we'll reveal all, I promise,' said Jualth.

'When?'

Jualth handed over her clothing, having undressed down to her costume. 'Far too busy to think about that now.'

'There you go,' said Lily, following suit. 'Take good care of them and don't run away. They'll be needed when we've finished.'

'We're heading to that spot over there,' said Jualth, pointing across the loch. 'If you could make your way around, please. We're not intending to swim back.'

The two women set off, leaving the newly identified bridge master with his arms full of recently worn clothing. His job had prepared him for many varied tasks, but never this. The seasoned anglers who had watched the swimmers wade into the loch now set their eyes upon him. Conjuring up what limited dignity he could, he backed away, mounted his horse and, holding onto the reins of the abandoned mares, started his short journey. When he reached the spot Jualth had identified and tethered the horses, he took a stroll along the shoreline determined to make full use of his spare time.

When the women emerged from the water, Lily was breathing heavily – her sister had set a hard pace.

'Well done. Almost there,' said Jualth, offering well-meaning encouragement.

'Of course I am,' Lily retorted, leaving her sister in no doubt.

They waded through the shallow water to a large, flat rock where they climbed on top and sat down. William returned having retrieved their clothing from the horses.

'Thank you,' said Jualth. 'Just drop them down there; we'll dry ourselves off in the sun first. Why don't you join us?'

William felt disinclined to sit meekly by such an open display of female flaunting. He stared up into the cloudless sky and quipped with a degree of satisfaction, 'No, I'll leave you two *sun worshippers* to dry yourselves off. Let me know when you're ready to depart.'

'Suit yourself, there's no need to be bashful, we have no plans to undress further.' Jualth poked her tongue out as William walked away – how dare he use her words to get his own back. She observed his path along the shoreline. 'What a sociable fellow he is, Lily. Our company is forsaken for that of a few unknown fishermen.'

'Sociable and dangerous,' Lily said warily. 'The wrong answers to his questions may hinder our new-found friendship.'

'Then we had better provide some answers of our own. We can't have him being misled, can we?'

Once dry, the inquisitive bridge master was summoned and they set off home. 'Did you enjoy your chat with the fishermen?' Jualth asked.

'Learn anything new?' Lily added. It was obvious to both that his roaming had been for a purpose.

'That this loch has fish,' William answered. 'I even witnessed the novel act of one being caught.'

'And what else?' Lily asked.

'That a certain loch to the south is considered a dead loch, with no fish to speak of.'

Jualth looked astounded. 'Lily, did you hear that? We have no fish in our loch.'

'I wonder if Ned knows.'

'*And*,' William continued, 'as I've seen no other person fishing in all the time I have been down there, it would indicate to me that you and Ned have been playing a game at my expense.'

'Ned would be very upset to hear you say that,' Jualth rebuked. 'I can see we will have to prove your fishermen friends wrong and our Ned right. But no telling your new friends, William. It's our secret and we'd like to keep it that way.'

'And how will you provide proof of something that evidently does not exist?'

The women smiled but refused to enlighten their companion.

'All right, tell me if I'll need Ned's rod.'

Lily turned her head to avoid showing her amusement.

'No, William, that's not the way to catch them.' William opened his mouth to speak, but Jualth cut him off. 'Wait. When we arrive at Velana, we will show you.'

Their return took half the time of the outward journey, with a direct route followed and no breaks – Lily had begun to brood for the sound of her daughter's healthy tonsils. They arrived at the edge of Velana, about a mile up from its feeder stream. Jualth and Lily quickly dismounted.

'What are you doing?' William asked.

'Keeping our promise,' Lily said wearily. 'Would you mind jumping down? This can't be done from on top of a horse.'

Jualth and Lily removed their footwear as William joined them. Then, at their immodest best, the women lifted their skirts and stepped into the water.

Jualth glanced over her shoulder. 'William, are you missing the point? If you'd prefer not to get your trousers wet, you can take them off.'

Although not enthused by the idea, William took off his shoes and socks, pulled up his trouser legs and, with a stiff upper lip, followed his guides into the ice-cold shallows. They stopped when the water was deep enough to hover above William's knees.

'What are we—'

'Sssh,' Jualth whispered. 'Look at your feet.'

Turning blue, but determined to match the sisters' resolve, he looked down. Within a few seconds, a long, thin, wavy figure glided along the floor of the loch to within a few inches, noted their presence, then slipped effortlessly away. He stared incredulously, first at the fish, then the two women. They were looking excessively pleased with themselves.

'Satisfied?' said Jualth in a hushed tone.

'And perplexed,' William said in an equally quiet voice. 'So why have I not seen or caught one?'

The women looked at one another and shrugged, still playing their little game. 'You tell us, William,' said Lily.

The point made, they waded onto the shore, remounted and continued their journey back to the inn.

Jualth noted how silent the bridge master had become. 'You're looking thoughtful, William.'

'Just thinking.'

'About?'

'Fish.'

'And?'

'And … maybe I shall have another attempt with Ned's rod. That will still be all right, I take it?'

Jualth glanced at Lily who had let out an involuntary and highly amused yelp, a reaction she had previously managed to suppress.

'That will be fine, William. You do all the fishing you want and when you catch something, bring it back to the inn and we'll cook it for you.'

William nodded, as Lily lost all control and burst into loud laughter.

'Tomorrow, I'll put you out of your misery,' Jualth said in a conciliatory tone.

'In what way?' William asked, doing his best to ignore the disconcerting laughter coming from her sister.

'By providing a trip to our distillery. As you have been so open with us today, you deserve it. I'm trusting you, William, taking you for an honest man that means us no harm. Just don't make me regret my decision. Wrong me and, I promise, you'll be sorry our paths ever crossed.'

The bridge master again noted how easily his host changed from one mood to another. However, he did not begrudge the warning – the landlady clearly took her responsibilities seriously, a quality they had in common. He would not let the threat come between them.

Chapter 20

With fears about the stranger alleviated at a late-night meeting of the Elders, Thomas was given the task of showing the protector of London Bridge around the distillery. With their confidence gained, William was then given free rein to wander, assist or merely observe. Any unasked questions he saved for the right time and the right person.

As the days passed, he continued to accompany the woman to Lonistle, to fish using Ned's rod (with the same lack of success) and to ride or walk alone. One such excursion found him heading up the southern slope of Velana Loch to the resting place of past generations.

He tied his horse to the hitching post in front of the church wall, intent on a brief stop before visiting Father Donald. Crossing a narrow track and following the slope's incline towards a sun-drenched loch, he reached a small, wooden gate set in a low picket fence. Save for a few cawing crows he had no company, a state of isolation that suited him well.

First impressions of the cemetery were mixed. Regimented lines in pre-planned order did not exist, even if the askew-facing stones and the short-cut grass looked well cared for.

He looked across the valley and noticed two horses ambling through a glade in the northern hills. Both riders were easily identified by their white clothing and red hair. His growing feelings for one of them was something he had not sought and, with his quest complete, the sensible course of action would have been to move on and let the memory of this Scottish encounter fade with time. But Jualth was not someone who could easily be forgotten, nor the strangely hidden community she lived in. Why the latter should trouble him so much, he was not sure, but leaving was not an option until he found out.

He dragged his eyes away from the two young women and started to stroll amongst the headstones. From the inscriptions he noticed that Lily was not the first McTavish woman to bear that name; it obviously bore a special significance to her family. He stopped by an interesting engraving. The stonemason had carved the vertical descent of a stream onto jagged, unfriendly looking rocks. The inscription read: 'Jade McTavish, daughter of our Mother'. It seemed a strange, almost unnecessary epitaph, one that did not make complete sense. What were they saying?

His eyes darted to the distant shore, to descendants who might know the answer. The riders were no longer visible. Assuming they had not vaporised into spirits, he presumed the trees to be the likeliest form of camouflage. His unproductive search came to a sudden end when he heard voices and the sound of a horse's hoofs approaching from the direction of the vicarage. One voice he recognised, that of Father Donald, but not the other. Its unexpected lack of inflection surprised him.

When they came into view, William's presence in the cemetery did not go undetected. Their conversation halted abruptly. Father Donald's companion mounted his horse and, with a parting word, headed off south past the church. The priest then made for the gate.

'It's good to see you, William, though you should have warned me if you wished to see me in private,' the priest said once he had reached the headstone.

'I was on my way, Father, but ...'

'You found yourself distracted,' the priest suggested on his behalf.

William could not conceal his curiosity. 'Your companion, I don't believe I've seen him at Matilda's.'

'No, you haven't. Strangely enough, he is not one for the inn.'

'I thought everyone visited—' William began.

'There are exceptions, as I'm sure you are aware, but it isn't for me or anyone else to question their ways.'

William recognised the priest's entitlement to protect his parishioner's privacy. There were no grounds to extend his curiosity, even if both knew how impossible it would be to live in a community and ignore its focal point.

'Your distraction, William?' said Father Donald, redirecting his attention.

William indicated towards the stone. '"Jade McTavish, *daughter* to our Mother"?'

Father Donald stared at the words that belonged to another century. 'The mother to them all,' he explained. 'They have great respect for their ancestry.'

'And who was Jade?' William asked.

'A McTavish redhead with an interesting history, and a very important person in the annuals of McTavish folklore as a result.'

Important enough to have a small waterfall named after her, William thought. He stared across Velana to the northern slope, searching for two present-day descendants. From under the cover of trees, they burst into view riding at breakneck speed.

Father Donald sighed fearfully at the sight of his most headstrong parishioners hurdling obstacles, weaving between rocks and plunging through streams as they galloped through the open glade. 'That's their mother's side you can see. They pursue danger as if it were a dear friend.'

William nodded. He had experienced something of the kind en route to the inn. 'How often?' he asked.

'Too often, and for no reason other than the hot-blooded thrill of a contest. It's a reckless race by two girls who believe they are charmed and thereby impervious to the consequences of a fall.' He sighed more deeply.

'The fire in their blood is hotter than at the core of our mortal coil. It is not wise to cross them.'

William took the warning on board but, unlike the locals, the landlady and her sister did not have the same hold over him. They had his respect, not his fear. 'There are some aspects of a person's fate you cannot control, Father. And you are right, it is reckless.'

The women soon disappeared, taking different paths through the trees. The spectators could only image the risks being taken beneath the canopy.

'Had enough of the cemetery, William?' Father Donald asked. 'If you have, we can retire to my lodgings.'

William remained rooted to the spot, gripped by the spell weaved on the distant shore. At his feet lay the stones of stories about McTavish women as yet untold. He was fascinated to know what they were but sensed the priest's reluctance to say more.

'Ned mentioned something about an Italian priest when he spoke of Velana. Did he live here? Did Velana? Do they lie in the cemetery?'

Father Donald shook his head. 'No, William, neither rest here. Velana we never met. If she did exist, it was in a distant land. When the priest left us, we never heard from him again.'

'He must have a special place in your history to have been allowed the honour of naming your loch.'

Father Donald smiled and gestured towards the gate; he would not be drawn.

William peered back to the northern hills. Jualth and Lily had remerged from beneath the canopy. In an open glade, they sat astride breathless mounts staring towards the southern shore. They could have been looking at him, it was hard to tell, but he did not intend a solitary wave to find out. He turned away and accompanied the Father to the gate, the mysteries of what the headstones told left to another day.

Chapter 21

'Well I don't know, it's a complete mystery to be sure,' said Ned, looking as baffled as one of his locals would if served a whisky with a cherry floating on top. 'You say the loch is teaming with fish yet you *still* haven't managed to catch one.'

'That's what I said, Ned. One moment there are no noticeable fish to be seen, the next, not only are they everywhere, but they're energetically leaping into the air as if the water's on fire. It's no wonder the girls have decided to trek all the way over to Lonistle for their swims.'

It was evening and well into the third week of August when, propped up against the bar, William had decided to tackle the barman on this strange phenomenon.

'Now, now, English exaggeration aside,' Ned chuckled before feeling obliged to point out, 'did you not say yourself that you and fishing were not the closest of bedfellows? To my way of thinking, you got that spot on.'

'Spot on or not, Ned, I remain the only person attempting to pursue this noble pastime in your loch.'

'Velana,' Ned reminded him.

'*All* I seem to meet are curious bystanders who refer venerably to your fishing implement as "Ned's Rod" and then struggle to keep a straight face. It's a phrase that extracted similar merriment from Lily a while back.'

William leant closer, causing the barman to straighten his back. 'So, Ned, why would they say that? Why with the help or hindrance of "Ned's Rod" am I achieving such a poor return?'

'You're blaming your equipment again, William, I can tell.'

'And that's all you'll be telling,' said Jualth, having quietly crept up to join them. 'Far end please, Ned.'

The obedient bartender tugged his forelock. 'Right you are, Matilda … eh, Jualth.' Ned received a swipe on the arm for his forgetfulness as he passed. In truth, though, Jualth did not mind the slip one iota. It was high praise that she reminded him of her mother.

'You and your sister do like bullying that poor man,' William observed.

Jualth leant alluringly forward. 'He loves the attention. It shows we care.' To her amusement, William edged slightly away, seemingly threatened by her close proximity.

'And it's as difficult to squeeze information out of him as it is you two. I've never encountered such a suspicious community.'

'You're one to talk,' Jualth said, making it perfectly clear how little his grievance mattered. But, having overheard William's comments to Ned, she considered a small explanation necessary. 'The fish are a wee bit perky,' she confessed. 'It won't last long, it never does. In a few days it will all be quiet again.'

'Will it?'

Jualth nodded. 'They pay us the briefest visit, then leave. It happens every year.' She reached down for a bottle to refill his glass.

William grunted, uncertain what to say. He took a moment to look around at the young men she had abandoned. 'Have you finished with them?' he asked.

'No, William, I am never finished with convivial company. I shall return after a brief word with you.'

He would have preferred a longer word and an extended period in her presence but, for whatever reason, such favouritism over the past few days had been lacking.

'So, what are you doing now, the landlady's rounds, making sure all your regulars have drinks and an allotted minute of your time?'

'That's right, William, and this is your allotted minute.'

'And the purpose?'

'The purpose … to put you out of your misery by informing you about tomorrow.'

'What's happening then?'

'Fish, William. You are going to catch one and I shall help you.'

'Are we going paddling again?'

'You are, William. First thing, tomorrow morning, I want you to follow the flow to Finlay Bay, ready to receive instruction.'

'From?'

'Whoever happens to be standing next to you. And after you've finished, you can relax until the evening when you will again follow the flow to the bay. Got that?'

Unsurprisingly, the answer was no. 'I haven't got a thing, Jualth.'

'You will, William, you will. Tomorrow you'll not only have your fish, but the answers to many of your questions.'

'Will I?'

'You will.' Jualth smiled and pushed herself away from the bar. '*Right*, that's your minute up, time to return to my young men.'

Jualth left the bridge master to drink alone. He had his whisky, a considerable state of confusion and an unwanted desire to follow the landlady along the bar. He sipped his whisky and fought to remind himself of the purpose for his travels.

William assisted in several tasks in and around Finlay Bay the following morning, chief amongst them the laying of a large net. It did not require many brain cells to work out where the fish would be caught, but as to the means ...? The large rock on the distant shore grew in ominous significance as he recalled the moment he had first gathered together Jualth's discarded clothing. The reason for all the swims and Lily's desire to participate so soon after having a baby was now becoming clearer – the two of them would have a prominent part to play in catching the fish.

By mid-morning, all tasks were complete. Finlay Bay would require his presence again in the early evening, but no sooner. He spent the rest of the day riding in the northern hills, fighting the image and lasting impression Jualth had made by disrobing next to him on that rock. He could not believe what she and her sister were about to do.

He returned to the inn late afternoon and, when the time came, followed the locals from Matilda's to the bay, where the gathering patiently waited for the evening's event to unfold. The wait was short, with the swimming party soon descending the hill. At the bottom, Ned led the women towards the stream and onto the northern shore.

'So, this is what the whisky does to you,' William murmured, wondering if he was the only one who feared for their safety. The fish, after all, were by no means small and their behaviour erratic to put it mildly.

The party stopped at the large outcrop and Ned turned to face the darkening trees. After flinging a robe over each of his shoulders, the two naked females tiptoed into the water, splashed themselves, then climbed onto the rock and walked out to its edge. Within seconds the sisters had dived in and were heading towards the bay.

William shuffled uneasily, sensing the nervous excitement of the crowd. He had come to Scotland to find and taste a malt whisky, not to witness two naked females swimming across a loch in order to fill a net with fish, an as unconventional a method of fishing as he was ever likely to encounter. The behaviour of this one, isolated community he found both perplexing and intoxicating. It was enough to provide second thoughts about a departure that grew closer by the day.

Jualth and Lily soon reached the bay amongst a maelstrom of fish swimming alongside and in tow. Once they were clear, the struggle to pull in the catch began and continued until tired limbs had completed the task and bodies had fallen exhausted into crumpled heaps. Wrapped in towels, Jualth and Lily turned to leave for their well-deserved hot tubs, but not before William had been the recipient of the broadest of smiles. He now had some answers, several more questions but, most of all, he now had his fish.

Chapter 22

Two days of celebration, which included the consumption of a peculiar but ultimately delicious fish, followed and then a day of calm, when Jualth and Lily were given space to breathe and a chance to relax. William, having gained the trust of the landlady and witnessed first-hand everything her isolated part of the countryside had to offer, was treated as an honourary member of the community and regarded as the acceptable face of the English enemy. He took an active part in the celebrations and had as good a time as any, benefiting from more attention from Jualth as a result. In return, his offer to go riding was accepted and they set out early one morning heading north.

'Where are you taking me, William?' Jualth asked curiously.

'You know where I'm taking you.'

By that, Jualth surmised it must be Jade's Fall. 'All right, why are you taking me there?'

'You'll find out when we arrive.'

'Will I?' Jualth raised an eyebrow; her companion was being very mysterious. 'Sure you can remember the way?'

'I'll remember.'

'Well ask if you can't. I know how difficult you find it without the sun to help you.'

William remained true to his word, having already retraced the route on a previous occasion. Leaving the horses to graze, they scaled the side of the waterfall and chose the same spot as before to rest.

Jualth playfully pre-empted the mysterious reason for their return. 'This is all very romantic, William. Have you brought me here to propose?'

The dignified authority that so typified the bridge master temporarily slipped, much to his companion's amusement. Highly embarrassed, he shook his head. 'No, Jualth, I have not brought you here to propose.'

'Pity.'

'*Jualth!*' Prior to meeting this particular young woman, he had rarely found himself so easily lost for words. 'Jualth, is there no holding you back, no consideration that it might be inappropriate to say the first thing that comes into your head?'

'I'm not with you, William. How else do we communicate?' Jualth's look of incomprehension gradually turned into a smile. She was being mischievous again.

Belatedly, the exasperated bridge master saw the funny side and relaxed. He was surprised at the ease he felt with someone he had known for only the shortest of weeks. In London, where he had yet to meet a woman like Jualth, such familiarity took years.

'So why have you brought me here or have you done it just to make all my other admirers jealous?'

William ignored the insinuation that he was also an admirer, choosing instead to address her initial question. 'To talk, Jualth.'

'About?'

'Things I have yet to understand.'

'Such as?'

'The distillery.'

Jualth groaned. This ground had been trodden over before – why the need to revisit it? 'What about the distillery, William? Were you not shown around and your questions answered at the time?'

'Not all, some I saved. Some I thought should wait for the right moment and the right person.'

'You don't have to ask, William. You're not going to take any of this knowledge away with you, you've already said. So why the need to know something you can never tell?'

It was a good question and one he could not easily answer. 'I have a need to understand. I cannot say any more.'

Jualth allowed him to continue, but with no guarantee of cooperation.

'Your distillery has no Excise hut, no Excise officer, no sign of a government official anywhere. How can that be?'

'We have an arrangement; we leave all the official stuff to Brethna. The duty is only payable when the matured whisky leaves the bonded warehouse. You probably know that.'

William did not say a word. He stared at Jualth and waited until she grudgingly relented.

'Okay, that's half the story, the part with a touch of honesty.'

'And the other half?'

'Illegal without the merest hint of honesty. We don't pay any duty on what we keep; we are very bad people.'

William closed his eyes. He had guessed as much, but wished, even prayed, to believe otherwise. 'Jualth, this could land you in big trouble.'

'Aye, I know,' she said indifferently.

'*Jualth*, are you listening to me? Not paying your taxes and running an unlicensed distillery are serious crimes. You could end up in prison.'

'I know that too.'

'*Jualth!*'

'*William!*'

The two stared at one another in equal frustration, one belligerently refusing to care, the other inwardly terrified at the potential consequences.

'Well ... tell me why ... and for how long ... and how you manage to get away with it?'

Jualth did her best to explain: 'The middle part of your question, since it was built, the latter part, I have no idea. We are careful, we are remote and the days when Excise officials combed the countryside looking for illegal stills has long since passed. Somehow we were never detected and we did not feel inclined to voluntarily hand ourselves in. And as for the why, because we don't like paying taxes that benefit the English and not us.'

'And ... nationalism aside.'

'And ...' said Jualth, sighing deeply, 'you saw the other reason a few days back and have had it for dinner ever since.'

'The connection between the fish and the whisky being ...?'

'The water, William. Remember the damp floor in the storeroom next to the outside wall where, drip by drip, we allow one or two of our casks to feed the soil, which, in turn, feeds the adjacent stream and ultimately the loch? It's also the reason for the unique fauna and flora in and around Velana.'

William held up his hands. 'No, that's enough, let's stick with the nationalism bit and forget about the water and what it supposedly does to those flawed fish.'

'*William!*'

'*No*, I'm fed up with fish and, if you don't mind, before I lose grip on reality for good, I shall choose to believe something that is in some small way rational.'

'Fine by me,' Jualth said flatly. She stared at her guest as he looked away, wondering if any of this really mattered to him. It did not matter to her, though. She had allowed her inquisitor to bring them to this spot for one reason and, however inappropriate, she had no intention of giving up so easily. 'William?'

'Yes, Jualth.'

'Do you mind if I try a wee experiment?'

'Go ahead. It will give me time to—'

William's words were cut off in mid-sentence as Jualth leant across and pressed her lips against his mouth, holding her kiss for as long as she could. She drew back, but only by the merest of inches, just enough for her blue eyes to focus on the dark brown ones in front of her. Jualth put her arms around his shoulders and moved in closer. Suddenly, without warning, William turned his head away.

Jualth momentarily held her grip, unaccustomed to such rejection, then eased away.

William took a deep breath and grasped both her hands. 'Jualth ...' He stopped, not certain how to go on.

Unsure of the problem, Jualth offered further encouragement. 'Do you want me to try again?' she suggested.

William shook his head, an action that held a contrary meaning to his will. 'No, Jualth; once is enough. Do it again and I might never want to stop *or* leave.'

'You don't have to leave, William. You can stay here and become a criminal too.'

The bridge master almost laughed, but he just could not bring himself to do so. Deceit went against the grain. He looked at her closely, as close as at any time during his stay. 'You are …' He hesitated.

Just in case he had suffered a sudden attack of shyness, Jualth helped him out. 'Beautiful?' she suggested.

'*Beautiful*, Jualth, and …'

She was about to aid him again when a finger pressed against her mouth. She pursed her lips and kissed the finger. 'It's all right, William. No need to explain further. It was a long shot, trying to seduce a man who actually has a brain. I shall make do with what I can find here.'

William released her hand and sat back, feeling both wretched and relieved at the same time. They remained silent but still relaxed in one another's company. Jualth raised her face to the emerging sun as it started to glisten through the overhanging trees. She closed her eyes, breathed in and listened. With little breeze to speak of, the only sound was the timeless flow of water falling onto the rocks below.

'What are you doing?' William asked.

'Listening.'

'To what?'

'The spirits. They're talking about you again.'

This time William could not help but laugh. 'Is there anything to this or am I just the victim of a joke that you and Lily choose to play on strangers?'

'No joke, William. This is real and both Lily and I can hear them talking.'

William closed his eyes and listened. He could hear nothing but the sound of running water. 'All right, you have the advantage; what are they saying?'

'That you are honest, trustworthy and would make a fine husband.' William tilted his head towards her. She smiled and opened her eyes. 'You have till the weekend to change your mind.'

'What happens then?'

'The Kvairen Cèilidh.'

'And?'

Jualth shrugged. 'Possibly nothing and, then again, maybe everything. That all depends on your answer.' She held up her hand, indicating to a bemused companion that the subject was closed. 'Wait and see, William,' she said firmly, but gently. 'Whichever it is, I promise you one thing, it will be a night to remember.'

'He should have kissed her,' Jade sighed. She glanced at Tily. 'Now what is going to happen?'

Her fellow spirit felt the same way. 'Jualth has given him another chance. Let us hope he takes it.'

'Why do we hope he takes it?' Lil asked.

'Do you not think he is right for our daughter?' Jade probed.

'How should I know? The man has barely been with us five minutes.'

'On occasions, that's all the time needed.'

Lil was not so sure. 'To fall in love maybe. But that does not mean he is the right man to stand at Jualth's side.'

Jade looked at Tily and the priest for support. 'Do you think he is the right man?'

Father Devra answered first, 'I have seen nothing in him to suggest otherwise.'

Tily nodded her agreement. 'I think he would make a worthy McTavish husband.'

'Well, there's a first,' Lil scoffed. 'Mother, you're being unusually quiet. Anything you'd like to say?'

'Only that my mind remains unchanged,' said the matriarch.

'Why?' Jade asked. 'However belatedly, he has been honest with us. And those weren't exactly dark secrets he was keeping.'

'Rejecting our daughter's hand, when every other man is falling over backwards to get it, troubles me. He obviously likes her, so why the resistance?'

'Has he not given a good reason – his bridge? It has a community just like ours and his loyalty to it is admirable. Why should we expect him to act any differently to us?'

'It's what makes him worthy in my opinion,' said Tily.

The priest agreed. 'The young man has all the attributes necessary to make a fine addition to your clan, though whether I can say the same for your daughter joining his ...?'

'If that is your opinion, Devra, I would rather not hear it,' the matriarch said brusquely. Her daughter's attributes were not up for question, especially by a man. 'I respect his loyalty to his community as all you do. There must be a very profound reason for it, either that or he has another reason to reject our daughter. And as I said, that troubles me.'

'So do you want him to stay or not?' Jade asked.

'I would like to keep an eye on him now he has made his mark on our family.'

'How do you intend to do that if he leaves?'

'I can't unless one of you girls cares to go with him? The matriarch looked around: there were no takers for her proposal. 'Then, as Tily has already said, he has been given a second chance, though why he deserves it ...?'

'We could help him, nudge him in the right direction,' Jade suggested.

'We could, but we will not. As his character is still in question – with at least two of us – it is best not to interfere. We will leave him to make up his mind and then deal with the consequences as they arise. Agreed? Or does someone have an alternative plan?'

No one chose to defy the matriarch's will. Her achievements had been years in the making and jeopardising them was at their peril.

Chapter 23

In the days leading up to the Kvairen Cèilidh, William spent much of the time riding in the adjacent hills, his thoughts wrestling in a disordered dance between life in London, his father, his work and the extraordinary community he had pursued for no reason other than to find its whisky. He had found much, much more.

At the inn, he was surprised to find Lily both an informative and agreeable companion when on breaks from her daughter. Several instructive walks alongside the loch provided a breadth of knowledge and enthusiasm about the local fauna and flora that she had been too busy to demonstrate before the swim.

Jualth, who had demanded time to bond with her niece, found out to her cost that, despite bestowing every ounce of attention possible, a McTavish baby always wanted more. She had no qualms about granting her grandmother's wish and handing Harriet over to someone with far more patience.

On the evening of the dance, William was escorted to the hall in a nearby hamlet. When fiddles rose, pipes blew and hands fell rhythmically upon drums, Jualth had one last word for him: 'Any change of mind, William? If you have, I can stop the music and make the announcement.'

William held his breath for what seemed like the entire length of the first reel. Eye contact never flinched; the unspoken answer in his dilated pupils was an unequivocal *yes*. Slowly, he shook his head. It was not the answer either wanted.

'So, you've decided London is where you belong?'

'It is and I must start my return journey without further delay.'

Jualth could not conceal her disappointment. 'Why so soon? It isn't autumn yet.'

'It will be by the time I get there.' His adventures in Scotland had to end at some point. A slow journey home would serve to distance himself from the dreamlike events of the summer back to a world and life where his real responsibility lay.

Jualth sighed, resigned to accepting the inevitable. 'So this is it then, and such a brief meeting. I shall not ask you to write; I'm not a great one for correspondence.' She took a step back, turned and slipped away for a quiet word with the band. William's last chance had gone.

The local hall was packed, the Kvairen Cèilidh attracting the entire community and, at Jualth's invite, a select few from Brethna. In her opinion, the most boisterous event of the year could only be enhanced by an influx of youth and spirit.

A young man with adoration in his eyes approached the leading lady as she headed back across the dance floor to the bridge master. 'Jualth, how about a dance?' he asked.

'Wait your turn, Jake. The first dance is already taken.'

A disappointed youngster backed away, rejected for the moment but determined to make his wait a short one.

'Well, William, it might be your only chance. Are you up for it?'

William studied the floor, noticing the diverse styles of hopping, stomping and raising of arms.

Jualth mistook his hesitation for apprehension. 'Anything goes, William. You will not make a fool of yourself.'

He nodded, his mind made up. 'Let's fight our way in, shall we? I've always wanted to do this.'

Jualth laughed, delighted to see the dignified outer persona substituted for the sense of fun beneath. 'Oh, William, if only ...'

Soon both bridge master and landlady were banging the floor as energetically as any of the youngsters that encircled them. Ned was present, having been busy during the day supplying the freely available alcohol that stood on tables at the opposite end of the hall to the band. The only notable absentee was Edith, who remained at the inn with her granddaughter. Her dire premonitions of what lay ahead that evening needed no affirmation from the spirits.

Jualth was soon parted from William, not by Jake, but by Craig and then Ted. She was at her most seductive best, in white as always, with her long red hair dancing to a tune of its own. When taking time to rest, she played her admirers as she always liked to play them, a few minutes' attention, then move on to someone else.

William stood back and watched, an interested, even fascinated observer. Nathan had blessedly come and gone, picking up a bottle of Kvairen on his way out. Freedom from her husband's jealousy allowed Lily to enjoy the dance as much as her sister. She made sure William had a dance and her occasional company, the last fleeting visit ending in a gently whispered, 'Not long now, William.' Bemused, he received no opportunity to seek clarification.

Jualth continued to dance with everyone, even permitting Ned the privilege until he trod heavily upon her toes and was dispatched with a swift kick to the shins. Frazer followed in the trail of Douglas, then Craig again and many others. Only the surly and hot-headed Jake found his persistent requests met with equally persistent refusals. He was out of favour, the recipient of the cold shoulder and nothing else. Instead of dancing, he spent his time brooding next to the drinks table, topping up on the courage needed to vanquish all competitors. When his patience finally snapped, he banged his glass down, stepped onto the floor and pushed his way towards the blurred image in white. One final lurch forward and he found himself between Jualth and her latest suitor.

'My turn, Jualth. Ye gonna dance with me now.'

Jualth knocked away his hands and moved resolutely to his side. 'I'm not ready to dance with you yet, Jake.'

He stepped back in front. '*Now*, Jualth.'

A hand grabbed hold of his shoulder, but it was repelled by an angry thrust of Jake's palm into the owner's throat. The suitor fell with both arms splayed, causing two more dancers to topple with him. Jake grabbed hold of Jualth.

'Let go of me, Jake,' she shouted, struggling to release herself from his grip. 'I'll decide who I dance with.'

In a flash, Craig and Ted were on top of Jake, wrestling him away. Jake lashed out, sending Craig crashing to the ground. Those that now turned had not seen who had started the fight and, when Jualth's original partner rose, he was greeted by a thump from Frazer and dispatched back down to the floor. Ted lifted Jualth off the ground, intent on getting her to safety. Jualth struggled and kicked out, unconcerned where her boots landed.

'Get off my sister,' Lily yelled from the side. She started to move in but was grabbed by William. Undeterred, Lily stamped her foot down hard, crushing his toes to regain her freedom, then charged forward and leapt onto Ted's back, her fingers gouging into his face. The young man fell backwards, taking both girls with him. Within seconds there were only a few not involved: the band who tried to play in rhythm to the fight, the elderly, the remaining womenfolk (who yelled encouragement from the side), Ned and the astonished visitor from London.

William now knew what Jualth meant by 'wait and see' and, although he did not fully understand their ways, he saw no reason why he should not join in, especially as the two young women were throwing punches to equal any around them. No sooner had he taken to the floor than he was on the ground; he had no idea where the punch had come from or who threw it. He got back to his feet and hit the first person he saw.

The band stopped only when the fighting had ceased, which in true inebriated fashion had gone on until everybody was too exhausted or too concussed to remain upright for more than two seconds. Only one combatant remained vertical, fists clenched, looking around for any last adversary willing to take him on. There were none.

Jualth pushed Lily to one side and sat up. The sisters had fought back-to-back until, through a wise tactical manoeuvre, they had sought the refuge of the floor. She stuck a finger in her mouth and wiggled a loose tooth. 'Damn,' she cursed, 'Jake will pay for that.' She glanced around at the sea of bodies, gratified to see William's prostrate and semi-conscious figure. She looked up and tried to focus on the one remaining upright figure. 'Ah … Frazer!'

Lily grabbed hold of Jualth's shoulder and pulled herself up. 'Frazer?' she said doubtfully.

'Frazer,' Jualth repeated.

Lily shook her head. 'No!'

'*Yes.*'

'Are you sure? We can always wait till next year's fight.'

'And witness the same outcome ...? No, Lily, I cannot afford to waste another year.'

With no fight left in her, Lily acquiesced. 'Oh well, your decision, Sister dear. Let it be the strong and very, *very* quiet Frazer.'

'Frazer,' Jualth called out. 'Come and pick me up.'

Frazer sprang into action, stepping on or over heaving bodies, until he had Jualth hoisted in his arms.

'Oh, you are strong, Frazer. Strong enough to carry me home?'

Frazer mulled over the weight of his prize. 'Aye, reckon so,'

'Okay, then, let's go. Coming, Lily?'

Lily looked up at the towering figure of Frazer holding her sister. She turned her head from side to side, choosing not to be outdone. 'Ned!' she cried as she searched. 'Ned, where are you? Come and pick me up.'

But Ned had quietly left whilst the fight was in progress and was already well on his way back to the inn to prepare hot water and bandages for the wounded. Lily caught William's eye as he and the other grounded rabble pushed themselves halfway up.

'William,' Lily smiled, rediscovering her sweet, alluring other self. 'Always around when I am in need and, as we're heading in the same direction, would you mind?'

William grunted and got to his feet. He did not mind at all.

Chapter 24

'William! Have you been fighting?'

The question came from across the kitchen table where Jualth had for some time been nursing her wounds. William had just slumped onto the chair opposite, the proud owner of a black eye, a bruised nose and several knuckles devoid of skin. Jualth had a matching black eye, a swollen jaw and a graze to her forehead.

'I do seem to remember an abundance of fists heading in my direction,' the bridge master recollected.

Jualth could not contain a wicked laugh as she struggled out of her chair to fetch a black coffee for her guest. 'Must have been a popular target,' she surmised, placing the cup in front of him. 'Care for anything else?'

William shook his head, an action instantly regretted. Jualth delicately returned to her seat and studied her foreign ally-in-battle. She was pleased with her night's work. 'Sleep well?'

William groaned a reply, 'With a demolition squad in full swing inside my head?'

'Plenty of them around after a Kvairen cèilidh. It will go in a day or two.' Jualth chuckled, basking in William's uncharacteristic overindulgence. 'Enjoy yourself last night?'

Feeling exhausted, William trolled through his memories of a night spent drinking and dancing, before being capped off by an every-person-for-themselves drunken brawl. He found himself making an extraordinary confession. 'Not only did I enjoy myself, but I also had the pleasure of witnessing another unknown aspect of your character.'

'I am full of surprises, William. Regretting your decision to leave?'

The visitor defied his internal fireworks and belligerently shook his head.

'Yes, you are. You will miss me, you will miss Lily, my inn, the whisky, even Ned's rod. In fact, everything about your short stay.'

William gritted his teeth at the thought of *that* fishing rod. He had the urge to break the damn thing in two before he returned home. 'Jualth?'

'Yes, William.'

'The purpose of initiating that fight was ...?'

'Frazer.' William looked puzzled. Jualth recognised the inadequacy of her explanation on dulled grey matter. 'All right, a man. I had to find a way to choose a man and it resulted in Frazer. If I'm not getting the brightest, then I might as well get the strongest.'

'Do you love him?'

Jualth felt an inner pang – they both did. 'I've known him for a long time and when he starts talking, I'll find out. He's a bit of a mystery man, just like you were and perhaps still are.' What mystery remained was now never likely to be learnt.

'Have you told him?' William asked, diverting the conversation away from himself and back to Frazer.

'Yes and he understood. Unlike most of the men at the dance last night, he does not drink heavily. He has no need of whisky, which is a quality I like, especially after Nathan. He's older, calmer and decent. He will make a good husband.'

William foresaw an obvious obstacle to matrimonial harmony. 'But you live here, and he lives and works in Brethna.'

'And he will continue to work there for the time being. When the opportunity arises, we will give him a job in our distillery. Until then, I will enjoy the freedom of only seeing him at weekends.'

William fell silent, the reality of another man taking his place adding clarity to his thoughts. It seemed to be what the whole summer had been about for Jualth. Her life would go on; she had no intention of pining for someone who would not or could not give himself to her. Belatedly, he offered his best wishes.

'I hope it works out, Jualth.'

'So do I, William. So do I.'

Lily entered the kitchen carrying Harriet and sat between the wounded couple. Studying the facial bruises of each in turn, she could not help but chuckle. In turn, her appearance had altered in no way, displaying not a single mark or blemish. She was the best fighter of the lot.

'Such a pity,' she sighed. 'You two have so much in common.' And in her unrestrained manner, she laughed out loud, leaving the recipients of her comment to contemplate the profound truth of those words.

William departed mid-morning the following day having completed the most interesting episode of his sabbatical. Jualth saw him off from the stables, then returned to the inn to join Lily and Ned at the bar. She received a hug and kiss from her sister and a warm hand on the shoulder from Ned, loving gestures that said everything. Then they industriously set to work, preparing the lounge for their first patron of the day. When done, the two girls sat at the end, permitting Ned sole charge of serving when the need arose.

'I'm surprised you didn't go with him,' said Lily.

'*To London?*' said Jualth, abhorred by the thought.

'No, stupid, to Brethna. You said he's heading back to the land of Jack Vardy before disappearing for good.'

'I was ready to go and I expected to go. William stopped me, said he could find Brethna by himself. It's a challenge, but challenges do not seem to worry him.'

'He led you to Jade's Fall unaided. It's not an easy place to find.'

Jualth leant back and shut her eyes. Memories of their last trip stirred and the agonising moment he had turned his head. Only losing her mother equated to her present feeling of loss. Hiding the pain was difficult.

'You could still catch him,' said Lily. 'You could still persuade him—'

'No, it's his decision not mine. I gave him a second chance and he chose to stand his ground.'

'But you love him?'

Jualth smiled, that much was obvious.

'You love him,' Lily repeated, 'and now you have Frazer instead, both men, both tall, dark and strong, and ... and there endeth the similarity.'

'You never know, Frazer might have surprising intellect underneath that wall of silence.'

'Just as long as he isn't another Nathan.'

Mere mention of the family's black sheep changed the mood. 'Where is that husband of yours today?'

'I no longer keep track. When I see him, I do not ask where he has been, I simply remind him he is a father now and it's usual for a father to accept the responsibilities that come with a child.'

'Any evidence to suppose he will?'

'None,' Lily sighed, regretfully. 'It appears I am her sole guardian.'

Each took a moment to reflect upon the man they had lost. If it was their fault, there was little they could do about it. Responsibility to their community came first.

'So, when are you planning to marry the silent one and, as we are in the wake of a riot, would you please make it a quiet affair?'

'It will be a civilised and modest occasion, but everyone will be invited. If the priest can marry us within the month, then so much the better.'

Lily sat up. 'Did I miss something whilst we've been sleeping together? Are you expecting?'

'I am expecting to be expecting.' There was no need for a deeper explanation. The timing of offspring was dictated by a higher cause.

'In that case, get on with it; you're not as young as I am. You'll not heal as quickly.'

'What about the sleeping arrangements?' Jualth asked. 'It should be you that's moving room, but if you want to stay put ...'

'No, Jualth. That room is for you and Frazer now. I'll have a word with Grandma, see if I can twist her arm.'

The impact of a sudden breakage shattered their cosy chat. They glanced around to a nervous-looking culprit.

'*Ned*, how did you manage to do that?' Jualth demanded. 'No one has come through the door yet.'

'I was just … whilst I …' Ned demonstrated with his empty hands what he had been doing to alleviate the boredom.

'Stock levels are low, Ned, bottles *and* glasses, so if you have a mind to keep living …'

'I'll clear it up,' Ned said hastily.

'You do that.' He disappeared out the back to fetch a pan and brush. 'I hope that's all he's broken, Lily. I've a mind that we're a bottle short.'

'William?' Lily suggested.

'I'm wondering that too. But with the dance, Nathan and all that's been going on, I cannot be sure. It might just be me.'

'Did you search him before he left?'

'I thought it best to keep my hands to myself,' said Jualth, with a hint of regret.

'You have no doubts about him?'

'We have his word, Lily, and remember what the spirits said.'

Lily recalled their trip to Jade's Fall. 'Ah, yes, the spirits and William. Did he ...?'

'Ask about Jade? No, Lily, he probably chose not to be curious.'

'A wise move had he but known. I wonder what he would have thought of us if he had?'

Chapter 25

1759

Jade stiffened behind the bar when she noticed the guide and his companion enter The Hidden Lodge. Anxiety was only natural when a stranger crossed the threshold, even when word had preceded his arrival and a room was waiting. Conversation shrank to a murmur and then into silence. Jade glanced across to Ruth, who sat alone in the corner of the lounge, and gave her a reassuring smile – she would deal with their unwanted guest, just as she always did.

Jade kept a close eye on the stranger as they approached the bar. He was looking around, assessing whether his prospective lodgings were up to scratch. It did not seem to bother him that he was the centre of attention.

'Good to see you, Stewart,' said Jade, greeting the guide.

'And you, lass,' Stewart replied.

The stranger's gaze had settled on Ruth, enough to make the young landlady feel uncomfortable. Jade cleared her throat: 'And your friend, Stewart?'

The stranger turned his attention to the barmaid, fixing his gaze on her in the same way as he had done Ruth. It was a touch too intense for Jade's liking, almost enough to cross the invisible line of what was considered acceptable.

'This is—'

'Auguste Braithwaite, miss,' the man interrupted in a self-assured, assertive tone. He did not need anybody to speak up on his behalf.

His intense stare softened; he seemed pleased with what he had so far seen. Jade noticed a worrisome sparkle in his eyes, the type designed to ensnare the fairer sex. It could easily end up upsetting the menfolk if care was not taken to conceal it.

She looked away, unable to hold his gaze. The locals were watching and, as far as she could tell, the stranger had not created a favourable impression in the few short seconds since his arrival. Strangers rarely did if they were not the type to blend into the background. The quieter and more reserved they were, the less trouble they tended to be. Unfortunately for Mr Braithwaite, he appeared confident and too handsome for his own good, despite several prominent scars to his face.

'Mrs,' the barmaid corrected, holding up her ring finger for inspection. 'However, I will not be offended if you call me Jade. Everybody else does.'

Mr Braithwaite smiled. Despite her regrettable marital status, he had already rather taken to the agreeable-looking redhead addressing him. 'You have a delightful inn, Jade. I take it that you are the landlady?'

Jade shook her head. 'No, sir—'

'Auguste, please.'

Jade half nodded – it clearly did not take much to embolden their new guest – and indicated towards the corner. 'Mrs Forsythe is both landlady and owner of The Hidden Lodge,' she informed him. Ruth could decide herself whether or not she wished to be on first-name terms.

Mr Braithwaite allowed Ruth the pleasure of one of his charming smiles. He received a nod in reply, but nothing more. Jade was quick to draw his attention back to the bar. 'Your room is already made up, Auguste.' She pushed a mug of whisky across the counter to Stewart and lifted the hatch. 'If you'd care to follow me.'

Mr Braithwaite politely stepped aside and, with bag in hand, duly followed. He had no objection to taking orders from a woman. Control always returned to him whatever the situation and, at present, he was more than happy to be alone in the company of the young barmaid, whether she was married or not.

'Is everybody as quiet as Stewart?' he asked as they reached the top of the stairs. 'I wasn't sure whether I'd said something to upset him on our journey here.'

'You'll find many on the shy side. I hope you'll understand if folks wish to keep their business to themselves during your short stay.'

Mr Braithwaite found the redhead's presumption amusing, though he was careful not to show it. The locals might well wish for his stay to be short, but that was for him to decide, not them.

Jade opened the second door on the left and stepped in. The room was not large, containing little more than a bed and a small cupboard. With its bare walls and floorboards, little was provided in way of comfort or aesthetic appeal. Mr Braithwaite, however, did not appear worried. If anything, he looked well pleased.

'You have other guests?' he asked.

'Just you at this time.'

The stranger nodded thoughtfully. 'Then these other rooms are empty apart from …?'

Jade breathed in, trying to be as patient and polite with the gentlemen as possible. It was a question he had no right to ask, but she felt the need to answer all the same. It would save him from trying to find out in another way. 'Those that belong to Mrs Forsythe, me and my extremely jealous husband, and two very noisy children who sleep with their respective parents when guests are present.'

Jade was starting to get a very bad feeling about their guest. She received another of his charming smiles, something she was already getting fed up with – the man was clearly not put off by warning shots.

'I think that's enough questions for now,' she decided on the stranger's behalf. 'I'll leave you to get settled in. Come and join us when you're ready.'

Jade closed the door on their guest before he had a chance to say anything more. As she walked along the corridor and down the stairs, she was thinking about Jamie. He would not take kindly to the stranger; not many would. Mr Braithwaite's manner was far too informal and the sooner he decided to move on, the better. Trouble of the husband kind she could do without.

Chapter 26

1896

It was late afternoon, a few days into September, when Jualth arrived at the Brethna Distillery only to find the Excise hut empty. With the desk tidy, the shelves in neat order and the cabinets shut, there was no sign of life to be seen. Jualth closed the door and watched as the black cat followed Daniel and the cask-laden cart towards the warehouse. Where was Arthur? He had never missed a meeting before.

On the other side of the main entrance she stepped into the office hallway and called out. There was no response, just stillness and then the slightest of noises from the back.

'Arthur, is that you?'

The floorboards above began to creak and Jack Vardy appeared at the top of the stairs. 'Jualth, I saw you arrive. Come on up.' He turned away without waiting for a reply.

Slightly miffed by his curt manner, Jualth instead chose to listen for another noise from the back. She heard nothing and, without the necessary authority to search the office, she felt unable to investigate further.

A glass of whisky stood waiting in Jack Vardy's office. She sat down on the opposite side of the desk, feeling ill at ease. 'I only popped in to find Arthur. I thought I heard someone moving around downstairs.'

'That won't be Arthur. Someone from the works, maybe.'

'Where is he then? Is he about?'

'He needed some time off. I sent him home this afternoon.'

That action in itself was mystifying; Arthur did not work for the distillery and was therefore outside Jack's jurisdiction. 'Can you do that?'

'I've done it.'

'Why?'

'I've already told you why. Even his type require rest at some time. I provided the necessary shove to untie him from his desk.'

'But what about—'

'Leave the delivery notes with me. Pop back in the morning, first thing. I'll have everything ready for you then.' Jack beckoned her towards the whisky. 'Have a taste. It's new. See what you think.'

Jualth stared stony-faced at the distillery boss; she did not like change, nor the unpleasant way he referred to Arthur. They both had reason to regard him as an ally and not the administrative nuisance that went with his position. She raised the glass, sipped and played the taste around in her mouth.

'Well?' Jack asked.

Jualth had little trouble in identifying the region and its derivative. 'A new blend from one of our friends on the Spey.' She sniffed, but did not care to re-taste. 'A tiny variation to Dougie's Hearth,' she concluded.

'But a big variation in its name – Celtic Fire.'

Jualth dismissed the notion as misleading. 'It doesn't have much of a kick to it. Best used for medicine, like all their blends.'

'Our friends will not be pleased to hear you say that.'

Jualth was not listening, her mind was still on the Excise officer. 'Will Arthur be all right?'

Jack leant back in his chair; the whisky had proved an unsuccessful distraction to his young and troubled business partner. 'Don't worry about him.'

'How can you say that, Jack? I'm bound to worry.' She irritably pushed the new blend away, having no stomach for weak whisky.

The distillery boss noted the assessment of the competition and directed attention away from the missing man again. 'Is there anything you need from us?' Jualth shook her head – for the moment that took care of business. 'And your daughter, how is she? Frazer says very little.'

Jualth made the necessary effort to be civil, though she still found the whole situation along with Jack's lack of empathy vexing. 'Jessica is busy finding her legs, like any other one-year-old, and managing to bump into anything and everything she should see but does not. That comes from my husband's side, not mine.'

She stifled a deliberate yawn – the falseness of the conversation was to the liking of neither. It provided Jack with the opportunity to end the meeting, recommending rest and a quiet night for the weary traveller.

Once outside, Jualth found the workshop closed and the workers already departed. It was the same case at the warehouse. Daniel had untethered the horse, but the cart remained loaded.

'Did you see Arthur before you left?' she asked as they walked up the track towards the stables.

'I dropped by his hut on the way out, told him you were due in today.'

'And how did he seem to you?'

'No different to normal. Why?'

'Because he isn't there now. Jack said he needed some rest and sent him home.'

Daniel, who had wondered why Arthur had not accompanied Jualth to the warehouse, was equally puzzled. 'Perhaps Frazer will know something.'

'I doubt it. My husband has no peripheral vision, he just follows his nose. If there's something I should know about, I won't get it from him.'

'Why not pay Arthur a visit then? He doesn't live far from the village.'

'No, I can't do that. If Jack's being honest with me, I could upset a very important person. I have to tread carefully, do nothing that will jeopardise our relationship. But there's something wrong, I can feel it.'

In the morning, and still troubled, Jualth returned to the distillery to pick up her papers. First though, she needed to know if Arthur had risen from his sick bed. She pushed open the door to the Excise hut and found him sitting at his desk, large as life, looking no different to when last seen. Jualth emitted a huge sigh and gave him one of the biggest hugs he had ever received.

'Arthur, never do that to me again. I barely slept a wink last night worrying about you.'

The hug lasted longer than it should – Jualth had been *very* worried. She let go and leant back to look at him closely.

'You look all right to me. Did you have a good rest?' Arthur opened his mouth, but his chance to speak quickly vanished. 'Of course you did, otherwise you wouldn't be here now.'

'J-Jualth ...' Arthur nervously stuttered, as beads of perspiration began to form on his smooth, hairless dome.

Jualth cut him off: 'If you had a woman to look after you, you wouldn't have been poorly yesterday.'

'Y-yes, but ...'

'No buts, Arthur. I want you taken care of, and if you don't do something about it before my next visit, I shall do it for you. Understood?'

Arthur nodded meekly.

'Right, then ... paperwork?' She looked over her shoulder. 'I can see nothing on your desk so I shall assume Jack has it waiting in his office.' Jualth kissed Arthur on his damp forehead, caring little for the moist, salty taste. 'Just remember what I said, and make sure not to worry me again.' With a quick wave and an affectionate smile, she left the hut feeling greatly relieved.

The papers, minus payment, were waiting as arranged in the lower office. The distillery boss did not deem to show his face and Jualth felt disinclined to climb the steep stairs to bid him farewell. The cash could wait until her next trip. She left and headed straight for the stables, saddled her horse and set off for home.

Behind her, Jack Vardy watched from his office window whilst, in the Excise hut, Arthur Whibley sat staring at the bare wooden door. Neither had said a word out of turn, neither had warned her. They had led the young woman to believe there was nothing to worry about on her journey home. She would soon find out how very much her friends had let her down.

Chapter 27

On her return, Jualth enjoyed a long hot soak to recover from two days of riding. Maternal duties then took over, feeding her playful one-year-old and an energetic, fast-growing niece. Lily had thought it only fair that her sister should re-establish the bond that her brief absence from both children had broken.

By early evening, Harriet and Jessica were safely tucked up in bed, with Edith sitting in the kitchen, an ear trained on the first floor. Lily, Ned and Jualth were behind the bar serving the locals as they arrived.

'How was your husband?' Lily asked in a quiet moment.

'Strong,' Jualth replied.

Lily smiled, envying her sister's good fortune. 'That wasn't quite what I meant.'

'But that's about it, apart from missing Jessica.'

'Does he not miss me?'

'I expect so. He just doesn't think to say.'

'Oh dear,' Lily sighed, sympathetically. 'You have to assume a lot with him unless you share his fascination for cask construction.'

'There's a great skill involved *and* it was very interesting learning the ins and outs on the first time of hearing.'

'But not the second, third and on all subsequent occasions.'

There was no use pretending – Frazer was the possessor of few thoughts and the entrusted keeper of no top-level secrets. Lily put her arm around her sister and gave her a loving squeeze. 'Disappointed?'

Jualth could not deny the obvious. 'Aye, though I have no right to be. I married what I knew, hoping it would turn into something different. It didn't happen, so I must make do with a decent man who treats me well.'

Jualth suddenly realised what she had said. 'Lily, I didn't mean—'

'That I have even more reason to be disappointed? Well, I do and we both know it. What I would give to have a strong, silent man to look after me, instead of an absent, idle drunk.' For all Frazer's failings, Nathan was far, far worse.

'I wish he'd stop visiting us, Lily.'

'So do I. When he returned to his folks, I thought he'd stay away. Unfortunately, he knows this is the only place he can make demands and get what he wants.' Lily caught Ned's quizzical-looking eye and decided to clarify. 'Whisky, Ned, nothing more. Now kindly stop eavesdropping.'

Ned's astounded look of innocence fooled nobody. Not one corner of the lounge was safe from his sharp ears, as the sisters knew only too well. He was ordered to the end of the bar where he could wait until his services were required.

'The sooner we get a job for Frazer, the better,' said Jualth. 'Nathan will think twice about visiting us with my husband close by.'

'Why didn't you stop longer in Brethna? You had no need to hurry back; Grandma and I could have coped with Jessica.'

'I know, but I couldn't have coped with Martha. She is hard work, even more so than Frazer, but for the opposite reason.'

Lily chuckled. 'Now there's a mother-in-law who's never lost for a good word to say about her eldest son.'

'Never, Lily. And she also knows everything about everyone in Brethna since the time its first settlers arrived. Add that to half a dozen opinions on every subject and the imploring "Why don't you bring Jessica to see me on these trips?". I'm telling you, before long I'll be asking Gus for my old room back. I enjoyed my evenings in the Whisky Makers' Arms.'

Lily smiled mischievously. 'Oh well, they just have me now, and I'm having a great time.'

Jualth felt a twinge of jealously but, with the problems Nathan had caused, she did not begrudge Lily her life away from the inn. She deserved the freedom. 'Just make sure word doesn't get back,' she warned.

'I couldn't care if it did. A girl needs attention and not the type I used to get from Nathan.'

'Have you stopped feeling guilty about bringing him to the inn yet?'

Lily heaved a long sigh. 'Will I ever? But ... he's gone now and as long as you don't kick me out, I'm staying.'

Jualth took a turn to put an arm around her sister and squeeze, proof, if proof were needed, that it would take hell or high water for anything to come between them. Ned cleared his throat and nudged the landlady on her arm.

Jualth glanced around. 'What is it, Ned?' There was no need for an answer; she could see for herself what was wrong. Her arm slipped down from her sister's shoulder, as a bottle that had been on the bar beside Lily swiftly disappeared beneath.

Standing in the hallway was the tall, slim figure of a man in his late twenties. In a collar and tie, he held a cloak and some sort of gloved implement in one hand and a small overnight bag in the other. He put his hand to his mouth and coughed away the dust picked up from his journey.

'Good evening,' he said in a firm, slightly aloft voice. This social nicety was greeted with a universal silence. He approached the bar. Jualth and Lily brushed Ned aside and skirted along to meet him.

'Good evening,' Jualth replied as two sets of penetrating blue eyes fixed upon their unknown visitor.

The traveller looked towards Ned as if he would have expected to deal with a man. He cleared his throat and turned his attention back to Jualth. 'If it is convenient, I should like a room,' he said in the same firm voice.

'*English*,' Lily murmured disdainfully under her breath.

Jualth looked at the three-foot-long, narrow, leather-sleeved implement in his hand. Arthur had a similar one resting in the corner of his little hut. Inside was the hydrometer he used to measure the alcohol content of the whisky. She glanced over to Thomas whom, along with many others, was also looking at it. 'That can be arranged,' she said guardedly. 'And who might I be addressing?'

'Pennan – Mr C Pennan.'

Jualth greeted his announcement with a further question: 'And what does the "C" stand for, Mr Pennan?'

His eyes flickered edgily between the unrelenting stare of the sisters and Ned. The gentleman appeared ill at ease dealing with women and would have preferred the barman to serve him.

'Cecil,' he said, feeling obliged to answer.

Jualth could not care less what name his parents had given him, she just wished to establish her authority over the hired help. 'Right then, Mr *Cecil* Pennan, I am Mrs Jualth McTavish, landlady to Matilda's, and this is my sister, Mrs Lily McTavish.'

'And no, we're not married to the same man,' Lily said flippantly. 'We keep our maiden names in the Highland wilderness.'

Mr Pennan's nose rose in disapproval. His dealings with the fairer sex was limited and rarely went further than asking after their health. He was certainly unaccustomed to them talking to him in such a manner. 'Do you?'

'Yes,' said Lily in a deadpan tone.

As Jualth had announced herself as landlady, the visitor directed his next assertive comment towards her, 'I have a horse tied up at the stables. Could you have it seen to, please?'

If it had not been for one of the locals choking on his whisky, several seconds of profound silence would have followed this request. Lily's already hostile behaviour took a turn for the worst.

'Look after your own—'

Jualth put out a hand to stop her sister, her eyes warning Lily to be careful. 'Ned, would you mind?'

Ned did not move. Apart from helping departing patrons into their saddles and pointing them in a homebound direction, his duties as barman had never entailed anything to do with the stables.

'*Ned*,' said Jualth more forcefully, '*go* and look after Mr Pennan's horse.'

Ned played the part of the aggrieved barman and made plain his reluctance. 'Right, I'll do that then, *shall I?*'

Jualth and Lily glared at him.

He got the message. In a tense atmosphere, he lifted the hatch, grabbed his overcoat and was gone.

Mr Pennan stood waiting – he had asked for a room.

Neither landlady nor sister were unduly concerned by his desire to escape their company. 'You're riding late this evening, Mr Pennan,' Jualth observed.

'You were lucky to find us,' Lily added. 'Was it by accident?'

'I never do anything by accident, Mrs McTavish. Now if you wouldn't mind—'

'Then how did you know the way?' Lily pressed.

The traveller looked at Lily with displeasure, clearly affronted by the persistence of her attitude towards him.

'I think that's enough questions for now, Lily,' Jualth relented. 'Perhaps tomorrow, when Mr Pennan has settled in. You will still be here then?'

'Indeed I will, Mrs McTavish.'

Jualth lifted the hatch. 'Right, follow me if you will, Mr Pennan. I'll show you upstairs.'

A room with a view of the front garden was found for Mr Pennan, after which the landlady returned to the bar.

'*Jualth*, why did you stop me questioning that man?' Lily demanded.

'Since when do guests have to undergo an interrogation before being allowed a room for the night?'

'Since now sounds about right to me, unless you can tell me why an *Englishman* has turned up out of the blue on our doorstep?'

'I think we both know why, Lily, but if he doesn't deem to tell us first, we'll ask him.'

'We most certainly will and until then, he can keep calling us both Mrs McTavish, however ridiculous it may sound. Have you ever known someone to act in such a pompous manner?'

'He did seem rather entitled,' Jualth agreed.' She felt the close attention of her patrons upon her. 'Lily, make sure everyone has a whisky; I've a bed to make up for our guest. As he won't be rejoining us this evening, a meal is required in his room. I'll have a word with Grandma.'

At the bar door, she stopped for a parting word with her sister, 'We'd better be up early tomorrow, just to be careful.'

Lily nodded. She understood. Mr Pennan would have a shadow at the inn for his entire stay.

Chapter 28

Lily was crouched down at the side of the loch, a short distance along the southern shore, when she spotted their sturdily booted and well-attired guest descending the hill. In his hand he held the leather-sleeved implement he had arrived with.

Noticing Harriet playing along the pathway, Mr Pennan judged it impolite to ignore them, despite the manner in which he had been spoken to the previous evening. 'Good morning, Mrs McTavish,' he said as he approached.

Lily stood up, took a couple of deep breaths and forced a show of civility. 'Mr Pennan. And where might you be going?'

'Yet to be decided. I need to walk along the shores of this beautiful loch before I make up my mind.'

'Why?' Lily asked. With any other man she might have felt flattered by the tinge of red emerging in his cheeks. But not this one.

Mr Pennan proffered a condescending smile and ignored the question, choosing instead to make reference to the scrapbook and pencil Lily was holding. 'May I ask what you're doing, Mrs McTavish? I saw you peering into the water, to my eyes deep in study. May I look?'

Lily felt like a schoolgirl being asked to reveal the adequacy or inadequacy of her homework. Begrudgingly, she opened the book to reveal sketches of plants, flowers and insects, with annotations relating to colour, size, time of year …

'Lily Velana,' Mr Pennan read inquisitively. He had clearly never heard of its like. 'Is the flower special to these parts?'

'You could say that.'

'Were you named after—'

'I probably was,' Lily said curtly, 'I should have asked whilst I had the chance.'

The sharp mind of Mr Pennan understood her meaning. 'Mrs McTavish and yourself …' he said in a sympathetic tone.

'Are orphans,' Lily said dryly. No mention was made of their relationship to the third Mrs McTavish living at the inn.

Mr Pennan touched his forehead, aware that it was damp. He was unaccustomed to holding his ground whilst blushing. 'They are fine drawings, Mrs McTavish. You take a great deal of care in your presentation and have an excellent eye for detail.'

Lily gritted her teeth. She felt irked by the possibility of a common interest. 'You like nature, Mr Pennan?'

'Indeed. It's a wonderful form of relaxation and makes for a very necessary diversion when so much of one's time is spent working and living in the city.'

'Well fortunately I live and work in the countryside, and *this* is a little more than a relaxing diversion for me.'

Lily snapped her book shut and made an unwanted observation of her own. 'You're very well dressed for a stroll, Mr Pennan. You do not have to wear a collar and tie in these parts if it makes you feel too hot. No one will see you.'

Mr Pennan took a step back. The remark was pointed and unnecessary and, in his world, women did not speak out of turn. 'Thank you for your advice, Mrs McTavish. Kindly be informed that I dress for a purpose and am well used to making such decisions for myself.'

Lily ignored the reproach and continued unabated, 'Which city do you come from, Mr Pennan?'

'From the capital, Mrs McTavish – London.'

Lily's countenance hardened, though it had little to do with the minor issue of what she considered to be the capital in that part of the country. *That place again*, she thought. Lily brooded over the possible implications. 'I should have guessed, Mr Pennan. You weren't told in London that this might be a nice place for a diversion, were you?'

Fighting the inclination to retreat and resume his walk along the shore, Mr Pennan shook his head at what he considered a strange question.

'Then why are you here? Why the sudden visit from your distant place of work?'

Mr Pennan peered down his nose at the young woman, again feeling offended by her forwardness. His immediate response, however, was interrupted by a movement over her shoulder. 'Your daughter, Mrs McTavish; she is disappearing from view.'

Lily turned sharply. The unsettling presence of the unwelcome southerner had drawn her parental eye away from her adventuresome child.

'Harriet! Harriet, dear, come back to Mama. We'll have a splash in the bay later on.' Harriet stopped and skipped around, forsaking a trip to Finlay Bay until her mother was ready.

'Will your daughter not catch a chill from the water?' Mr Pennan felt duty-bound to point out.

Lily did not care for the interference. 'My daughter will be fine. She is made of hardy stuff, as are all my family.'

'Even so ...'

'My daughter's welfare is my concern not yours, Mr Pennan. Now, do you have an answer to my question?'

The visitor stared open-mouthed at the feisty redhead. Not even his superiors addressed him in such a blunt manner. 'You are very direct, Mrs McTavish. When I wish to inform you of my business, I shall do so but, until then, I shall bid you—'

'Where are you going?' Lily asked again, refusing to be intimidated by his show of authority. This was her home not his and she did not react well to those who did not respect that.

Mr Pennan stopped, having already turned his back. He pointed across the loch, having now decided. 'If you must know, I intend to follow the stream in the corner there up into the hills. So, if you will—'

'Mr Pennan, how long will you be staying?'

Deigning to answer one last question, the visitor replied, 'My intention is to leave tomorrow. Now, good day.'

Lily watched him depart, her eyes boring volcanic ventholes into the back of his head. She looked up towards the inn where Jualth and her grandmother stood watching in the garden. She shook her head. The message was clear – Mr Cecil Pennan was bad news.

Harriet wandered back and tugged her mother's dress, showing her impatience at having to wait. Lily knelt down to tidy her daughter's hair, straightened her blouse and remove specs of dirt picked up on the hem of her skirt. Her hand brushed against a silver necklace – an heirloom given at birth. It had belonged to her mother, Matilda, whose passion for the inn, the loch and the community's traditions she had passed on to her daughters. Mr Pennan's presence now put that legacy in considerable danger.

'We'll go swimming in a minute to the same place your grandma used to take me.'

Harriet nodded, not understanding the significance of her mother's remark, only the affection behind the kiss and prolonged hug that followed.

Jualth's curiosity did not allow her to wait for her sister's return. Her impatience had her descending the hill in minutes, Jessica held in her arms. When she reached Lily, her daughter was released and left in Harriet's care.

'Well, Lily. How serious is it?'

'He's following the stream up its course.'

Both girls fixed their sights upon their potential nemesis. Mr Pennan's interest in the flora was slowing his progress along the western shore. It was another source of irritation for Velana's wardens.

'So now we know,' Jualth whispered.

'He will find out and return to inform his masters unless …'

'Unless what, Lily?'

Her sister typically spoke from the heart. 'Unless … we stop him.'

'Without managing to send us to the gallows, how do you intend to do that?'

'We have our ways, you know we do. Why not take him to Jade's Fall?'

Jualth had hoped for something better. 'No, Lily. That place is not for the likes of him and we will do him no harm.'

'Then what *do* we do? Allow him to leave and then sit around waiting for English justice?'

'Harming Mr Pennan will not stop that. We need a different approach, one based on reason and not wishful thinking.'

Maybe that would come later but, for the moment, all Lily had to offer was raw, cold-blooded emotion. 'Why now, Jualth? After all this time, why now?' Her sister had no answer. Lily stared accusingly at her. 'He comes from London, you know.'

The insinuation was not to Jualth's liking. There was no evidence to suggest another party's involvement. 'This has nothing to do with William. He gave us his word.'

'He said no harm would come to us. His idea of harm may be very different to ours.'

'Lily, *enough*. Do not blame William. You cannot land this on his shoulders.'

Lily felt another tug at her dress. Two worried children stared up, frightened by the sight of their mothers arguing.

Lily stroked her daughter's hair to sooth her fears. 'Jualth, we cannot let that man take everything we have. No one has that right.'

Mr Pennan reached the corner of the loch and started to ascend the small rise to the stream.

'I didn't say we would, Lily. I said we have to find a different approach – another option. This is hardly something you plan for. You just hope the day will never come.'

'Should we get the horses and warn the distillery there's an inspector on the way?'

'A warning will not stop him. He has a right to do and go where he pleases. They're half expecting his visit anyway. Leave it to Thomas. He'll fill us in this evening.'

Mr Pennan now stood by the stream, taking in the view over the loch. He soon detected the distant scrutiny of his hosts. Their disapproval of his presence mattered not; he had a duty to perform and the law to uphold. He turned away, set on his purpose to follow the line of the stream up through the trees.

'I will have to ride to Brethna after Mr Pennan has done his work,' said Jualth. 'A meeting will be needed.'

'I'm riding with you. You are *not* leaving me here.'

'I had no intention of leaving you, Lily.' The thought of a speedy return to Brethna was a timely reminder of her recent visit. 'Arthur,' she whispered.

'What about him?'

'He wasn't in his hut when I arrived. I didn't see him until the following morning. He said nothing, not a word.'

'Perhaps he didn't know.'

'He knew all right. He and Jack Vardy, they both knew.'

'And you reckon they told Mr Pennan where to find us.'

'How else ...?'

Lily felt the world imploding. 'Great! What happened to trust between business partners?'

'Arthur isn't a business partner. He's as much to lose out of this as we do.'

'And yet he said nothing!'

'His position doesn't allow him to stand up to the likes of Mr Pennan. He does as he's told. If Arthur gets into trouble, we are responsible, Lily.'

'Why? He didn't have to do it?'

'But he did, and he did it for nothing more than a warm hug and our friendship. He gets no other reward, we don't pay him.'

'What about Jack Vardy, then?'

'He'll be in the same trouble as us, everyone that colluded in our arrangement. And if news spreads wider than official circles, which I'm sure it will, our notoriety will make us the most sought-after loch in the Highlands.'

Lily looked horrified. The implications were untenable. 'Jualth, you have got to think of something. *We* have got to find that other option.'

'I know, Lily, but *what?*' Her sister could not answer. Jualth's frustration mounted. 'I can't do this alone, I need help from you, Thomas, Jack, the Father, even Frazer – anyone with the slightest notion that could lead to a way out.'

'Then we had better gather ideas and be quick about it. We'll start this evening, when Mr Pennan is not about, and then take the first opportunity to leave for Brethna together.'

'What about the girls?'

'I'm not leaving Harriet, not with Nathan behaving the way he is. She's coming with me.'

'They both are then. Frazer's mother can have her wish.'

Lily received her third tug on the skirt. 'Finndy Bay, Mumma.'

Lily bent down and kissed her on the forehead. 'Okay, Harriet, Finlay Bay it is.' She almost wished Mr Pennan was still on hand, just so she could witness his disapproval. There was no sign of him any more on the other side of Velana. 'Coming?' she asked her sister.

Jualth nodded. When there was little else to do except worry about the future, and the probable lack of it, why not embrace the simple pleasures of everyday life whilst they could? There was no telling when it would all end.

Chapter 29

1759

Jamie slammed the front door, his mood no better than when he had left first thing that morning. His excursion to the distillery, where after seven years he still remained the junior member of the workforce, had provided little more than exercise. It rarely amounted to anything else at that time of year whilst they waited for the tilling of barley to begin. Every conceivable job had already been done and, for the hell of it, redone. Jobs elsewhere were not easy to come by and the pay a pittance for their short-lived duration.

No work, yet here he was living in a thriving inn that did not require his services. He was the man of the house, but Ruth (his sister-in-law) owned it and Jade (his sweet, overly sociable wife) did the lion's share of the work and made most of the decisions. The women managed without him and the patrons liked it that way.

It should have been a source of pride, making a living from a successful inn. But it wasn't, and the minor role he played in providing for his family was not the only niggling problem that currently plagued his mind. There was also the small matter of Braid, his six-year-old daughter.

One solitary child that had required a swift marriage between her parents was all he had; a redhead like her mother, whom she resembled to an uncanny degree. 'No one would know you're the father,' his mother had commented when alive and he, too, may well have doubted his own part in her conception if Jade's unabashed flirting with the regulars had started before their marriage. That, however, did not stop him dwelling on whether he had the right to be called a true blood father and, in the absence of another child, his doubts would remain.

There was no one in the lounge when he looked in, or behind the bar. He called through to the kitchen but received no reply. Then he heard footsteps on the stairs. They were heavy and brisk, and did not belong to any of the females living at the inn. He stiffened as the person appeared through the archway.

'Good morning,' Mr Braithwaite said cheerfully, as if there was no reason to be anything other than good-humoured.

Jamie had given up trying to respond in kind. The women could be civil if they wished, it was their job to do so, but he was under no obligation to provide a false demeanour to an unwelcome guest. 'Seen my wife?' he asked gruffly.

'Eh, today? No, not so far.'

Jamie was not satisfied with the answer. He stared almost accusingly.

'Perhaps she's gone for a walk,' Mr Braithwaite suggested helpfully. 'Shouldn't you be …?'

The stranger's interest in why Jamie was in one place instead of another was interrupted by the creaking sound of floorboards above. Before he could move, the young man brushed past him on his way to the stairs. Mr Braithwaite watched him disappear, then chuckled quietly to himself. Insecurity in marriage was a sad part of life that he had witnessed in various social circles many times. He knew where the blame lay but felt under no obligation to change his ways. Where was the fun in that?

'So, the missing wife?' he said, pondering Jamie's predicament. He suddenly felt duty-bound to assist in finding the young woman.

Jamie slammed the last door on the landing, the final room yielding nothing. There was no one up there, least of all his wife. And yet he had not imagined it, he had heard someone moving about – they both had. He thought for a moment. Had the guest reacted to the sound or had it just been him? He ran down the stairs determined to find out, but when he got to the lounge there was no one there. Now the stranger had disappeared as well. His frustration was growing. No work, no wife, no stranger – nothing in any form that could occupy his time. The stables, he would try there. If he did not find Jade, perhaps he would find something to do.

He returned fifteen minutes later. The stables were in order. Like the distillery, everything that needed doing had been done. And still he had not found his wife. The Hidden Lodge was as he had left it, with no one answering his call.

He walked through to the kitchen and then into the garden. If he could have retraced his steps back the way he had come, he would surely have done so. Sadly, he had already seen them. Jade and Ruth were down by the loch and they were not alone. It infuriated him – their guest was taking inexcusable liberties! The three of them were strolling along the northern shore in amiable conversation, with no apparent sign that their gathering was inappropriate. Beyond the inn's bar, that man had no right to dwell in the company of another man's wife without the husband's presence or say-so. Even from the distant garden he could see that Ruth was on the edge of the conversation. Four days with Mr Braithwaite was already too long. If his behaviour remained unchanged, his stay would come to a rapid and enforced conclusion.

'Where are the kids?' Jamie murmured to himself, scanning the shoreline.

They were too young to be left to their own devices and yet ... not a sign. Usually, they were making enough noise to wake the dead, which often involved doing foolhardy things like jumping into the loch's freezing waters from large rocks. He was uncertain whether to admire the spirit his daughter displayed or be angered by the manner of her upbringing.

And there she was again, even though neither in sight nor sound his thoughts were on his daughter. If only he could be sure she belonged to him, then maybe he would be proud of the life and daring the young girl possessed. As it was, it only increased his anger and hardened his bad mood.

He had no intention of watching his wife and her wanton behaviour any more. Although she had not cast a glance in his direction, he sensed she was aware of his presence. With no work and no wife on hand, there was little to do other than follow the trail back through the kitchen to the lounge where, if he wished, he could drown his sorrows. After all, he had the bar to himself.

Chapter 30

'Jade, for goodness sake, tell him to go away,' Ruth implored in a hushed tone. She felt exasperated and uncomfortable in Mr Braithwaite's company, and saw no reason why they should extend civility at The Hidden Lodge to a stroll around the loch. She glanced around to the stranger, who was presently staring into the shallows studying the spasmodic ripples with interest.

'I tell him every day to go away and he ignores me each time. What am I supposed to do?' Jade replied.

'Something. *Anything.* Your word is usually enough.'

'Well, it isn't with him and, as he's a guest, we have little choice but to play along. He'll get the message eventually.'

Ruth breathed in irritably and looked away. Her dislike and mistrust of strangers had not changed. In her view, the entire male species were capable of dark deeds. It was the reason she had never remarried – there was too much hurt involved – and why she regarded Jade's presence as so important to both herself and The Hidden Lodge. She could rely on her friend to deal with the guests. If additional support was needed, Jamie and Madoc could be called upon.

'He might regard playing along as encouragement,' Ruth pointed out.

'Encouragement for what?'

'What do you think? I've seen the way he looks at you.'

Jade smiled. 'If he wants to add some additional scars to his collection, let him try. And besides, he knows I'm married, so the reason for his close attention cannot be for me.'

Ruth looked aghast. 'Yet his eyes tell a different story. Honestly, Jade, you tell such lies.'

Jade received a playful nudge for her impudence, but her friend was right – she did tell lies. To conceal the true parentage of her daughter, what choice did she have? It had been surprisingly easy until recently, when her powers to placate Jamie's moods seemed to have lost their usual effectiveness. Why Braid lacked for a sibling was unknown. Jade could only surmise the problem lay with Jamie. She was certainly doing nothing to prevent having another child.

'How do you think he got those scars?' Ruth asked. His face was a battleground that looked like it could tell many a sinister tale.

'Fighting, what else? And in many an alehouse, judging by his night-time indulgences.'

'He could be a soldier,' Ruth suggested. 'He could be honourable and brave besides being a drunkard.'

'True,' said Jade thoughtfully, noticing that the stranger was again approaching. 'Let's ask. It might serve to get rid of him.'

Ruth put an arm out to grab her friend, but it was too late.

'Mr Braithwaite, Mrs Forsythe and I were wondering whether you are an honourable and brave man or a drunkard who came by those scars in barroom brawls. Would you care to enlighten us?'

Mr Braithwaite stopped in his tracks. He had never expected a question concerning his facial trophies to be so forthright. For a moment it was hard to tell if he was offended, but then his mood lightened. A show of temper would only have proved the latter.

'Would it concern you if I confessed to being nothing but a bar-room brawler?'

'It would indeed. That's why we thought it best to ask.'

Ruth looked on in embarrassment. Despite the well-established principle that the least known about strangers the better, she was just as interested to hear what the man had to say for himself.

'You are worried about my conduct at your inn?'

'Now you mention it,' Jade replied. Knowing so little about someone, it was a dangerous game to play, this pushing of social boundaries, but it was done under the assumption that he needed to behave himself whilst he remained a guest.

Mr Braithwaite at last showed a glimmer of a smile. He reserved an easy-going manner for the ladies, even when being probed for information that was best left hidden. 'I am grateful for your hospitality and admire the peace of your home,' he said, gesturing to the surrounding landscape. 'It is how I would wish for it to remain.'

'Pleased to hear it,' said Jade, the lack of a direct answer an answer in itself. Ruth edged away, leaving Jade to deal with the stranger.

'You strike me as the type of man who has acquired an enemy or two in your time. Would that be true, Mr Braithwaite?'

The stranger's mouth dropped open then quickly closed – the young woman was as bold and forward a female as he had ever encountered. He felt affronted but also saddened; saddened that he had needed to travel to the ends of the earth to finally meet his match, only to find the woman married. 'I can look after myself, if that's what you mean.'

Jade hummed non-committally. Mr Braithwaite's informal behaviour indicated a disregard for its consequences. He appeared unable to deviate from type, even when such behaviour exposed him in an isolated community he knew precious little about. He was on a dangerous path that could very easily attract trouble. 'Looking after yourself is admirable but there comes a time when everybody needs a friend to call upon. Do you have such a friend, Mr Braithwaite?'

The gentleman nodded. The message was being spelt out very clearly. 'You want me to behave like an English gentleman, do you not?'

'Which I am sure you are,' said Jade, telling another of her lies.

Judging by her husband's surliness, it was a warning Mr Braithwaite felt obliged to heed. 'In which case, and if you will permit me, ladies, I shall leave you and venture into the hills along one of these paths. I shall endeavour to look forward to the hospitality of your inn once again on my return.' He provided a courteous nod and departed.

Jade watched him go and beckoned to her friend to return. 'There. Happy now?'

The way Ruth stared after the stranger, it was clear she was not. 'He's trouble that one, I can feel it.'

'It would be naive to think otherwise,' Jade agreed. 'We had all best be on our guard until he leaves. In one way or another, I do not think we will have long to wait.'

Chapter 31

Mr Braithwaite mopped his brow. It was a warm day and, through no fault of his own, his short stroll around the loch had turned into a much lengthier hike into the Highland wilderness. Bearing in mind it was only the second time he had walked along this trail, it was surprising how easily he had found his way. On the first occasion he had discreetly followed two young children, curious to see where they were heading, and had stumbled upon the waterfall. It had provided a cold but refreshing bathe once they had departed, so much so that, when his plans had changed that morning, he had decided to repeat the experience.

He was in good spirits, despite his unaccustomed lack of success with what he regarded as two conquests in the making. Considering the opposition, he was not disheartened and still held high hopes with either or both of them. It was a game he loved to play and one that he was rather good at, whatever the odds. He was a past master of secret liaisons that continued until the neediness of his conquests became too great. As the women he entangled himself with were usually married – or of a station far above his own – it then became wise to detach himself and move on, leaving vengeful but powerless victims to fester in their own self-destructive thoughts.

The odd husband, relative or guardian was bound to find out, hence the very visible battle marks earned along the way. They had nothing to do with military gallantry or the acquisition of a few useless feet of land on behalf of rulers who wished to own everything. It was just such a pity that these daring, sensual forays into society had – for the moment at least – all come to an end, that he had aimed too high and the woman's husband had sought a bloody and fatal revenge. Pistols at dawn were simply not his thing.

The troublesome situation, together with its obvious danger, had necessitated a rapid flight which, with the aid of his ill-gotten gains and the few 'friends' he possessed, had landed him in a place he could never have found on his own. It was the perfect hideaway and, until things cooled down and he received word that it was safe to return, he had no intention of leaving.

Taking a breather, he stopped to listen. He could hear running water not far away. Having waded through several small brooks, the noise was nothing out of the ordinary, only the sound of its energy. With his jacket slung over his shoulder he pressed on, the prospect of a cool, revitalizing bathe never more appealing.

Mr Braithwaite felt it before he saw it. Something was wrong. He slowed down – it was all too still, all too quiet. Overhanging branches stood rigid and birdsong was conspicuous by its absence. As he approached the falls he looked up: she was standing at the top, the redheaded child, staring down as if in a trance. She did not seem to register his presence. He followed her gaze to the edge of the pool, where the water dropped over a small step of rocks before running away into the distance. There he saw an arm dangling and the fair hair of a head that was all but submerged.

Stirred into action, he leapt into the water and turned the girl over. She was not breathing, and the cold water disguised any lingering heat in her body. It was impossible to tell how long she had been there. He slapped her across the face, then shook the unresponsive body. It ushered forth a gasp, but not from the dead child. He looked up again. The redheaded child had woken from her trance and was staring at him in horror. She moved quickly before he could do anything, down the side of the falls and off into the forest.

Mr Braithwaite shouted after her, but his throat was dry and his voice lacked any force. As the redhead disappeared into the trees, he carried the girl to the side of the pool. In desperation, he dangled her upside down and shook again. With no response, he laid her on her front, massaged her back then turned her over and pushed down on her chest, but all to no avail. It was hopeless; the child had either drowned or died in a fall. There was nothing he could do.

He felt a surge of anger and stood up, rubbing his brow vigorously. 'Damn it!' he cursed. A few minutes either way and who knew? He might have prevented whatever had caused this mishap or stopped that redhead from looking upon him as if he was responsible.

'*Damn it!*' he cursed again. What the *hell* had just happened? He had not fled the length of the country to become entangled in a death he had nothing to do with.

He had to think. He still had time on his hands if he acted quickly. That redheaded child could easily blacken his character if she implicated him in the girl's death. And if the locals chose to blame him, well, there was no telling where that would lead.

So, what was he to do? Abscond? Abscond where and by what means? He did not have a horse or knowledge of the territory. And why should he flee anyway? He had not done anything, so why make it look as if he had?

He desperately sought other options: he could catch up with the child – but, judging by her terrified state when she ran off, that would only make matters worse – or he could get back to the inn ahead of her and lay out his own account first. The latter option seemed the only sensible choice. Feeling regret at the need to abandon the dead girl, he took to his heels, heading back as fast as he could run.

If Mr Braithwaite had looked back to the top of the falls at that moment, he might have noticed an unusual glint of light. By following the girls and taking a bathe that first time, he had introduced himself to the spirits and given them an opportunity that had long been in the waiting.

'What has happened?' the priest called out in a broken voice as he hurried to Lily's side. A man was rushing away into the trees, leaving the body of a young girl lying on the ground at the side of the pool. 'Lily! That's your daughter's friend! What have you done?'

Lily barely reacted. She was deep in concentration, her eyes in a place well beyond the falls and the dead child's abandoned figure.

'Lily!' the priest cried. 'Will you answer me? What has happened here?'

Lily blinked. She was back at the falls when she needed to be elsewhere. 'You can see what has happened, Father. Your worst fears have come to pass.'

'But how? And by what means? If you had anything to do with—'

'What, Father? If I had anything to do with ... what?'

With polar opposite views of right from wrong, they stared angrily at one another: the one, pious and determined; the other, manipulative, stubborn and steadfast. It was the priest who eventually gave way. He looked back towards the trees.

'Well, who was that man then? Did he have a part to play in this?'

'Almost certainly. By how much, others will decide on his behalf. Now, if you don't mind ...'

'Lily,' the priest said with mounting frustration. 'If you have interfered with the living and are responsible for that child's death—'

'Ask the girl,' Lily interrupted.

'What?'

Lily pointed down to the body. 'Go and retrieve the girl's soul and then ask her if I had anything to do with her death.'

'Her soul has already left her body,' the priest said angrily. 'And we both know where it's gone.'

'Then you had better hurry, if you want to head her off before she gets to the loch and bumps into Agnes.'

The priest growled angrily. 'I will find her, whether it is now or later and, doubt you not, I will ask her.' The priest scurried away and disappeared into the first conduit of light.

'Irritating man,' Lily seethed. The interruption could not have come at a worse time. She narrowed her eyes and refocused. The stranger would not find his way back to the inn as easily as he had retraced his steps to the falls, not if she had anything to do with it. Although he did not know it, the luckless Mr Braithwaite had become a very important person to the spirit and her daughters. The day of reckoning for all his misdeeds was fast approaching.

Chapter 32

'Enjoy your walk?' Jamie asked coldly, as Jade and Ruth arrived back from their stroll around the loch. He was sitting at the kitchen table with a mug of whisky cupped in his hands.

Jade did her best to conceal her disappointment. She was reminded of another person who had sat at the very same spot in a similar pose seven years previously. That time had not turned out well for anyone. 'What are you doing here?' she asked. 'Do you not have work to do?'

Ruth walked over to retrieve the whisky. 'You shouldn't be drinking this early,' she said reproachfully.

'And you two shouldn't be enjoying the company of strangers without your menfolk present.'

'Uninvited company that we did not set out with,' Jade hastened to explain. 'I told him to go away, more than once.'

'She did,' said Ruth in support.

'And that's exactly what happened. If you'd spied on us a while longer, you would have seen that for yourself.' Jade felt no reason to go on the defensive. As far as she was concerned, the situation had been dealt with in a fitting manner.

Ruth reached out for the mug.

'Leave it,' Jamie hissed. 'It's just a drink.'

'And it's my inn, not yours, and it's for me to say—'

'*Leave it!*' Jamie shouted.

Ruth hastily stepped back. She was not used to being spoken to in such a manner, especially in her own home.

'*Jamie!* Don't speak to Ruth like that,' Jade reprimanded.

Her husband stood up; the women were siding against him and he did not like it. Furthermore, when it came to their 'guest', he did not believe them. *They* were in the wrong, not him.

Ruth abandoned the mug and moved away. She did not like confrontation or wish to be part of an argument. She disappeared into the lounge, slamming the bar door behind her.

'Happy now?' Jade asked, raising both hands to her hips.

Jamie was not. It was his wife he was angry with, not his sister-in-law. He sat back down. 'Where are the girls?' he asked. 'Why are you not looking after them?'

Jade took up the seat opposite. 'Unlike you to be so worried about them.'

'I have a right to ask, don't I? They *are* young.'

'They're the same age as Ruth and myself were when we decided the need for elders to watch over our every move was unnecessary. You're never too young to grow up in a place like this or do you think differently?'

Jamie grunted and looked out of the window. 'A place like this,' he murmured dejectedly. 'There's no escape, is there – this place, this community? We all have a rope tied to one ankle that can never be cut.'

'Why do you want to escape?'

'Why do you want to stay?'

'Because it's my home.'

'It's not the only place where we could have a home.'

Jade looked at her husband, mystified by what he was saying. 'What's wrong, Jamie? You've never mentioned anything about leaving before.'

'There's lots of things I've never mentioned.'

'Then why now?'

'Because of our guest. And if it wasn't because of him, it would be because of our forefathers or the loch and the so-called spirits that others swear they can hear.'

'Perhaps they *can* hear them,' said Jade.

'And perhaps it's all rubbish. Perhaps it's just old wives' tales told to reel in the gullible.'

'I wouldn't say that in Ruth's earshot.'

'Why not? Ruth thinks she will hear Gregor down there in that damned fog because of those tales. She needs to be told otherwise.'

Jamie brooded, thinking over what he had just said. 'The fog,' he repeated, tapping his mug. 'Where does it come from? We don't see it in Lonistle, not like here, not appearing as if from nowhere.'

Jade sighed. 'Who's to say and if you don't believe in the spirits, why does it matter?' She stared at her husband, hoping that he had at last calmed down. 'Have you finished moaning now or do you want to tell me what's really bothering you apart from our guest, the girls, the loch and a lack of work up the hill?'

Jamie pushed the mug away. He did not need it or really want it. And as for his wife, she knew exactly what was bothering him. 'The lack of a child, that's what.'

'We have a child,' Jade reminded him, 'and we will have another.'

'When?'

Jade shrugged – how did she know? 'It's happened once, so it can happen again. All we can do is be patient.'

She could hardly point out where the problem lay. They had a child or rather she did, fathered by a man whose family had inhabited the inn since the day it was built. Without Tapper they would have no child at all.

The side door to the inn opened and banged loudly against the wall. Both looked around sharply as the sound of feet rushed towards the kitchen door. An exhausted child stumbled in, her hair matted and cheeks rosy-red with the effort made to get there. Panting wildly, Braid stopped in front of the table. Ruth hastened in from the lounge. They all stared at the wide-eyed girl wondering the same thing – where was Isobel? If something bad had happened to Ruth's daughter, it seemed only a child who appeared too terrified to talk could tell them what.

Chapter 33

Silence reigned, the inn deserted apart from the mother and child sitting in the kitchen staring blankly into space. Both were in deep shock. Braid had mentioned the falls, but little else since her return. It had been enough to send Jamie and Ruth scurrying to the stables to saddle up and ride out.

Jade had washed her daughter, then dressed her in clean clothes. She was being as patient as she could be, but there was a need to know more and to know it whilst they were still alone. 'What happened, Braid?' she asked quietly.

Not for the first time, her daughter did not react. It was hard to tell if she had even heard.

Jade tried again; time was slipping by far too quickly. 'Braid, dear, can you tell me what happened? What you were doing?'

Braid glanced between mother and kitchen window, her eyes wide and unfocused. 'We were lying down …' she began.

'Asleep?'

'We both were. We'd finished playing …'

'And you were drying off?'

Braid nodded.

'And did you hear those voices again?'

Braid thought for a moment. 'I don't remember. I was listening out for them and I kept waiting, but I don't remember … and then I woke.'

Jade waited, holding onto her hand, trying to calm her down. Her own trips to the falls had become few and far between. They had rather lost their purpose since Tapper died, but she was happy for her daughter to meet her ancestors in the same way that she had done. Until that moment, she had seen no harm in such encounters.

'Are you sure, Braid? Are you sure you didn't hear them?'

Braid shrugged. 'I don't think so.'

The spirits were always present at the falls. Jade had never known an occasion when they had failed to speak to her. So, if they had not spoken to her daughter, had they chosen to speak to Isobel instead? 'Was Isobel still by your side?'

Braid shook her head, trying to recall. 'I woke … and then I was at the edge of the falls.'

Jade soothed her hand around her daughter's shoulders as Braid began to tremble. It was hard to imagine Isobel suffering an injury at the falls. To Braid, maybe, but Isobel shied away from real danger, just like her mother.

'What did you see?' Jade asked.

'That man by the edge of the pool. He was holding Isobel.'

'The man? The one staying here?' Braid nodded. 'Then what happened?'

'He hit her first, then shook her.'

'And what did Isobel do?'

'Nothing. She didn't move.'

'Or make a noise?' Braid shook her head. 'Then what?'

'The man looked up and saw me. He looked funny.'

'In what way?'

Braid struggled; it was hard to describe. 'Scared. Then he looked dark and angry.'

'Did he say anything?'

'I don't know.'

'Why not?'

'Because I started to run and then I heard him shouting, so I ran faster, till I couldn't hear him any more.'

'Did he follow you?'

Braid shrugged again. 'I didn't look back.'

So, he could have followed her and then got lost, in which case he was on his way back either with or without Isobel. Alternatively, he could also have remained at the waterfall in the hope that Braid would summon help.

'Listen,' said Jade softly but seriously. 'The voices we hear at the falls. It's our secret, remember? It's important you tell no one. They will not understand.'

'Our secret,' Braid whispered by way of confirmation.

'Good girl,' Jade said gently.

They sat quietly whilst Jade considered what best to do. If Mr Braithwaite was on his way back, what would he do when he arrived? She doubted his involvement, but there was no knowing for sure what sort of man they were harbouring. All they did know was that he had visible scars that he had been reticent to talk about.

The front door opened and closed. Then silence.

Jade stood up. There had been no need to summon anyone, she instinctively knew a certain person was on the way. 'Wait here, dear. I won't be long.'

Jade walked through to the bar to have a word. Help in the form of the gravedigger had arrived.

Chapter 34

Jade was standing next to the bar when Mr Braithwaite stumbled through the front door. He had taken longer than expected to return, a good half an hour after Braid. His appearance could not have contrasted more from the person last seen at the side of the loch. He no longer had a jacket and the rest of his clothing was dishevelled, torn and dirty. Lines of blood covered his arms, evidence that he had not followed the easiest route back to the inn. When his eyes fell upon Jade he stopped, giving himself a much-needed moment to recover.

'Where is everyone?' he asked, looking around the lounge. There was no charm or politeness in his voice. That had gone, replaced with a demand for information that he expected to receive.

'Out. We're the only ones here.' Jade was nervous but determined not to show it.

'Your daughter must be back by now. Where is she?'

'Gone.'

'Really.' Mr Braithwaite sounded dubious. 'All right, what did she tell you?'

Jade made no attempt to answer. However unpredictable his present state, she was not about to be ordered around.

Mr Braithwaite looked to the archway and then up to the ceiling. The lack of an answer indicated to him that the woman might be lying. 'I don't believe you,' he said. 'I want to hear what that girl has to say for myself.'

Jade backed away as he came towards her, but he lifted the hatch and veered off into the kitchen. She followed him through as he satisfied himself that no one was hiding there or in the garden. He moved past her and smartly onto the stairs and to the rooms above. From the kitchen, Jade heard the doors being flung open as he searched each room in turn.

Jade moved back into the lounge. She had not lied and Mr Braithwaite would not find anyone. Braid was by now far away and Jade intended to keep it that way until their guest was in no position to bother her again. There was no telling what accusations he might throw at her daughter. Madoc, who considered himself more than a match for the stranger, had been reluctant to leave but Jade had insisted.

Mr Braithwaite reached the last room, his own. The banging of drawers could only mean he was packing. Rapid footsteps on the landing and then the stairs soon followed.

'Going somewhere?' Jade asked as he reappeared through the archway.

Mr Braithwaite dropped two small bags tied by a rope. He had further business to conduct before he left. He had not changed his clothing and, if anything, he looked more possessed with the injustice of the situation than he had before he went upstairs.

Jade backed away as he approached. Judging by his appearance, not to say his scars, she doubted whether Mr Braithwaite was a man who could control his temper.

'Whatever your daughter told you, I had nothing to do with it,' he asserted angrily.

Jade swallowed hard. 'Then why are you leaving? It's hardly the act of an innocent man.'

'That girl was dead when I arrived, I swear it.'

'We only have your word for—'

'Damn it!' In his rage, Mr Braithwaite swung his fist, hitting an imaginary assailant inches in front of Jade's face. 'I did not touch her!' he yelled. '*What* did your daughter say?'

By now, Jade had her back to the wall. She could see nothing of the charm previously displayed, just the countenance of a nasty man who did not wish to account for his actions. 'That you were standing next to Isobel at the bottom of the falls.'

'And she was standing at the top of the falls staring down. It could have been her.'

To Mr Braithwaite's astonishment, Jade agreed. 'It could have been, but if folks want to blame someone, who do you think it will be?'

'It could also have been an accident.'

'So why run?' Jade watched as he struggled to fathom out his next move. She thought it only fair to warn him. 'There's no escape. Wherever you go, we'll find you.'

Whether that was true or not, Mr Braithwaite could now see that the only real option he had ever had was to flee. Blaming one of their own would only antagonize them and claiming it was an accident without the girl's support was far too risky a strategy in an unfriendly environment. Suddenly his eyes were back on his cornered prey. He thrust a marauding hand into her chest and squeezed painfully hard.

'Such a pity we never had time to get better acquainted.' He grabbed the top of her dress and yanked her to the side, caring little as she fell amongst the tables and chairs.

When a bruised and highly shaken Jade got back to her feet, the bags and Mr Braithwaite were gone. A whisky was quickly poured and consumed. The man's decision to go was a good one. If he had stayed, she would have poisoned him first chance she got. The type of man they had been sheltering was no longer in doubt.

'They'll catch you,' she seethed. 'And when they do, it's *bye-bye*, Mr Braithwaite.' She raised her mug and drank with satisfaction at the thought of his imminent demise.

Chapter 35

1896

Mr Pennan wiped the perspiration from his brow. His notion of what constituted an invigorating walk was being severely tested. With his trousers torn, jacket snagged and shoes scuffed, he looked anything but the respectable gentleman he aspired to be. His choice of attire for a trek through the rugged landscape was clearly unsuitable – the young woman had been right all along.

Up until that point, the day had gone well. When he had left the distillery he had felt pleased with himself, enough to take a rewarding hike through the countryside. He had already accomplished a large part of his inspection and had only to sit down with the landlady to complete it. Then he would be able to leave. Considering the hostile environment, leaving was something to look forward to. Why he had been sent there with no assistant to watch his back was hard to fathom. The job demanded it.

The Excise officer looked around for a way out of the wilderness. A short distance away he saw the sun's rays feeding through the canopy of trees. It was as good a place as any to head towards. He set off and soon found the going much easier.

When he arrived, he perched on a rock and took a moment to reflect. He thought about his last remaining task again. In normal circumstances, it would have been the easiest of all to perform and, once done, he could leave knowing that he had done his best, as he always endeavoured to do. But for him, dealing with women had never been easy. Generally speaking, they made him nervous – a drawback in his character that he had never managed to rectify. Conversations with the opposite sex were mostly short and, up until his present assignment, had never involved work. Work, however, now compelled him to say more than a few words and to submit to their presence for a much longer period than he was accustomed.

From his earlier trip to Brethna, he knew that the landlady's husband worked in the distillery there. He had watched him put a cask together in the workshop and admired the proficiency of a highly skilled craftsman. He had envied the man's ability, almost enough to express his admiration. But he had said nothing. It was best to remain detached. His job did not encourage familiarity.

As for the sister's husband, their paths had not crossed. In a small, closed community, he found that strange. All he did know was that the sister was not well disposed to his visit. It should not have mattered, but for some reason it did. Why? Why did it matter? Neither woman had made life easy for him. The respect that should have been present for the position he held was absent. Moreover, even though they were in the wrong, they acted as if the blame lay with him, forcing him to stand his ground.

'They should be ashamed,' he muttered bitterly. So why weren't they? Perhaps when he got back to London someone would tell him. He would dearly like to know.

'Well, Matriarch? You brought him here, now what are you planning to do with him?' Tily, the latest addition to the McTavish spiritual clan, asked.

'Yes, Matriarch, what do you intend to do?' Jade asked her grandmother. They had differing opinions when it came to actions that affected the living and, in Jade, the absent Father Devra had a worthy ally.

Lily watched silently as the company of spirits encircled the Excise officer, each studying him closely as they made up their own minds about what should be done with him.

'He is lost and without our help will remain so,' said Lil.

'Who wants to help him?' another spirit asked.

'He is not on our side. Why should any of us help?' a different spirit responded.

'A good question,' said the matriarch. 'Can anyone give me a reason why we should?'

'How about the problems our community might face if we do not,' Jade answered pointedly. 'Things could get worse, Matriarch.'

'Then what do you suggest?'

'Work on his feelings. Let him fall for one of our finest.'

'And what good will that do?'

'You never know. One day his sense of duty may favour us instead of the rulebook he follows so closely.'

'You are hoping for a lot if you think this man's loyalty can be swayed by emotions that he cannot express.'

'But hope I shall, nevertheless. It is far better than the alternative.'

'What do you think, Tily?' the matriarch asked. 'They are your daughters.'

'He is not the sort of man I would have chosen for either of them, though I do not think he is a bad man, just someone who is bound by a rigid set of principles. He's unlikely to switch allegiance.'

'Quite,' said the matriarch. 'So what should I do?'

The spirits stopped circling the Excise officer and instead gathered at the matriarch's shoulder. 'I agree with my daughter for once,' said Lil. 'There is no benefit in keeping him here if it means another will come in his place. We must fight in a different way.'

'Fight in a different way,' one of the spirits repeated in accord.

'Let him go, Matriarch,' another spirit agreed.

The matriarch heard consensus from all sides. 'Very well, as you please. Fight we shall, but if this man causes any of my daughters harm, he will pay for it and no one here will stop me. Clear?'

The spiritual clan of McTavish women nodded. No one disagreed when vengeance was necessary.

Chapter 36

Jualth and Lily counted every minute of every drawn-out hour as they waited for Mr Pennan to return from his stroll. When Thomas and his fellow workers appeared, their expressions said everything that needed to be said. In sombre mood, they gathered in virtual silence.

'Horrible, just horrible,' Thomas muttered, as he took up a stool next to Father Donald. The landlady passed a dram of sorts into his hands. 'What's this? I want a proper drink, not a pale imitation. Where's the real whisky?'

'Hidden away. Lily and I felt it best to conceal it this morning.'

Thomas sniffed the offering, then gritted his teeth before downing it in one. He stared in disgust at the empty glass. Jualth gave Ned the nod to refill Thomas's glass and freely distribute the *pale imitation* to all new arrivals.

'How?' Thomas growled. 'After so long, *how* is this possible?'

'That's what we all want to know,' said Lily. 'We thought he might have said more to you, being men.'

'Not a word. He withheld all explanations and volunteered no helpful information.'

'What did he do, then?'

'To begin with, nothing. We noticed him outside, making notes, pacing up and down, measuring each part of the building. When we went out to see what he was up to, he kindly identified himself *officially* as an inspector in the Excise Service. From that point on, he was in control.'

'You showed him everything?' Jualth asked.

'Several times over: upstairs, downstairs, along the corridor, up and down more stairs, then back and around with him making notes all the while. Once he'd done that, he pulled out his hydrometer from its leather sleeve and dipped it into our casks. Apparently, our whisky is very strong.'

'We didn't need his device to tell us that,' said Jualth.

'I'd have dipped his head into the cask instead,' Lily said vindictively.

Thomas repeated the disappearing act with the whisky. He waited in vain for the after-kick. It was little better than drinking tainted water. He studied the quickly refilled glass and said without looking up, 'He asked to see the paperwork, Jualth. I had to tell him where he could find it.'

The landlady kept it at the inn. Wishing to be regarded as a serious businesswoman, she was no less organised than Arthur or Jack.

'We could light a fire,' Lily suggested.

'A sinful thought and an illegal act,' Father Donald chastised.

'Never stopped us before.'

Jualth agreed with the priest. A paper trail would confirm the link with the Brethna Distillery, but as the inspector had visited Brethna first, there seemed little point in attempting to conceal it. 'Best we cooperate, Lily.'

'Why? It's hardly likely to make any difference to our defence.'

'Even so, why make matters worse?' Jualth turned back to Thomas. 'How did he react to what he found?'

'In a business-like manner throughout. When he asked, we answered. He spent the whole day gathering information and only when he was satisfied that no stone lay unturned did he take his leave.'

'So where is he now?'

Thomas shrugged. 'He did not ask for directions and we did not think they were needed.'

Lily relayed what the inspector did for an *interesting diversion*. 'He's wandering the countryside, relaxing, distracting his mind from all the trouble he's about to cause us.'

'Well, he'd better not take long, 'cause there will be no search party sent out to find him if he gets lost,' Thomas declared.

Lily nudged her sister. 'Ideas, Jualth. We need that option.'

The landlady put the question to the floor. With the priest present, not even the preferred choice of a lynching was put forward. The gloom deepened.

Thomas spoke up. His statement was brief: 'I cannot see a way out of this. None at all.'

Father Donald agreed. 'A miracle is what we need, nothing less will do.'

'Then get to work, Father,' Lily said coldly. 'Remember, if we perish, you perish too.'

Mr Pennan returned to the inn only when the shadows of evening had begun to darken the unfamiliar paths. Looking anything but the smart professional who had set out that morning, he approached the bar with as much dignity as he could muster.

'Nice walk, Mr Pennan?' Lily asked pointedly, making it obvious that she had noticed the torn and snagged clothing.

'Indeed, Mrs McTavish,' the Excise officer lied before rapidly changing the subject. 'I shall require dinner in my room tonight, Mrs McTavish. Could you arrange to have some water brought up, please?'

As his eyes had moved on to Jualth, she assumed herself to be the Mrs McTavish he was now addressing. She replied with minimal warmth, 'I shall see to it straight away.' She waited for his next demand.

'Good, perhaps the two of us can have a word at the same time. If you will kindly excuse me.'

They watched as Mr Pennan strode away, walking at his most authoritative height.

'I wonder what that word could be about?' said Jualth, knowing full well.

'I still have time to light a fire,' Lily offered.

Although sorely tempted, Jualth held back. 'There'll be no fires tonight, Lily. I'll give him what he wants.'

'Then how about some proper whisky now Mr Pennan has come and gone?'

'No, Lily, not yet. Wait until tomorrow when he has *properly* gone. You can drink all you want then. We all can.'

The locals did not stay long. With little to say and their favourite dram unavailable, they did not make for good company. Ned was allowed an early night and departed for his cottage, a short distance beyond the stables.

Jualth and Lily remained at the bar, neither feeling inclined to extinguish the lanterns and close up. It was a black night for solemn contemplation about a bleak future. The gloomy atmosphere was only interrupted when they heard the familiar echo of footsteps descending the stairs. They waited until shadows cast by a moving lantern flickered through the archway. Mr Pennan emerged in fresh attire with his sturdy shoes now sparkling clean. In his arms he cradled a bottle.

'Perhaps if we could sit over here,' he said, directing them to a table. 'Would you mind bringing three glasses with you, Mrs McTavish?' He sat down, expecting immediate compliance with his request.

Jualth reluctantly raised the hatch and, with only one question in mind, led her sister over. 'Where did you get *that* bottle?' she asked sharply once they were sitting opposite.

The inspector did not answer. He pulled the cork from its neck and poured whisky into each of the three empty glasses. Jualth and Lily stared at him icily. Mr Pennan took the lead by taking the first sip. For all his dignity, he could not help but gasp at the power of the liquid that swelled up and burnt the back of his throat. After a couple of short breaths, he lowered his glass and recovered his poise.

'Your first taste?' Lily enquired, condescendingly.

Mr Pennan indicated towards the two remaining glasses, his voice lacking its normal authority. 'If you wouldn't mind, ladies.'

'We know what our whisky tastes like, Mr Pennan,' Lily snapped back angrily. The inspector waited, he had issued an instruction. Begrudgingly, the women did as they were told, each breathing the blazing embers into the inspector's face.

'There ... satisfied?' Lily asked.

'And that is your whisky?'

'You know it ...' Jualth stopped. She realised Mr Pennan needed to be sure that the whisky he had pilfered from the bar the previous night came from the distillery up the hill.

'Thank you, Mrs McTavish,' said the inspector, his voice having regained its accustomed assurance. 'I shall settle up first thing tomorrow morning and then depart.'

'Hang about,' Jualth said speedily. 'Before you go, would you mind telling us what you intend to do?'

'Certainly, Mrs McTavish. I shall return to London by train the day after tomorrow and file my report.'

'And what will your report say?'

'That an unlicensed distillery is operating and avoiding the taxes due on its produce. In addition, whisky is being sold to the public at this establishment where further taxes are knowingly being avoided.'

'Duty *is* paid on what we produce,' Lily said furiously.

'But not in the proper way and only on part of it. No doubt you will be notified of the correct procedures to follow, the back taxes due and any other matters resulting from this inspection.'

'Back taxes!' Jualth exclaimed. 'We don't have any money to pay back taxes. The little money we make, we need to live on. Look around you: this isn't the life of luxury we're enjoying here. It's plain, it's simple and it's how we survive in the Scottish wilds.'

'How you pay is not my problem or my concern,' Mr Pennan stated factually. 'My work here is done and any issues that now arise from it will be dealt with by other people. They will be in touch in due course.' The inspector made to stand up.

'Is that it?' Lily all but shouted. 'One whole day poking around in our community and you take away the power to destroy it.'

'The consequences are not …'

Lily growled. Jualth moved swiftly to prevent her sister demonstrating the power in her arms. '*Stop it, Lily!*' she yelled.

'But what's that man going to do to us?' Lily yelled back, struggling in her arms.

The frightened sound of rudely awakened children started above their heads. 'Oh great, now look what you've done, *Mr Pennan*!' Lily roared.

The flustered inspector attempted to restrain his own anger. 'I think it's about time I retired. Good night, ladies.' He replaced the cork in the bottle and stood up.

The heat in Lily's head rose. 'What do you think you're doing with that?'

'This is evidence to go with my report and has been confiscated as such. In addition, I shall also be taking back to London the papers you gave me this evening, Mrs McTavish. They will be returned once this matter is concluded.'

'Make sure we get the whisky as well,' Lily yelled.

The unwaveringly officious Excise officer glared at his verbal assailant, then picked up the lantern, turned his back and returned to his room. The cries from Harriet and Jessica grew louder. Lily flung her arm across the table, smashing the glasses against the wall.

'I hate that man, Jualth. I want to *kill* him. I want to *kill* them all.'

'*Lily!*'

'You've got to do something, Jualth, and you've got to do it now before he delivers his report, otherwise we're through here and you, me and everyone else will be living in rabbit holes, teaching our children how to swallow worms.'

'*Options, Lily*, I need *options*,' Jualth shouted back for the umpteenth time of asking.

'*Kill him!*'

'No, Lily, and if that means guarding his room till he leaves, so be it. We will do him no harm.'

'No harm. *No harm!* Where have I heard that before?' Lily banged her fists on the table, frothing at the mouth.

Jualth refused to argue anymore and stood up. 'I'll go and help Grandma with the children and then I'll be back to talk some sense into you. Do not move from this spot.'

Jualth stomped angrily away, following Mr Pennan's trail up to the first floor. Her only hope, as far as she could see, lay in Brethna. But having been badly let down once, who was to say it would not happen again? In a couple of days, she would find out.

Chapter 37

1759

'It's out there somewhere, the girl's soul,' the priest lamented.

Father Devra had returned with Lily to the loch as dawn was breaking. Like most mornings, a veil of grey moisture hung in the air. *'You should have helped me whilst we had the chance. Then we could have got to her before Agnes.'*

'I was rather busy at the time, if you care to remember,' Lily said in sufferance. *'And as it is far too late now, why have you dragged me all the way down here?'*

'Because it is never too late. I want the child and her father as well. He has been imprisoned between these shores for far too long.'

'And you intend to get them by …?'

'By …' The priest gritted his teeth … *'By getting to know Agnes.'*

'So-o, I'm here to liaise between the two of you, is that it?'

'No … Yes … To …' The priest threw up his arms in exasperation. *'To find common ground between us. For the sake of those poor souls, this standoff has to end, and it can only be done by establishing a means of communication.'*

It was an idea Lily approved of. *'I do not think common ground will be difficult to find. Shall I summon her now?'*

The priest shook his head. *'Not yet.'*

'When then? And why not now?'

'Because I need to understand her first, and to do that you need to tell me why she is here and why she is so angry.'

'You do not know?'

'As far as Agnes goes, I know very little. When I sensed her spirit down here – as with you less than a year later – I went to meet her. It was a day just like today, with everything shrouded in this accursed mist. I did not know the cause of her passing and it was only when I approached that I realised all was not well. She was standing with her back to me, staring out into the gloom. I stopped when she glanced around. She looked confused, as if unable to comprehend what had happened. She then stepped into the water and I called out for her to wait. She ignored me and, instead, climbed into a boat as ghostlike as herself and started to row. I soon lost sight of her.'

'What happened after that?'

'Nothing immediately. I returned on a number of occasions, but it was several months before I saw her again. I heard her at first, rowing on the loch, and then she appeared through the fog drawing towards the shore. She turned the boat around to face me. There was no sign of the confusion that I

had seen before. It had been replaced by an assured anger. What had troubled her, she had worked out.

'"Stay away from me, Father," she had seethed.

'"I only want to help," I had called out.

'"Then stay away or I promise you will regret it."

'Before I could say anything more, she had leant on the oars and rowed back into the fog.'

'But you had to try again, didn't you?' Lily said reproachfully.

'Of course. As with you, I consider it my duty.'

'And as she forewarned, you have regretted it.'

'She has done nothing but interfere ever since. I fear for any spirit she gets to first.'

'She got to me first.'

'As I am well aware ... For some reason, she is consumed by a sense of injustice and when she finds it in others, such as yourself, she stirs it up. As a result, my work has become a trial of perseverance.'

Lily reflected on what the priest had said. 'You're right, Agnes is consumed by injustice and if you want to know why, I shall tell you. It's about time you understood her. Then maybe the two of you will stop fighting and instead join forces.'

'Join forces!'

'Yes, Father. You, Agnes and me. None of us are going anywhere and if that means keeping one another company for all eternity, it is best done on the common ground you're looking for.'

'That being?'

'The defence of our community.'

'That is a task for the living.'

'And with us the living will have all the help they need. You owe it to them, Devra, and this is the best way you'll ever have to repay your debt. Think about it and once you've learnt about Agnes, join us.'

The priest grumbled unhappily. In life he had sworn to serve the community, but in death he had serious misgivings that such an alliance would be in anyone's interest other than his companion's. Learning about Agnes would, on the other hand, do no harm if it lessened the ill-feeling between the two of them. 'Is she listening?' he asked.

'I should think so. I am not betraying a secret or talking behind her back. What you are about to hear, she agreed upon long ago. It was just a question of you asking and it being the right time.'

The priest looked about uncomfortably – he did not like being spied upon. 'Go on, then. I'm listening.'

To greet the moment, they heard the sound of oars scraping on rowlocks as they were lifted from the water and rested on the boat. Lily had a captive audience.

'One morning, on a day when light, patchy mist hovered over the loch, Agnes was walking along the shore with nothing on her mind other than her betrothed: Murdoch, the person who served the community as gravedigger and woodcutter.'

'Madoc's father?'

'Aye, that's the one. She had almost reached the pathway leading up to his cottage, when a voice called out from across the loch. She thought it strange to see her young man waving from the other side and could think of no reason for him to be there. He indicated to the boat grounded in the shallows and called for her to row over. Apart from the mist, there was nothing to worry about. So, with her boyfriend's encouragement, she set off, content to reach him as quickly as possible. Such excursions onto the loch were numerous, they enjoyed the peace and solitude it presented. But water soon began to appear around her feet, just a little to begin with and then all in a rush. Not being a strong swimmer, she began to panic and shouted out for help. There was no reply and when she turned to look, there was no sign of her young man. Even in the mist she should have been able to see him. The boat sank quickly and, with its rope tangled around her leg, she followed it down.'

'Poor child,' said the priest. 'An accident?'

'That was the general consensus to everyone living, but not to a very discontented spirit. In the weeks and months that followed, Agnes brooded on one of the tiny islands, with her boat pulled up on its shore. When there was fog or the mist thickened, she took to the water. No one ever saw her, but she was there biding her time.'

'Why biding her time?'

'Because she had long since worked out the reason for her untimely death. She had been wronged and a woman treated in such a manner is a woman who will never rest unavenged. When we met, she took me to her island and we got to know one another. She told me what had happened and, naturally, I felt obliged to help.'

'So that's when your interfering started.'

'That's when I learnt it was possible to influence the living.'

'Even though it is forbidden!'

'Who says it is? If it's possible, why should it be forbidden?'

The priest sighed – it was an argument for another day. 'All right, tell me what she had worked out.'

'That Murdoch had another woman and not just any woman. He had taken up with her sister and when Agnes saw them together and noticed that she was with child, the extent of his betrayal became clear.'

'Romance could have blossomed through shared grief. Maybe that is what brought the two of them together.'

'A noble thought made by a priest and a man. A woman knows better, Father.'

The priest grunted, he doubted that very much. 'So, how did you meddle with the living?'

'As was necessary. My daughters are not the only ones privy to a quiet word from the spirit world. With Agnes's help, the gravedigger and his descendants came to know about us and our part in his misfortune.

'On one late summer evening, Murdoch was returning home along the shoreline in a state of whisky-induced merriment. With the light fading, he spied a boat pulled up on Agnes's little island and thought he saw his wife disappearing into the trees. Agnes and her sister were alike enough to be mistaken for one another at a distance. He called out, but his wife did not respond. She should have been at home, looking after their child, and he wondered whether they were both out there. His boat, which should have been moored nearby, was missing and he could only assume they had taken it. He called out again and waited. The light was now failing fast and there was still no reply. In his less-than-lucid state, and with an encouraging word in his ear from me, he decided to strip off and swim out.

'He was not the best of swimmers, but the distance was not great. Even so, with the darkening sky, it soon appeared farther away than he could manage and, with no answer to his cries, he resolved to turn back. That was the moment that Agnes struck. Suddenly, his way back was blocked by her boat. In disbelief, he trod water and looked up into the angry face of the girlfriend he had betrayed.

'He tried to swim around the boat, but Agnes blocked his every attempt. And then, as he began to scream and shout in desperation, he felt a large, scaly form slap against his body. It was followed by another and then another. He felt teeth nibbling and gnawing away at his skin and, without a way to protect himself, he started to panic.

'Survival instinct kicked in as more beating salmon gathered around him. Flailing his arms, he scythed through Agnes's boat and made it ashore, bleeding in many unpleasant places.

'The fish had done their worst and Murdoch bore reminders of Agnes's vengeance that he would never forget. His encounter with her he confessed to his wife but none other, though he had to provide an explanation for the visible scars that covered his body. It instilled a dire warning to anyone else with the foolish idea of swimming in the loch at that time of year, a lesson *that no one has since forgotten. And as you already know, no more children. They were lucky they already had the one.'*

'Why have they stayed at their cottage?' Father Devra asked. 'After such an experience, I would have been severely tempted to leave. What stopped them?' The priest waited patiently for a reply. 'Lily?'

'He knew too much and had a debt that, as far as Agnes was concerned, he and his family could never fully repay. And besides, I needed them here.'

'To …?'

'Look after my daughters, what else? He and his descendants will be called upon as and when we need them, for as long as we need them.'

'Your daughters know about this?'

Lily smiled. 'Not directly. As long as they know help will always be on hand, they can speculate as much as they wish.'

The priest looked no happier than he had done at the beginning of the story. 'So, Agnes makes sure the gravedigger – Murdoch, Madoc or whomever – does your bidding.'

'Get to know her, Father, and we can all work together. Agnes may then be less possessive with the dead souls that suffered in life and you will find your wish granted far sooner. Have a think about it, just don't take too long. Neither Agnes nor myself are blessed with patience.'

To emphasize the point, there was a loud splash in the water as Agnes took up her oars. The priest had been warned – he was either with them or against them.

Chapter 38

1896

In the morning, Mr Cecil Pennan left for Brethna, choosing to depart in the same sudden manner as his arrival, and carrying in his bag all the evidence needed to bring ruin to a community he had known for little more than a day.

Twenty-four hours later, Jualth, Lily and daughters followed the inspector hoping that, by the time they reached Brethna, no physical trace of the wretched man would remain.

It was nearing dusk when they arrived at the distillery and found the gates locked. With two small children to accommodate, the journey had taken even longer than expected. Their first stop, before Jualth headed on to her mother-in-law's, was the Whisky Makers' Arms to find Lily and Harriet a room and to glean what information they could from the landlord. The inn was muted, no different to their own, its few regulars in reflective mood.

'Daniel was set to ride out tomorrow to see how you were coping,' Gus said pensively.

'Badly. We could not be worse,' Lily said bluntly.

'It's a pity Jack had not decided to find out for himself,' said Jualth. 'My business partner has much explaining to do.'

'Arthur as well,' said Lily, refusing to let the Excise officer off the hook.

'I'd leave Arthur alone, if I were you, unless you have something good to say to him,' Gus advised.

'Why?' said Lily, seeing no grounds for such leniency.

'He could have warned us,' said Jualth, agreeing with her sister.

'You know he will lose his job over this,' said Gus. 'And finding another in these parts, or any other come to that, is highly unlikely.'

'Did you know there was an inspection taking place at your distillery, Gus?' Jualth asked.

'No one knew except those in charge and Arthur. The inspection happened after you and everyone else had left for the day, so I'm told.'

'Has Arthur gone?' Lily asked.

'Not yet. At the moment he's still up there, but only until a replacement arrives.'

Lily held Harriet closer, gently kissing her sleepy head. 'My world is falling apart, Jualth. We're going to lose Arthur as well.'

With two weary children, it was not the time for a prolonged reunion. 'You'll want your room tonight, Lily?' Gus asked.

'Do you mind Harriet staying with me?'

'Is she past the crying stage?'

'Almost.'

Gus grunted but, as there were no other guests, did not voice any objections.

'Did Mr Pennan stay here?' Jualth asked.

'No. With Arthur, I should think. We've seen little of the poor man since his superior turned up. Like I say, it's been a tough time for him.'

Jessica yawned in her mother's arms and shut her eyes. 'My little girl's worn out. I'd better find the way to Martha's doorstep. I'm sure she and Frazer are wondering where we've got too.' She bade her farewells, having one last word for her sister. 'Tomorrow morning, Lily – *early*.'

Lily nodded. She was ready to take on the distillery boss now, but tomorrow morning *early* would have to do.

At 9.00 a.m., Jualth knocked on the front door of the Whisky Makers' Arms. 'Lily! *Lily!*' she shouted.

Lily, who was in the lounge with Harriet, hurriedly opened up. 'What is it?' she asked urgently.

'It's my stupid husband, that's what.'

'Jualth!' Frazer grunted in protest from behind.

'*Shut up*, Frazer. I'm talking to Lily.'

Lily scowled at him fiercely. 'What's he done now?'

'Known all along that Jack was holding a special meeting this morning, starting right this very minute. He thought to tell me five seconds ago as he was about to depart for work.

'Well done, Frazer. Nice to know you're on our side.'

'Lily, we have to go, *straight away*.'

'What about Harriet, I need time to—'

'There's no time! Frazer can take care of her.' As her husband began to protest, Jualth lost patience. 'Bring Harriet with you. Look after her until we're finished. Lily, *come on*, we're missing the meeting.'

Lily yanked Frazer inside. She had surfaced at dawn and spent most of the intervening period pacing the floor. Harriet, who had understandably slept late, was only now being fed. 'I'll leave you to figure out what to do, Frazer.' She kissed her daughter and hurried after her sister.

At the distillery, accustomed formalities were dispensed with. They rushed into the office hallway, clambered up the stairs and burst into the boardroom. The meeting had just started.

'Did you not think to invite us?' Jualth asked breathlessly, as both she and Lily pulled up chairs next to one another. 'We are entitled to come to these meetings, are we not?'

The four men in the room politely stood up before retaking their seats.

'You were invited, as you put it,' said Jack. 'I mentioned to Frazer that you should be notified if he saw you. Did he not—'

'He did, Jack, five minutes ago. When I see him next, he'll need every ounce of his strength to protect himself.'

Jack was well accustomed to hearing Jualth's fearsome proclamations. Most were considered bravado and, as a consequence, merited sufferance rather than serious contemplation.

'You've missed nothing, Jualth, and the board is pleased to see both you and Lily in attendance today. I had scheduled Daniel to ride out to keep you informed if you had not arrived in person.'

'Saved me a trip,' said Daniel, greeting the girls with a welcoming smile.

Jualth mustered up the smallest of smiles to reciprocate the pleasantry. Daniel was a friend but, at that moment, a distraction from the main business.

'Jack, I wanted a meeting with you *before* we sat down together.'

'Jualth, catch your breath,' the distillery boss ordered. He rose from his chair and, from a jug perched on a side cabinet, poured two glasses of water and placed one in front of each of the late arrivals. 'Please, ladies, take your time.'

The boardroom now consisted of a gathering of seven: James Gravid, the sales manager; Lewis Cravett, the purchase manager; Samantha the secretary (who was sitting at the opposite end of the table to her boss); Daniel, who represented the workers; Jualth and Lily.

Jack returned to his seat and addressed his secretary: 'Samantha, would you amend the minutes to include the presence of Jualth and Lily McTavish? Both are present to represent the interests of their community.'

'Thank you, Jack,' Lily said tersely, 'though I had no intention of leaving, whether you included me in the minutes or not.'

'Do we have to go through a long list of irrelevant items before we get to the one matter I want to talk about?' Jualth asked as calmly as she could.

The question was addressed to the distillery boss only. He controlled the meetings as tightly as he controlled the distillery. All others present towed a careful line.

'It's all right, Jualth. There is only one item under discussion this morning and that's the recent visit of Mr Pennan, an inspector from the Excise Service.'

'Why did you not inform me of his presence the other day? You knew, Jack, and you allowed me to ride out of here with no warning.'

'My hands were tied, Jualth. If I had given you the nod, it would have done you no good and only added to my own troubles. His sudden appearance here was as big a shock to me as it was to you.'

'That must have been some shock you had then,' said Lily. She was not prepared to sit back and let her sister do all the talking. The distillery boss would face her added volatility in a two-pronged attack.

'And not one I wish to repeat, hence the meeting. We are here to discuss how to respond to the visit and to assess the future once the findings are known.'

'When you say "the future", Jack, *whose* future are you talking about?' Jualth asked.

Jack looked gravely at the late arrival, not as a friend, not as a girl he had known since before she could walk, but as a business associate and nothing more. What needed to be said would be said.

'All matters are up for discussion.'

'Meaning?' Lily demanded.

The distillery boss sat upright and breathed in, so swelling his considerable chest with self-importance. The effect was to provide a highly unwelcome, if excellent, impression of a recent visitor to Matilda's.

Jualth chose to answer her sister's question on his behalf: 'Meaning the relationship with the Kvairen Distillery. Do you want an end to our association, Jack?'

'It might be over already, regardless of what I want.'

'But if you had to, and it saved your skin, you'd leave our fate to the dictates of those hyenas?'

'That's not fair, Jualth. We have been in this together and the Brethna Distillery has taken many risks on your behalf. We will be lucky if we can save our own skins.'

Lily did not like what she was hearing. She would not play the role of sacrificial lamb for another's cause. 'Is that your solution then, Jack? Is that why this meeting was called? Dropping us is your way of finding the best way forward.'

'My responsibility and yours, as part of this board *and* as shareholders, is to this distillery. We have a duty to act in its best interest to secure a future for the customers, ourselves and the workers.'

Lily slammed the table with a force that almost toppled her glass of water. 'But what about *us*, Jack? What about *our* community, *our* workers? What about all the years we've been coming here – Jualth, myself, *our mother*? Have you forgotten about her? Would you be where you are today without *her*?'

'*Lily*, calm down and leave Ma out of this,' Jualth said forcefully.

'*Why?*' said Lily, already red-faced with rage. 'After everything she did for him, why not mention Ma? He would never have dropped her. He would never have left her to fend for herself.'

'*Lily!*' Jualth cried, 'shut up or leave the meeting. This is not helping anyone, least of all us.'

All sat motionless, waiting to see what Lily would do. Samantha looked at Jack, motioning towards the minutes. Jack shook his head; Lily's comments did not require an official entry.

Lily stayed put, brimming with anger and adamant that she had no need to apologise. It was left to Jualth to proceed.

'Jack, I understand that you have to look after the Brethna Distillery, but is there nothing you can do to help us? Can you not give one word or piece of advice that may help us to keep the Kvairen Distillery operating and our relationship intact?'

Jack did not answer. He looked at Jualth and then his fellow board members, inviting suggestions. None came. He opened his hands to indicate there was no help on the table.

With her last possible hope crumbling away, Jualth continued with difficulty. 'Mr Pennan said we would owe a considerable amount in back taxes. We have no money and, when I say no money, I mean *none*. Can you help us?'

Jack shook his head. 'We have pecuniary consequences of our own to consider. I would be lying if I gave any such assurance.'

Jualth took a long, deep breath. 'So that leaves us alone. You cannot advise, you cannot maintain our association and you cannot provide finance. In fact, you cannot help in any way, shape or form.'

'Regretfully, not as things stand.'

Jualth looked at the other three members of the board. Lewis and James nodded their agreement. Daniel looked at Jack, then Lily and finally Jualth.

'Sorry, girls, if there was anything I could suggest, I gladly would. I … I …' He tailed off, at a loss what to say.

Lily stood up and left the room, her footsteps thundering down the stairs. The sound of the front door slamming made the whole building shudder.

'Would you like to follow?' Jack asked. 'There's no need for you to stay, if you'd prefer to leave.'

'I *will* follow Lily momentarily, Jack. Firstly, though, our respective distilleries have outstanding business to complete.'

'We do?' said the distillery boss, looking perplexed. He thought the line that separated their association had just been drawn. 'And what form does this business take?'

'How we settle up. You owe me money, Jack, and I want it now.'

Chapter 39

Lily ran across the track into the workshop. 'Where's Frazer, he's got my daughter?' she called out.

One of the workers pointed to the field behind, but was given no chance to enquire after the young woman who had immediately run off between the workshop and warehouse.

Lily climbed the small wooden perimeter fence and found Frazer sitting at the edge of the riverbank attempting to amuse a playful child. Harriet ran up as she approached and was hoisted, twirled around, then hugged to satisfy the needs of her mother more than her own.

''Ors-ses,' Harriet implored softly.

'What's that, dear?'

'She wants to see the horses,' Frazer informed her.

'You want to see the horses do you, darling? And your Uncle Frazer has managed to find an empty field with nothing but grass.'

'She wanted to see the ducks first,' said Frazer, his explanation tinged with frustration. 'Then, when we got here, she changed her mind.'

'As women often do, you should know that by now.'

Frazer did know that and had done so for quite some time.

Harriet received another volley of kisses. 'We'll take you up to the stables and see lots of horses in a moment, darling. First of all, though, Mama wants to throw a few heavy rocks into the water.'

Lily released her daughter and settled down at the top of the small grassy bank next to her unpopular brother-in-law. 'You're not in Jualth's good books, Frazer. Be very careful when you next see her and, in future, try to remember to pass on important messages.'

Frazer grunted. Upsetting his wife was never wise yet, somehow, he had developed the knack without even trying. He picked up a stone and lobbed it into the river, saving his sister-in-law the trouble. 'Short meeting,' he said.

'It's still going on. I disgraced myself by making an undignified exit. Being trapped in a room with Jack Vardy and his obedient lackeys had lost its appeal.'

Frazer mulled over Lily's answer. Eventually, he reached the correct conclusion: 'Bad news?'

Lily emitted a pained sigh. 'Yes, Frazer, bad news. Perhaps with a little more time to prepare *and* a prior meeting with Jack, as we had planned, we might have achieved something more rewarding. Instead, I rather lost control and we achieved ...' Lily sighed again; everything seemed so hopeless and her refusal to accept the situation for what it was had made matters worse.

The reality of where they now stood had come as a very unpleasant awakening.

'Sorry,' Frazer said belatedly.

'Aye, so am I. We all are.' She took her turn to seize the nearest stone and hurl it into the water.

'Jualth?' Frazer asked.

Lily was momentarily thrown. 'What?'

'Where is she?'

Lily shrugged. 'No idea. I thought she'd follow me, but here I am, all alone. Perhaps she stayed to wreak revenge, in which case I regret leaving.'

Lily buried her face in her hands and rubbed her forehead, wishing the action could erase the nightmare of the past few days from her memory. 'None of them said a word on our behalf, not one. Even Daniel just sat there, all meek and silent, allowing his boss to twist his specially welded dagger into our already bleeding bodies. We were alone in that room, Frazer, totally alone.'

With her mother's and uncle's attention fixed on the river, Harriet had quietly made her way to the perimeter fence. She stood looking up at the vast side of a stone building that, to a little girl, could have been anything – an inn like her home, a church or even a stable full of 'ors-ses. Finding a small gap under the fence, Harriet quickly tumbled onto her tummy and crawled through. She stopped, caught in a moment of distress by a tug at her neck. She pulled once, then again and finally a third time. The last determined effort secured her freedom and she crawled forward, leaving her silver necklace glinting in the morning sun.

Harriet merrily scrambled back to her feet and scurried up to the tall building, pressing her hands against its stone walls. 'Ors-ss,' she whispered in delight and quickly scurried to the end and disappeared around the corner.

'I cannot believe that man,' Lily lamented, still struggling to accept how the distillery boss had turned against them. 'He and Ma … well you know about him and Ma. If she had lived, he could have become part of our family. Now he's what? Someone who puts business before everything else and cares only when it is convenient.'

'Mr Vardy's a good man. I respect him,' said Frazer.

Lily groaned. 'Thanks for that, Frazer. Don't feel the need to support your family, will you?'

'I was only saying—'

'I know what you were saying, Frazer, and up until a few days ago, so did I. Today I realised the shallowness of our relationship. Now I'd like to line him up with Mr Pennan and … and …'

Lily's attention wobbled as her eyes tried to focus on the warehouse. She attempted to make sense of the blue and orange colours refracting in the sunlight. She hesitated, struggling to believe her eyes. 'Frazer, those are flames ... aren't they? The grass – the grass and the roof – they're on fire!' In a moment of sudden panic, she looked around. 'Where's Harriet? *Frazer, where's Harriet?*'

Lily leapt to her feet. Frazer gripped her shoulder. 'I'll find her, you stay here.' Frazer bounded towards the fence, hurdled over and ran between the buildings into the courtyard.

Lily watched him disappear, then turned in circles and shouted, '*Harriet!*' As she stood watching the flames take hold of the aging warehouse roof, the call went unanswered. She screamed again for her child, then hurried after her brother-in-law.

Frazer stood in front of the warehouse looking for his niece, firstly up the track and then in the direction of the main entrance. She was nowhere to be seen. '*Fire!*' he yelled. '*Fire!*'

With no visible movement or acknowledgement, he could have been shouting to the heavens for all anyone seemed to care. '*Fire!*' he yelled again.

As if delayed by the shock of such a call, figures began to appear, first from the malt barn, then the workshop and, finally, Arthur from the Excise hut. All stood staring at Frazer.

'Behind the warehouse, flames!' Frazer pointed.

Lily came running around, frantically looking in all directions. 'Have you seen her?' she cried.

Frazer shook his head. 'Try the stables.'

Lily set off, running for all she was worth up the wide track flanked by the granary on one side and the malt barn on the other.

Jualth and Jack Vardy had been in the distillery boss's office completing their business when they had heard Frazer's cry. One glance out of the window had them heading for the stairs.

As people began to move in haste around the courtyard, Frazer stood outside the warehouse door wondering whether to follow Lily in search of Harriet or help with the hose to put out the flames. He began to move towards the fire hut but stumbled as the distillery cat scuttled past his feet. He cursed and made to move again but stopped – he heard crying, a child crying. He turned to see if Harriet was behind him but saw only the padlocked doors of the warehouse. His eyes darted down to the bottom corner. Clinging to the rotten, jagged timber that surrounded the hole for the cat to move freely in and out was a piece of cloth that belonged to Harriet's skirt. As the crying grew louder, he realised his niece had managed to trap herself inside a smouldering warehouse full of highly flammable casks.

Within seconds, he was in and out of the workshop and attacking the lock with a crowbar. He yelled out to Lily as the rusty metal bracket yielded and the smell of burning wood flew past.

Lily heard Frazer's cry and turned to see him disappear into the warehouse. A loud explosion lit the interior with an orange glow. '*Harriet!*' she screamed. If her daughter knew where the stables were, Lily would have seen her by now. Terrified and fearing the worst, she charged towards the brightly lit entrance, avoiding arms that stretched out to stop her. As she approached, a far greater explosion tore through the building and lifted the roof.

Lily tumbled back heavily over the cobbled flagstones as the burning heat set fire to her dress. Screaming, she dug her fingers into the gaps between the stones to drag herself clear.

Jualth yelled above the roaring blaze for someone to help her sister. Two men braved the searing heat to grab an arm each. At a safe distance all three were smothered in clothing to douse the flames.

'Get some water!' Jualth cried.

'The bloody fire equipment isn't working,' someone shouted back.

Before Jualth could think, Lily had been hoisted up and, with great haste, was being carried towards the far end of the granary. At the top, she was passed over the fence and rushed down to the river. By the time Jualth had scrambled over, Lily's wailing body had already been soaked in water and was lying on the bank. She pushed everyone aside and grabbed her sister.

'*Harriet!*' Lily screamed, flailing her arms as she tried to get up. '*Where's my daughter?* Jualth, go and get Harriet … *I want my Harriet!*'

Jualth knocked her arms aside and pulled her close – that's all she could do. She could not retrieve the life of a lost daughter from the dead.

Lily's rescuers respectfully withdrew, leaving Jualth to tend to her sister and endure the screams and agony of their loss.

Jualth listened to the shouts and cries of men desperate in their fight to save the surrounding buildings. Their plight seemed nothing against that of a grieving mother and the eternal pain that would follow. She felt cold to their needs – the distillery could burn to the ground and Jack Vardy along with it. This was his fault.

It was not long before Daniel came rushing around the end building. He called down, 'You're going to have to move, Jualth. We don't know if we can stop the fire spreading.'

'Can you give me a hand, Daniel? I cannot move Lily by myself.'

Daniel summoned help and Lily was carefully lifted up to the courtyard.

'We will have to take her across the field to the lane,' said Daniel. 'We've moved all the horses and carts away from the buildings.'

'Do you have a doctor in Brethna?' Jualth asked.

'Of sorts,' he replied.

'They're all "of sorts", Daniel. Whoever he is, he'll have to do. Can we use the cart to get Lily to the inn?'

Daniel nodded. 'Of course we can.' Nothing would stop him from helping them now.

Jualth held onto her sister's hand as she was carried across the field. She looked back at the silhouette of white light beyond the intervening buildings and quietly whispered her husband's name. She had seen him outside the warehouse from Jack Vardy's office, but had not seen him since. Her eyes flicked to Daniel. He shook his head. The pain in his eyes providing Jualth with the answer she had dreaded.

Chapter 40

1759

The atmosphere in The Hidden Lodge was tense when Jamie returned from the stables. Two days had passed since the heartbreaking event at the waterfall and a day since Isobel's funeral. Those that had gathered were waiting for word from Braithwaite's friends and with little to do except kill time until it arrived. Only then would they know how to act.

For the sake of enquiry, the official reason given for Isobel's death was misadventure, an accident due to the over-exuberance of two children in a dangerous game. Unofficially, no one believed that. According to Braid, they had not been playing at the time of the incident and nobody doubted the word of the six-year-old. So how had Isobel managed to get from the top of the falls to the bottom? There was only one possible way in the minds of those that lived in the area – with the involvement of Mr Braithwaite. His desertion since had only strengthened their view.

Madoc moved away from the bar as Jamie approached. He was not best pleased with how the young man was behaving.

'Where've you been?' Jade asked from behind the bar.

'Where do you think?' Jamie responded curtly. He did not feel obliged to account for his actions to anyone, let alone his wife.

'You should have been here, not riding about looking for trouble.'

Jamie glanced at Madoc and the group of men in the corner. 'What, sitting around with that lot whilst that murdering lowlife gets away?'

'He won't get away,' Jade said in exasperation. 'You just need to be patient like everyone else.'

'You should have stopped him leaving.'

'How? You've seen the bruises. What was I supposed to do?'

Jamie looked away. He was angry, frustrated and in need of a victim. Yet no one was helping, they were just sitting on their backsides doing nothing. 'Where is she?' he asked gruffly.

'Ruth?'

Jamie nodded.

'Where she's been all day, in her room lying down. I gave her a potion, a strong one. Why don't you go up and see her?'

'Ye, why not?' he said irritably. 'Anywhere's better than being down here.'

Jade was relieved to see him go. However moody, her friend needed familiar company.

It was early evening when the front door swung open. Conversation hushed into muted tones as Stewart, the man who had guided Mr Braithwaite to The Hidden Lodge, walked in. Madoc stood up and beckoned him over to the table in the corner. Others gathered around. Jade poured a whisky and took it over, but did not join them. She would learn the outcome of their meeting soon enough.

Instead, she nipped into the kitchen and then upstairs to check on her patient. Ruth was lying down, her face turned towards the window. Her eyelids were heavy and she did not react to Jade entering the room. Jamie was still seated by the bed, his demeanour unchanged.

'Stewart's arrived,' Jade said quietly.

Jamie nodded. He understood what it meant. Without a word he left the room.

Jade sat down, grateful for a few minutes' rest. She felt the loss of Isobel as well. If it had been the other way around, with Braid dead instead, she might also have been inconsolable and, like Jamie, seeking a bloody revenge. As it was, all she could do was hope that Mr Braithwaite's reckoning would satisfy everybody's need for justice. When she returned to the bar, Madoc came over.

'Mr Braithwaite's *friends* have already forgotten about him,' he informed her. 'There will be no repercussions if he does not return.'

Jade nodded, it was as she had expected. Those that had brought Mr Braithwaite into their midst now washed their hands of him. The death of a child severed the tie of any friend, however much money was involved.

'When will you start?' Jade asked.

'Tomorrow, first thing.'

'How many?'

'Three will suffice. Myself and preferably two of my choosing.' He glanced around to Jamie who was hovering over those sat in the corner. 'Is there any chance you can persuade your husband to leave the business to us?'

'Why?'

'Because it's not a matter of seeking revenge in any manner that he sees fit. Care must be taken and less is likely to go wrong if we can keep him away.'

Jade shook her head. 'It won't happen, Madoc. Whatever I, you or anyone else says to him, he will want to go.'

It was not an answer to Madoc's liking. Someone he could not control was a liability. 'Well, have a word all the same, lass. We're in this as a community, not as individuals. It's important he knows that.'

Jade watched as Madoc returned to the group. The die had been cast and the stranger's fate sealed. His time had come and if not here, it would have happened elsewhere soon enough. Whatever evils he had committed in his life, he was about to answer for every last one of them, with the addition of one that, as he himself had so rightly said, he had had nothing to do with. Poor, innocent Mr Braithwaite.

Chapter 41

Jade sat in the lounge dressed in her night clothes. Apart from a small fire and the light from a lantern, the inn was in darkness. Sleeping had proved impossible despite having barely slept the previous two nights. A third on top was exhausting.

She raised a mug and sipped. The whisky provided much-needed comfort and as her mother had stayed away, support had to come from somewhere. She had tried to speak with Madoc, but he had not been forthcoming, either with talk about the spirits or in explaining his uncanny ability to turn up at times of misfortune. If he also had contact with the afterlife, it was hard to understand his reticence to share it.

She took another sip. There was no one else. With her husband she had to be careful and the priest she did not like for some reason and never had. As for the benefit of taking a sleeping potion, that luxury sadly did not extend to the person with a bereaved friend and a highly anxious daughter to look after. And besides, even with a potion, there were too many troublesome thoughts rummaging inside her own head to sleep, including one she had taken a while to realise: not far down the line, as things stood, Braid was now directly in line to inherit the inn.

Her daughter was Tapper's heir by blood and, if it had not been for his accursed vengeful nature, she would have been by law and openly bearing his name. As it was, Braid bore the surname of another but, through Jamie's relationship to Ruth, still had a formal right to the inn. Isobel's sudden, unexplained death had made that possible.

Seven long years has passed since Jade had returned with the purpose of securing the inn. Tapper had ultimately proved to be an obstacle and paid the price. His demise she could live with; he was bad for the inn and the community. Isobel, whom she had watched grow up and had loved like a mother, her demise she could not bear. Nothing justified her death.

Jade sighed deeply. She was desperate to visit the waterfall but was tied to the inn and, until the stranger was dealt with, that was where she would remain. She needed her mother. Whatever the spirits were presently up to, she had not signed up for. Tapper, yes; Isobel, *no*.

And, although it barely seemed possible, events that night had taken yet another, unexpected turn. Earlier, when she had checked in on her friend, she had found her missing, her bed empty. The potion administered should have knocked her out for the night but, somehow, she had managed to creep out without being noticed.

Having discovered the side door open, Jade had then ventured into the garden where she had heard Ruth down by the loch, calling out her daughter's name. In the low cloud, her voice had echoed up from different places, sometimes loud and clear, at other times muffled and faint. Jade had decided to wait in the lounge for Ruth to return. There was no point rousing Jamie – neither of them would have been able to find her in the fog.

It was difficult to tell how much time had passed when she finally felt the chill from a rush of air. It was still night and the fire was low. She picked up the lantern and walked over to the archway. The side door was ajar and there were wet footsteps leading onto the stairs. Jade followed them up and along the landing to Ruth's bedroom. She pushed open the door.

Ruth was lying on the bed, her face turned towards the window. She was soaked head to toe, her entire body trembling. 'I found her,' she whispered softly. 'I found my baby.'

Without speaking or showing the slightest sign of emotion, Jade crossed the room and opened the windows. As the fog crept in, she backed away to the door and returned downstairs.

It was light when Jamie roused her with a shove on the shoulder. 'What are you doing down here?'

Jade had no idea how long she had been asleep, but it could not have been long. It was still early.

'*What* are you doing down here?' Jamie repeated.

Jade looked at the extinguished lantern, the burnt-out fire and the empty mug of whisky. She felt disoriented. She had only moments earlier been with Ruth. 'Ruth!' she exclaimed.

Jamie looked puzzled. 'Ruth? What about her?'

Jade pushed past him and hurried towards the archway. The side door was shut, the floor and stairs dry. She rushed up to the landing and into Ruth's room, with Jamie following close behind. It was empty. The windows were closed and outside the fog had lifted sufficiently to see the loch.

'Where is she?' Jamie asked anxiously.

Jade could barely bring herself to utter the words: 'She's been gone half the night. There's only one place she can be.'

Jamie could scarcely contain himself. 'For Christ's sake, Jade!' As he tore out of the room he yelled back, 'Send the others down when they arrive.' The search party for Mr Braithwaite, due to assemble out front at first light, would have to wait.

Terrified and angry in equal measure, Jade collapsed onto the bed. Although only in a dream, she had opened the window to let out her friend's spirit. She knew what it meant and could not believe it. This was another death she had not signed up for. It had to stop here. The spirits were out of control and, with her husband already vying for blood, far from the only ones capable of vengeance. If punishing the stranger did not satisfy Jamie's need, who else would be in the firing line? She did not need to look beyond herself for the answer. A day that had started badly, seemed intent on getting much, much worse.

Chapter 42

1896

Lily spent the next two days in bed at the Whisky Makers' Arms, staring at a vision only she could see. There was little that could be done with her hair, so Jualth had cut it back until it was closely cropped. Her physical wounds – the burns to her legs, arms and body – would heal, but not the emotional scars that came with the loss of an only daughter. That wound would last a lifetime.

On the same day as the fire, Daniel had ridden out to deliver the terrible news. As Jualth would not leave her sister's bedside, Edith had returned with him to look after Jessica, who was presently lodging with Martha – Frazer's grieving mother – so sparing Lily the sound of a young child's cries.

On the third day Lily insisted on getting up – she wanted to return to the distillery to be near her daughter. Daniel assisted with the cart and took her and Jualth into the field where Lily had last held Harriet. There they stared at the collapsed walls of the old warehouse and the burnt-out remnants of the workshop, fire hut and pump house to either side. All other buildings remained – scorched, charred, but still standing.

'We were lucky, if a word like that can be used in such awful circumstances,' said Daniel. 'The buildings flanking the warehouse were not large enough to spread the flames. If they had been, the village would have lost its reason to be here.'

'I wonder what that feels like,' Jualth muttered bitterly. It was a fate in the waiting for her own community but, sapped of all energy, the inclination to care could also wait.

'How do I find her?' Lily whispered. 'Where do I start looking?'

Jualth put her arm around her shoulders, allowing Lily to rest her head. 'You won't find her and I won't find Frazer. But they are here together. Each has the other for company.'

The field was bathed in sun, summer having a late fling before autumn took over. There was no wind or breeze to scatter the smoking ashes.

'Everything happened so quickly,' said Lily, struggling to make sense of the tragedy. 'A few flames and then … all hell. There was no chance to get her out.'

'Someone was moaning about the fire equipment,' said Jualth. 'I never saw it being used.'

'They couldn't get it to work,' said Daniel.

'Why not?'

'I don't know and we never will now it's been destroyed. Apparently, Mr Pennan spent a while in the fire hut during his inspection. What he did in there and what I'd give to find out …'

Lily murmured on, oblivious to the words being spoken around her, her voice reflecting the pain felt by a mother imagining the cries of a daughter needing protection. Tears started to flow as she wept on her sister's shoulder. Daniel stepped down from the cart and, like all the villagers that had come to stare, left them to mourn by themselves.

A service in the field took place two days later with Father Donald presiding. Jualth and Lily stood dressed in black, their sympathetic resemblance to the charred remains only heightened their sense of loss. It was a state of attire loathed by both that, regardless of local opinion, would be replaced by white the moment they returned to the inn.

Lily trailed her gaze upon the layers of ash, searching for a clue that would tell her where her Harriet lay. She had relived the nightmare a million times over and had cursed herself each time for allowing her daughter to wander off. *Why* had she not taken her to the stables straight away? Now it was too late. She would never be able to do so again.

The service was solemn and blessedly brief. The many sympathisers then formed an orderly queue to offer a few awkward but well-meaning words of condolence. Most then departed, some heading for the main entrance and their posts in the distillery. It felt like an insult to see the cogs of life continuing to turn when Harriet and Frazer lay only feet away, unable to join in.

'Those who could not make it will have congregated outside Matilda's to pay their respects,' the priest informed them. 'They wanted the gathering to coincide with the service here.'

'I know where I'd rather be,' said Lily, staring into the ashes.

'Thanks, Father,' said Jualth. 'When will you return?'

'Without delay. I said I'd be back this evening.' He followed the gaze of the two women, feeling the depth of their sorrow. As with all others, there was nothing he could say that would ease their grief. He moved away.

Jualth and Lily lingered well after the last person had gone. With the sombre formalities behind them, a small flicker of life began to reignite in Jualth's veins. Sooner rather than later she would need an outlet to vent her growing frustration.

'Look at them, Lily. We've lost Harriet and Frazer, and our livelihoods will soon follow – together with the roof over our heads. Yet there they are, carrying on as if our plight means nothing. It isn't fair, *it just is not fair*.'

That was one observation that Lily did not need. 'Have you spoken to Jack Vardy since the … the …?'

'Apart from receiving his sympathy, he has had nothing to say for himself. What is there to say? He won't change his mind, he never does once it's made up. He's saving himself, saving *his* distillery and we—'

'We should be fighting,' said Lily, rediscovering her resolve.

The women turned their gaze from the languishing wisps of smoke to one another, recognising the same grim determination witnessed in each other as at the time of their mother's sudden death. Then, as now, the protection of their home, community and traditions came first and, despite manifest danger and opposition, the sisters prevailed.

'Aye, Lily, we should, and I, for one, am fed up with standing around doing nothing.'

'You have an idea?' Lily sensed that Jualth had been holding back. She understood why, but if an option now existed, she wanted to hear it.

'Aye, Lily, and a crazy one at that, but I can think of none other.'

'What is it? What are we going to do?'

'Not *we,* Lily. *You* will remain here and get yourself better. I'm going to London.'

'*What?*'

'London, Lily. I've got to do something and as *that* is where Mr Pennan has gone, *that* is where I intend to follow.'

'It's far too late to kill him. We should have done that when I suggested it.'

'I'm not going to kill him, Lily. At least, I'm not planning to.'

'Then what are you intending to do?'

'I don't know, but I will not sit around waiting for my fate to be decided by some distant government official. We have got to fight and I cannot do it by standing about up here.'

'I'm coming with you,' said Lily, with more determination than sense.

'No, Lily, you are staying put.'

'*I am—*'

'*Lily, listen to me.* Regardless of the fact that you can barely walk and are incapable of travelling, I need you at Matilda's. I want you to carry on as if there is a future and I want you to make sure every local and every resident feels the same way. On top of that, there's Grandma, Jessica and Ned, and despite all your injuries and everything that has happened, you are the strong one and I need you to look after *all* of them. If you're holding them and our community together, I will not have to carry that worry with me whilst I'm away.'

'But, Jualth, you've never been farther than here, *Brethna,* and you have no money. Where will you stay?'

'I have *some* money but not much. Most of it is going home with you. Like I said, the idea is crazy, but it's the only idea I can come up with and, as no one else has thought of another, I'm going.'

Lily recognised the futility of continued objections. Something had to be done, even if it meant her sister travelling to that distant, dangerous place, where the chances of success were slim. For her part, all she could do was stand in a field next to a pile of ashes that contained her daughter and her sister's husband and hold the closest person she had left as tightly as possible.

'Okay, Lily, I'm off home,' Jualth said, gently releasing herself. 'I shall return as early as I can in the morning. I know there's a midday train south tomorrow and I aim to be on it. Now, let's get out of these morbid clothes and start doing our bit to defend what we inherited.'

Jualth headed for home and returned early the next morning, having risked the depth of night to begin her journey back to Brethna. She had packed what she deemed to be essentials in the lightest bag she could find. At her mother-in-law's, Jualth said her farewells to Jessica and her grandmother, but Lily had no immediate intention of doing the same.

'I'm coming with you to the railway track. If I can't accompany you to London, I'm damn well going to make sure you get on that train safely.'

Jualth did not have time to argue the point. Lily fought her way onto a horse and, grimacing with pain, rode with her sister to the railway track where they did not have long to wait for the blackened, wheel-grinding steam engine.

'Right, Lily, remember what I said: I'm relying on you to take care of Jessica and all those other rogues we love so much.'

'Just as long as you promise to come back the same person that's leaving. I don't want anything happening to you.'

'I'll be back. Whatever happens, Lily, I'll be back.' The guard who had taken Jualth's bag onto the train called down. It was time to leave.

A final, painful hug ensued and then Jualth was on the train, waving from the window, watching as Lily's tiny white frame grew smaller in the distance.

Eventually, she sat back and, in the midst of an empty carriage, started to cry for her sister, for her niece and then, and for the first time, for the loss of her husband.

Chapter 43

1759

Mr Braithwaite pulled on the reins – enough was enough. The wretched redhead was right, there *was* no escape. All he had managed to do by fleeing was to make matters worse and look like a coward in the process. With the lie of the land as unfamiliar as the Celtic language, reacquainting himself with civilization had proved a feat well beyond his capabilities. He was lost, hopelessly so.

'Friends!' he spat dismissively. 'Thank you one and all.' He should have relied on his own guile to avoid the shooting match with his pursuers – it had served him well enough in the past. Instead, he had trusted others and if their aim had been to get rid of him, they had succeeded masterfully.

He slipped from his horse – after nearly three days, in testing conditions, it deserved a rest. Having set out west, poor visibility had hampered his progress to the point where all sense of direction had deserted him. It was only now that a dim glow penetrated the gloom. Considering it was still early morning, it had to be coming from the east, the one direction he did not wish to travel in. It was almost as if the light was calling him towards it; there was no sign of the fog lifting elsewhere.

'Why not?' he muttered. He grabbed the reins and, after ten minutes, began to feel the sun's warmth for the first time since leaving The Hidden Lodge. Then the sound of birdsong started up. After another five minutes, he heard something else. He stopped to listen more carefully. The sound was unmistakable. There was no longer any mystery where the light was leading him. Its miraculous reappearance was to draw him back to the very place he had started.

'Damn it all!' he cursed. He was not escaping, he never had been, just wandering the hills according to the wishes of the loathsome people he had been trying to flee from. They were a strange lot, every last one of them. He should have been more observant when he had arrived and not behaved as only his nature would permit. He blamed the redhead for that; the woman had lowered his guard. That had been a bad mistake.

He cursed again, then forced a smile; perhaps he had overstepped the mark once too often and upset too many important, powerful people. Maybe running was an option that no longer existed, something he felt certain he would soon find out. All he had to do was to follow the light and wait. He would make sure he was ready. If they thought his demise was a formality, they were in for a shock. The guest, late of The Hidden Lodge, would not die easily.

Chapter 44

Jade found herself back in the lounge, brooding in the company of a liquid friend that was fast becoming far too familiar. If the night had not been lengthy enough, she now had a tense wait to endure whilst the search party did their business. As the probable whereabouts of Mr Braithwaite were known, his punishment – just or otherwise – was unlikely to take long. A midday return was expected. Any later than that and she would have cause to worry.

Braid was in the garden, as yet unaware of the night's event. Jade would have to break the news gently but, before that, she needed to soothe her own nerves. When her husband had returned from the loch with Ruth's body earlier on, the shock of recent events had finally opened his eyes. Jade no longer recognized the boy she had seduced all those years ago – he had become a very different person.

With the other two members of the search party waiting outside, his mood had been dark as he stalked the bar. His parting words had been anything but pleasant. 'This place is cursed, I've always thought it and now I know for sure.'

'Don't be silly, you're in shock like the rest of us, that's all,' Jade had replied.

Jamie had jabbed an accusing finger at his wife. 'Not so long ago, I had a brother and a mother. Then Ruth joined us and Isobel followed soon after. You came next and a daughter that now resembles you and only you. As of this morning, I have close to nothing. And I put it down to this *accursed* inn.'

'That's ridiculous. You're not thinking straight, Jamie.'

'And maybe that's exactly what I *am* doing, and all it's taken is the loss of my family.'

'I am family in case you've forgotten. Braid is family.'

'Is she?'

'Of course she is!' Fighting a losing battle to remain calm, Jade had thrown her arms up in frustration. 'You're not making any sense. You need to go. We can talk about this when you get back.'

'The inn,' Jamie had spat out.

'What about it?'

'It's killing us, that's what.'

'Jamie!'

'And when I get back, we're leaving.'

Jade shook her head vigorously. 'No we're not.'

'Oh yes we are. This inn belongs to me now and very soon I will make sure it belongs to another.'

'We can't leave.'

'Why can't we? Ruth doesn't need our help any more and we have no other tie.'

'We have a tie with everyone that comes here.'

'Aye, and I'm fed up sharing my wife with the lot of them. I want her back to look after her husband's needs, not those of a community.'

And so the conversation had ended, with Jamie laying down the terms of their future life together as he strode angrily out of The Hidden Lodge.

Jade lifted her whisky and took her fill. Jamie was not the only one suffering. She had lost people close to her as well, but she could not lose the inn on top. It was Braid's for the taking and it was up to her to make sure her daughter got it. But how? The man that had left was not a man she knew how to control.

Jade could see no way forward, not without consulting the spirits, something she was now loath to do. Recent experience told her they would have only one answer. It was a thought she could not stomach. There had to be another way.

She refilled her mug. If only her husband had the same taste for the whisky that she had developed. It had a way of taking hold and refusing to let go. Leaving then would not be so simple. It was something to bear in mind. Losing her husband to the whisky was a price worth paying if it meant retaining her daughter's inheritance.

Chapter 45

In Mr Braithwaite's view, sitting on the edge of the pool was as good a place as any to wait. It was, after all, where he had carefully laid out the young girl for the locals to find, sacrificing his jacket in the process. How had she died? He wished he knew even if it barely mattered now. Whatever the cause, the locals needed to hold someone accountable and that someone happened to be him. The offence of allowing two young children to play in such a dangerous place required a culpable party and retribution on an outsider was a far easier choice to shoulder than blaming themselves.

'Cowards,' he seethed. He despised people who did not have the backbone to admit to their own failings and merely lashed out at whomever happened to be in the vicinity at the time. Presumably it eased their burden of the guilt, the need to take responsibility. Admitting to a wrong for them was far too grown up.

The fugitive chuckled. He was not a good person, he knew that without the need to be told, but were his pursuers any better? Were they not seeking vengeance for their own misdeed? It was cowardice, pure and simple. How dare they judge him as something different to themselves.

In the lull whilst he waited, the type of confrontation that loomed had undergone plenty of thought. When battle commenced, he would seek higher ground to give himself the initial advantage. Then, with the help of lady luck and his superior fighting skills, prevailing was possible. More than possible. Fist-fighting was second nature to him and defeating a worthy opponent usually served to pay off his debt. He was not under any illusions it would do so today, though.

He sensed the approaching horses before he saw or heard them. The question was … how many? When they came into view, he had his answer – three. That was all. He had taken on three before. He studied them as they dismounted ten paces in front of him. The redhead's young husband was there, looking mean but nervous. The other two – one, ironically, he recognised as the gravedigger – were stronger-looking and stockier, but well beyond their prime. He could handle them, he was sure of it.

There was to be no greeting, no preamble. This was not a trial that would allow him to plead his case. A verdict had already been reached and the punishment decided upon. He momentarily stood his ground as his pursuers stepped forward, then, without warning, set off for the slope and scurried up the side of the falls.

As expected, the redhead's husband was the quickest to follow. The other two did not have the same speed, which meant the young man was isolated when he reached the top of the slope. Mr Braithwaite gave him enough room to stand up, but no more. He sneered into Jamie's face.

'Do you know what, I believe it was your daughter, the one that looks nothing like you, that pushed the other child to her death.'

The provocation worked. The young man swung wildly, a left followed by a right. Mr Braithwaite ducked and swerved, but due to their close proximity could not fully avoid the blows. He regained his balance quickly and, after a couple of quick jabs, lifted his leg. Jamie received a hard shove in the midriff and then another in the chest. He fell back into the arms of one of the men following and they both toppled back down to the bottom, one falling on dry land, the other in the pool. The gravedigger now stood in Jamie's place, squeezed in the same way at the top of the slope.

'I didn't kill her, you know that,' said Mr Braithwaite, trying to buy himself a second.

Madoc was not listening. Having already assessed the strengths of his opponent, he lunged forward – fist-fighting was not for him. As Mr Braithwaite swiftly darted to the side, Madoc grabbed his shirt, swung him around, lowered his shoulder and rammed his full strength into the stranger's stomach. Both men tumbled back the way they had come.

At the bottom, Mr Braithwaite felt the immediate presence of the man who had fallen with Jamie looming over him. Instinctively, he threw a handful of dirt into his face, jumped up and deftly dispatched a fist into the man's jaw, felling him instantly. No sooner had he done so than he again felt Madoc's shoulder in his midriff, this time pushing him towards the pool. He dug his elbow into Madoc's back, hoisting himself up and pushed his assailant down in the process. When they landed in the water, Mr Braithwaite was on top. He pressed his weight down onto Madoc's body and held him under.

Mr Braithwaite grimaced. The gravedigger was strong, but without oxygen he would soon tire. He took a quick glance to either side. The redhead's husband was in a bad way. The fall into the pool had not been kind to him. He would cause no more trouble. The man on the side was still dazed and unable to get to his feet. In a moment, he would join his friend in the pool.

Mr Braithwaite felt a surge of adrenaline; he could already taste victory. The gravedigger was weakening, the boy looked crippled, the man on the side could not stand up and the woman … *The woman?*

Mr Braithwaite gaped open-mouthed at the redhead standing at the side of the pool. Dressed in translucent white, she had not been there five seconds before. For a moment, he thought it was the redhead from the inn, but there was something different about her, something odd. And just as he realized *what* it was, an arm reached up from the water and a large, strong hand grabbed his neck and forced him over and under. Madoc surfaced gasping for air and, with two hands and the weight of his body, held the stranger down.

The apparition Mr Braithwaite had just seen would be the last thing he ever saw.

At the top of the waterfall, a spirit stared down upon the aftermath of battle. As he reflected on its outcome, another spirit, who had momentarily left his side, re-joined him.

'A timely intervention,' the priest commented.

'It has its uses, Father,' Lily replied pointedly.

'Pity you could not have done more to help the young man.'

'Pity *we could not have done more, Devra. No one was forcing you to stand by and watch.'*

The priest was being taken to task again, though maybe on this occasion with good reason. Lily's actions had saved a member of the community – possibly three – and although he was edging closer to understanding its need, interfering was still a difficult step to take.

The spirits watched as Madoc and his stocky companion helped Jamie out of the pool and onto a horse. All further assistance was waved away. Hunched over and holding the reins awkwardly, Jamie set off through the trees. Attention then turned back to the body floating in the pool.

'I have a soul to help, one that is unlikely to head to the loch,' said the priest.

'Agnes would not welcome him,' Lily agreed.

'But I would like to go to the loch all the same. After I have helped this man rest, I want to hear about Gregor. It's about time I learnt how he suffered his fate and why he has lingered in the mist so long.'

'Are you ready to join Agnes and myself?'

'Let me hear the story first and then I will give you my answer.'

Lily nodded. She knew the answer already. For all his protestations, the priest was with them. Deep down, he always had been.

Chapter 46

Jamie stumbled through the front door, blood dribbling down his chin and onto his shirt. Clutching his chest, he leant back slamming the door shut, then staggered forward. He had the look of someone who had just killed or was set on doing that very thing.

'Whisky,' he growled hoarsely. Speaking was an effort. Moving was agony. Wincing with every step, he reached out to rest against the bar.

Apart from Jade, the inn was deserted. Those that had knocked in Jamie's absence had come to offer condolences. Once delivered, they had left.

Jade raised the hatch and quickly provided the desired medicine. She had not expected to see her husband in such a state. Her thoughts were now on what had happened and the condition of the other members of the party. 'What's wrong with you?' she asked, leaving the jug on the counter so she could better aid him.

Jamie took a mouthful of whisky. It immediately came back the way it had gone, soaking Jade.

She held her ground; the injury to her husband's chest was clearly unbearable. 'Sit down,' she pleaded. Her arm was pushed away, the offer of help firmly rebutted. His behaviour when he had departed had verged on menacing. If anything, it was now worse.

With considerable effort, Jamie straightened up to face his wife. 'Where's the girl?' he said, grimacing with the exertion.

Jade backed away as he edged towards her, fearful of what he might do. 'If you mean your daughter, she's out.'

'Out where?'

'The churchyard. She wanted to see Isobel. The priest took her.'

The inn was no place for a child when its parents were fighting, and Jade had wanted her daughter well out of harm's way. But she had expected the fight to take the form of a heated argument, not something more violent. 'You need to see someone,' she urged.

'Who do you suggest?' His body was broken. No one could mend it, they both knew that.

'Lie down then and I'll go fetch my mother.'

'You'll go fetch no one.'

'Jamie!'

'*You're staying.*' He doubled up, instantly regretting the surge of anger.

'Jamie …' Jade tried again.

Jamie held out a hand until he had recovered. His wife was going nowhere – they had unfinished business. Clutching his chest, he forced himself up. 'The girl,' he said, spitting out blood with saliva, 'is she mine?'

Jade took a deep breath and another step back – the subject was never going away. 'Her name is Braid, Jamie. We named her after your mother.'

Jamie took an unsteady foot forward – he did not need reminding. '*Is she mine?*'

'This isn't the time …'

'When you're bleeding inside and you're at death's door, it's time. Even that man seemed to know.'

'What man?'

'The one who just paid the price for being overfriendly with my wife.'

That could only mean the disreputable Mr Braithwaite was dead. Her heart was briefly gladdened. At least she now knew his fate. 'And the other two, how are they?'

'In better shape than me.'

'Where are they, then?'

'Taking your lover to the churchyard. They dug his grave yesterday evening. Two graves in one day with one to follow. How many more were you planning on, *sweetheart*? Or am I the last?'

Jade took a further step back as he edged closer. His face was a mask of searing discomfort and he spoke in an unrecognisable drawl. In his present mood he was capable of anything.

'You lied to me,' he said scathingly. 'That girl ain't mine. I have no family, *none* at all.'

'That's not true, Jamie.'

'All of us are dead and for what? A pile of stones and a stupid pond. Is that what you wanted? Is that what all this has been about?'

Jade found herself up against the wall where she could retreat no farther.

'The girl belongs to Tapper, not me, and you were using him just like you used me and everyone around you!' Jamie spat on the floor, the foul taste in his mouth made all the worse by the thought of that union. He could not raise his right arm, but Jade felt his left hand inching up her dress. The fingertips reached her throat as he slumped forward, his weight pressing her neck back against the wall.

'No more, Jade. No one else is going to their grave because of you.' He tightened his grip.

Jade could feel the strength in his arm. For all his agony, he was still capable of choking the life out of her. She tried to prise his fingers away, but they were locked solid. As black patches began to form in front of her eyes, she moved a hand onto his chest. Left with no option, she pressed – it was the only way to survive. She placed her other hand over the first and pressed harder, then harder still. The sound of a bone cracking was agonising.

Jamie flinched and the pressure on her neck eased. As his mouth frothed with blood, his grip loosened, and his strength faded. Slowly he slipped to his knees.

Jade slid down with him and then moved quickly to make sure he fell back into her lap. She held on, making his last moments as comfortable as possible. She had never meant for this. Jamie was her family – Ruth and Isobel were her family. She was the one that had been used and, if she had known what was going to happen, she would have stopped it before it began. And all for *'a pile of stones and a stupid pond'*. Considering what had happened, the reward seemed trivial.

When the front door opened, she could barely whisper let alone shout out for the person to leave. Fortunately, it was Madoc. She held up a hand and waved him away. Madoc understood and departed – he would return later.

Not long after, Jamie choked on his last breath. Jade's husband had died in her arms. The Hidden Lodge was now occupied as others had ordained, with just Braid and herself.

'What now?' she rasped, a hand held to her bruised throat. She broke down, exhaustion and the events of the past few days taking their toll. She hated what had happened and wished for nothing more than to avenge her family. But what could she do other than curse the day she ever took Ruth to the waterfall? The spirits had a lot of explaining to do, their future relationship depended upon it. Leaving, according to her husband's last wish, no longer seemed such a bad idea.

Chapter 47

Lily and Father Devra were back at the edge of the loch, the thick morning mist hanging doggedly over its surface. Lily and Agnes had deemed it time for the priest to learn about the unhappy man who had eluded him for so many years. Recent events had made the telling imperative. The issue concerning the priest's allegiance required a final nudge.

'It all started with a stranger arriving at the inn that, fourteen years afterwards, involved the rarity of a second visit,' Lily began. 'Stewart brought him in the first time; the second was unannounced. The name given was Elliott Ludbrace though, as he forgot to answer to it half the time, no one gave it much credence. Not that it mattered – as with all strangers that are brought in, the less known the better.

'The first occasion was uneventful, how the locals liked it and, after a couple of weeks, Stewart came back and escorted him away. There was, however, one unremarkable incident that went largely unnoticed.'

'Why would it be noticed at all if it was unremarkable?' the priest asked.

'Because it made the person who noticed it suspicious and, where strangers were concerned, that person always kept an eye on them.'

'And who was that person?'

'Lil, my daughter.'

'And she told you?'

'Naturally. We barely lost contact after I died.'

'And was it just her that noticed?'

'Her and the boy who used to run errands and do odd jobs up at the inn.'

'You mean Gregor, when he was … what …?'

'Seven, maybe eight. An obedient little thing but not too bright, as Lil was sadly to find out.'

'Not bright enough for your purpose you mean.' The priest sighed and allowed the storyteller to go on.

'Ludbrace enjoyed the scenery and often took to the paths, ending up, more times than not, somewhere around the loch. He was watched closely to begin with then, after a week, he was left to do as he pleased. He couldn't really get up too much and if he did happen to suffer an accident, who was there to care?'

'Many I hope. Most had a heart in my day, that's why the community meant so much to me. I believe that to still be the case, even if it is lacking in a few.'

'Yes, Father, let's conveniently forget that love and hate and all other types of opposite can exist in the same heart, but …' Lily held up a hand to deter another interruption, 'if it means you'll shut up and listen, by all means have it your own way.'

The priest grumbled but chose to listen rather than argue.

'One day, in the middle of the second week, Lil was resting in the garden of The Hidden Lodge. Ludbrace was standing on a distant part of the northern shore, staring across at the little islands dotted in the loch. He then walked up and down the shore until he found a rowing boat. Lil thought he was going to row out, but he chose not to. Instead, he inspected the boat from all sides and, having done so, headed back to the inn along the shoreline.'

'He was up to something?'

'Aye, and Lil had an idea what it was and why he had chosen not to act in broad daylight. When she saw Gregor later that day, she asked him to go down to the loch when the light faded and keep an eye open for their guest. He was to make sure he wasn't seen.'

'And was he?'

'He hid in the boat.'

'What?! She didn't mention …'

'She didn't think there was a need. Lying in the boat that the stranger had paid a particular interest in was not a good hiding place.'

'He was only a boy.'

'And as I said, not the brightest, as Lil quickly realised. Fortunately, it worked in his favour.'

'How?'

'When he was caught, each was as shocked as the other. Gregor just made out he was lying there for the night.'

'And Ludbrace believed that?'

'No. It was an awful lie, which made him suspect the boy was poaching, something he eventually got Gregor to confess to. He wasn't to know no one can catch fish in our loch and, if they could, it would be a free for all. He didn't suspect for one moment he was being spied upon.'

'So, what happened? Why was he there?'

'He had a purpose and now he also had an accomplice. He took a shine to Gregor, judging him a rogue not unlike himself, but one he could control. Ludbrace was not what you'd call an English gentleman, though he clearly aspired to be one. He had a rough voice, rough skin and a rough manner. Add that to his size, and very few would have sided against him. A terrified youngster was easy prey.

'So, he showed Gregor a couple of coins, and promised them to the lad if he did what he was told and kept his mouth shut. It was a fortune to Gregor, and he agreed, especially when Ludbrace promised to make him a man of means when he came of age.'

'*A bit rash, wasn't it?*'

'*Maybe, but it got Gregor to agree, which was all he needed. They pushed the boat into the water and headed for one of the islands. Once they'd arrived, Gregor was made to stay in the boat whilst Ludbrace disappeared into the trees. He waited there for over ten minutes, not daring to get out. When Ludbrace came back, they returned to the shore and Gregor got his reward. Ludbrace said he was leaving in a few days, but he would come back one day, when the lad was much older, and he would keep his promise if Gregor kept his eye on that island for him. If anyone ever went near it acting strangely, and Gregor heard about it, he was to tell him who when he returned.*

'*Gregor promised and, with a sworn pact to keep the matter to themselves, they parted.*'

'*He didn't tell Lil?*'

'*Not at first. He lied, said he hadn't seen a thing all night.*'

'*How did she know he was lying?*'

'*Because he's a very bad liar for one and, for two, Lil heard Ludbrace creeping out of The Hidden Lodge late at night. A guy as big as him does not tread lightly. From the window, she watched the pair row across to the island. She decided to let it rest until Ludbrace had departed, after which she made it clear to Gregor what she thought about boys that did not tell the truth. He was left in no doubt whose side he should be on.*'

'*Lil's or the community's?*'

'*Hers, though through Lil he naturally served the community as well.*'

'*Of course he did,*' the priest muttered.

'*They kept the matter to themselves and Lil told him he should not return to the island again by himself. Ludbrace had obviously hidden something valuable there and she needed to think about the best way to proceed.*'

'*Why valuable? Why not something he wished to get rid of?*'

'*Because he had no need to visit the island to get rid of something. He could have weighed it down and dropped it in the loch.*'

'*Did she find out what he had hidden?*'

'*No.*'

'*Why not?*'

'*Because she walked out of The Hidden Lodge soon after, leaving its problems and mysteries to others.*'

'*Ah,*' said the priest. '*That was unfortunate timing.*'

'*As far as subsequent events went, very.*'

'*So, Lil never found out what the stranger was up to?*'

'*Before she left ... no. It was a while after and only because the unfortunate Elliott Ludbrace had chosen the wrong island to hide his wares on.*'

'Don't tell me,' the priest sighed, 'he hid them on Agnes's island.'

'And Agnes knew exactly what he had hidden and where. She had stood looking over his shoulder whilst he dug a hole with his hands to bury a pouch containing all kinds of colourful stones. He had been unable to resist a last look inside before dropping it into the hole. Later, Agnes showed me.'

'How? If they were buried ...'

'That's right, I could not have seen them.'

'So ... you mean ... the boy. He must have returned and dug them up.'

'How? Gregor didn't know where they were buried.'

'Then someone must have told him.' The priest looked scathingly at his fellow spirit. 'Is that when you took it upon yourself to interfere?'

Lily smiled. 'With Gregor, not directly, though I thought it only right to keep an eye on him. Without Lil, there was no one else to do it. But, that said, it wasn't Gregor who dug them up.'

'Who then?'

'Agnes's friend. I told you about him, remember?'

'Murdoch? You got Murdoch to dig them up?'

'Not me. Agnes. She had kept in touch with Murdoch in the same way I now keep in touch with my daughters. You would have been surprised to know how often they saw each other before the whisky took him.'

'The poor man.'

'He got everything he deserved. What Agnes has to "live" with, so did Murdoch. He and his family will never stop paying for what he did.'

'Why didn't he take the stones and disappear?'

'Guilt for what he did is the easy answer.'

'And the difficult one?'

'He knew Agnes would have pursued him and tormented him every day he was absent. If Murdoch and his family wished to go mad, that was the sure way to do it. Staying was the sensible option.'

'Did he rebury the stones?'

'No. Agnes has them in her own hiding place where she can see them. It makes her happy and anything that makes Agnes happy we should be grateful for.'

'In normal circumstances, yes. But I believe you said our friend Elliott Ludbrace returned.'

'He did, long after most had forgotten he had ever visited. No guest had ever managed to find their way back without a guide's assistance. To do so after such a lengthy absence impressed some and worried a good deal more. If one person can find us, then, through him, the whole world can. And with Lil gone and that idiot Tapper running the inn, there was no one able to offer the leadership required to deal with him.'

'There must have been someone: the Church, those that ran the distillery ...'

'There is always someone, but not necessarily of the right calibre. A helping hand was needed.'

The priest grumbled again. Agreeing with his fellow spirit on such a matter meant agreeing with interfering. 'Left to their own devices, they usually pull through.'

'But without the proper leadership, the situation was far too dangerous to leave alone. Do you agree or not?'

Reluctantly, the priest nodded. The safety of the community was paramount. 'What reason did he give for returning?'

'Gratitude and nostalgia. He felt a need to return and thank everyone for the service they had provided. It was about as lame as saying he was just passing through. No one ever thanks us. Most are grateful to get away and to forget the fact that they ever came.'

'Everyone was suspicious, then?'

'And capable of little more than scratching their heads, wondering what to do.'

'So, you took it upon yourself to provide the helping hand.'

'*Me* and *Agnes*. There was no choice. Ludbrace had returned for his precious stones and they weren't where he had left them. He would find out quick enough and, having come such a distance, we could only assume the discovery would not be well-received. Our help was given with the best of intentions, but we could not control events, just the ultimate outcome.'

'And a poor lad died because of it.'

'In spite of it and he was a young man by now. With Murdoch dead, it was up to Madoc to assist us and, with his help, we saw a way through our problem. It was not our fault that Ludbrace did not behave as we had hoped.'

'Why Madoc?'

'Because he was the only one who knew the stones had been moved. Gregor had no idea. At the time, Gregor was the sole person to welcome Ludbrace's return. He was now married to Ruth, had a baby and was desperate for a place and life of his own.

'Madoc warned him that Ludbrace was bad news and it was for his own safety to stay away. In the circumstances, Gregor could hardly be blamed for ignoring the warning. The truth may have saved him, but valuable stones hidden on a small island was knowledge best kept to a few.

'Agnes told Madoc what was required of him. Given no choice, he was forced to have a quiet word with Ludbrace at The Hidden Lodge on the first evening of his return. Ludbrace was stunned by what Madoc told him – the importance of the stones to him could not be underestimated. Madoc left him to fester in his own thoughts, certain that the matter had not been laid to rest at his word. Ludbrace would check for himself.

'And so he did, in the early hours of that night. But he did not row out alone, he had prearranged to meet with Gregor. We were relying on him rowing out by himself to discover the truth. If he was then mindful for vengeance, it would not have mattered, we could have handled it. Unfortunately, events turned out differently.

'When they pulled up on the island, Ludbrace invited Gregor to accompany him, citing a bad back and the need for a younger man's strong arms. They found the spot and Ludbrace asked Gregor to use his hands to dig down. Gregor did as he was told. He dug and kept digging. Just to make sure he was not mistaken, Ludbrace widened the search, but found nothing and he soon realised Madoc was right. He had been betrayed. The young man had not kept his mouth shut. He had told someone about the trip to the island, probably that Madoc fellow, and the gems had been taken. As the Englishman knew where the gravedigger lived, he knew he could deal with him and his family later. For now, though, there was a price to pay for treachery. He produced a knife and Gregor was dead before he knew he was in danger.'

'Poor lad,' said the priest. 'He had no idea?'

'None at all. He thought Ludbrace was his friend and Gregor believed him when he said he was going to change his life. Sadly, Ludbrace did but in the worst possible way. As I said, we could not control the events, only the outcome.'

'So, what happened to Ludbrace?'

'He returned to his boat set on paying Madoc an immediate visit. It was a surprise to him to see how much mist had gathered in the short time since arriving at the island. The light that had reflected from the moon had all but gone. Hurriedly, he climbed on board and started to row in the direction of the southern shore. However, the mist quickly thickened until it was dense and visibility was restricted to no more than a few yards. And then something quite unexpected happened; there was the sound of another boat on the loch. Ludbrace stopped rowing and listened as the sound of its oars got louder and nearer. It was hard to tell where it was coming from but, with his knife to hand, he would be ready if necessary.

'And then the strokes stopped and, very slowly, a boat slipped into view and slid quietly past, heading in the opposite direction. It was covered in mist but he was still able to make out the figure of a young, hooded woman. Need I say, it was Agnes and she was looking at him and smiling. In the poor visibility, he watched as she raised her arm. On the flat of her hand she had managed to conjure up a few coloured stones – to Ludbrace's mind, his stones.

'Before he could say anything, she turned her palm down and splayed her fingers. One by one they fell into the water and began to sink. Hoping to save some of the precious jewels, Ludbrace leapt from one boat to the other only to find there was nothing there. With a mighty splash, he landed face first in the water. He could not swim and started to flail his arms. His boat was close by, but he had pushed it away when he had jumped, and it was now slowly disappearing into the mist. Unfortunately for Ludbrace, he drowned, as bewildered by his death as Gregor had been by his own only minutes earlier.'

'Poetic justice that in no way makes up for what happened to Gregor and his family,' said the priest. 'A heavy price was paid for the right outcome.'

'True. Agnes then led Madoc, who had been waiting in his boat, to the body of Elliott Ludbrace. By morning, the reprobate had been buried in the graveyard and the threat posed by someone who could find their way into our community without a guide no longer existed.'

'Poor lad,' the priest repeated.

'You're really upset about him, aren't you?'

'Very. Are you sure there was no other way, one that could have avoided such a pointless death?'

'Why do you ask?'

'Because it has not gone beyond my attention that he was married to The Hidden Lodge's heir and his death started a trail of events that ultimately benefitted your family.'

'It did, didn't it? And you think that was deliberate?'

'Was it?'

Lily smiled. 'If that's what you want to think, Father, you think it. I know what I did and the reason for doing it. Trust me or believe otherwise, it's totally up to you and changes nothing. Now, are you with me or not?'

'You don't make it easy, do you?'

'We are all on the side of the community: you, me, my daughters and Agnes. That's as easy and uncomplicated as it gets.'

The priest nodded; when put like that, he had to agree. 'I'm almost there,' he said. 'Almost.'

Lily smiled, a rarity in the priest's company. 'Then a gift to help you those last few inches, Father.' She directed his attention towards the loch.

In the thinning mist, the priest could see Agnes rowing towards them on the shore. She was not alone. Once she reached the shallows, the boat was turned and the passengers allowed to disembark. Gregor waded towards the shore, with Ruth at his side holding onto Isobel's hand. Bringing up the rear was Jamie, who was looking towards the western shore in the direction of The Hidden Lodge. The interest was brief – it no longer held any attachment for him. He ploughed on through the water to join the only family he had *ever really had. The priest took them into the forest, where they vanished from view.*

Having watched them depart, Lily stepped into the boat; she was not the only one with a contented smile on her face. Agnes heaved on the oars and they were soon shrouded in the morning mist. The future was shaping up as they had intended and, with a watchful eye and the right people in place, there was no reason to believe that it would not stay that way.

Chapter 48

Jade was sitting in the kitchen when she heard the side door open then gently close. Only Braid had a right to use that entrance and she was in the garden. As the inn currently lacked for a man, she would have to think about keeping it locked in future. For now, though, she had to find out if the unexpected visitor presented a threat.

She picked up the poker from the kitchen fire and moved quietly into the bar. There was no one in sight. Whoever it was had decided to loiter at the bottom of the stairs. She listened intently but heard nothing, not even the whisper of a dead soul.

Eventually, a floorboard creaked, and a small, middle-aged woman appeared through the archway and stopped at the end of the bar. There was a short period when neither mother nor daughter spoke. Jade lifted the hatch and placed the poker on the counter.

'Sure you won't be needing that?' her mother asked. Lil strolled forward, calmly looking around her old home as she did so. She settled into a seat by the fireplace and waited.

'You're too late for the funerals,' said Jade coolly, as she sat opposite. 'The last one took place yesterday.'

'So the priest kindly informed me. Our paths crossed at the graveyard a short while ago.'

'You went to visit him?'

'In a manner of speaking.'

'That must have been quite a shock for the old man.'

'He took it well, considering …'

'That you might in some small way have been responsible for the recent deaths?'

'Now, now, dear, I'm sure he thought nothing of the kind.'

It had been a number of years since Lil and the priest had last laid eyes upon one another. That was her doing. She had never forgiven Tapper for the loss of her home and, as the path of vengeance had no room for a priest, it had been necessary to part ways with the Church as well as the inn.

'Why not?' Jade asked.

'Because we all know the blame lies elsewhere.'

'Of course we do. So you went to the graveyard to thank Mr Braithwaite, did you?' Jade asked derisively.

'To look after his spirit now he has departed. I dropped some grain around the grave to aid his transition into the afterlife.'

'How thoughtful of you, Mother. Pity you could not have been more protective when he was alive.'

A sympathetic smile fleetingly touched Lil's lips – considering what her daughter had just been through, her chilly manner was understandable. She reached across, put a finger under her chin and lifted. 'Those are nasty bruises you have there. Your husband's doing?' She received a curt nod. 'Has anyone seen them?'

'I kept them covered at the funerals.'

'No one, then?'

'Just Madoc and the doctor.'

'How did you explain them?'

'I didn't, there was no need. Neither are likely to say anything and, as the inn is in mourning and therefore closed, nobody else is likely to find out. I will send word when I wish to reopen.'

Lil nodded her approval but she would have a word with Madoc and the doctor just to make sure. 'I can make a lotion to help the healing if you like.'

Jade shook her head. 'I can manage.'

Her mother smiled thinly. She was not used to rejection.

'Why now?' Jade asked.

'Why now … what?'

'Isobel, then Ruth and finally Jamie. Why decide to come back now?'

'It wasn't easy staying away.'

'But you managed all the same, despite my need. All I've had is the support of a tight-lipped gravedigger whose mortal perception defies comprehension. Why *now*, Mother?'

'You coped.'

'But I needed you. *Braid* needed you. These last few days have been unbearable.'

Lil remained unapologetic, despite her daughter's less-than-effusive welcome. 'And if Madoc had sent word, I would have come. As he didn't, I went to the waterfall instead.'

'And what did the *spirits* have to say for themselves?'

'They were pleased. They want to speak to you.'

Jade shook her head. 'Well they can go on wanting to speak to me. I will not be returning and neither will Braid. You can tell them that if you wish.'

'I can but if you do not visit them, they will come to visit you. I'd keep them away myself. They interfere less if kept in one place.'

Jade scoffed, 'That's how it works, is it? That's the only way to hold them at bay?'

Her mother smiled. Her daughter still had much to learn. Now she had possession of the inn, she would not be allowed to lose it.

'And Madoc, is it the same with him?' Jade asked. 'I did not seek his help, yet he knew on each and every occasion when it was needed.'

'He is told in some way, but we must respect his wishes if he does not choose to tell us how.'

Jade looked away dejectedly. She felt mentally drained, trapped in a life she no longer desired to live in. 'Why now?' she repeated. 'If you thought I could cope, why visit at all? I might have come to you.'

'I have no further reason to stay away.'

'You could have come when Tapper died.'

'True, but it was best to leave the running of The Hidden Lodge to you. I could not be seen to interfere.'

'Why?'

'Because of what eventually transpired with Isobel, Ruth and Jamie. It would have looked far too suspicious.'

'You knew all that time ago?' Jade asked angrily.

'And so did you, even if you refuse to admit it,' Lil answered patiently.

'I do refuse. They were my family!'

'It was your choice to return, then stay after Tapper died. It was your wish to own the inn. Now you do, even if the manner in which it happened is not to your liking.'

'It is not and it *still* looks suspicious.'

'It looks unfortunate and very sad. From what I have heard, everybody is pleased no harm came to you and extra vigilance by the community will make sure nothing ever does.'

Jade could not contain her frustration and bitterness. 'And that's the end of it, is it? We got away with our shameful deeds – our betrayal of all those who stood in our way – and life will now go on in some twisted version of normality.'

'There is no other way. The arrival of our family in these hills was not by chance. We now have roots and a purpose.'

'Which is?'

'To safeguard this inn. By doing that we safeguard the community and the special qualities that makes it so unique.'

'*Qualities*,' Jade virtually spat. 'You mean the whisky?'

'Yes, the whisky. This community was rudderless before we arrived and very little has changed since. It needs leaders at its centre who appreciate what it has and are prepared to fight to keep it. Those leaders are us.'

'Why? Why does it have to be us?'

'Because we are fighters; we wouldn't be here otherwise. Women we may be, but our suffering has made us strong and determined. This is our home and nothing is going to shift us or our spirits from it.' Lil was unyielding in the face of Jade's anger and despair.

'So if the inn survives, the community survives. Is that what you're saying?'

'Glad you understand, dear. It's your responsibility from this day forth, a responsibility you must hand on to Braid and all future generations.'

'Lucky them,' Jade said, feeling immense pity for every last one of them. 'Will you help me? Are you intending to come back?'

'Initially – no. But it will look strange if I do not put in the odd appearance with you two being on your own here. Then we'll see.' She looked around. 'It hasn't changed much, has it? Do you mind if I have a look?'

Jade was soon sitting alone and feeling no better than before. Her mother was clearly not dwelling on the past, however recent. Only Jade had to live with that. She wondered how history would treat her and how she would fare in tales that would be handed down to future generations. Her conclusion was a simple one; she would be damned. Not the outcome she would have wished for but one she probably deserved. She could think of only one way to deal with it. At the bar, she poured herself a whisky – a very large whisky – and, like so many before, drowned her sorrows.

Chapter 49

1896

Jualth arrived at King's Cross railway station on the second day of her travels. The journey had been long, tedious and – as the beautiful countryside had gradually turned into the hungry, sprawling suburbs – a depressing insight into what the future held for her descendants.

A different person to the one that had boarded the previous day disembarked. Through necessity, her period of mourning had ended – it would not accomplish the task she had travelled so far south to undertake. In its place was an inner resolve and hardness that blended in perfectly with the colourless, functional surroundings of the vast double-hangar shed. She concluded that the structure was perfectly suited to the iron monster that had brought her there. She had no qualms about leaving it, only the manner in which her journey was to continue.

On enquiry her spirits had plummeted several fathoms deeper; it appeared that the underground service provided the best means to continue her journey. Reluctantly, she descended the concrete steps to join the throng of passengers in the third-class carriage of the Inner Circle line. Her lack of familiarity with the system meant she caught the hissing fire dragon heading west rather than east, causing her to endure many more stops than would otherwise have been necessary. Having passed through the delights of South Kensington, Victoria, Westminster and many other stations, the smoke and foul-tasting air forced her to re-emerge at Temple, several stops short of her intended destination.

She emerged into daylight hoping to fill her lungs with the sweet taste of fresh air. Sadly, she was to be disappointed – it was barely better than that already experienced in the Underground.

'The river!' she choked in desperation.

Finally, at the brow of Waterloo Bridge, air of some breathable description surged into her lungs. Although anything but pure, it contrasted greatly to the stagnant, smelly air so far endured.

She peered over the balustrade into the river. Despite blue sky, there was no corresponding reflection, only a grey-brown, lifeless surface full of floating debris and chugging steamboats transporting their passengers from Blackfriars to Westminster. She groaned. Even the bridges could not provide a safe haven from the soot and smoke.

They drink this muck? she wondered, having never seen such disgusting-looking water.

Horses, buggies, taxis, omnibuses and carts competed for space between the bordering footpaths of the bridge, and all vied against the horn blasts of the attention-seeking automobiles that, by their privileged, modern status, forged a preferential passage. Before her trip south, Jualth had never seen a train let alone endured the sight and sound of an angry metal carriage that roamed the highways as it pleased. How could anyone survive in such an environment? She cursed the Londoners' apparent immunity and, in particular, that belonging to Mr Pennan. If anyone was to succumb to this filth-ridden town, it would probably be a wee, hapless Scottish lass on her first visit.

Looking downstream, Blackfriars was the first bridge she could see. There were several beyond, but the bend in the river meant she had to move back the way she had come to see the tip of the rebuilt Old London Bridge. It was a welcome sight.

'Now then, William,' she mused, 'all I have to do is follow the bank and see if you remember me. If you don't, that lovely new bridge of yours is going into the river.' She took off her cape, picked up her bag and set off.

The 1880s had seen the completion of Joseph Bazalgette's Victoria Embankment and although it stretched for four miles, it did not extend beyond Temple. Instead, a narrow walkway broken by wharves and warehouses lay between Jualth and her destination. As she weaved her way east, it was not long before she encountered the first sign of trouble.

'What 'ave ye got in ye bag, missis?'

She glanced back and locked eyes with a scruffy, ravenous-looking lad. 'Naught that a wee boy like you would look good in.'

She kept walking, but a couple of youngsters moved past to block her path. With some distance still to cover, Jualth had managed to attract an unsavoury pack of hungry urchins.

'C'mon, love. Ye got some money to giv' us, 'aven't ye?' said the same lad.

Jualth turned to face him. With the tide out and evening approaching, the shoreline was relatively quiet. Jualth glanced over to the warehouses, searching for anyone who could provide much-needed assistance. Seeing no one, she clasped both arms around her bag and held it against her chest. It was not the welcome to London she had expected.

'Clear off the lot of you,' she shouted, giving them a taste of the forbidding temper they were up against.

The urchin that had spoken to her scuffed the sole of his tattered shoe over the hard, concrete walkway. This was his patch of land and he did not take orders from hapless strangers who were careless enough to wander in. He wanted the bag and whatever was in it, and he was well used to taking what he wanted.

The twisting of his foot stopped. Jualth readied herself as tired, protruding eyes stared longingly from his gaunt, hollow face. She felt the urchins on either side close in. She glanced at them – they were staring at their leader, waiting for the word. A nod of the head was all it would take yet, for some reason, it did not come. Instead, the leader seemed caught in a moment of uncertainty. The hunger in his eyes remained, but not the will to act. And then, without another word and for no apparent reason, he took a step back and walked away.

Jualth watched him go and then the slow, gradual retreat of his surly-looking accomplices. She breathed a sigh of relief, surprised but thankful that it had been a relatively simple matter to scare them off. Perhaps her fearsome Scottish accent had provided an unexpected but effective weapon and made them think twice about the wisdom of taking her on. She wheeled around, satisfied that the danger was over, only to immediately bump into a further threat.

She staggered back in disbelief, dropping her bag in the process. Blocking her path this time was a smaller, tidier and, up to that point, unnoticed young lad. One look was enough to establish that he was different. Although thin, there was nothing dissolute or emaciated about his appearance. Even his clothes, showed the after-effects of soap and water. A spark of life – that was so absent in the urchins – lit his eyes revealing a confidence well beyond his years.

Jualth caught her breath and took a step nearer, ready to impart a Scottish greeting in the form of a hefty clip. She held back seeing nothing more in his pale hazel eyes than the innocence of a child. A cloth cap covered his blond hair and his smart, grown-up clothes made him look ridiculously cute and an impossible figure to suffer her wrath. Noticing the bag on the ground, nearer to the lad than herself, she moved to pick it up.

'That's all right, missis. Allow me,' said the lad.

Before Jualth had chance to utter a word of refusal, the boy had swooped an arm down to grab it. He stood to the side.

'You were 'eading this way I believe, missis. I'll accompany you if I may, until I know you're in safe company.' The boy motioned to move, but Jualth remained rooted to the spot. 'It's all right, missis; no 'arm will come to you whilst you're with me.' His diction was an exaggerated mixture of well-pronounced words and an obvious and dominant East End accent.

'Do you know what you nearly did to me, then?' Jualth growled. 'Have you any idea what I've been through these last few …?' Her blood was boiling. London Town had so far proved unhygienic, unfriendly and undeserving of any reverential respect. The darker side of its notoriety was all she had experienced.

'Sorry, missis. I didn't mean to scare you.'

Jualth took her time to weigh up the young lad and his offer. She glanced back at the deserting urchins as they shuffled away, empty-handed, to pursue their means of mischievous gain elsewhere.

'Did you do that?' she asked, pointing towards them. 'Are they running away because they're scared of a wee lad who's no bigger than a Shetland pony?'

The young lad's chest swelled in importance, though he had not an inkling as to the miniature size of a Shetland pony.

'Yes, missis ... and no, missis. They're running away because of me, but not *because* of me.'

'You just said yes and no twice. What do you mean?'

He struggled to elucidate, though in truth he had little choice but to be vague. 'Umm ... I mean, they're not running away *because* of me—'

Jualth put up a hand. 'All right, that's enough. You might be young, but you're still a man, however small. Why should I expect any more sense out of you than I do from one of your kind back home?'

The boy again motioned to move. Jualth hesitated and then edged slowly forward, keeping a close eye on her unsolicited escort.

'How do I know I can trust you?' she asked. 'You've got my bag and I dare say you could disappear in the same secretive manner in which you appeared.'

'No problem there, missis. You can trust me.'

'I hope so ...' Jualth stopped, unable to complete her sentence as she would wish to. 'Do you have a name, young man?'

'Cutter, missis.'

'Do you have a proper name?'

'That is a proper name.'

'No it isn't. It's the name of a boat or a villain with a thirst for blood. What name were you born with?'

'Don't know, missis. You'd 'ave to ask my parents if you could find either.'

'Have you tried?'

'Na. No point.'

'Why not?'

'They wouldn't know me and I wouldn't know them.'

Jualth cautiously resumed her passage towards Old London Bridge, a tinge of sympathy softening her tone for the common pain they shared. 'That's tough, Cutter. I lost my father when I was too young to remember, my mother when a teenager. At least I have some memories. Any brothers or sisters?'

'None that I know of.'

'Who looks after you then or do you make a living carrying the bags of defenceless females?'

'I'm well looked after, missis. You 'ave no need to worry on my account.'

'That wasn't an answer, Cutter. I asked *who* looks after you, not whether I should worry.' Jualth eyed him suspiciously as he made no attempt to explain. He was holding something back, though why there should be a need ...?

Coming up to Blackfriars Bridge, they were unable to pass underneath so scaled the steps to cross the road. It was Jualth's first opportunity to see Old London Bridge from one end to the other. Although a completely new structure, its historic character remained. Houses supported by wooden staffs overhung the buttresses, whilst the Chapel of St Thomas à Becket to the north and Nonesuch House to the south each stood upon a large pier at either end of the prominent and open central arch.

'They did a fine job rebuilding your bridge, William,' said Jualth with a touch of pride in her voice.

'I reckon so,' Cutter agreed. 'The Master took his time to get used to it, but I think even he 'as a liking for it now.'

Jualth stopped in her tracks. 'The Master! You know the master of that bridge?'

Cutter shuffled uneasily. Jualth looked back the way they had come. 'Now I understand. Not afraid of you, but they are afraid of ... the *bridge master*. And your connection is what, Cutter?'

'I'm one of 'is 'awks, missis.'

'One of his *what*?'

'One of his 'awks: his eyes and ears. We keep a lookout to make sure nothing bad 'appens.'

'Lookouts or spies?' Jualth asked.

'Lookouts, missis! Too many people know who we are for us to be spies.'

'Like those urchins back there?'

''Specially them.'

Jualth nodded, the young man's intervention now made a lot more sense. Without it, there was no telling what might have happened to her.

Once back on the walkway, they soon passed under Cannon Street, the next bridge along.

'The bridge master must hold considerable respect if unruly urchins respond like that to someone so small, even if he is an *'awk*,' said Jualth after a short period of silence.

'I'm not much smaller than you, missis.'

'I'm minute, Cutter. I was carved out of a very small rock. How old are you?'

'Fourteen, fifteen.'

'You don't look it. How about eleven or twelve?'

'No, missis. I'm older than that, I'm sure I am.'

There was an obvious need for the boy to feel grown up. Jualth pitied him. Being a child in the Highlands had been a wonderful time that she had wished would never end, but in this dirt-grey, suffocating town, beyond growing up there seemed little else to aspire to.

'Cutter?'

'Yes, missis.'

'Are you just carrying my bag or are you doing something more?'

'Like what, missis?'

'Like providing protection whilst taking me somewhere of your choosing.'

'Just helping out a lady in need, that's all, 'onest. It's all part of my job.'

Jualth remained sceptical, but it was ridiculous to think their meeting could have come about by anything other than good fortune. Still, she did have a mind to go *somewhere* and, being in the company of one of the Bridge's *'awks*, had chanced upon a safe passage and the best means to get there.

'I'd like to meet your master, Cutter. Can you take me to see him?'

'Of course, missis, if that's where you're 'eading.'

She offered no explanation and wondered why the young man did not ask for one. It would have been a reasonable question to ask.

'My name's Jualth, if you want to use it.' Cutter nodded but looked puzzled. 'What's wrong? Don't you like it?'

'It's not that, missis.'

'What then?'

What was wrong soon became apparent. '*Jawff?*' Cutter attempted. Necessary assistance was provided.

'*Jewel-ff.*'

Cutter scratched his head. 'That's a new one on me, missis. If you don't mind me asking, where'd it come from?'

'It's a new one on all strangers I meet and as for where it came from … well, let's just say I missed my chance to ask.'

'No one knows?'

'Not even my grandmother. My mother made it up and managed to fool everyone into thinking it originated in the country of her birth, which, I might add, is on the other side of the world.'

'That's a long way, missis.'

'It couldn't be farther.'

'So you have no idea?'

'Not one I'd care to admit to. It might make me appear too big for my boots with folks back home.'

When they reached Old London Bridge, Jualth chose not to climb the long flight of steps on its west side, but instead followed the walkway under the first arch. She stopped in the shadow, captivated by a view worthy of her long journey. Barges moored to jetties floated lazily and unobtrusively between the banks whilst, a short distance farther along, the majestic crossing of Tower Bridge newly spanned the river, with its central drawbridge raised to allow passage to a tall schooner.

She took a pace forward and emerged into the sunlight. Her eyes were immediately drawn to a small stone building on the southern bank.

'That's the Bridge 'Ouse, missis,' Cutter informed her. Jualth did not need to be told – she had already sensed the presence of his master in that building.

From the walkway, they climbed half-a-dozen steps to the narrow passage between the side of the bridge and the freshly renovated church of St Magnus the Martyr. Jualth hovered momentarily at the church entrance, feeling the call of the Holy Father to go and account for her sins. She quickly shuffled past – spiritual salvation would come later, if needed.

Jualth followed Cutter up a double flight to the cobblestone platform of Old London Bridge. It was busy, but not packed, and orderly pedestrians replaced the mayhem witnessed on Waterloo Bridge. She had, at last, discovered a civilised world within a city of apparent madness.

Looking up, she captured the menacing glare of the fearsome gargoyles staring down from the parapet of the first terraced block. They protected the bridge from all foes, whatever their form. She had a mind they were watching her closely.

They walked through Princes' Gate to a small space that preceded the first arcade of shops. The centre passageway was wide, far wider than she had imagined, with a mixture of open sky and overhead *hautpas* (gangways) linking the two sides. A traditional signboard, displaying the craft and nature of the trade within, hung above the door of each narrow residence, and lamps – powered by electricity and attached to the walls – shone throughout the night to provide both illumination and security.

'People and nothing *but* people,' Jualth observed with satisfaction as she wandered through.

'There used to be 'orses and carts, but they did too much damage to the platform and it was before all the other bridges got built,' Cutter helpfully informed her.

Another gap followed the arcade and then came the east-facing Chapel of St Thomas à Becket that jutted out into the river over its supporting pier. The bridge then opened into a central arch that curved gently up and then back down towards the southern half. Jualth held onto an imaginary hat as they made the crossing.

'Always gets a breeze over 'ere, missis,' Cutter pointed out. 'Sometimes strong enough to blow you clean away.'

'Aye, and I bet those shops would not be far behind.'
'Never had one fall down yet.'
'Give them a chance, Cutter. They've only just been built.'

At the brow of Central Arch, they stood next to the balustrade, facing east. Jualth stared at the small two-storey building on the southern shore, then averted her eyes – it would not be long now.

'What's that bridge called, Cutter?'

The schooner had completed its passage upriver and the platforms were in the process of descending.

'Tower Bridge, missis. Not long been there. Took about eight years to build.'

'It looks ancient for something so new.'

'Think that was the idea, missis. Blends in with The Tower.'

Jualth eyes flicked to the imposing sight of the Tower of London on the north bank, a well-known landmark with many centuries of morbid history. 'How can a place like that attract visitors?' she muttered. Her eyes fell upon a building with a glass roof. 'And that, Cutter?'

'Billingsgate, the world's finest fish market. I can take you for a visit if you like.'

'You can indeed, Cutter. I have a close affinity with fish; I might meet some old friends.'

The Hawk was lost for words and too perplexed to seek an explanation. For a respectable lady, his companion certainly said the strangest of things.

'It's far busier downriver,' Jualth observed.

'That's cause of the docks, missis. Used to be a lot busier than this, too busy most say. Things 'ave died down in recent years.'

Jualth could remember someone else telling her the same thing. It was time to reintroduce herself. 'Lead on, Cutter. Much as I prefer the air in the middle of your bridge, I have business to attend to that cannot wait.'

At the end of Central Arch, they passed through Nonesuch House followed by another gap called the Square that preceded the second arcade of shops, the Drawbridge and finally the Great Stone Gateway leading into Southwark. The tower of St Saviour's Church rose to the southwest, another temple of worship with a colourful history. For over four hundred years, it had suffered indignities similar to those of London Bridge, being at times used as a pen for pigs and the premises for a bakery.

They descended a double flight of steps to the southern walkway and soon reached Bridge House. Jualth halted and turned back.

'You have a fine view from here, Cutter.'

'You can see the whole of the bridge, missis, but you need eyes upon it to see inside. That's where we come in.'

'Not just on the bridge, Cutter. You didn't find me on the bridge.'

Cutter squirmed, as if caught out again. 'On and *around* the bridge then,' he clarified.

'And how many is "we"? How many pairs of eyes does the bridge master have?'

'Four as it stands.'

'All boys of your age?'

'A bit older, a bit younger and sometimes girls, but not at the moment.' He pushed against the door. 'Shall we go in, missis?'

Jualth kept her eyes on the bridge. It was hard to be anything but impressed, even if it had been chosen in preference to her. She felt pride and envy at the same time, pride for what William had achieved and envy for the hold it had over him. But that was all now by the bye. Time had moved on and personal feelings towards its master had nothing to do with her trip south. She turned her back on her rival and followed the Hawk into Bridge House.

Chapter 50

Cutter knocked on the impressive office door to the left of the open hallway. Jualth put her hand on his shoulder. 'It's okay, I can manage from here.'

'But I've got to announce you to the master, missis.'

'*Cutter,* he knows me,' said Jualth more sternly.

The young Hawk hesitated, momentarily fearful of a failure in his duties. On reflection, he could see no harm in this particular transgression. He handed over the bag and stepped aside. Jualth twisted the handle and, with an appreciative parting smile for her saviour, slipped through the narrow crack and closed the door behind her.

The bridge master had a large office and a grand desk with its back at an angle to the front window, where a quick twist of the head provided an immediate view of the bridge. Bureaucracy (in the form of in-trays and cabinets) mixed with carpets, family portraits and other homely comforts. In his executive seat behind the desk sat a much smarter-looking, fuller-faced William.

Jualth stood motionless by the door staring at the unreadable countenance of the bridge master, so reviving their own very special form of greeting. It was left to the visitor to break the impasse.

'I see your black eye has healed, William.'

The bridge master leant back, a flicker of a smile but no more. He looked her up and down: the uncovered red hair, the sullied white clothing, an aging bag in one hand and a worn cape in the other.

'My skirt was white a couple of days ago. I could wash it but, having seen the colour of your water, I'm not confident it will ever be so again.'

William's lips imperceptibly curled at the edges as he continued to stare and play the waiting game.

'You *do* remember me, William? If it would help to jog your memory, I can easily start a fight.'

William relented. 'You still do that?'

'When provoked, though, I might add, I've been a good girl on the whole these past couple of years.'

'Glad to hear it. So married life has proved a calming influence.'

Jualth looked away. William could tell by her manner that the subject had provoked a degree of distress. He stood up.

'Jualth, please, let me take your things.' He hung up her cape, placed the bag against the stand, then drew up two chairs and sat beside her. 'Your husband?'

'Dead, William.'

'Dead!' He had not expected the full gravity of her distress. 'I'm sorry ...'

Jualth imparted the full horror of events back home. 'My niece too.'

William sat back, stunned and deeply shocked, unable to comprehend such dreadful news.

'A week ago, in a warehouse fire at the Brethna Distillery. Harriet somehow found her way inside and Frazer, hero that he was, tried to save her.'

William felt horrified and angry with it that no word of the tragedy had reached his ears. Someone should have told him. 'That is terrible, Jualth, absolutely terrible. Your sister, how is she?'

'Burnt ... scared. She did what she could to save her daughter and very nearly perished herself. I shouldn't be here, William, I should be with Lily, but ... I had to come, *I had to.*'

There was a quiet tap on the door. William glanced irritably over his shoulder. 'Excuse me a moment.' He stood up, walked to the door and disappeared into the hallway. Within a couple of minutes, he had returned.

'Sorry, Jualth, bridge business. We will not be disturbed again.' He settled back into his seat and grasped a tiny hand that on most occasions belied its strength. 'Right, first things first, have you a place to stay?' Jualth indicated that she had not. 'All right, a room can be made up for you here.'

Jualth smiled gratefully, though in truth she had counted on his hospitality.

The sleeping arrangements out of the way, William had some pressing questions. 'Now, Jualth, I want to know why you are here. What could possibly have brought you so far at such a time?'

'Trouble, William.'

'What sort of trouble?'

'The biggest sort. We could end up losing everything we have as a result. An unwelcome guest paid us a visit. He is intent upon our ruin.'

William nodded. It could mean only one thing.

'I did not know what to do and could think of nothing else. I need help and if you are unable to provide it, I will have to seek out this man myself and try to stop him.'

Jualth's plan provoked immediate fears. Her volatile nature, especially in its present state, was unlikely to aid her objective. More likely, it would cause a regrettable and irreversible act and only add to the trouble she was already in.

'Tell me what happened, starting with the name of this unwelcome guest.'

'Pennan, Mr Cecil Pennan, inspector from the Excise service. He turned up from nowhere two weeks ago, first at Brethna and then us. We told him nothing, but he found out all he needed to know for himself. He took my papers and a bottle of Kvairen, and he's here, somewhere in London.'

'Was he alone?'

'He braved hostile territory without an army, if that's what you mean. His arrogance proved a powerful defensive shield.'

'And he's been back in London for …?'

'Little more than a week.'

William stood up and walked over to the window, staring out at the river, the boats and the buildings that lined the bank on the opposite shore. Jualth gave him a moment whilst he searched for something unseen that would rescue her from the abyss. She stared at the portrait of a man on the side wall. With his dark, strong features and authoritative posture, there was no doubting the family connection, nor the depiction of a troubled and tired man. The artist's portrayal of William's father showed an honest likeness that captured the struggle he had endured as bridge master.

'I did say, I did try to warn you,' said William, turning to face her.

'You did, William, but it was a bit late in the day for a rethink.'

'*Jualth!*'

'*William!*' Jualth responded with matching exasperation – this was ground they had already covered. '*Why* should we change? *Why* should we allow ourselves to be ruled by a distant government? *What* harm does a tiny community like ours do to anyone else?'

'That's not the point and you know it. It's the law and your community chose to break it.'

'But the law has ignored us for centuries. Why has it bothered to come and find us now?'

William shook his head, dismissing the pretence of misfortune. 'It was always likely to happen, in your generation or a future one. You can't keep secrets for ever, not any more, not in an age when the world is changing so rapidly.' William returned to the seat next to her and sighed gravely. 'You are not exaggerating, Jualth. You *are* in as big a trouble as you can imagine.'

The statement of the obvious was not what Jualth had travelled so far to hear. What she had come for was something quite different. 'Can you help me, William? I don't care how slight, but I have had no support; not one word that could comfort me since Mr Pennan walked into my inn. Anything at all. *Anything.*'

She knew little of what she was asking or of the help William could provide. But he was not a man without influence and, like Jualth, he did not stand back and accept defeat unchallenged. Many hard-fought battles had strengthened his own resolve.

'If I can help, I gladly will, but you'll have to be patient.'

'How patient?'

'*Just* ... patient. The process will not be quick. There will be no early return to Scotland if you are steadfast in pursuing this matter.'

The prospect of an extended period sitting on her hands presented Jualth with a problem. 'I have no money, William, not even my fare to get home. I will need to earn my keep.'

'You're a guest in my house; I shall take care of your needs. My staff is small: a housekeeper, my Hawks – you've met Cutter. I shall put them at your disposal.' William looked down at her bag. 'You've brought little in the way of clothes.'

'Little in the way of anything. I only intended a short stay, not a permanent resettlement.'

William fought to conceal his admiration. He respected her directness and the strength of character that had brought a person born to the countryside to an unfamiliar and daunting environment in search of the one person she knew to be a friend. She demonstrated a depth of courage that was lacking in all but a few.

'I wish the circumstances of our meeting were different, Jualth, but it's good to see you all the same.'

That was more in keeping with what she had wanted to hear. 'You too, William, and I like your bridge – even if you don't. When do you intend showing me around?'

'How long did you make me wait to see your distillery?'

'I'm not as patient as you.'

'As I seem to remember.'

'And I want to meet "her" or "him" as well.' William looked curious, he did not follow. 'The one you helped bring into this world – that gave you your skills as a midwife. I take it the child resides on your bridge.'

'She does, and I will gladly introduce you to Lucy and all other tenants. First though, I shall summon Mrs Tuckle, my housekeeper, and sort out a room and your cleaning. When did you last eat?'

'Haven't felt much like eating recently.'

'Well, we'll find something. You can decide what you want. As for clothing, you will need some additional garments. White is not the ideal colour to wear in the city.'

'I'm dressing in white, even if it means washing my clothes twice a day. I always dress in white, it reminds me of home, the countryside, everything that's clean.'

'You'll change your mind.'

'No, I won't.'

William reached over to his desk, picked up a bell and shook it.

'Don't tell me people come running to the sound of that thing!' Jualth exclaimed.

'Different ways,' said William, by way of an explanation if not a laudable excuse.

Presently, there was a knock on the door and the housekeeper entered.

'We have a guest, Mrs Tuckle. This is Mrs McTavish. She has just arrived from Scotland.'

'Jualth, please,' said the guest, wishing to dispense with any unnecessary formality. Different ways were not for her.

'*Mrs McTavish* will be staying with us for a … well, let's just say for a while. Could you make up the room next to mine and prepare some hot water?'

'As you wish, Bridge Master.'

Jualth received the shortest of polite smiles. Mrs Tuckle was the last member of the domestic staff retained and tended to all the needs of those that stayed in Bridge House. In effect this meant two people, William and herself, though she did wash and cook meals for the Hawks as well.

In her mid-fifties, and supporting a portly girth, she liked everything in an order of her choosing. Any deviation was treated as a burden that she shared to the point of generosity. Upsetting her routine upset her. She prided herself in her work, if exaggerating its vital role in the running of the bridge. But as long as she demonstrated a sufficient standard of care, William tolerated her somewhat difficult and grumpy nature. Mrs Tuckle left the room.

'You're supposed to follow,' William indicated to his guest.

Jualth looked bemused. 'She didn't say anything – just walked out.'

'Different ways …'

Jualth flapped a dismissive hand, not wishing to hear the same excuse again. She quickly grabbed her bag and scampered into the hallway after the housekeeper.

William remained in his study listening to the sound of footsteps, firstly on the stairs and then the landing boards in the open hallway. From his desk he had not so much as seen Jualth but sensed her, his eyes drawn to the shadows of the northern walkway, an area that had not previously ranked high in its estimable attraction. He had instantly recognised the tiny figure in white and discerned a ruffling of the muddy waters between them. It had not boded well.

At the bow window, he noticed Cutter approaching from the southern gate. He glanced to the ceiling and decided their meeting should take place outside. 'Well, Cutter?' he asked when on the walkway.

'All set up, Guv. They'll expect you at eleven o'clock tomorrow morning.'

'And you're sure no one saw you?'

'Made myself invisible. The only ones that knows are you, me and—'

William quickly cut him off. 'Okay, that will do. Just keep it to yourself.'

Cutter understood – he was in the bridge master's confidence. Although the youngest of his Hawks, Cutter was the most trusted. He knew when to be discreet.

'Quite a lady, your visitor. Not the typical type you meet in London. I likes a woman who talks direct and says whatever comes to mind. Most women 'ardly say a word, a compliment 'ere, a direction there, all very reserved. She says what she thinks right from the start.'

'She has a good side, try to stay on it. Make her angry and you may start wishing she was reserved.'

'Glimpsed that side of 'er earlier on, Guv. I can 'andle it,' the young Hawk boasted.

'I'm putting you in charge of looking after our guest, showing her around, keeping her out of harm's way and, when necessary, out of my way.'

'I can do that, leave it to me, Guv. It will be fun.'

'Don't be so sure, you barely know the woman. I'll introduce her to the others first thing tomorrow. Then I want you to take her into town before I go to my meeting. There are certain essentials she needs for her wardrobe. Take her to Silk 'n' Lace Street. Make sure she buys what's appropriate for the town.'

'No worries, I'll put her right, Guv. When can I bring her back?'

'There's no hurry. After she's finished with the shops, show her what you like – just keep her busy.'

Cutter was well taken with his new assignment. 'The other 'awks are gonna be dead jealous.' He chuckled and walked off, his errand run.

William's eyes flicked across the grey, murky river and through the masts of a sailing boat to a large, imposing building on the far side. He showed all the signs of being a man with deep troubles, the type that he could not share with anyone, least of all his visitor.

Chapter 51

Jualth's room faced the rear and fashioned a beautiful view of the workshops and the back walls of the surrounding buildings. That minor issue, however, mattered little on her first night in London; she was exhausted and, as a consequence, experienced her best night's rest in a week of considerable sorrow. Many troubles still lay ahead but she at last had a companion in a struggle that, before her foray south, had shown not the slightest sign of hope.

Overnight, Mrs Tuckle had obeyed her master's instructions to the letter, presenting Jualth with surprisingly clean clothes at the foot of her door in the morning.

'Mr Halar is attending to important matters on the bridge,' Mrs Tuckle reported at the breakfast table in a manner pertaining to her high rank. She busied herself with domestic chores whilst Jualth contentedly savaged a plateful of toast. 'He will shortly return to have a word.'

Jualth interpreted the message as an instruction to stay put and, although she had every intention of being amenable during her short stay, obeying orders induced an innate desire to rebel, especially when delivered second-hand. She tapped her fingers on the tabletop as she made swift work of her toast and took a moment to compare Mrs Tuckle's kitchen to her own back home – it was a different world.

There was no such thing as 'Here's a pan, find a spare hook to hang it on if you can, otherwise toss it on the side'. Here each pan had its place, its order, its angle of alignment. Metal and earthenware pots sat spotless and imperious upon shelves or placed in cupboards and, when not in use, the chairs stood in regimented lines on their allotted floor tiles. Jualth couldn't stand such rigid order, where any little detail out of place became an issue of importance. Surely there were better things in life to be concerned about than extreme tidiness? She concluded that the room was crying out for an unruly riot. As a leaving present she might arrange a drinks evening to promote Scottish traditions – William knew the type. With a mental note made for future plans, she judged it appropriate to tell a wee white lie.

'I like your kitchen, Mrs Tuckle – very modern. I didn't know a range could pump hot water up to a bathroom above.'

The haughty housekeeper jumped at the opportunity to put the ignorant country girl in her place. 'Yes, well you're bound to discover such things to be more advanced in the town, it's only natural.'

'Is it?'

'I'll show you how it works if I get a chance. It serves to provide considerable heat for the building and has some interesting features for the *knowledgeable* user.'

Jualth stifled a yawn that only a simple country girl could get away with. Her polite attempt to converse had only served to put her in her place. 'Worked here long?' she asked, already fed up with the advanced range.

'Since before Mr Halar was born. As with all the bridge staff, we have served his family well and they have taken good care of us in return. It's just such a pity that circumstances have recently reduced our number to so few.'

Jualth already felt there would be one fewer if she were in William's shoes. 'How many?'

Mrs Tuckle drew in a deep breath to demonstrate the huge effort being made on the guest's behalf. 'Well, the masons, smithies and carpenters who used to repair the old bridge have largely gone. Mr Halar found them jobs, every one of them. None were left without means to provide for their families. The eldest carpenter and blacksmith were retained, the ones that have been with us longest, but when they retire …?'

'… a very special breed will have died,' Jualth stated on the housekeeper's behalf. That was at least one thing they could agree upon. 'And besides you, who else cares for William?'

Mrs Tuckle stopped in her tracks; her master had no need of anyone else to care for him. She stared at the young woman, her worst fears realised – the country girl, with all her endearing simplicity, had arrived on a mission: to entrap her employer and become his partner in life. With no one to talk to on such issues, who might temper her views, Mrs Tuckle could be forgiven for drawing the most obvious and paranoid conclusions.

'He has relied upon me his whole life and I have never given him cause to question that reliance,' Mrs Tuckle responded assertively.

Jualth mulled over the reaction to her innocent comment. How strange that her concern for William had elicited such a defensive posture. Mrs Tuckle had been kept on after the great purge, so why the insecurity? Unless … *unless* she had installed herself as sole appraiser of all women that came into contact with William. The thought infuriated her. Ignoring the housekeeper's sensibilities, she offered her own take on the situation.

'I've a mind that William works far too hard. He needs time to relax away from his responsibilities, otherwise he will go the same way as his father. He deserves the same chance as any other man to have a family and a home life. I'm sure he would like a son to pass the bridge down to, just as his father did to him.'

'It doesn't work like that, young lady. William had to be elected to his position and so will his successor.'

'But surely it helps having a father to follow on from,' a rather peeved *young lady* suggested.

The inference that her employer secured his job by anything other than merit was not well-received. The guest understood little of how the world worked away from her petty rural existence. 'Mr Halar has his own special qualities and a love for the bridge, as you will gather when you know him as well as I do. Now, if you will excuse me, I have some *essential* housework to perform.'

And with that, Mrs Tuckle picked up a broom and headed for the hall to perform some *essential* brushing, the breakfast chat between the two women abruptly concluded.

Jualth took her time to chew her last remaining piece of toast, sizing up the spotless kitchen and its wonderfully modern range with waning interest. She realised there was little chance of hitting it off with Mrs Tuckle; the cultural and age differences between the two, coupled with a predilection to be in charge, were too great. Pity, a rapport with the housekeeper might have provided a greater insight into William's life.

Eventually, Jualth tired of waiting – if the bridge master wanted a word, he would just have to find her. Passing through the washroom and scullery beyond the kitchen, and then the staff quarters, she strolled out into the courtyard at the rear. Hearing the echo of a lone hammer, she followed the worn path to the front door of one of the workshops.

Through the distorting heat of the forge, the sweat-drenched blacksmith looked up to gaze upon what appeared to be a rather out-of-place redheaded angel. He wiped his brow, blinked, and stood back from the heat – the wraithlike angel was smiling. The furrow-faced and fire-hardened smithy could not help but smile back.

'My, you do have a big workshop, Albert,' said Jualth, once introductions had been made. 'I can only imagine the amount of work performed in here at one time.'

'Couldn't keep up with the demand and there were five of us in days gone by,' said Albert, having taken the trouble to lay a clean cloth across a stool for his unexpected visitor. He towelled himself down and pulled up a stool to sit opposite. Even then the tall, muscular figure with thin, greying hair towered over the angel.

'Boats ran into the piers smashing the brackets; fire and rust provided a constant stream of repair work; shopkeepers needed fittings of a particular type … and so it went on … and on. In time, the costs became too high, the repairs insufficient and the decision was made to rebuild from scratch.'

Jualth felt a sorrow for his loss, the dedication of a life for a structure that no longer existed. What did it all mean if he and others had nothing to show for their efforts? 'Is there not enough of the old bridge in the new to ensure it will not be forgotten?' she asked.

'And that was only thanks to the young master, his father and their supporters. If others had had their way, we'd have nothing to remind us of the past. And then how many generations before it would be forgotten altogether?'

'But, if the repairs were insufficient, was it not right to rebuild the new bridge?' Jualth had a feeling it was, despite its history.

Albert took his time to respond – it was a difficult admission to make. 'Now I've got used to it, the answer is probably yes, I think it might have been.'

Jualth thought about the noise and congestion she had witnessed on Waterloo Bridge. Old London Bridge had houses, shops and pedestrians; that was its noise, its congestion. It was a community with a heart – not unlike her own – and the only one of its kind in the country. Perhaps its very destruction had saved what lived and breathed upon it from the same fate.

'So what happens now, Albert, when there is no call on your time from the bridge?'

Albert gestured to the workshop. 'Look around, see for yourself.'

Jualth happily accepted the invitation and slipped off her stool. There were many items in various states of evolution on workbenches, leaning against walls and resting on anvils. Albert led his guest on a closer inspection of fireguards, gates, locks, brackets ...

'Some of this I make from scratch to customer designs. Others are just mere repairs. It's more than enough to keep me busy.'

Jualth stopped when it appeared Albert had omitted one corner. 'What about all these ... these ...? What are they, Albert?'

'What indeed,' the blacksmith grumbled.

'They look a little ... what's the word?'

'There isn't one, at least, not a polite one. Some of my commissions are damn-right peculiar. What the customers figure on doing with them is anyone's guess.'

Jualth stared at coat stands, screens and bowls of a most unusual shape and design. The twisted and curved metal held a fascination that was hard to explain.

'*Modern!* That's it, Albert: peculiar and *modern.*'

Albert grunted his disapproval. He had a leaning for a more traditional use of his skills.

'You still do the work, however peculiar the designs,' Jualth pointed out.

'I know, I'm a fool to myself.'

'So why do it?'

Albert opened his arms, searching for a justifiable excuse. 'Because it's a challenge and I suppose I like a challenge. Unfortunately, I have now established a reputation for the peculiar, and commissions are turning up from every which way.'

The blacksmith raised his eyebrows, but, for all his protestations and hankering towards tradition, Jualth detected a soft centre for someone who cared about people and their needs. Having completed the circuit, they returned to their stools.

'I like your shop and I like your work,' said Jualth, having already warmed to her new friend. 'It's just a pity you cannot see anything beyond these walls.'

'It can be claustrophobic,' Albert admitted. 'Trips to the bridge are rare events these days. It seems a strange thing to say when working so close, but I miss the river. I miss the openness.'

The sadness of the admission tore at Jualth's own love for the countryside. She decided there and then upon a mission to free a lost soul crying out for the wilds. 'Albert, go and live in the country. I promise you, it's as many times better than the town as you can imagine. Have you ever thought about it?'

What person who tasted soot in each city breath he inhaled had not? Regrettably though, jobs in the country were scarce. 'Perhaps when I retire.'

'I wouldn't leave it till then. Once gone, you'll regret the time you wasted.'

The blacksmith nodded; he had also warmed to the angel. Although not one to listen to idle tittle-tattle, rumour had it that the bridge master had met his match amongst the fairer sex during his long period of absence. Until that moment he had not believed it.

William appeared in the doorway. 'I can see you did not feel the need to wait for your host to show you around, *Mrs McTavish*.' His playful sternness turned into a look of concern. 'And you have no chance of keeping that dress clean sitting in here.'

'I said I'd wash it twice a day, *Mr Halar*, and, if necessary, I will.'

'A darker colour would be more practical.'

'I'm sure it would, but darker colours are not for me.'

William exchanged a nod with the blacksmith – as on every working day, their paths had already crossed at an earlier meeting. 'Have you finished with Albert or would you like some tea brought out?'

Jualth's face lit up. 'Now there's an idea. Have you brought your little bell with you?'

Having just encountered the housekeeper in a rather gruff mood, William regretted making light of her duties. 'Mrs Tuckle did not seem in the best of humours when I walked through.'

'I noticed that, William.'

'Any ideas?'

Jualth shrugged. 'Probably something to do with me.'

'Probably?' the bridge master sighed. 'If you could please try to get on,' he urged.

'Promise,' Jualth replied meekly. 'And yes, William, I have finished with Albert – for now.' She thanked the blacksmith for his hospitality and was invited to return any time she liked, and in whatever dress she chose.

After a brief visit to the workshop of Three Fingers White, the carpenter, they used a side gate to escape the confines of the courtyard. The sight of the river and the rush of moving air never felt more welcome. Albert would receive further visits and, if necessary, persistent nagging to forsake his enclosed workshop for the countryside.

On the bridge, Jualth received a tour, a history lesson and an introduction to the shopkeepers in the southern arcade. Amongst the bookshops, printers, tanners, haberdasheries and linen shops, one abode stood out – the photographic studio. Jualth had never seen such a thing and laughed openly at the formal poses taken, understanding little about exposure time and the dignity and status of the subject. She did not succeed in her request for a joint pose with the bridge master, though it was added to the list of topics upon which to nag. At the top of Central Arch, they stopped to capture the view downstream.

'Not bad and probably quite warm when the sun is out,' Jualth conceded for her companion's benefit. She inhaled deeply. 'And the only open place so far discovered that does not leave a foul taste in the mouth.'

'The dust from the coal fires, it tends to hang in the air,' William explained apologetically. 'You'll get used to it.'

'No I won't. I have no intention of developing a sympathetic layer of tar on my lungs. I will not be here long enough. I've told Albert to go and live in the country and I intend to do the same with everybody else I meet, starting with my young Hawk.' She looked around. 'Where is Cutter?'

William noted the claim already made on his Hawk. She had obviously taken to the boy and done so without any coaxing on his part. Putting his fingers to his mouth, he whistled south and then north.

'Don't tell me they answer to whistles as well.'

Two boys appeared running past the chapel, soon to be followed by Cutter and then a boy from under the archway of Nonesuch House.

'I recognise that one,' said Jualth, as all four stood to attention in front of her. 'He was lurking in the background whilst we were visiting the shops.'

'That's Nipper,' said William, proceeding with the formal introductions.

'Who gave you that name, Nipper?'

'Always 'ad it, missis.'

'I dare say. My name's Jualth, as Cutter has hopefully already mentioned.'

'And this is Stretch and Jamba.'

Jualth sighed in disbelief. 'Does anyone have a proper name around here?'

'Cutter you know.'

'How ye doing, Jualth?'

'In excellent hands, thank you, and glad to hear you remembered my name. Try to do likewise when your master is not present.'

The other boys tipped their caps and made polite greetings. They were neat, tidy and clean, and easily identifiable to those in the know as Hawks to Old London Bridge. All were bigger than Cutter and two were bigger than Jualth.

'Cutter, wait down by the chapel,' William ordered. 'The rest of you, back to work.'

The Hawks ran away as quickly as they had gathered.

'So, there you have it, you know their faces and, if needed, you know how to summon them.'

Although never previously witnessed, William did not doubt for one moment that she had the knack, however unladylike. For her part, Jualth resisted the temptation for an immediate trial run.

'William?' she said, quizzically. 'The Hawks – your spies – where do they come from?'

William ignored the somewhat provocative description. Although he recognised a certain greyness to some of their duties, he considered them indispensable protectors of his bridge.

'All urchins, all orphans that I found in rags, begging on the street.'

'I guessed that, but why these four? There must be hundreds of boys like them.'

'Because all showed a quick wit, a determination to survive and a willingness to answer back. None, despite their deprivation, were prepared to be humiliated.'

Jualth approved of their fortitude. She delved deeper. 'What did Cutter do?'

William half-smiled in recollection. 'I dropped a coin into a pile of horse dung for him to pick up. He did so along with a handful of the muck that he then hurled at my back. He subsequently invited me to drown in the river and expressed the hope that my corpse would be ravaged by rats.'

'Good for him, though that was not a very nice thing to say.'

'But it was the right thing to say and more important to his pride than the farthing I had thrown. He then pocketed the coin and bid me return the next day if I cared to repeat my act of generosity.'

Jualth laughed approvingly.

'And they are not spies,' William stressed, 'they are a defensive shield that protects my bridge. The first sign of a flame or trouble, they raise the alarm. Fires have been started deliberately before now, and houses made largely from timber do not last long once a fire takes hold.'

Jualth looked away into the distance, allowing the breeze to blow her hair over her face.

It suddenly dawned on William what he had said. He inhaled sharply, feeling very angry with himself. 'Sorry, that was a thoughtless thing to say.'

Jualth shrugged away the apology. She could not expect an expression of regret every time the word fire and its effects were mentioned. 'Go on, William, you were saying.'

The bridge master gratefully returned to the subject of his Hawks. 'There's a room at platform level either end of the bridge that sleeps two apiece. They take their meals at the bridge house and Mrs Tuckle sees to their washing. As for when they get older, well, that's more complicated than it used to be.'

Jualth saw the same pain she had witnessed more than two years previously when William had spoken so passionately about the original bridge and its centuries of tradition. No resolve, however hard he tried, could ever overcome that trauma.

William explained. 'When we had a courtyard full of craftsmen, we could teach each a trade and find employment for them when they left. Now we're teaching them to read and write and that's it. We'll help as much as we can, but it will be down to them to decide where their futures lie.'

Jualth felt a common bond with the urchins – none had a future without the bridge master's help. The thought carried more truth than she cared to contemplate.

William put his hand into his breast pocket and pulled out his timepiece. He looked in the direction they had come. 'Time presses, Jualth. The rest of the tour will have to wait till tomorrow.' He nodded towards the Hawk stationed by the Chapel. 'Cutter is waiting to take you shopping. He will advise you on appropriate clothing. Please listen to him.' The bridge master made to depart.

Jualth called after him, 'Eh … William, one tiny thing you might have forgotten – money? Either Cutter is a young man of unexpected means or the two of us are about to embark on a premeditated wave of shoplifting.'

William waved his hand as he called back, 'Cutter will handle it. Leave it to him.'

He disappeared, striding speedily towards the Bridge House, a change of clothes necessary before his important meeting.

Jualth ambled down Central Arch to where her Hawk waited. He looked anything but his age in his smart attire and the confident, ready manner in which he carried out his duties.

'Looks like it's you and me again, missis.'

'Doesn't it, Cutter. Your master informs me that you are a man with a generous heart who wishes to take me shopping.'

Cutter stepped aside and they set off, heading for Fish Street Hill and then beyond to Silk 'n' Lace Street, an arcade of fashionable shops that boasted ladies' outfitters of high repute.

'Cutter?' said Jualth, when they were halfway up the hill.

'Yes, missis.'

'Why are we not shopping on the bridge? Did I not see ladies' garments displayed in at least two window fronts?'

'Yes, missis, and very elegant clothes at that.'

'Do you not think I would be comfortable in *elegant* clothes?'

'It's not that, missis.'

'*Cutter*, have you forgotten how to pronounce my name?'

'No, missis.'

'What is it then?'

'Jualth, missis.'

'Well remembered.' The young woman foresaw a considerable struggle ahead. One name appeared to suffice for all women in the young Hawk's eyes. 'So why are we not using those shops?'

'Choice, missis. There's a much better choice the way we're 'eading. The master himself wanted you to see them.'

Jualth did not appreciate the implication of Cutter's remark. The man was exerting pressure to enforce conventional clothing of his choosing upon a woman who knew her own mind. 'What's wrong with white, Cutter? Does he not like me in white?'

'Course he does, missis. It's not so much what he likes though, as what's right for the town.'

'But as I do not intend staying long in the town, why should I buy clothing that I will hardly ever wear?'

'Cause the master's buying?' Cutter suggested hesitantly.

Jualth brooded over the inner mysteries of a man's mind. 'He likes me in white and yet he wants me to buy black.'

'Or something in-between. Gold jackets with upturned collars are very fashionable.'

Jualth was not listening. 'Men. You normally know what's going on inside their heads – next to nothing. Then you meet one who can actually put sentences together and you suddenly encounter a challenge to the control you took for granted. Now I'm wondering which of the two I prefer.'

'He is the master, missis.'

'He's your master, Cutter, not mine and I will not give in. Besides, I have an inkling that William likes a girl with independent thoughts, even if she does not possess independent means. And if he wants a fight about it, he'll get one.'

Cutter nodded – he had an uneasy feeling that she meant it.

Chapter 52

Jualth had never previously spent more than five minutes deciding upon which clothes to purchase. However, once in the shop, Cutter made sure she chose between at least half-a-dozen outfits, contrasting jackets with blouses and skirts. Her thin waist made tortuous corsets superfluous. The carefully selected hats were initially brushed away politely, but persistence had them flying through the air aimed at the infuriating culprit. The footwear was something else entirely.

'These shoes are alive, Cutter. Every step I take, they groan with pain.'

'That's because they're good-quality leather, missis.'

'As opposed to the comfortable sheepskin us country clodhoppers wear?'

'How about this 'at, missis?'

Cutter's never-say-die attitude left him susceptible to permanent hearing loss as another swift clout brushed against the side of his head. 'That's for not taking "no" for an answer *and* for calling me "missis" again.'

By the time they were ready to leave Silk 'n' Lace Street, Jualth had become the owner of two additional white blouses, skirts and undergarments, a handbag – an accessory she had never previously owned – and been measured for a pair of squeaky shoes and one dark, morbid outfit that she was only prepared to wear on the happy occasion of Mr Cecil Pennan's funeral. They would return later that afternoon to pick up what was ready.

'That was quite a fun way to spend an hour and a half, Cutter. Are there any more shops William would like us to visit?'

'Stationer's, missis.'

'*Cutter!*' Jualth growled. She was already sensing the futility of continued correction. 'What does he want me in a stationer's for?'

'It's not for you, Jualth, it's for me. The master thought it might be somethin' you could 'elp me with.'

Jualth took a moment to figure out what William had in mind. The penny dropped. 'My skills as a teacher, I see. Repayment in kind if I'm not mistaken.'

'More of a way to keep you occupied, I think, missis.'

Jualth weighed up the Hawks over-honest comment. She was nonplussed. 'Keeping a tab on me, just the sort of thing I would expect a spy to do. Does your master not trust me?'

Cutter could not think of anything convincing to say, so he did not attempt to lie. 'Don't 'ave to go to stationer's, Jualth, if you'd prefer not to.'

Jualth heard her name mentioned for the second time in quick succession. The considerate child was willing to relieve her of the burden of teaching him. But it was payback time, Jualth to William and William to Cutter. In such circumstances, she felt obliged and did not resent the imposition. Cutter would get all the instruction he could cope with and a considerable amount more than he was used to.

'Where to now?' Jualth asked, after they had finished at the stationer's. 'The bridge? Some other shop?'

'No 'urry, missis. My orders are to show you around. Anythin' you want to see I can show you.'

'What do you suggest?'

He followed his master's carefully laid-out instructions. ''Ow abouts some garden or maybe a park?'

Jualth's heart leapt. 'That sounds like a wonderful idea. Get me into an open space surrounded by nature, and as quickly as possible. Where is the nearest park?'

'That will be Victoria Park, still quite a trek though, so I'll take you past some sights on the way.'

'Victoria Park! That woman gets everywhere.' Jualth had already encountered an Underground station in her name. 'Does no one else get a look in?'

'Don't seem like it.'

Jualth sighed. 'Oh to be the queen of a tiny island. If only she were a Scot. All right then, lead the way. Just remember, I do not regard automobiles, trains or their stations as sights of any interest whatsoever.'

They headed northeast, keeping to the pavements as much as possible but risking their lives to various modes of transport every time they ventured to cross a road.

'Cutter, they're coming from all directions,' Jualth ranted nervously.

'No one will hit you, missis, not whilst you're with me.'

'And as for the mess in the street ... I hope someone clears it up.'

'It sort of blends in with the rest of the mud when it rains. Probably the reason it smells so much.'

'Urgh!' Jualth exclaimed in disgust. 'Get me away from these plague-ridden streets, Cutter. Where is the park? I want to see trees, grass, clean-blue running water ...'

They turned up a narrow alley and within fifteen minutes had reached an area where large buildings stood back from a road all but free of traffic. It would have taken only ten minutes, but for an unnecessary diversion that Jualth had observed without mentioning.

'What's that place?' she asked, at last seeing something worthy enough to delay their foray into parkland.

A large, impressive building with a façade of lightly coloured grey stone and tall windows stood two stories high within a perimeter of neatly kept gardens. Strategically placed works of art surrounded the building; the statues of Roman gods and Greek philosophers contrasting with embryonic structures that offered no recognisable form.

'That's where all the great artists go to learn 'ow to sculpt, paint and draw,' Cutter informed his companion.

'Does it have a name?'

'Frostfairs, missis. You must 'ave 'eard of it.'

'Not me, Cutter. Obviously not famous enough for me. Do the artists make all these sculpture things?'

''Spect so.'

'Can we go in, take a look around?'

'Don't think it's allowed, missis.'

'Why not?'

''Cause we ain't art students and we can't draw.'

'But who's to know? Could we not mingle? Could we not just watch?'

Cutter shrugged, he didn't want to do anything without the Master's say-so, especially when it came to gate-crashing a renowned educational establishment.

'Shall we see?'

'Let's go to the park instead, Jualth. It's much nicer in the sun.'

For the third time that day, Jualth heard the unusual sound of her name being mentioned. She sensed the invisible hand of a higher authority denying them entry. On this one occasion – and for the sake of her chaperone – she acquiesced, making a further mental note to sharpen her teeth on the 'hand' if it continued to interfere with her wishes.

In another ten minutes they reached Victoria Park, a welcome expanse of green with a large pond, fountain and bandstand, bordered to the southeast by the Hertford Union Canal.

'That was quite a walk, Cutter. A pity it took so long to get here.'

They kept moving towards its centre. A well-spoken young woman passed by reading out loud to attentive children.

'I see you've brought me to where the nobility resides, Cutter. Do they mind us using their park?'

'Public park, missis. Doesn't matter if they mind.'

Jualth smiled politely at passing couples: the women smiled back and most of the men raised their hats. Those that did not looked sheepish, leading Jualth to speculate unfavourably upon their characters. But why shouldn't the so-called good and the not-so-good inhabit the same park? Surely it belonged to unwashed urchins as much as smartly groomed children playing with hoops; to pickpockets and beggars as well as sketching artists and poetic writers. It belonged to them all, all who made the effort to seek out nature and clean air within a metropolis of filth.

'Cutter?'

'Yes, missis?'

'I've had an idea.'

Although with no previous experience of Jualth's ideas, there was something in the way she made the announcement that filled the young Hawk with the same foreboding as those that had.

'As punishment for your continued reference to me as "missis", a term that I now realise to be too ingrained to dislodge, I have decided to anoint you with a real name. It is about time you were properly christened.'

'What's wrong with Cutter?'

'It's villainous. People will get the wrong opinion. You need something that is friendly and dignified.'

'Like yours?'

'Like mine, but not unique,' said Jualth, taking Cutter's comment as a compliment whether intended or not. 'How about Robert?'

Cutter screwed up his face. 'Nah, don't like it.'

'Okay … Michael?'

His expression surpassed the first.

'Andrew?'

'Nah.'

'Roderick?'

Cutter gasped. 'Definitely not Roderick!'

'Right,' said Jualth, quickly grasping the direction in which each suggestion would travel. 'I can see you intend to be difficult but, I'm telling you straight, you're not keeping that name. You cannot go through life with a name that would do Jack the Ripper proud. The next suggestion I make, you will keep.'

Cutter shifted nervously, dreading what was coming. Jualth winked. 'Save your worries for another day. I'll have a nice long think and then surprise you when you least expect it. Something for you to look forward to.'

Jualth resumed her game with passing couples, gratified, in the process, to see some of the young men blushing. Sadly, conversation was limited to polite pleasantries.

'What's that?' Jualth asked when they had reached the midpoint of the park.

'The Victoria Fountain.'

Jualth sighed mournfully – did *she* reject nothing? 'They should rename London after her and be done with it,' she suggested. Perhaps a royal pardon could be negotiated in return for allowing her to name a certain Scottish distillery after herself. She would speak to William later, get his thoughts on the matter.

After a peaceful walk and having enjoyed a nice rest, they embarked on the long sojourn back to the bridge, picking up all but the morbid outfit from the dressmakers as they passed.

'You'll collect that other thing for me, Cutter?'

'I think you are supposed to try it on first, make sure it fits.'

'I wasn't ever intending to wear it. The mere fact that I have a dark dress should be enough to keep William happy.'

'And he won't be pleased that you 'aven't bought an 'at.'

'But he will be pleased that I have an outfit that is not white. Hats we have not discussed.'

They turned into Fish Street Hill, the steep feeder road that sloped at a slight angle to the bridge. Jualth's footsteps shortened then ground to a halt.

On the eastern flank, halfway down, the Monument – a Doric column mounted on a huge, ornately carved pedestal – stretched two hundred and two feet into the sky. Designed by Sir Christopher Wren and Dr Robert Hooke, it commemorated the great London fire of 1666, the destroyer of half the city. Farther down, St Magnus the Martyr chimed the hour, a small but proud church that had caught fire many times but had risen from the ashes like an irrepressible phoenix on each occasion. The bridge itself – with its gates, chapel and buildings – stretched across the river to Southwark, where the bells of the distant church of St Saviour's answered the call from St Magnus. Changed guises or not, this was one place in London they had managed to get right, a path through history that everyone could share.

'I never thought Man could create anything to match the wonder of nature, but they didn't do a bad job here,' Jualth whispered. 'I hope William is proud of it. I would be.'

'Missis,' said Cutter, wishing to move on.

'Give me a moment. This might be a daily sight to you but it isn't to me.' Her first impressions of London had not been favourable, but the walk and visit to the park that day had gone a small way to raising her spirits and her opinion. Staring at the view south from Fish Street Hill, she understood better now the strength of her rival's attraction.

'Do you know the history of your bridge, Cutter?' Jualth asked.

'Course I do, missis. The master tells us stories all the time.'

Jualth nodded approvingly. 'Listen well. Those stories must never be lost. It's up to you to retain all you learn and pass it on.'

'That's what the master says, keep the public informed. It's our duty to do so.'

'And do you?'

'It's part of the fun of living on the bridge. The public loves 'earing it and we loves tellin' 'em.'

Jualth noticed the chest swell again. It was easy to see the reason for such self-esteem – the bridge had a scale and place in London's landscape to match any other historic landmark. It made the task of bridge master seem all the more daunting.

'He needs your help, Cutter, the Master. He can't look after all this by himself.'

'We 'elps 'im, missis, 'is 'awks and 'is friends.'

'Who do you mean by friends? Proper friends or the likes of Mrs Tuckle?'

'She's 'is friend, the best sort, does all 'is cookin' and cleanin'.'

'One woman who is nearly sixty is not what I had in mind. That man needs a woman, a young one that is capable of providing a little more than cooking and cleaning.'

This was not something Cutter had previously contemplated. Since he had been taken on it had always been the Master and them, and it had worked well up to that point. 'You mean a wife?' he asked cautiously.

'Aye, a wife. Have you seen him with any young ladies?'

Cutter shook his head, no thinking time needed.

'Do you know of any, then?'

'Beyond you, missis, none.'

'Well look beyond me, Cutter. My future is unknown apart from one certainty – I shall be returning to Scotland.'

'He won't go there, missis.'

'Which confirms that I am not the solution.'

'But you'd like to be, wouldn't you? And so would he.' Having got used to the fleetness of Jualth's intended clips, he managed a fleet, defensive manoeuvre of his own to avoid one.

'*Cutter*, this is only the second day in which our lives have crossed and if you can read me like a book already, will you kindly keep the book closed. And next time I want to hit you, *stand still*.'

The lively and impulsive joust did not go unnoticed. As the passing numbers steadily increased, it suddenly occurred to Jualth that detours were being made around the blockage she and her companion were creating.

'It's very busy, Cutter. Where are all these people going?'

'Home, missis. It's that time of day. They walk over the bridge to catch the train. If you're ready to join them,' he almost pleaded, 'dinner should be waitin' in the Bridge 'Ouse by now.'

Jualth looked into the disarmingly cute eyes of her hungry young guide – her wish to linger and absorb London's finest view had kept him from his dinner. Having put up with her for most of the day, it was the least he deserved. William and his need for a woman could wait. A shove in his back was greeted with no defensive manoeuvre, only a welcoming smile as they joined the growing rush of pedestrian traffic moving south towards the Thames.

Dinner was held around the large table in the kitchen, where William, Jualth, Mrs Tuckle, Cutter and Nipper all enjoyed Irish stew, dumplings and bread. The accomplishment and proficiency of the cook was appreciated by all, even the guest. However, to her eyes, the gathering lacked its full membership.

'Where are Jamba and Stretch, William?'

A strict rota existed at mealtime, which never included more than two Hawks. 'They'll have their turn once Nipper and Cutter have returned to the bridge.'

'Keep them out all night, do you?' Jualth quipped.

'Especially at night. The hours of darkness can be the most dangerous, the time when mysterious fires take hold more often than not.'

'Like the fire of 1733,' Cutter coughed up to show how well he listened to his master's stories. 'Lost a considerable number of the buildings during that one, didn't we, Guv?'

'There's still a threat?' Jualth asked.

William nodded. 'It pays to be vigilant. I would have expected something to happen during or soon after the rebuilding. As it hasn't, maybe we are guarding against the past and not the present.'

'No one would dare with us around,' Nipper said boastfully.

'Too good at our job,' Cutter agreed in the same vein.

Mrs Tuckle – the bastion of good manners – tutted, warning both not to talk at the table unless invited to by the bridge master. Jualth naturally ignored the warning.

'So, I've told you about my day, William, and shown you the evidence ...' Jualth had emptied the boxes to display all items purchased from the shopping trip, undergarments included.

'You really didn't need to do that,' William said awkwardly.

'*Quite,*' said Mrs Tuckle, wishing to register her own disapproval and that she stood shoulder to shoulder with the Master on this issue.

'Just thought you'd like to know where your money went,' Jualth explained.

'Money well spent, missis,' said Cutter, speaking totally out of turn, which in the ensuing silence he quickly realised.

'Anyway,' said Jualth, returning to the subject she wanted to talk about, 'your day, William. Do you have any news?'

William was not forthcoming. 'I told you, Jualth, you will have to be patient.'

'Not easy, William. Things are happening and I need to find the man who is making them happen.'

'Can we 'elp, missis?' Nipper asked. 'What's 'e look like?'

A profound look of displeasure from his master told Nipper to rein in his tongue. Cutter did likewise. His pledge to keep silent on secret errands remained in force.

'There's more to your problem than finding one man. If anything, that's the simplest of our tasks.'

'So, why can't we ...?'

'Because meetings have to be arranged and a course of action decided upon. What *you* might do without thinking it through first is something I would rather avoid.'

'If I'd wanted to kill him, William, that simple undertaking could have been achieved whilst he was still on Scottish soil. I want to avoid that course of action as well, which is why I have come to reason, plead and beg, and if all that fails, then I'll—'

'More bread, young lady?' said Mrs Tuckle, holding the bowl under her nose. Her exceptionally stern and grumpy demeanour indicated that the conversation had strayed into an area of questionable integrity. Nipper's and Cutter's slightly ashen expressions backed up this theory. Jualth took a piece of bread but refused to be silenced.

'So, what time will my tour recommence, William?'

He chose to be more forthcoming on this subject, having already planned the next day's schedule. 'Nine o'clock. Once we've been to the chapel, we'll meet the rest of the shopkeepers.'

'And then visit St Magnus?' Jualth asked, identifying a gap in the itinerary.

'I'll introduce you to the minister. He'll be the best person to show you around.'

'And what about the Monument? I want to see that too.'

Mrs Tuckle sighed loudly, obviously disapproving of the endless stream of demands being made upon an important and busy man.

'We'll be off then,' said Nipper, indicating to the master that they had finished and wished to return to their duties.

William nodded. 'Send the other two along. I'll be out later.'

'If you'll excuse me a minute,' said Jualth, rising from the table, 'I'd like a word with Cutter before he goes.' Jualth ushered him away from the table, through the hallway and out onto the walkway.

Mrs Tuckle was left to sigh her heaviest yet. If she had received an offer of help in her kitchen from their guest, it would naturally have been refused. But it would have been nice to receive it all the same. Bearing the full weight of her burden, she rose from the table and started to clear the abandoned dishes – two more hungry Hawks required imminent feeding.

William stared at the vacated chair to his side, more worried than he cared to show. As Jualth had previously stated, she was not a patient person and was bound at some point to force the issue. He had assigned Cutter to keep her occupied, diverting her attention to give him the time he needed. It was a tough assignment and maybe beyond the boy's capabilities.

The front door opened and closed. Footsteps quietly approached. Ignoring Mrs Tuckle, Jualth sat in the chair opposite William, clearly contented. 'Right,' she said, making no attempt to explain her brief absence, 'the Monument, William. You were just about to add it to tomorrow's tour.'

Mrs Tuckle turned from her cooking pot intending to afford the precocious country girl the sternest of glares. Instead, she hurriedly turned her back, having witnessed the softening of the bridge master's features to reflect the young woman's smile. In little more than a day, her worst fears had been realised – the little madame was intent upon becoming mistress of the house. The thought was untenable. Allowing her into their home had been a terrible mistake.

Chapter 53

William could feel something was wrong the moment he stepped onto the walkway. His custom was to rise early, meet up with his Hawks and listen to their night-time reports. It was a well-honed routine of vigilance that provided a twenty-four-hour guard to his bridge and yet, that morning, he sensed all was not right.

He searched through the haze hanging over the river, past the steamboats and moored barges, to the darkened mass of buildings on the opposite shore. Even at that time of day life stirred within. His eyes moved towards the bridge but stopped when his vision snagged upon a blurred image in white. His blood ran cold as he recognised the rebellious morning ghost and the young Hawk standing next to her. '*Cutter!*' he growled. 'Who are you working for, lad?'

He set off towards the Great Stone Gateway to join the burgeoning commuter tide heading into the town though, in his case, with no grey office interior as his destination. The famous and infragrant Billingsgate fish market could never be called that.

Jualth and Cutter stood at the rear of the large Victorian market hall, where the doors to trade had opened at 5:00 a.m. Under the watchful eyes of the inspectors, quayside rigs had winched the perishable sea cargo ashore for bobbin-hatted barrow boys to cart into the hall.

At the front of the market – in Lower Thames Street – a chaotic scrum of horses, fishmonger vans and delivery wagons filled every inch of the road. With the advent of the railways, a faster, more efficient means of conveyance brought salmon from Scotland, cod from Hull and mackerel from Bristol – the final leg of the journey (from station to market) completed by horse-drawn railway wagon.

 Inside the hall, latticed girders (spanning sixty feet in width) supported a louvred glass roof more than thirty feet high. The traders' floor contained stalls arranged in rows, whilst lining the interior walls – and aided by steam-powered lifts running to and from the basement – merchants' shops delivered shellfish ready-boiled to waiting customers.

At one of the thirteen quayside arched entrances, Cutter shifted uneasily. He had been saddled with an impossible choice: to obey his master's instructions and report *everything* or to betray a secret – 'We're just going to look, Cutter, no harm in looking' – and lose the respect of their guest. After a restless night, youthful intuition had come down on the side of his *missis*.

'Shall we go in?' Jualth asked.
'*In,* missis!'
'Have a look around, see if the fish are up to scratch.'

Cutter looked insulted. 'Course they're up to scratch, missis. Billingsgate is the best fish market in the world, everyone knows that.' He bit his tongue – such praise was inviting trouble.

'Good. All the more reason to take a peep. Coming?'

Cutter attempted to head her off. 'It's a bit smelly, missis. Mighten be a better idea stayin' put and just lookin'.'

Jualth brushed him aside. 'Nonsense, Cutter. We can hardly absorb the more unsavoury odours of the sea in the time it takes to peep.' She stepped into the Great Hall and squeezed her way through the crowd of onlookers surrounding the stalls.

Cutter jostled in behind, straining to follow a lithe figure that slipped through the pack of bodies as easily as the fish did through salt water. 'Try to keep close to me, missis,' he called out in a voice studded with panic.

Jualth chose not to hear. She was intent upon discovery, peering between bodies and over shoulders at the fascinating array of cod, sturgeon and haddock, amongst many others, all laid out on trays.

Soon Cutter's chase became a lost cause. Passages that opened effortlessly to the redheaded tearaway remained blocked for the pursuing Hawk. With his charge concealed amongst the crowd, he hastened back to one of the entrances bordering the wharf.

In the niche above his head, dome-shaped grills displayed fish crossed in the shape of crescent moons, along with the fishmongers' coat of arms and insignia: '*Dominic Dirigenos*' – 'We smell of fish'. Jualth had earlier expressed scepticism at Cutter's translation.

He stood on the top step of half a dozen that rose from the wharf, set to scale the open iron gates to catch a better view. Before he had the chance, a hand grabbed his shoulder from behind and lifted him partially off the ground. Much to his professional embarrassment, he had not noticed his master's approach.

'Cutter, where is she and why are you not with her?' William asked angrily.

'I was with her, Guv … just now, but she … she …'

'If you've lost her, lad …'

Cutter gulped. 'I haven't, Guv. She's in there … somewhere.'

Both looked into a hall crowded with dawn raiders. Even in white she could not be seen.

'What is she doing in there in the first place and without me knowing?' The repentant Hawk had no answer. William released his collar – his priority was to find his missing guest, not reprimand his disobedient Hawk. 'Later on, I want to see you in my office. Understood?' Cutter nodded. 'Now, wait here.'

Leaving his Hawk to rue over what lay in store, the bridge master moved from entrance to entrance, craning his neck in a frustrated search for the smallest person in the hall. After several fruitless minutes, he took the plunge, forcing his way through a scrum towards a briefly glimpsed target. Several bouts of laughter ensued, culminating in a cheer and a miraculously parting of the waves. A woman in white emerged through a sea of bodies with two hands pushing her firmly forward. In her arms, wrapped in layers of paper, was a salmon, a bribe paid for by her captor to extract her from the hall.

'I only wanted to get something for your dinner, William,' Jualth protested. 'You *do* like fish; I *know* you like fish. You ate enough of them in Scotland.'

'Guests do not have to buy the food, Jualth. That is a function of Mrs Tuckle's office.'

'Shall I invite her next time?'

'There will be no next time,' William said sternly. Jualth pulled a face as he laid a course for the bridge, though in truth she rather liked his assertive display.

'I had to make sure it was the *right* salmon, William,' she said flippantly.

William glanced around, firstly at Jualth and then the fish. 'And … is it?'

Jualth smiled furtively.

'Well?' William demanded.

Jualth laughed, enjoying the doubt she had cast. 'Ours have a distinctive aroma, William. These do not. It will do though, even if the flavour will be slightly lacking. Do you think Mrs Tuckle will mind me cooking the meal this evening? I take it a wee country girl touching her modern range will cause no problem.' Her cheeks glowed in barely suppressed amusement.

William muttered a few inaudible words, dreading the thought of putting the proposition to the housekeeper. 'We shall ask at breakfast and, in future, that's where I want you to be first thing in the morning. *Cutter*,' he commanded.

'Yes, Governor?'

'The fish. *You* may carry it.'

'Yes, Governor.'

Jualth stopped to hand it over. 'Hold on tight, Cutter, I think it's still alive. Can you feel it wriggling?'

He nodded. 'Shall I drown it in the river, missis?'

Jualth would have laughed if she hadn't found the quip profoundly depressing. 'Poison more like, and only if you wish to follow it in.'

They scampered quickly after the bridge master, up the steps to the platform and into the opposing flow of the early morning commuters. Strange glances were met with innocent smiles. Jualth decided it necessary to berate her young Hawk: 'Told you we'd end up smelling of fish if we went inside that hall, Cutter. Why did you not listen?'

Cutter's mouth fell open in speechless astonishment at the injustice of the remark. He was learning many hard lessons about women that morning – a foretaste, he feared, of what lay ahead.

Chapter 54

At the breakfast table, William made the request on behalf of his guest. Mrs Tuckle agreed to relinquish her already carefully planned cooking duties for the evening, but only because it would give her more time to deal with the additional washing provided by both Jualth and Cutter. In return, the range was further praised in the exuberant expectation that it would soon be in the hands of an unsophisticated, country girl.

After a wash, Jualth was a vision in white in her new clothes and, on the second half of her tour, more than happy to deflect praise towards the man who had provided the funds.

The northern arcade resembled the southern in most respects; a woven patchwork of quaint, narrow shops that covered a range of different trades. Variety was of the essence and the means to individual survival though, even on Old London Bridge, evictions were a sad part of the bridge master's duties. Jewellers stood next door to drapers; haberdashers next to small picture galleries; bookstores and map sellers next to chandlers and basket makers. There was even enough room for an inn that, due to a lack of cellar space, had not been possible in previous times.

The last call on her guide's time took place halfway up Fish Street Hill. Spiralling around the Monument's inner railing – and illuminated by slots in the wall – three hundred and eleven steps were tackled in a test of mountaineering endurance. As fortune had it, nobody chose to descend as they struggled up the last few narrow steps.

At the top, a doorway opened onto a small, square viewing platform bordered by a chest-high ring of metal rails. In the centre, and rising an additional thirty feet, was a drum that supported a copper urn and a billowing, ornately carved, golden flame. It was a visible symbol of fire throughout London.

Jualth walked slowly around the balcony, once, twice and then a third time, initially revelling in the distant view, then looking with greater circumspection at the shambolic arrangement of buildings. As with seeds scattered over the land, all sorts of edifices had battled for the tiny piece of space they now occupied. On her last circuit she finished facing south, staring past the tall tower of St Magnus towards the river and the bridge. A smile crept across her face.

'This is the best view, William, your bridge ... and maybe that one farther along as well.' However false an impression, Tower Bridge resembled a structure from a distant era and, in that capacity, was a worthy addition to London's historic skyline.

Jualth gazed at a constant stream of tiny shapes passing through Princes' Gate – some, familiar faces to the bridge, others, first-time visitors drawn by its historic pull. They would return home with a story to tell and the knowledge gained from a day spent on a renowned London landmark.

'How do you feel now, William?' she asked gently. 'Are you impressed by what you have done?'

William had climbed those three hundred and eleven steps on more than one occasion and witnessed many different views. The strongest image he carried with him was that of the old bridge in the midst of its demolition.

'I'm getting there,' he said without conviction. 'I lost a dear friend; it takes time to get used to a new one.'

Jualth felt saddened that he could not assess the change more objectively. Perhaps with the right person beside him, a more enlightened view would prevail.

'What you see before you is the best I could have hoped for – a new bridge that resembles the old, which is visible and accessible. You have only to look in whichever direction you choose to see how heritage can be concealed without foresight and proper planning.'

Jualth looked. Beyond church spires, the infamous Tower of London, the dome of St Paul's and the distant Palace of Westminster, there was little of note.

'And what you see is unlikely to improve. With concrete walls growing ever higher, we will gradually see even less of our old town. Why we go to such lengths to suffocate and imprison ...?'

Jualth could see the pain in someone who cared deeply about his home. It was a mutual pain they shared for two worlds far apart.

'Imagine what would have happened if we'd lost the bridge,' said William. 'What would have happened to the small church of St Magnus or to this column?' He answered the question himself. 'They'd be forgotten relics, that's what, with no one aware of their history, importance or probably even their existence.'

'So are you proud of what you have achieved or not?'

William struggled with the notion of his right to feel proud.

Jualth provided the answer he felt unable to give. 'Well, you should be and it's about time you did, and if you're hanging onto any remaining misgivings, *let go*. Be proud, William, be *very* proud.'

With no reaction from the bridge master, Jualth's endorsement was allowed to settle then float gently in the breeze towards the river. At Billingsgate, the wharf was quiet, its business for the day concluded. By tradition, the gates closed at 10:00 a.m. Elsewhere, rigs and quays had sprung into life, whilst flotillas of barges moved both west and east.

'By the way, William,' said Jualth, breaking the silence, 'somewhere back there you mentioned being imprisoned. If you could kindly be more careful. It has a rather unpleasant connotation to me.' She looked at him closely, her thoughts now firmly on herself. 'It could come to it, couldn't it?'

William could not deny it; pretence would serve no purpose. 'You have friends and they will do everything they can to help you.'

'Who are my friends, William? Other than you, who is looking out for me?'

'Be patient, Jualth.'

She emitted a long, tired sigh. That word 'patient' was already getting on her nerves. 'I'm beginning to struggle here, William. As each day passes and whatever happens behind closed, official doors happens, my resolve to sit idly around is weakening. I need to do something, otherwise what is the point in me being here?'

'I can't help you, unless you trust me. Take measures into your own hands and you could end up in even more trouble and without a thing I can do to help.'

Jualth heaved deeply; she couldn't be patient for ever. Her eyes settled on St Magnus and the arch over the front of its main entrance – the starting point of the old bridge. 'It's about time I paid the priest a visit. I want to find out if there's a chance of redemption if all else fails.'

The bridge master removed the timepiece from his breast pocket. 'And I need to check up on my Hawks.'

'Will you put Cutter on the church door whilst I'm inside?'

'Nipper for the moment,' William replied. 'I want a word with Cutter first.'

'A pleasant word, I hope. I'm growing very attached to my shadow and I shall require him in a good frame of mind for his first lesson this afternoon. I thought an hour to begin with.' Jualth ignored the bridge master's doubtful look; she had a knack of making men do as she pleased, whatever their age. 'I can manage an hour, so why not Cutter?'

'Because he's a struggle and that's putting it mildly. If you can get him to learn for that length of time, you deserve another dress.'

'Make it a dress for Lily and it's a deal.'

At the bottom of the Monument, they parted company, William for the Bridge House and Jualth to study the inscriptions that covered three sides of the base pedestal and figures carved in relief on the fourth. She concluded it was the worst place in the world to escape such reminders of the devastation caused by fire.

The door to the church remained open during the day, an invitation to all who wished to enter. Walking past the foyer screens, Jualth marvelled at the beauty that had not been evident from the outside. At the front, beyond the central aisle and pews, curtains fell from ceiling to floor behind an enormous altar and an elevated pulpit. The main source of natural light came from the right, the side facing the Thames, where three large, stained-glass windows each depicted a saint: Michael, Margaret and the eponymous Magnus. To the left, overseeing Lower Thames Street, a row of smaller, round windows skirted the ceiling.

Jualth sat in a pew near to the rear, not wishing to disturb those sitting closer to the altar. The echo of every movement made a pleasing sound. It reminded her of another church, but with a view over a far superior waterscape.

Presently, a figure clad in a dark, ground-hugging gown appeared in the central aisle intent upon a word with the highly conspicuous new arrival. 'Is there anything I can do for you or would you prefer to be left alone?'

The words were spoken in a soft whisper by a genial-looking, bespectacled, middle-aged man, slim in build but tall in stature. Jualth smiled and beckoned him towards the pew – she had a feeling that her visit was not unexpected.

'I haven't got a lot to say, Father, but I thought I'd come to meet you, just in case I have a greater need at another time.'

It was an interesting opening gambit that had the priest intrigued from the start. 'And why would that be … ah …?'

'Jualth, Father, and I'll own up to my needs if, and when, they arise but not before.' There was to be no early confession and the priest obligingly withdrew his interest.

'Anthony,' he said, offering his hand.

'Father Anthony?' Jualth enquired.

'I answer to either, whichever you prefer.'

The informality was accepted and the offer of both friendship and respect welcomed.

'I had not expected your church to be so beautiful, Anthony.'

The priest had heard the same sentiment expressed on a number of occasions, though why the beauty of a renowned church was such an apparent secret he never fully understood. 'You're from Scotland,' he observed.

Jualth smiled politely. 'There you go, that old accent giving me away again. I expect you see quite a few of us on our travels.'

'Not only on your travels. With modern transport, the numbers that now dwell in London have grown considerably.'

'Really!' There was a note of disapproval in the voice of the visitor. If the noise and soot were not bad enough, the trains were now enticing her fellow countrymen to desert their homeland for this filthy, distant city.

'Why do they do it, Anthony? What is so wonderful about a place that turns grass into roads and trees into buildings?'

The priest was likewise sceptical about the benefits, though for a different reason. 'It has certainly done little for the poverty in the town. If anything, attracting more people has made it worse.'

It was an issue close to his heart, having dedicated much of his time to those seemingly abandoned to their fate by a government unable to see beyond a drive towards modern-day advances. Sadly, the transformation in technology had not been mirrored by a leap in social reform that would have alleviated the plight of the poor.

Jualth decided it was time to dispense with the charade. Trust between two people could not be founded on falsely held ground. 'I'm staying at the Bridge House, Father, a guest of the bridge master. Did you know?'

Not only did the priest know, but he had also received a request to be as helpful as he thought wise. He was interested to see the direction such help would lead. 'Let's just say a guest of the bridge master, and a young woman at that, is not a common event. In the small community we have on the bridge, word was always likely to travel fast.'

'No different to where I live then, though please do not read too much into my visit. Unlike my fellow countrymen, I have every intention of returning home and in the shortest period possible.'

With the pretence vanished, and Mrs Tuckle already a lost cause, Jualth decided to test the priest's willingness to be open. There was much she wished to learn about her host and perhaps now was her best opportunity.

'There's a portrait of William's father hanging in his study. I have a feeling William is very proud of him, but he says very little, almost as if he feels that he has let him down in some way. Did you know him?'

The personal nature of her question had him wondering about the true intent of her visit. It was a long way to travel for just a short stay.

'I knew Edward very well. William bears a strong resemblance to his father and in more ways than one. What you see in William – his strength, dedication and determination to fight for his beliefs – Edward put there. Together they formed powerful protectors of the bridge and it was perhaps Edward's early death that made William strive to overachieve in the battle. I believe it is the lack of a father to pat his son on the back that weighs so heavily on William's shoulders. If Edward were around to express his opinion, I'm sure he would have been proud of the bridge his son has built.'

Jualth profoundly agreed and was sure that the priest had expressed such views to the bridge master. Why, then, did William torment himself with the notion that a partial victory meant a larger defeat? Why did he not listen to those that offered honest praise?

'Did you know his mother? William's never mentioned her to me.'

Father Anthony shook his head. 'No, it is a great sadness that I did not and, to my knowledge, neither did William. It was Edward that raised him.'

Jualth had suspected as much. William lacked the assurance that a woman could provide. No mother, no sisters and his time spent fighting for an inanimate object that could show no warmth or affection in return. 'He has had no female company, Anthony?'

'Not unless you count Mrs Tuckle.'

'I do not,' she answered flatly. It was an unhealthy alliance where each did not need to depend upon the other but, through loyalty to an iconic and historic wonder, did just that.

'What company did you have in mind?' the priest asked.

A wife and children, Father, that's what. Somehow Jualth felt it was a little early in the day for such candour and chose a less frank approach. 'William works too hard; there should be more to his life.'

'As I said, he is a dedicated man. Getting him to leave during the rebuilding was a struggle in itself. He needed the rest and a perspective on life outside the daily confine of fighting to preserve the bridge.'

'And did he have one when he returned?' Jualth asked.

The priest again shook his head. 'He had the same drive as before, though this time I fancy it was not for the bridge alone. He spent more time in the town, increased his circle of contacts, business associates—'

'Friends?' Jualth said hopefully.

'No, I wouldn't call them that. Few to my knowledge visit the Bridge House informally.'

'Then it is not the company I would have wished for him. That man needs a proper home life. That is the only way he will gain another perspective.'

It was an issue upon which both agreed.

'Anthony,' said Jualth more quietly. 'Did William ever mention what he got up to during his period away?'

The mere question told the priest a great deal more than he had previously known. Certain aspects of William's behaviour now made a great deal more sense. 'He did mention his travels in Scotland, but William is not one to expand if he chooses not to. I have a notion though that he might have crossed the path of a certain clan, one of whom I am sitting next to right now.'

'And between you, me, these four walls and the Almighty, your notion would be correct, though I am slightly vexed that I did not impress enough to merit a mention. That said, I haven't come all this way to claim a lost possession. My business lies in another direction and if it doesn't turn out as I would wish it, I'll be back on your doorstep needing that chat.'

'I hope you will come and see me whatever the outcome, Jualth. You'll be welcome at all times.'

A small figure appeared at the doorway. After a brief moment of searching, footsteps advanced along the central aisle and stopped at the pew on the opposite side of the aisle.

'Cutter! Welcome,' said the priest, with an equal measure of surprise and delight. 'You do not often venture inside these walls.'

'He likes to stay in my shadow,' Jualth whispered loud enough for the Hawk to hear.

Cutter attempted to show just how sophisticated a shadow he had become. 'The master told me to wait outside but, just in case you found another way out, I thought I'd wander in – keep you company.'

'Very thoughtful of you, though I'd prefer it if you did as William asked,' said Jualth. Noticing a lack of give in her shadow's stance, she tried another tack – she had come to meet the priest for more than one reason. 'Anthony, there's something I'd like you to do for this young man.'

'Cutter! How can I help Cutter?'

'You just mentioned the *how* twice. His name, it's about time he had a proper one, a Christian name. If I think of one, can you bestow it upon him in an official manner?'

'I can help you register it, but only if Cutter is a willing participant.'

'Cutter's fine by me,' said the Hawk, now regretting his decision not to obey his master's order to the word.

'But not by me and this isn't the place to argue,' said Jualth. 'Now, do as I say and wait outside. I promise I will not use the side door.'

Cutter hesitated. 'Sure you won't?'

'Did I not just promise?'

The zealous Hawk rose and slowly withdrew, pensively taking guard just underneath the bell tower.

'I thought you would see more of the Hawks, Anthony. Does William not insist on their attendance?'

'I see plenty of them on the bridge. As I've said, it's my parish and if this is where their hearts eventually lead them, the door will be open as it is to everyone.'

'What about the chapel? Could they not go there?'

'The chapel is for the people who travel upon the bridge, not for those that live there. It's had no parish through the centuries other than its wayfarers.'

'Sounds like I should be there, then, rather than here,' said Jualth. 'But now I've found you, Anthony, I think I'll stick with St Magnus.'

'As I said, anytime regardless of need.'

Jualth took her leave, satisfied that she had met a dependable ally in the clergyman. Outside, she brushed past her shadow and made for the steps. 'See, you can trust me.'

'Yes, missis,' said Cutter, clinging onto her hem. 'But from now on rules have changed.'

'Have they indeed?'

'The master says I have to tell 'im everything you gets up to, and no more early morning trips without his prior knowledge and say-so.'

'Just testing the water and you will get a fine dinner as a reward.'

'Even so, missis—'

Jualth cut him off. 'Rules, Cutter. I do not like rules. They're made to obstruct the freedom of others by people who are far too used to getting their own way.'

They reached the bridge platform and Jualth, in belligerent mood, studied the skyline in all directions.

'Now then, before I give you your first daily lesson, where shall we take our walk?'

'*Daily*, missis!' The threat of an enforced and frequent period of learning was greeted with little enthusiasm and considerable shock. The bridge master sat down with him twice a week at most.

Jualth smiled contentedly. 'That's right, Cutter, *daily* lesson. Did your master not tell you whilst he was explaining the rule changes?' She chucked and indicated that she wished to head back up Fish Street Hill. They could plan their day from the top of the Monument. The view from the platform was well worth a second look.

Chapter 55

William quietly cursed as another groan from the floorboards threatened to wake his household. Standing outside his guest's door, he held his breath and listened: he heard nothing above the faintest murmur of soft breathing. He edged around the remainder of the landing, then down the stairs to the hallway and finally into the kitchen. The passageway through to the wash area and Mrs Tuckle's living quarters was as silent as the rest of the house. For the moment, the occupants slept undisturbed. He left them to their dreams and took his troubles into the smoke-filled atmosphere of the still, chilly night.

On the walkway, an opaque layer of haze obscured all light from the heavens. Only the hum of distant factories permeated through, their chimneys spewing out unseen smoke and ash to further choke the narrow streets and tightly packed buildings. The bridge master headed for the bridge – in his present state, there was no point in returning to his room.

Once through the Great Stone Gateway, he stopped at the edge of the first arcade of terraced houses. The gargoyles stared down fiercely, unable to identify the shape as friend or foe. Sensing their uncertainty, the figure of a dark-skinned adolescent emerged from the first building on the left and stepped forward to occupy the middle of the platform. Jamba was the lightest sleeper of all the Hawks, with ears as sharp as a fox.

'Governor!' he said in a surprised low drawl, having feared the worst by his sudden call to duty. 'Somethin' wrong, Guv?'

William had barely made a noise in the short distance between the Gateway and Jamba's lodgings. He felt gratified in his choice of Hawk. With Jamba and the gargoyles, he knew Old London Bridge was well protected.

'Nothing's wrong, Jamba, leastways nothing for you to worry about.'

Jamba stirred uneasily as Stretch appeared belatedly at the doorway. 'You like me to walk with you, keeps you company?' he asked.

William shook his head – company was the one thing he did not need. 'No, Jamba. Go back to bed. You too, Stretch. Get some sleep.'

His orders given, William resumed his late-night inspection. Ahead, a row of lamps hung intermittently at first-floor level on either side, enough to give a pale illumination to an empty passageway.

Jamba took a few paces along the arcade, trying to figure out the bridge master's meaning. Something was wrong and if it wasn't the bridge, then what was it?

Stretch whistled softly, calling him back – they knew better than to disobey a direct order. Jamba slowly retreated, but only returned to his room once his master had disappeared into the fog covering central arch. Both lay awake until they heard the footsteps return. Jamba then watched, unnoticed from the doorway. A few moments later, Cutter edged alongside his fellow Hawk, having followed his master from the northern arcade.

'Any ideas?' Jamba asked.

'Only one,' Cutter replied.

Jamba nodded. If they had not known before, both now realised the importance attached to the guest residing at the Bridge House.

William leant against the front door, having gently closed it behind him. His eyes were drawn to the kitchen door where a dim light flickered through the small gap at the bottom. Someone else was awake. He crept forward, irritated that he could not control the surging beat in his chest. Slowly, he pushed the door open.

On the table, a cup of steaming black coffee languished without an owner – the work of the housekeeper who sat at the side of the range.

'You'll need something to warm you up after doing your duty,' said Mrs Tuckle. Bedecked in dressing gown and slippers, she glanced up fleetingly over the rims of her spectacles, all the while battling gainfully to darn a hole in one of the Hawks' trousers. It was not a sight that William had previously been privy to.

His pulse slowed as he sat down in company he had not expected or sought. 'Can you see what you're doing in this light, Mrs Tuckle?' he enquired politely.

Mrs Tuckle replied wearily, 'I'll make do, Master William, as always. You'll hear no complaint from me.' A pained sigh accompanied her words of suffering allegiance.

William sipped his coffee as Mrs Tuckle concentrated on her darning. He recognised the falseness of the determined act. Both, for whatever reason, had found sleep difficult to come by that night.

As the minutes ticked by, his cup was refilled in an atmosphere of silence. In a way, Mrs Tuckle was an ideal incumbent to the position she held. A widow with no children of her own, she had instead made do with her adopted family, comprising the master, his family (when they were alive) and whatever youngsters filled the shoes of the Hawks. She was rarely visited by those that moved on, but the few that did made the efforts she rendered seem a touch more worthwhile.

William started to turn the cup in his hand and tap the porcelain. He thought about another refill, but instead placed it on the table and pushed it away. He forgot about Mrs Tuckle and reverted to the reason for his insomnia – the thought that played over and over in his mind and could not be shared with anyone else.

'She isn't the one for you.'

William looked up, startled by the sudden break in the silence. It took him a moment to focus on Mrs Tuckle's words.

'She isn't the one for you,' Mrs Tuckle repeated, 'not that one. You need a young lady that will care for your needs, obey your instructions; someone who will not speak or act out of turn. The lady for you will recognise your standing in London society and provide the support required of that position. She'll understand those responsibilities, just the way I do.'

Mrs Tuckle stopped darning to observe the bridge master. From his impassive expression, she could not interpret the effect of her words, but at least they had been heard. The trousers were folded, and the needle and thread packed into a small bag. She rose, bade the master goodnight for a second time and retired to her room.

William remained motionless, his thoughts with the one person that did presently sleep under his roof. How could Mrs Tuckle have possibly known? How could anyone? If only his dilemma was as simple as letting her go.

Chapter 56

'That was a very interesting park you took me to this morning, Cutter,' said Jualth several days later. They were sitting in a tiny room close to the Princes' Gate, one of two lodgings on the bridge allocated to the Hawks, where yet another difficult and lengthy lesson was in progress. 'How many does that make – five, six …?'

Cutter spoke with exaggerated cerebral fatigue. 'Three, missis … only three.'

Jualth looked perplexed. 'Only three! Are you sure?'

Cutter held up his hand and counted them off his fingers: 'St James's, Southwark and Victoria, plus the gardens.'

'Ah,' said Jualth, seeing the light. 'It's the gardens that are confusing me – why are they not called small parks?'

'I could take you to see Hyde Park if you were prepared to go on the train.'

'I am not, Cutter. Find me a horse and a pony for yourself, and maybe.'

'Can't ride, missis.'

'Share one with me, then. Our two wee bodies will not break the back of a sturdy mare.'

'All the same, missis,' said Cutter, preferring to keep his feet on solid ground. 'And besides, only posh people ride in Hyde Park.'

Jualth tutted, 'If only you'd made me buy a hat.'

Cutter fidgeted in his chair, a tormented figure unable to free himself from invisible restraints. 'Have we nearly finished, Jualth? All this reading and writing has damn near worn me out. You make me work ten times harder than the governor.'

'You do want my sister to have that nice new outfit, don't you?' his teacher said sternly. It was a timely reminder why they were making such an effort.

The pupil grudgingly nodded. 'Yes, Jualth.'

'Then kindly revert back to calling me "missis", 'cause using my name will not help you one little bit.' Jualth was a tough taskmaster and required her pupil to make visible signs of improvement at each lesson. As it happened, though, they had reached a point where she wished to reveal a carefully concealed surprise. She broke the news gently.

'We only have one more word to learn today, Cutter, and then we shall return to our drawing.'

The young lad perked up at the new subject Jualth had introduced. 'I like drawing, missis.'

'I know you do and you've been a great help to me. In return, I've taken considerable pains to make sure your learning has increased *ten*fold.'

Cutter returned to his sullen state. 'Thanks, missis.'

'Now then, this word.' Jualth printed five large letters on the piece of paper and pushed it in front of the unenthused recipient. 'There you go, what does that say?'

Cutter instantly struggled with the challenge. 'Ler, Ler… Flippin'…'

'*Cutter!* None of that.'

'But the word starts with two "L"s, missis. What sort of a word starts with two Ls?'

'This one. Now curve your tongue and have another ago.'

The young lad recommenced his mighty struggle. 'Ler, Ler–orr–d. Ler–ord. Lord.'

'No, Cutter, there's an "oy" in the middle, as in "ahoy". Try again.'

Determinedly, he stuck to his task. 'Ler…oy…d. Ler–oyd. Lloyd. *Lloyd?*'

Jualth patted him on the back, impressed by what mutual effort could achieve. 'Well done, Cutter. Now you know how to spell your new name. What do you think?'

The pupil suddenly regretted his struggle. 'Prefer Lord, missis.'

'And one day the title may well be bestowed upon you but, until then, Lloyd will have to do.'

Cutter screwed up his face. 'Can I have Robert instead?'

'No, Cutter …' Jualth flapped her hands in annoyance, then cleared her throat to correct her mistake – it would be the one and only time she would make it. 'No, *Lloyd*, you cannot. That option has long since passed.'

'But it makes me sound posh.'

'It makes you sound distinguished and capable of great things.'

'It makes me feel like a completely different character.'

'It makes you sound like a man who can stand on his own two feet and that is what William wants when you leave the bridge and cross swords with the big, ugly, sooty world. Subject closed. Just remember how to spell it. It will be the first word I test you on tomorrow.'

Cutter's enthusiasm for the drawing waned. He did not like his new name but, at Jualth's prompting, he pulled out his sketches from a table drawer and laid them out. 'Is that what you had in mind, missis?'

She scanned the designs, studying the detail closely. 'Excellent, Lloyd. You have a steady hand and an observant eye, just like my sister. This is a talent you should pursue. Now then,' Jualth looked more closely, 'our one remaining task is to decide which bits to keep, and how to arrange them in an overall design. Perhaps I'll add some words as well.' She thought for a moment, hoping for inspiration. An idea came to mind, an intriguing idea, which instinctively made her smile. 'Why not?' she whispered with palpable wickedness.

'Missis?' Cutter questioned cautiously, his curiosity winning the battle over the wisdom to know.

For the time being, however, Jualth had no intention of corrupting an innocent child. 'It's a Scottish greeting for strangers to pay special attention to, Lloyd. Let's leave it at that.'

Besides her walks with Cutter and his lessons in the afternoon, Jualth had little else to do to pass the time. Anthony had thoughtfully provided introductions to a number of his parishioners on the bridge that, in turn, had led to invitations to morning tea but, even so, the fear that she was waiting for nothing more than the date of her execution would not go away. Worried and at a loose end, her trust remained in others, but the promised help seemed as elusive as a safe passage across the busy London streets.

In Scotland she had her family to look after, an inn to run and the means to swim and indulge in uninhibited horse riding. Hanging around was an alien and stressful condition for one born to be active. If nothing happened soon, there was every possibility that cracks would start to appear in her so far well-behaved and unblemished persona.

By mid-afternoon, Jualth had assumed her customary position leaning on the balustrade of Central Arch facing east, where her visibility satisfied all those charged with her protection. Sadly, no amount of protection could safeguard her from the unseen powers that had pulled her so far south. London, for all its fascination, was no friend to her and she now longed to submit to the reverse pull north.

Through a gap in the buildings on the northern shore, she spotted Father Anthony returning to his church and, judging by its lightness, carrying an empty bag. Much to his credit, the church missionary had probably been out delivering aid and short-term relief to the needy. Jualth looked away, her conscience pricked by a selfless, compassionate act that she felt no desire to emulate. All she cared about was her own plight and the burden she shouldered on behalf of her distant community.

She pushed away from the balustrade and a view that served only to soothe her fraying temperament. She no longer welcomed its calming effect. Crossing the platform, she adopted the same position on the opposite side. There was nothing soothing to see in the view west.

Presently, she found company approaching from the Southwark end.

After a curious glance to the east, William settled beside her. 'You're normally looking in the other direction, downstream.'

'That's because it's a much nicer view downstream; Tower of Torture and its rat-infested dungeons aside. The river and the one bridge you can see are worth seeing.'

'So why look west?'

Jualth sighed – why indeed? A metal railway bridge did its best to block the view upstream, a belated addition that cluttered the river in the same way as the traffic and unplanned buildings clogged and suffocated the streets.

'Look at them, William,' she said, her voice muted. 'Hundreds, thousands of lives scurrying this way and that, none daring to fall behind in their pursuit of the new age. Barely one knows another as they weave in and out of traffic and from one end of the day to the other. So much energy and for what? Do they ever stop weaving to consider why they live their lives is such a hurry?'

She pointed a tired, dismissive finger towards Southwark Bridge. 'One of those horseless, smoky carriages stopped in the middle a while back. You can see it through the gaps in the metal girders. It chugged up to the brow – gunpowder blazing – gradually slowed and finally ground to a halt. A strange-looking man pushed open the door, got out, slammed it shut, then walked around to the front to watch steam rising from beneath the metal lid – a bit like watching a kettle boil but without the reward of a cup of tea at the end. He scratched his head, gestured with his arms, completed half-a-dozen troublesome circuits, and finally concluded that he should kick each wheel in turn. That didn't seem to help; the horseless carriage appeared to be a very stubborn one. Perhaps it needed a consoling word or a lump of sugar, rather than such rash, ill-tempered treatment. It got neither and the man was forced to abandon his contraption and hail a hackney carriage. He helped his female passenger aboard and the two were last seen riding towards the glistening sun, pulled by a reliable and willing, four-legged horse.'

Jualth wrenched her eyes from the uninspiring iron girders and rested them upon the bridge master. 'So, William, there must be some deep, meaningful point I am missing here, where an *unnatural*, soot-spewing wagon – a product of today's revolution that doesn't work – is preferred to a *natural*, dependable and proven means of clean, healthy transport. And another thing …'

William was given no chance to comment, Jualth had not yet finished moaning.

'From what I have seen, the only people that drive these metal boxes are men. Women satisfy themselves with holding onto their hats whilst providing amiable and picturesque company. This world is frightening: dirt, the death knell to horses and women content to fulfil subservient roles.'

She stopped and rested her chin on the palms of her hands staring into the distance, her energy levels to moan temporarily spent.

'Jualth,' said William, knowing that no explanation would ever placate the young woman.

'Hmm.'

'You are not quite yourself today, are you?'

Jualth sighed. 'William, there's a place where none of this manic behaviour matters. It's a place where I should be instead of … instead of what? Visiting parks, teaching a boy how to read and write, and … and absolutely nothing else.'

'I can take you riding if you'd like.'

'If you're thinking of Hyde Park, forget it; Lloyd has already warned me. I am not riding side-saddle and I refuse to look elegant.'

The mention of an unfamiliar acquaintance momentarily threw the bridge master. 'Lloyd? *Who* is Lloyd?'

For the first time, a small smile flickered across Jualth's bored features – the young Hawk was obviously being secretive about his new name. 'Has he not told you?'

'Has *who* not told me?'

'Cutter that's who, or rather, who was. He now has a real name like everyone else and if I get the chance, so will Nipper, Jamba and Stretch. When Lloyd has realised how distinguished his new name sounds, I shall arrange with Anthony to have it made permanent.'

'You call the vicar by his Christian name? What happened to Father?'

'He told me to. Why, what do you call him?'

William did not answer. He turned back to the subject of his Hawk. 'Jualth – Cutter! It might take him a very long time to get used to his new name.'

'In which case, I'd better get to work on him, 'cause I'm fed up with waiting for things that take "a very long time" around here.' She was at last becoming animated.

'*Jualth*, you've got to be patient.'

She groaned and gritted her teeth. The mention of *that* word, *yet again*, came close to igniting the gunpowder.

'Are we far off, William?'

The question drew no response.

'*William*, I am in the dark here, relying upon a man to do the work I would normally undertake myself and, as you know, I am *not* a patient person. You have told me nothing. I have waited and waited and it's beginning to seem like for ever. *One thing*, William, tell me *one thing* that is happening.'

William stood up and backed away, refusing to yield.

Quietly seething, she watched her unhelpful host depart – *why* could he not mention *one thing*? She settled back down on the balustrade and decided there and then upon one goal: to return home and to do so within a week.

Chapter 57

'Where to today, missis?' Cutter asked, brimming with enthusiasm for a new day and a new challenge. He was more than satisfied with his work up to that point; the master had praised it so. Had he known on that fine autumn morning that his strong-willed Scottish charge was determined to use all means at her disposal to make it her last week in London, he might not have appeared quite so happy.

'The park I think, Lloyd.'

Cutter grimaced, as on every other occasion he had heard his newly anointed name mentioned. 'Which park, missis?'

'Victoria. We can retrace the steps of our first intrepid walk together. I want to feel noble again.'

'Only one way to feel noble, missis.'

'And what's that, Lloyd?'

'Buy an 'at.'

Cutter received a well-deserved clip around the ear for his cheek. Similar punishment would follow if he dared to continue in such a vein.

'Not the shops, just the park, so let's get a move on, shall we? And kindly remove that ungrateful expression from your face. The name suits you and it's staying.'

Victoria Park was not Jualth's main destination of the day and, after a brief spell of admiring the colourful leaves as they fell upon the paths and lawns, she informed Cutter that she would like to return the way they had come.

'But … but we usually spend a couple of 'ours at least in the parks, missis,' he protested.

'Not today, we don't.' Jualth stood up ready to leave, but Cutter remained resolutely stuck to the bench. A clearly needed insight into the feminine mind was dispatched: 'As you grow older, Lloyd, you will realise that women change their minds whenever it suits. Grasp that minor detail and you'll go a long way towards understanding that the female can never be fully understood.'

Cutter unwillingly wrestled his tired limbs from the bench. 'Are they all like you, missis?'

'The redheads are the worst.'

'Glad to 'ear it. I'll make sure never to 'ooks up with one.'

Cutter received his second clip of the day and was given a lengthy rundown of the fights his companion had been involved in, just in case he thought the clips were the worst thing he could expect. After fifteen minutes of walking, Jualth took a wrong turn.

'Umm ... missis, it's this way back,' Cutter said nervously.

'And this is another way back, Lloyd. The streets all lead in the same general direction, do they not?'

'Yes, but some aren't for ladies like yourself. We'd be much better 'eading back the way we came.'

'Nonsense, Lloyd. With you to protect me, what could possibly happen? Oh, look!' Jualth pointed straight ahead, 'Usquebaugh Street. Now fancy naming a wee London backstreet in honour of us Scots.'

Jualth headed around the corner and crossed the road. 'Now, you're not telling me there is something wrong with this street. Have you not yet learnt how friendly we Scots can be?'

The flustered escort grunted distractedly, praying that she would not notice the one establishment he had been told to keep at arm's length. He breathed a surreptitious sigh of relief as they passed, unaware that the faintest whiff of a very familiar nectar had just filtered into her nostrils. Before he could prevent it, Jualth turned on her heels and swept through the open door into the Highland Fires.

'Missis ...' Cutter called out, desperate to stop her.

'Out, boy!' came a deep bark from behind the bar. 'No kids allowed in here, and lady—'

'North of Glasgow, west coast, Mallaig maybe,' Jualth interrupted, using her broadest possible accent to place the origin of the barman. He stared back in astonishment. The young woman had judged the source of his inflection to perfection.

'You're a Scot, madam.'

'Indeed and on my first trip to London. It's good to meet a fellow countryman at last.'

Jualth stood opposite a middle-aged man of average height, with only a light dusting of hair on top, but huge red whiskers and sideburns to compensate. His forearms were immediately noticeable for their size and strength, enough to impress any young aspiring female.

'Are you a Highland Games man, ah ...?'

'Samuel, madam.'

'Jualth.'

Yet again the barman was impressed by his visitor's perception. 'I did my turn as a young man.'

'You still are, Samuel,' said Jualth, spreading the commendations as thickly as possible. 'And now you have travelled south to run the famous Highland Fires, with the biggest selection of whiskies beyond the borders of our homeland.'

With a face fit for the most enigmatic of poker players, Samuel fought a momentary dilemma. He lost. Sixty seconds was ample enough time to succumb to his visitor's allure. In defiance of the house rules, he reached under the counter.

'We rarely serve young, unaccompanied ladies, madam, but as you're a Scot …'

Jualth smiled furtively, satisfied that her charm had won the day. 'Not today, Samuel,' she refused politely. 'I shall return another time for my whisky, quite possibly tomorrow as things stand. Tell me, that boy who came in after me, is he waiting outside?'

Samuel did not need to look. 'He ran off a few moments ago. Was he troubling you?'

'No, Samuel. That was Lloyd, a close friend who will be a very distinguished gentleman when he grows up. At the moment, however, he is not grown up and I did not require his company.' She smiled, 'Till tomorrow, Samuel.'

'A drink will be waiting for you on the house, madam.' Samuel and all his customers watched in silence as the young mysterious woman departed as swiftly as she had arrived, leaving nothing more than a huge, lasting impression.

It was late afternoon before she strolled casually down Fish Street Hill, sporting a visible glow to match a contented, inner warmth. Cutter charged up the hill to greet her.

'Where the 'ell—?'

'*Lloyd* – language!'

Cutter bit his tongue and, as Jualth breezed past, rephrased his initial outburst: 'Well … where the bloomin' 'eck—?'

'*Lloyd*, that is just as bad and before you are tempted to further discredit your name, I shall *blooming* well tell you.' She paused, as was her habit when she wished to play.

'Well!' said Cutter, fit to burst.

Jualth relented. 'I've been having my picture drawn.'

Cutter slowed. '*What?*'

'You heard,' said Jualth, continuing to feel thoroughly pleased with herself. 'I'll show you once we get inside.'

Cutter scratched his head, wondering how she could possibly have had … The answer suddenly struck home. '*You've been inside Frostfairs?!*'

Jualth smiled and nodded as Cutter, who had fleetingly ground to a halt, ran to catch up.

'I did, was warmly greeted by all and allowed to watch the artists at work. I then volunteered to replace a rather shabby-looking model. They hadn't drawn a redhead before.'

'Missis, we've had a search party out looking for you. The master went to the Highland Fires himself and when he was told you just ups and left, he sent all us 'awks out to scour the town.'

'Was he angry?'

'Very.'

Jualth's smile grew with impish satisfaction. 'Oh dear. Now that will never do. Tell you what, the moment we finish your lesson, we'll let him know I'm back.'

'Straight away sounds like a better idea.'

'Hush, Lloyd. I shall take full responsibility. You have no need to worry.'

That was easy for Jualth to say, less so for Cutter to accept. When they reached the small room Cutter shared with Nipper, Jualth calmly conducted a lesson with her anxious pupil.

'Well done, Lloyd, you're making real progress. I'm very proud of you.'

Cutter shrugged away the praise – he was only too relieved that other matters could now be attended to.

'I'm proud *and* delighted that my high hopes are being realised,' said Jualth. 'You deserve a reward.'

'We need to speak to the master, missis,' Cutter said urgently.

'And so we shall, Lloyd, the moment I've shown you my picture. Now then, where did I put it?'

Jualth bent down and picked up a carefully rolled-up piece of paper, tied by a piece of red ribbon.

'All right, Lloyd, scan your artist's eye over this masterpiece, tell me what you think.' Jualth untied the ribbon and let the picture unroll.

As Cutter's eyes widened into a fixed stare, his mouth dropped open and his bottom lip began to quiver. 'Gord'n Bennett, missis! You shouldn't be showin' me that!'

'Well, I am and as you're still staring at it, tell me what you think. *Well?*'

Cutter seemed unusually tongue-tied but, as Jualth had observed, was finding it impossible to look away. 'Say something, Lloyd. That's yours truly – a picture of me.'

'It's ... it's ... all of you,' Cutter spluttered.

'I know, it's what they call a life drawing. You have seen a naked ...?' Cutter shook his head. 'But you have seen paintings and sculptures.' Cutter nodded. 'Good and now you've seen one of me. So, what do you think?'

In the circumstances, Cutter struggled to be critically objective. 'They certainly knows how to draw, missis.'

'I think they did me justice,' Jualth agreed. 'This was the best picture and was naturally drawn by a woman. Her name's Collette. I received it as my prize for being such a good model.'

Cutter pointed through the wall in the direction of Fish Street Hill. 'So, whilst we were out combin' the streets …'

'I was having my picture drawn, I know. There's no need to worry about me, Lloyd. I can look after myself.'

Having cause to know London slightly better, Cutter wished that was true. 'Can we go and tell the master you're still alive now?'

'And show William my picture? Why not? It will be a nice surprise for him.'

Still glowing, Jualth rolled up her masterpiece and, patting her rather startled companion on the back, departed for the bridge house.

Dinner was held in silence. William's austere exterior concealed an inner amusement; Mrs Tuckle did not approve and Jualth did not care in the slightest. Cutter remained in deep shock and Nipper appeared deeply envious. He was the only one present who had not seen the drawing.

At the end of the meal Jualth had one question for the bridge master: 'Any news, William?'

A long period of thoughtful silence ended in the word, 'None.' An enquiry of his own followed. 'And what do you have in mind for tomorrow, Jualth?'

'I intend to stay out of trouble, William, just like I did today.' Jualth pushed back her chair. 'If you'll excuse me, I'd like to spend the rest of the evening staring at my goddess-like image in my room.' She smiled and left the bemused gathering in peace.

William waited until he heard the landing door shut before addressing his young Hawk, 'Well, Cutter, looks like you have another busy day ahead of you tomorrow. Let's hope you can acquit yourself better than you did today.'

Cutter nodded. He did as well. His reputation as a Hawk depended upon it.

Chapter 58

'Where to today?' Cutter asked his charge through force of habit. *Nowhere or a quiet day on the bridge* would have suited him fine, anything but …

'You know, Lloyd, I rather enjoyed yesterday. Why don't we go back to the park?'

If they went to any park other than the one intended, no reason at all. Ever the optimist, Cutter offered a selective choice on the south side of the river. 'Southwark, Potters Fields—'

'Victoria, Lloyd.'

'Went there yesterday, missis. Sure you wouldn't like a change?'

'Nope.' Jualth recognised a reluctance in her custodian to play her game. 'I'll go by myself if you'd prefer. I can find my way.'

Cutter shook his head. 'Can't let you do that, missis. You need protection.'

'Do I?'

'Master says so.'

Jualth sighed endearingly. 'Now, isn't that thoughtful of William.'

As they ascended Fish Street Hill for the second time in two days, William watched closely from Princes' Gate.

'Follow them, Nipper. When our Scottish friend gives Cutter the slip, be on hand to take over. I want no harm coming to our guest.'

Nipper had his orders. Like a bloodhound on the trail of a rodent's scent, he set off to track them.

By midday, Jualth found herself back in the Highland Fires. A reference to their stealth-like shadow had been enough to distract Cutter and allow her to breeze into the bar. With Nipper standing watch, Cutter had dashed back to the bridge to summon reinforcements.

'Your whisky, madam, and as promised, the first is free,' said Samuel.

Jualth played around with the glass, holding it up to the light before running it back and forth under her nose. She sipped, held the moisture on her lips and the tip of her tongue, then swallowed.

'A Lowland blend … dry … mellow.' She stared impassively at the barman, then smiled with a contented smirk. 'Copper Grouse Smooth. Not my favourite, far too light, but I'll give them credit for trying.'

As the wall clock ticked without a tock and then tocked without a tick, a stirring of disbelief spread throughout the bar. Those standing nearby glanced from customer to barman. Those seated at the tables hushed, then murmured quietly. Jualth, never one to enter an establishment unnoticed, had announced her presence.

'You know your whisky,' said the astonished barman.

Jualth detected an ailment commonly held amongst members of the opposite sex. 'Why is it that men think they are the only ones who can do anything or know anything?'

'Because that's usually the case,' Samuel declared flatly. His poker face and whiff of arrogance indicated his firm belief in this view.

Jualth took a deep breath, a *very* deep breath. 'Oh, Samuel. You say things like that and you and me are heading for trouble.'

Samuel stared back, unmoved, as he sized up the young woman and her audacious comment. 'That sounds like a challenge to me, madam.'

Jualth lifted the glass again and ran it under her nostrils. 'Care to make a wager, Samuel?'

Not one to back down, Samuel, in true Scottish tradition, laid out his terms: 'I'll select the whisky; if you get it right, the dram is on the house. Get it wrong and an evening's bar work will be the price.'

'You think I'll be good for business?'

'And without the need for training.'

Jualth acknowledged the compliment – it appealed greatly to her vanity.

'The wager will continue until you either identify the whisky incorrectly or decide to stop.'

'Free whisky or the pleasure of serving behind your bar. Samuel, this is a wager I cannot lose. Please, make your first choice, whilst I make light of this wee taster.'

William arrived within half an hour, Cutter jogging to keep up. Nipper met him at the door and indicated that she was still inside. The bridge master entered virtually unnoticed. Crowded by a dozen or more interested spectators, Jualth, with a steadying hand gripping the side of the bar, faced Samuel. Five glasses stood empty and a sixth – ready to be assessed – rested expectantly between the warring parties.

The barman paid scant attention to the figure that quietly joined the rear of the pack. The whisky in front of Jualth was the rarest he had. He did not enjoy losing wagers or dispensing whisky with no return.

Jualth grasped the bottom of the glass with her finger tips. She smelt but did not sip. Instead the glass returned to the bar. She stared into the barman's vicelike gaze – neither wavered, not even to blink. A blanket silence sharpened the atmosphere in the salon, heightening the expectation to fever pitch.

Jualth scraped the glass along the bar's oak grain as she mulled over her hardest challenge yet; then half a turn one way and half a turn the other. The whisky rose and passed under her nose one more time. Samuel admired her stillness, her calmness, but not the incessant suspense with which she kept them waiting. The woman was playing a hard game.

Jualth tasted the whisky as with all previous drams, first with the tongue, then the lips, and finally an effortless, impassive sip. Samuel sensed victory. His finest and most secretive malt had provided the stumbling block to fox the young connoisseur. A thin, mean smile stretched across his lips as the mental count of his elevated takings ushered forth a flush of colour to his cheeks.

'From those tiny islands to the north of my homeland,' Jualth declared. 'A full, fruity flavour, smoky with a hint of pepper and … and wood – that will be the heather added to the peat when the barley is dried.'

The barman's smile hardened into a scowl as fear of financial loss replaced visions of an overflowing cash register.

'More to my taste, Samuel. Single malts have always ranked in preference to blends. I do love the kick of a full malt, especially that of the Highland Talisman.'

Jualth raised the glass and, taking a wholesome mouthful, gasped in delight. The blaze that surged from her lungs singed her opponent's whiskers. For a sixth time she received a round of applause as Samuel – glowing red in ignominious defeat and wretched poverty – again conceded. William approached the bar, the only one present that showed no sign of surprise at her remarkable victory. Samuel backed sure-fire winners or nothing. He had never been known to lose a wager.

'What's next, Samuel?' Jualth enquired contentedly, quite prepared to try every whisky in the house. The barman glanced to her left to a well-known London figure, indicating that the decision no longer lay in his hands.

'William!' Jualth exclaimed in delight. 'I didn't see you come in. Care to join us? Samuel and I are in the middle of a game. It's very simple and very cheap.'

William put his arm around the ever-so-tipsy redhead and gently wrestled her away from the bar, much to the disappointment of those who had gathered to watch. Honour-bound, Samuel shook his head when money was offered. The acute pain he already felt quadrupled.

'If you need a barmaid and you pay well, you can find me at the Bridge House, Samuel,' Jualth called over her shoulder. William shook his head as he pushed her through the door, making it clear that no such offer should be considered.

Jualth stepped merrily but unsteadily onto the pavement, requiring the assistance of a guide to keep her moving in a straight line. Samuel had not held back on the strength of each carefully selected dram or in the quantity dispensed. His dignity and hard-nosed reputation for fiscal acumen had suffered a severe dent in a challenge he had perceived to be heavily weighted in his favour.

'Not having your picture drawn this afternoon, missis?' Cutter quipped cheekily.

Jualth stopped, the brilliance of the idea a revelation. She executed an immediate one-hundred-and-eighty-degree turn only to find her feet leaving the ground and manfully pointed back in the direction of the Bridge House.

At mealtime that evening, Jualth sat with her head in her hands: William was again inwardly amused, Mrs Tuckle disapproved, Cutter was grateful to have missed a lesson and Nipper was still hoping for a chance to see the life drawing.

With effort, Jualth turned her head marginally to catch sight of William through splayed fingers. 'Any ...?' she asked drowsily.

William shook his head and was not troubled again.

Chapter 59

Jualth's need to retire immediately after the previous evening's meal enabled her to be up bright and early the next morning, early enough for the lingering darkness to conceal her clandestine exit.

Through painstaking reconnaissance, she had plotted a path from bedroom to front door to avoid all creaks and groans that would alert anyone to her movements. Mrs Tuckle's discovery of her tapping the floorboards one afternoon had been covered up by a reference to the Celt's love for Highland jigs. Her tuneless rendition of an obscure Gaelic poem – full steps included – had sent Mrs Tuckle scurrying for the kitchen none the wiser.

Once on the bridge, the next obstacle was inescapable. It mattered not how quietly she moved; by the time she reached the first terraced arcade, there he would be, fully awake and attending to his duty. Jamba could sense the descent of a feather cast aside by the flight of a passing sparrow's wing, if it fell within fifty yards of his lodgings. His greeting was, as ever, respectful.

'Morning, Miss Jualth.'

'Morning, Jamba. Anybody watching will think we've arranged a secret rendezvous.'

'Nobody will be watching at this time less you count the night owls or the river rats. A couple of hours and more will pass before we 'ears the sound of our first City worker.'

'Just how I like it, peaceful and quiet, and a world that belongs to no one but the early riser.'

In the distant darkness, and just to shatter their illusion of perfect isolation, a belligerent voice trumped up. To the east, the river, if not the land, was reawakening.

As Jualth moved forward, Jamba fell in alongside. For this part of the journey, she welcomed his company. It meant he had no immediate intention of alerting his master to the whereabouts of a persistent absconder.

At the crest of Central Arch, they settled on the balustrade and waited for Billingsgate Market to open its doors. When the bells of St Magnus eventually tolled the fifth hour, the first sign of movement from within heralded a similar awakening outside. Vessels moored to the quay and anchored to the river floor chugged into life as their captains prepared to manoeuvre them into position for unloading.

Jualth and Jamba watched as fully laden containers were hoisted from the holds and guided onto waiting carts for transport into the vibrant, boisterous hall.

Presently, Jualth stirred. 'I think it's about time I joined them, Jamba. Are you coming or ...?'

'Part of the way, Miss Jualth, but no further.'

Jualth understood his reticence and did not cajole him again. At the City end, Jamba watched as she descended the steps. Belatedly, Cutter crept out of his lodgings and joined Jamba by the balustrade. Without a word or gesture, he followed Jamba's gaze. Jualth was on the walkway approaching the steps to the hall, her white dress ablaze with the market's cascading yellow light.

'Ye better go and fetch the master,' said Jamba, turning to the space Cutter had briefly occupied. There was no need for the prompt – Cutter was already halfway through the first arcade running for all his worth.

Jualth weaved a deliberate path between stallholders and customers as the serious business of selling got underway. She felt gratified to be instantly recognised by the vendor from whom she had acquired her first salmon.

'Hello, sweetheart. You sleepwalkin' again?'

'Aye, Sid, and dreaming of you as always.'

As catcalls rang out for Sid's uncanny knack of attracting the attention of the only redheaded female from the Highlands to have ever ventured into the hall, he rubbed his chin in sudden concern and stared around at the overflowing trays.

'Not sure I can spare a whole fish this time, love. If I'd've known you were comin', maybe I could've put one aside.'

'Like the last tiddler you sold me?' Jualth chastised. 'Honestly, can you not wait for your fish to grow up before you catch them down here?'

Sid's fellow traders jeered as, for the first time in living memory, the quality of Sid's produce came into question. His hands gravitated to his hips, the business of the morning temporarily suspended.

'And just 'ow big are the fish in your *wee* part of the world, darlin'?'

Jualth smiled and raised her hand level with the top of her head. 'About the size of a mermaid and, being one, I should know.'

The dereliction of trade spread to adjacent stalls as they witnessed the unusual sight of Sid struggling to hold his own.

'Are you really, darlin'?' he said, sizing her up and down.

'Aye,' Jualth said sweetly, before adding, 'my sister's one too.' It was fun lying, knowing that half the joke belonged to her alone.

'And are our fish not good enough for a wee Scottish mermaid?' Sid asked, his hands resolutely stuck to his hips.

'They are pale imitations. I'm surprised you can sell any at all.'

'Are you?'

'Yes.'

'Right then, I'm goin' need some help, darlin', aren't I. Nobby,' he said to his assistant, 'get me an empty crate.'

Cutter flew into the Bridge House, ran up the stairs and knocked on his master's door.

'Governor ... Guv! It's Cutter,' he called out.

A light appeared beneath the door, followed by hasty footsteps. The door opened and William, dressed in his nightshirt, looked down upon his gasping Hawk. 'Okay, Cutter, just tell me where she is ... as if I couldn't guess at this hour.'

'Fish market, Guv.'

'And ...'

'And ...?' Cutter did not follow.

'And ... *who* is with her?'

'Jamba's watching from the bridge, Guv.'

'The bridge?'

'Yes, Guv.' Cutter looked away, knowing instantly that *with her* did not mean watching from the bridge.

William sighed in deep irritation. 'So, she's in there alone.'

Cutter nodded sheepishly. 'Yes, guv.'

'Yes, Guv,' William repeated to his crestfallen young aide, though in truth he attached no blame to the Hawk. In her present mood, Jualth was as controllable as the river tide.

Within minutes they were across to the north bank and standing outside one of the thirteen riverside entrances to the crowded hall. In the middle, a gravitational pull had compelled a sea of spellbound faces to stare upon the ethereal redheaded figure who, with words aplenty and in possession of a Gaelic slant, had assumed the role of vendor. The task that William had previously undertaken to extract his mischievous miscreant from the hall now seemed as simple as finding a certain Scottish distillery compared to what lay ahead now.

'Stay here, Cutter. I'll whistle if I need help.'

'Right,' Jualth announced, 'two left in this tray, brothers, inseparable since birth, looking for a kind-hearted, compassionate owner.' A hand duly rose. 'Thank you, sir. Sid, the honours please.'

Sid tugged his forelock, only too happy to watch his produce disappear at the best possible price and with such effortless speed.

Nobby quickly replaced the empty tray. 'From the Western Isles, love ... your neck of the woods.'

'Excellent,' said Jualth, rubbing her hands with glee, 'the price has just doubled.'

Out of the corner of her eye, she noticed a dark-haired figure struggling to find a path through the crowd. She clapped her hands to summon the minimal attention that she did not already have.

'Got to be quick, gentlemen, I fear the point of our parting is fast approaching. Right, Scottish Salmon, lean, fit, do somersaults to entertain, hugely popular with the Master of London Bridge, so better be sharp if you want one.'

Jualth got to work dispensing a tray and a half before her unwanted knight could push his way through to rescue her.

'Go away, William, can you not see I'm busy? I've got five thousand fish to sell in the next half an hour – do you want me to lose my job?'

William ignored the remonstrations and, with one fell swoop of his arm, lifted the charlatan trader off the crate. The action summoned an immediate barrage of protest.

'Oi, put 'er down, Guv,' Nobby remonstrated. 'It's the fish that are for sale, not 'er.'

'Perhaps he's whisking her off to the altar before Sid gets the chance,' a fellow fishmonger jested.

Jualth held out her hands in resignation. 'This happens all the time back home.'

William smiled as he was barracked from all sides, but adamant that the day of the female fishmonger had arrived and, if he had anything to do with it, swiftly passed. A fish wrapped in paper found its way into the arms of the helpless abductee as she hung over his shoulder.

'Is that the biggest you've got, Sid?'

'Put aside especially for you, love. We'll be here same time tomorrow if you can manage to escape.'

At the exit to the hall, William dropped Jualth to the ground and pushed her in the direction of the bridge.

'Got this fish for nothing, William. Aren't I a clever girl?'

William, as on the first outing, did not respond. He had an air of authority to uphold in the eyes of the three Hawks looking down from the platform and the one trailing behind.

'Would you like to tell Mrs Tuckle what's on the menu this evening or shall I?' Jualth asked flippantly.

'Mrs Tuckle's sense of smell will save us both the trouble,' said William, as he glanced back to his Hawk. 'Cutter.'

'Yes, Guv?'

'The fish.'

Cutter followed his orders and relieved Jualth of her salmon.

'Have you any other plans for today or was the early start *it*?' William asked.

Jualth toyed with the bridge master's uncertainty, intentionally straining his patience.

'*Well?*'

'*Well,*' Jualth mimicked, continuing to tease. 'I have plans for Lloyd that will keep us both occupied for the rest of the morning.'

'Plans, missis?' a worrisome Hawk repeated. 'You means the park again?'

'No, Lloyd, not the park. We won't be leaving the bridge again today.'

That seemed like good news as far as the Hawk could tell. If he knew precisely what her plans entailed, he would know for certain.

'First, I have to make amends for yesterday's missed lesson, and then, after our *double* session, we will take a stroll amongst the shops. Oh and, William, if you could see to lending me a little more of your money? I can assure you it will be put to good use.'

'The double session really isn't necessary,' said Cutter, already longing for a reinstatement of their trip to the park.

'Yes it is, Lloyd. My sister wants her dress. I shall nip in to see Albert this afternoon, and then, later on, and with Mrs Tuckle's willing acquiescence, assume sole use of her kitchen to cook everybody's favourite supper. So, there you have it, William, providing you give me that little bit of money I've asked for, I shall be no trouble at all to you or anyone else for the rest of the day.'

Chapter 60

Jualth's first job on her return to the Bridge House was to wash her own clothes and those belonging to Cutter. With Mrs Tuckle's approval rating rock bottom, she sensibly did not wish to further strain the housekeeper's waning patience. Cutter received his extended lesson in the morning and, as a reward, was allowed to accompany Jualth to the photographic shop where the bridge master's money was wisely spent. In the afternoon, and prior to visiting Albert, Jualth made a visit to St Magnus to chat with and cajole Anthony into an unscheduled but necessary stroll through the arcades.

At the dinner table, after all had consumed an ample portion of salmon, Jualth sat back reasonably content. But for one expected disappointment – the lack of news from William – the day's scheming had gone well. The following day she hoped would prove even better.

It started quietly – ominously so. Apart from Cutter's lesson, Jualth spent much of her time on Central Arch leaning on the east-facing balustrade, looking for all the world like a serene vision of untroubled youth. Inside, it was a different story. There was still no word, not even the slightest hint of one, her look of enquiry to William the previous evening having merited nothing more than a truncated shake of the head. Her wait had assumed an element of cruelty and, if it was nothing more than a prelude to prison, she would rather the wait took place in the company of her sister and family. Idling away her time in a foreign land had lost much of its infinitesimal attraction and most of its hope.

'Has she still not moved?' William asked the young Hawk he had assigned to keep a close eye on her. The two of them stood in the lee of Nonesuch House, concealed by the shadows.

'Apart from my lesson and a wander along the arcades, she's been there most of the day, Guv. She dropped into one or two of the shops but spent no length of time in any.'

'The shops again. Today, yesterday with the priest …'

'One other thin', though,' Cutter volunteered, 'she ain't always been alone.'

William looked curious. 'What do you mean?'

'She's had company; strangers 'ave wandered up for a word. One woman had a nice long chat and then Jualth permitted 'er to draw a sketch. Thought it might be 'er friend from Frostfairs, Guv.'

William nodded. It may well have been, in which case he would dearly have loved to meet the woman. 'What's going on, Cutter? Strangers seeking her out, strolls along the bridge with and without company …?'

'I could ask Father Anthony,' Cutter offered.

'No, Cutter. That would intrude upon the priest's business, the very reason Jualth chose to plan her visits in his presence.'

'What about the shopkeepers, then? I could ask them.'

William ignored his Hawk whilst he contemplated his guest's unusual behaviour. 'Why has she not asked to go to one of the parks, to Samuel's or the college?'

'She isn't herself today, Guv, I'll say that much.'

William grunted, distracted by a conundrum that made no sense. 'What's happening up there, Cutter? She isn't patient enough to play this type of game.'

Whilst she was active, the bridge master had felt reasonably assured he could control the outcome, but these lulls…? Periods of inactivity were out of character and that made his guest unpredictable.

'It's about time I revisited our friend,' he said, at last deciding upon the very course of action he had sought not to pre-empt. 'Make sure I am not followed.'

Cutter grew in stature as he always did when singled out for an important task. 'No problem, Guv. You can count on me, you knows that.'

William departed and was soon on Lower Thames Street. Jualth glimpsed his upright figure and measured stride as he headed east. She looked along the walkway at the buildings lining the street, seeing nothing of any distinction between Billingsgate Hall and the Tower of London, just one sombre, grey stone building that resembled the dull, lifeless, muddy river that ran alongside. Jualth lost interest, rested her head on her hands and stared into the distance, re-engaging with the dark images that had preoccupied her mind prior to the distraction.

At mealtime, a letter propped up against the salt cellar, lay in wait for the visitor. It was unceremoniously ripped apart and eagerly read.

'Damn,' Jualth cursed, 'I knew I'd spelt it wrong.' She gnashed her teeth and glanced in the direction of the workshops.

William cleared his throat; although Jualth was eminently capable of shutting out everything and everybody in the world around her, the surrounding world struggled to do the same with her. 'Anything wrong?' he asked.

She held the neatly written letter aloft. 'A letter from my sister enquiring as to my health. She hopes I am well but if I have succumbed to some plague-like disease, then I'll be forgiven for having not written home. She saved some of her favourite Gaelic phrases for you, William, just in case you're holding me captive. If you'd like, I can translate?'

Bearing in mind the company at the table, William declined the offer.

'I had better write back, although …'

William prepared himself – he knew what was coming.

'... although, I have nothing to say unless I'm very much mistaken.'

As on the three previous evenings, the salient subject drew no response from the bridge master.

'And besides,' Jualth continued, not wishing to exacerbate an uneasy silence that early on in the evening, 'how can I get a letter delivered to the remote, untamed wilds that I call home?'

Jualth pondered this dilemma for a few seconds whilst Mrs Tuckle's chest heaved in disapproval at a point clearly aimed in her direction. Jualth hit upon the obvious solution. 'Gus – I'll write to Gus. He'll see it finds its way to Lily.

'If you'd care to write the letter this evening, I'll have it posted in the morning,' said William.

Jualth smiled sweetly. 'Thank you, William. How very thoughtful. If you like, I can include your right of reply.'

Dinner passed quietly, with Jualth making no additional enquiry. When the Hawks departed for the bridge, William remained to browse through his paper, Jualth to just sit and Mrs Tuckle to clear up. All glances directed from housekeeper to unoccupied guest were ignored.

Jualth's tack with Mrs Tuckle, when she had previously complained of long days and tired limbs, was to unhelpfully suggest the employment of a *much* younger helper. After all, Mrs Tuckle could not be expected to go on for ever and, at her age, could there not be a more appropriate time to acquire the services of an eager assistant? With the threat of being edged out of a job, Mrs Tuckle had had little choice but to put a lid on her immeasurable suffering.

From the hallway, three thuds of the heavy knocker on the front door produced three wooden echoes. The housekeeper made to move.

'That's all right, Mrs Tuckle, I can see that you're busy,' said Jualth, pretending at last to be helpful. She slid off her chair and all but skipped into the hall.

'Well!' Mrs Tuckle exclaimed indignantly. She bent over the table and started to rub it vigorously with a cloth. 'Do I not get a say in such matters any more?'

William grunted distractedly. He had his ear trained on the door, listening to muffled voices.

Mrs Tuckle grumbled on, taking the chance to speak her mind: 'That girl, Master William, she's taking over the running of this place, doing as she pleases whilst the rest of us run around her. She even has Albert making something on her behalf.'

William responded curtly as he fought to hear the voices above the drones of his housekeeper's moaning. 'She's still our guest and I want her treated in no other way.'

'Even so, Master William, the young Hawks, *think* of them.' The housekeeper would not be silenced. After so many years of service, she had the right to make her opinion known. 'Our Cutter is being exposed to things way before the natural time. What if he tries to copy her wild ways? He could end up no better off than when you first found him.'

William wrestled with the distraction, his ears still trained on the hall. He was having great difficulty identifying who Jualth had let in. The kitchen door opened and Jualth reappeared followed by a group of unexpected visitors. After a momentary lapse, William stood bolt upright, his paper hastily put to one side.

'William, I thought it would be nice to have some company this evening. You know Polly, Emily and Josephine from the bridge.'

William's social composure swiftly returned. 'Eh … yes, of course, good evening, Polly, Emily and Josephine, and …' His eyes suddenly softened. '*And* Lucy.'

Jualth could not bring herself to be so welcoming. 'And *Lucy*, younger sister to Emily,' she repeated tersely. 'Apparently she refused to be left behind.'

William bent down to greet the self-invited addition to the party, calculating the time that had elapsed since a very special occasion, as he did so. 'Seven years, three months and two days.'

Lucy beamed proudly. 'Most people think I'm older and I feel a lot older. My reading is as good as a twelve-year-old's and …'

'Thank you, Lucy,' said Jualth, deciding that that was quite enough to be going on with. Much as she had wished to meet the young girl William had delivered into the world, her presence at the Bridge House that evening was not desired. 'Ladies, if you would like to take a seat around the table.'

'Indeed,' said William, 'and perhaps a hot drink for each of our guests, Mrs Tuckle.'

The housekeeper's cheeks flushed pink, a prelude to what seemed an inevitable explosion. In sufferance, she stomped off into the scullery to fetch some water.

'I'll take my paper to the study and leave you ladies to enjoy …'

'No, no, William, there's no need for you to go. Please ...' Jualth held out her hand, indicating that he should return to his seat. It was a cordial invitation that lacked any right of refusal.

After obeying her employer's request with the maximum of pot banging and spoon rattling, Mrs Tuckle cast her gaze over the group of ladies that had settled around *her* table, as ill-informed of their invitation as her master and, in her case, without the slightest attempt at an introduction. It was time to snort her disapproval and leave. With all the melodrama she could harness, she untied her apron, hung it on a peg in the corner and, nose in the air, trod a noisy path to her private quarters at the rear.

The housekeeper's departure merited nothing more than a few amused giggles and was just what Jualth had been waiting for.

'Now then, William,' she said, 'naturally, you are acquainted with our three guests—'

'Four,' Lucy interrupted, to demonstrate her proficiency in arithmetic as well as reading.

Jualth executed a pained smile – for William's sake rather than the child's – and soldiered on, 'Acquainted with our *four* guests this evening, being residents on the bridge, before and after its reconstruction.

'Indeed, I—'

'Emily,' said Jualth, allowing no interruptions until she had completed her carefully tailored preamble, 'is a teacher of English and also works in her parent's bookshop. She is, if I am permitted to say, considered to be a bright young lady by all those who know her.'

Emily blushed at the commendation.

'Polly is the daughter of The Tavern's landlord and need I mention the high esteem attributed to such an establishment's proprietors in my part of the world?'

'You've been in there?' William asked.

'Briefly, and with Anthony as a chaperone. It is a hub for conversation, opinion and a female perspective on all matters.'

Polly nodded her agreement.

'Now, Josephine is, if I understand correctly, what is termed a social activist and volunteer. She spends much of her time assisting the priest by helping those in need. In addition, she attends meetings to discuss the rights of the poor and – just as importantly – the rights of women, so they may better assist where their level-headed and enlightened views are of greatest value. In short, to assist everywhere.'

Josephine bowed her head. The description was reasonably accurate, even if she had yet to build up the confidence to assert the opinions in open meetings that Jualth had alluded to.

To Jualth's mind, all her guests were young – younger than herself – and deserving of more than a passing acquaintance with the landlord's agent. 'So, that's the barest of essentials to be going on with,' she said. 'Who wants to be the first to expand?'

'Well,' said Lucy, set upon rectifying the extraordinary oversight of not hearing any mention of her own considerable qualities, 'I live in the bookshop with my sister Emily, and we have a brother Edgar—'

'Lucy!' said Jualth bluntly, stifling the progress of the precocious and exceedingly annoying child. 'If there's anything we need to learn about your home, I'm sure Emily can tell us. We will look no farther than you should any gaping holes arise.'

It did not bypass William's attention that this ruse by his house guest served no purpose other than to introduce him to eligible young women who lived under his nose. It was a ploy he found amusing but which provided no serious ground for future courtship. Despite his preoccupation with bridge business, many women, including those around his table, had not gone unnoticed; only the will to commit the time necessary to establish a meaningful friendship.

To Jualth's annoyance, her triumvirate of carefully selected suitors were too much in awe of their handsome, authoritative host to offer the forthright and controversial opinions she had hoped to hear. Had she known it, all three had received stern instructions from their tenant parents to be polite, good-mannered and guided by the bridge master when in his company. Commenting on the menial and limiting roles for women, their lack of influence on important issues and their position in society were forbidden. The bridge master should not be bothered with such ideas or issues. The one thing Jualth did learn about she had no interest in hearing; namely Lucy and her school, her aptitude for embroidery and her Aunt Dvora's beautifully manicured pet spaniel.

'My favourite book is *Alice in Wonderland*, which I read aloud to my sister Emily every evening before prayers and bed,' Lucy rattled on. 'My second favourite book is …'

'Isn't it about time you *went* to bed, Lucy?' Jualth suggested in frustration. 'Why not read your *second* favourite book to your brother Edgar this evening?'

'I think it is about time we were all retiring,' said Emily. Polly and Josephine concurred.

'Oh no, I didn't mean for you all to go,' said Jualth, stricken by the sudden fear of failure. 'One of the Hawks can walk Lucy back to the bridge.'

Emily was as firm as she had been polite all night: 'I am responsible for taking my sister home. Thank you for a lovely evening, Jualth, Bridge Master. It is late. We must all now return.'

Jualth soon found herself alone at the table, her search to remedy good manners maddingly unsuccessful. Brimming with impatience, she waited for William to return – he had dutifully accompanied their guests back to the bridge.

When the door eventually opened and closed, the bridge master reappeared and casually took up his seat at the table. Ignoring his guest, he picked up his long-since abandoned paper and resumed his intense scrutiny of homeland affairs.

'You're trying to annoy me, aren't you?' said Jualth. She had no reason to be at the table other than to talk to him.

He grunted in a manner calculated to emphasise that most of his attention lay elsewhere.

'Bridge Master!' said Jualth, spitting out his official title. 'You made those poor girls call you "Bridge Master" all evening. How was that meant to be a relaxing, informal occasion if you were making them address you by a title and not a name?'

'Lucy called me William.'

'Lucy is an annoyingly clever seven-year-three-month-and-two-day-old, who can count herself lucky that she'll live to add another day to that total. If I'd have known Emily intended to bring Lucy, our company tonight would have been minus two sisters.'

William nonchalantly turned the page of his paper. 'Always had a soft spot for Lucy; bright, observant, well-educated—'

'*William*, are you going to keep reading that paper?' Jualth asked, her fury mounting. She was frustrated by an evening that had strayed into a pointless waste of time all due, as far as she could see, to an incorrigible child. Despite her endeavours, another day had passed without accomplishment. One sign of irritation at the intrusion into his private concerns she would have regarded as a victory, and a display of interest in any of the females, other than Lucy, a triumph. Success in either of these aims would have suited her, but failure in both suited nothing but her anger.

She was left to stew, irritated by a lack of response that would have done William's three inadequate suitors proud. All attempts to cause trouble and disturb that exaggerated level of authority had failed. Nothing she had so far done that week had advanced her aim to make it her last away from her family.

'*William*, put the paper down,' said Jualth in a manner that clearly displayed her irritation. She received nothing but a small grunt in reply. It was enough to push her over the edge. The paper was forcefully removed and dispatched in several pieces. Jualth, her chest heaving with the sudden exertion, had at last grabbed the bridge master's full attention.

'William,' she began again in a low voice that simmered with the expectation of rising, 'I have come to England in need of your help and so far I have received none. In three *whole* weeks I have dithered under your roof whilst my sister, daughter and grandmother face potential eviction from our home. And instead of being there, planning the best way to defeat the English army when it invades, I have been here, being escorted from one pretty park to another.'

'I've told you, Jualth—'

Jualth screamed and banged her hands upon the table. 'William! Do not tell me to be patient any more. I am fed up with being patient. Unless I know something is happening, I shall start searching for this man myself and, if I cannot do anything when I find him, I shall return home. *William! Is anything happening?*'

Jualth's mood was now several degrees above boiling point and her anger cried out for a victim. William was not, however, prepared to let such behaviour force him into disclosing information that he did not have and raise hopes that might never materialise. He responded with equal determination.

'When I hear, I'll tell you.'

'What does that *mean*, William?'

'Governor.'

Jualth's rage was interrupted by a call from the hall. William looked around, then pushed back his chair and headed for the door.

'*William!*' Jualth shouted, 'I'm talking to—' The door shut firmly between them.

Jualth looked for something to fling at the door; there was no shortage of ammunition. A noise from the rear proved a timely intervention – there was no point in initiating warfare with Mrs Tuckle as well. One fight was enough. Instead, several chairs were knocked aside, and the kitchen door wrenched from its hinges as she followed the bridge master into the hall. Cutter and Jamba were giving their last report of the day.

'*William*, I have not finished talking to you,' Jualth yelled.

'In the morning, Jualth, when you are calmer. A reasonable conversation is impossible when you are in this mood.' William curtailed any further riposte by striding up the stairs, walking around the landing and disappearing into his room.

Jualth turned away in fury, grinding her teeth as she contemplated a violent act. Cutter and Jamba backed closer to the front door, trying to dodge the Gaelic curses growled in their direction. Jualth stopped, as a sudden dart of her eyes to the first floor indicated the formulation of a new strategy. She picked up a lantern from the hall table and swept into the bridge master's study.

Alarm bells, louder than the call of a hundred town criers, rang in Cutter's head. 'You can't go in there, missis, not without the master's say-so.'

But Jualth was gone, hidden behind a half-closed door, the light dimming as it moved farther into the room. She looked around, grimacing at its tidiness: nothing lay undealt with on the desk; everything on the shelves was neatly aligned and the cabinets were closed. Jualth tried the drawers to the desk: they were all locked, likewise the cabinets. Everything was locked with one notable exception. She grabbed a glass and poured a large whisky, the mere act only heightening her desire to be home.

Cutter stuck his head around the door. 'Missis,' he whispered as loudly as he dared. He watched as the intruder downed her first glass. 'Jualth, the governor will be livid. You shouldn't be in 'ere.'

'As livid as me, Lloyd?'

'Somethin' like that. C'mon, missis, you knows it's against the rules.'

'I do, Lloyd,' said Jualth, staring in resentment at the empty glass – it had had no beneficial effect whatsoever. Another swiftly followed before the room shuddered to the echo of a glass rolling on its side after being forcibly rammed down. No attempt was made to conceal its use. She walked over to the desk and picked up a heavy, two-centuries-old, wooden paperweight carved by the Bridge Carpenter into the shape of the chapel. With her nerves calmed and her initial strategy of delving through his papers unfulfilled, there was now only one course of action left open.

'Right, let's try again,' she murmured, thrusting the lantern into Cutter's hands as she brushed past both Hawks en route to the stairs.

Cutter looked at Jamba for guidance, unsure whether they should try to stop her. Jamba hesitated, his eyes fixed on the potential calamity fast approaching the Master's door. Belatedly, he reached a decision and quickly followed, reaching the master's room just in time to see the hem of a white skirt disappear as the door slammed behind it. A loud thump quickly ensued as the stolen object missed its intended target and splintered against the wall. An alarmed cry of 'Jualth!' was followed by a pained cry of '*Jualth!*' as a second object was successfully thrown at the innocent victim. Cutter and Jamba stood transfixed, listening to the unfolding one-way battle that consisted of Jualth's violent screams and their Master's cries of pain.

'That's one angry woman,' Jamba surmised. 'Wonder what the governor did to upset her?'

Cutter, his ear to the door, nodded his agreement. 'Must've been something pretty bad.' He motioned towards the door handle. 'Should we …?'

Jamba paused, deeply tempted to act on his fellow Hawk's suggestion. He had a feeling though that this was one fight where any intervention would be considered an intrusion. He waved Cutter's hand away. 'The governor should be all right,' he said with little conviction. 'After all, she's only a woman.'

Cutter and Jamba stood like drapers' mannequins, listening to the evolving noise: the screams had turned into the sounds of a struggle and then into something quite different.

'They've stopped fighting … haven't they?' Cutter said indecisively.

Jamba pursed his lips and nodded. 'They ain't fightin' no more, that's for sure.' He crouched down to peer through the keyhole and sighed in disappointment – there was a key on the other side.

Slowly the two mannequins straightened – the need to burst into their master's room to save him from his attacker had passed.

'Listen,' said Cutter, keeping his voice down. 'Those moans, it's almost sounds like 'e's tryin' to kill 'er.'

Jamba shook his head. 'And, I, for one, ain't goina stop him, least he tries to kill me.' He grabbed the sleeve of Cutter's jacket. 'We have a job to do, my friend, and we ain't doin' it standin' here.'

'Best keep this to ourselves,' whispered Cutter, as he was dragged away.

In the hall, the noise of a door shutting along the passageway made them turn sharply. The kitchen was in darkness.

'Looks like we ain't the only ones that knows,' said Jamba. 'But we won't be the ones to tell.'

They took one last glance towards their master's bedroom and left for their posts on the bridge, hoping for a far quieter, and less eventful, night ahead.

Chapter 61

'William?' Jualth sighed from the comfort of his bed, a strong arm holding her close.

The call went unanswered. In the first blessed moment of silence to befall the Bridge House that evening, the bridge master wished for nothing more than for it to last a bit longer. He was to be disappointed.

'Sorry about the paperweight,' Jualth said with a slight touch of guilt.

William's lazy groan turned into a rather more pained groan of remembrance. Several generations of bridge masters had managed to pass that precious object down unscathed. It now lay in several, splintered pieces on the floor. He allowed the blissful state of silence to return.

Jualth raised her head from his chest. 'And the vase, your washbasin, the small picture that stood on—'

William rested his hand on the side of her head and gently returned it to its starting position – they were both sorry but none of it mattered.

Contentedly, Jualth snuggled up again, an eye still upon the dimly lit debris. 'William?'

'Umm.'

'Should I offer to lend a hand or do you think Mrs Tuckle will want to clear up the mess by herself?' Jualth chuckled. She knew she was being wicked.

'We shall clear it up together, spare Mrs Tuckle the trouble,' said William.

'What about the buttons on my blouse?'

'The buttons on …?' William groaned again – the objects were no longer attached. An uncontrolled eagerness had rather forcibly relieved Jualth of her clothing. 'Can you not ...?'

Jualth pulled a face. 'S'pose I could. Never enjoyed needlework much; always left it to Grandma.'

William glanced at the pale-white figure lying on his side, reflecting skin tones of yellow, blue and orange from the lamp. He fidgeted awkwardly. 'Comfortable, Jualth?'

Jualth glanced up and smiled contentedly – it was sweet of him to ask.

William sighed, wondering how to rephrase the question in a more obvious but still tactful manner.

'Jualth?'

'Yes, William.'

'Are you planning to stay in my bed *all* night?'

A satisfying moan of pleasure indicated that his bedfellow was well set till the morning.

William sighed again. 'Right ... that answers that question.'

Jualth chuckled once more. 'Everyone knows, William. I didn't exactly sneak into your room, did I?' And bearing in mind the subsequent events, she certainly had no intention of being ordered out. 'The Hawks will be discreet, you know that.'

'I shall have a word with them all the same.'

'I think you should. We can't risk upsetting Polly, Emily and Josephine, can we?'

William's groans continued as did Jualth's amusement. 'Did you really think that would work?' he asked.

'In one way or another ... yes. Word will get around that, after many prolonged years of dedication, the bridge master has finally turned his attention to matters of the heart.'

William raised his one free hand and pressed it against his forehead – it was an outcome to Jualth's scheming that he had not foreseen. 'Well, do not expect me to marry Polly, Emily or Josephine. It was hardly an enthralling evening and if it hadn't been for Lucy ...'

'Lucy is seven, William. You cannot marry a child.'

Jualth was still vexed that her plan had not worked. Her three candidates had been meticulously chosen and, with her presence to break the ice and guide the conversation ...

'All the same, if you feel the need to do that again ...'

'I will look for twenty-year-old Lucys,' Jualth acknowledged.

Down in the hallway, a large upright grandfather clock chimed the half hour. In normal circumstances, a small bedside clock would have chimed in unison.

'How did you convince them to visit the Bridge House in the first place? I thought I had a fearsome reputation amongst my tenants. A summons to my office is meant to conjure up trepidation and foreboding.'

'Not when convinced they were here to rescue a young, lost woman crying out for friends in a cold and forbidding town. They had no idea, William, none at all.'

'Hence the misunderstanding with Lucy.'

'So it seems.' A stunted sigh turned into a giggle. Gradually, her companion's defiant sense of authority fell apart and he conceded to seeing the funny side. It was about time. Jualth recalled the man that had visited her home – it had taken far too long for her to free him from his burden of responsibility and to rediscover the person she had known.

Resting comfortably, she again spied the mess of what had been a perfectly ordered room. She felt quietly pleased with herself – there was no imagination in order. Order was dull.

'Does this mean more time with new acquaintances and less work for Cutter?' William asked.

'*Time*, William! What time? If nothing happens soon and, by that, I mean in the next couple of days, I shall return home and wait for whatever is to happen *to* happen.'

'But you came here to fight?'

'Which is precisely what I'm not doing. I'm doing nothing and I can do that at home.'

'Jualth?'

She shook her head, unwilling, in this special moment, to return to the remorseless world of her problems. They could wait.

A cosy interval of silence passed, providing a long-enough hiatus for William's thoughts to stray to a topic that had troubled him for more than two years.

'Jualth?'

'Yes, William.'

'How did Jade's Fall get its name?'

Jualth flinched, as if struck by a sudden burst of static. She pushed herself up, profoundly astonished by the unexpected question.

'William, before I consider answering that question, will you please tell me how the mind of what I took to be a perfectly normal man, actually works? We've had a lovely evening with some invited guests, then a row, a fight and capped it all by ripping off one another's clothes – two years too late in my opinion. Then, from somewhere in the depths of your distant travels, you dredge up a question like that. I thought it was women that were supposed to have the unfathomable minds!'

'Emma, Polly and Josephine do, but not you, Jualth. I know what's going on inside your head, you tell me. It may take a few seconds or a few days, but you always tell me.'

Jualth leant down to kiss his chin, then settled back onto her side, leaving an arm to rest on his chest. 'I will tell you, William, but not tonight.'

William did not outwardly react, but Jualth could sense his disappointment. She yearned to know what had sparked the interest. 'Trust me, William, the wait will not be long, but Jade's Fall is not a story to go to sleep on.'

She kissed him again, closed her eyes and said no more.

Chapter 62

Breakfast was a quiet affair, with Jualth and a brooding Mrs Tuckle the only ones present. Words were kept to a minimum.

'Mr Halar informs me that *you* will be attending to his room this morning.'

Mr Halar had probably also informed her that *she* had already agreed to this arrangement and required no further direction from another quarter. Jualth did not, therefore, deem to reply to what was really just a statement of a previously known fact.

Instead, with her elevated glow slowly fading, she sat quietly at the table sipping coffee, contrasting the joy of the previous evening with what William's life must otherwise be like by allowing someone who could not provide such warmth to look after him. She concluded it was a false life and one that William should reject. Maybe now, with the encouragement provided, he had a reason to broaden his desires.

When she had woken, she had done so alone. Without rousing her from a contented and peaceful sleep, her night-time companion had disappeared and – as the housekeeper had also dutifully informed her – was not expected back until much later. This would allow her plenty of time to gather together the broken artefacts of the previous night's battle. However, the inclination to immediately rectify her misdeeds drew a decided blank – she had till evening, after all. Instead, she decided upon a different course of action and, in the full knowledge that Mrs Tuckle would poke her nose around William's bedroom door in her absence, slipped out the back to see Albert.

Fanning herself against the blast of heat that swept past her face on entering the workshop, she smiled brightly upon the blacksmith and headed for one of the corners.

Having had the privilege of many such visits, Albert felt relaxed enough to finish what he was doing before towelling himself down and joining his wraithlike angel.

Jualth tutted, 'Quite extraordinary! That is definitely the strangest thing I have ever seen.'

Albert sighed morosely; he could do nothing but agree. The misuse of his skills was on open display to all who ventured in to see. Jualth offered sympathetic encouragement, 'But the craftsmanship, Albert … breathtaking.'

If the heat of the forge had not already turned Albert the colour of a ripened tomato, Jualth would surely have noticed him blush. True admiration was precious and, despite his modesty, he enjoyed honest praise.

'The customer's designs were on the vague side and three nuns in the shape of a cloud formation was quite a challenge, I can tell you.'

'Is that what they are?'

Albert nodded.

'For a public house?'

'What else.'

'Then maybe it will make more sense on the way out than the way in.' Jualth patted the forlorn blacksmith on the back, empathising with the demands modern society had placed upon his skills.

Having had enough of Albert's peculiar commissions, she looked around searching for an item of much greater worth. 'Where is it, Albert?' she asked. 'I hope the three nuns have not kept you from your most important work.'

Her frequent visits had permitted the blacksmith no slack. Despite the fact that the benefit came purely from praise, the angel stood head and shoulders above all others as a taskmaster.

He grumbled from the heart. 'You know, I'd have left years ago if Master William drove me as hard as you do,'

Jualth smiled, that sounded like a compliment to her. 'Is it finished, Albert?'

The blacksmith led her over to one of the workbenches on the opposite side of the workshop where a dark metal plaque lay next to the designs drawn by Cutter. He tilted it forward and rubbed the surface with his finger.

'As you can see, almost there but not quite.' He flicked it over to better explain. 'Look, you can see where I've traced your design onto the back.' Jualth inspected closely. 'Some of the detail requires additional work to knock it through. Embossing cannot be rushed.'

Jualth nodded pensively, studying the back first, then the front. She ran her eye over the outer rim, quietly reading the inscription.

'As I couldn't understand a word, I was very careful with the spelling,' Albert explained. 'I hope my innocent labours have not abetted a call to arms.'

'Hardly, Albert,' Jualth chuckled. 'We Scots are far too placid a character for such a thing, you know that, and as for the spelling, exactly what I gave you. The only person who's likely to be incited when she reads it is my sister.'

'A gift to her?'

'It is but not her alone. It will serve to remind one and all of our ancestral resilience in the hope that it will continue.'

In the light of that comment, and despite the denial, his *call to arms* jest did not seem so farfetched. 'And the inscription aside?' he asked, inviting her opinion.

Jualth had no need to compare the plaque to the drawings – she recognised every detail. 'Just what I had in mind, Albert: a montage of the whisky-making process from raw material to end product together with a small waterfall in the background. What could be more appropriate for a Scottish innkeeper?'

What indeed? And it was certainly more appropriate than his three nuns sculpture. 'Last chance if you want a name included. There'll be no room after today.' The lack of a name for the whisky, the inn or the region had puzzled Albert from the start. He had still to receive a proper explanation.

Jualth politely declined. 'I have my reasons, Albert. Please don't ask me what they are. If anyone ever manages to decipher these words, they'll understand why the distillery and the whisky are not mentioned.'

'Would I think badly of you if I knew?' Albert asked.

'You might, so please, no more questions.'

Albert relented. It was not for him to cross-examine the motives of his patrons, even the ones that did not pay. 'You'll hang it in your inn?' he asked.

Jualth was noncommittal. 'I have two possibilities and whichever I decide, I shall make sure all know about it. Like your gargoyles, it will serve to protect my community from outside forces.' Jualth shuddered – the gargoyles were vile-looking creatures. Perhaps her next commission would enable Albert to replace them with something less grotesque.

'Do you mind if I stay with you a moment?' she asked. 'I thought you might like to hear a wee bit more about the countryside.'

Albert looked around. He had more work to do than he had ever had in his life but, when equated against the few remaining opportunities he had to entertain his ethereal angel, he perceived only one choice. He sat down and permitted Jualth another attempt to turn him from a hard-working townie into a man of rural leisure.

After Jualth had finished an agreeable interlude with Albert, and spent a not-so-agreeable hour picking up the broken objects scattered around William's bedroom, she relocated to the bridge to seek out the company of her young Hawk. A shove in the back directed him away from his duties towards Princes' Gate, from where they headed west along Lower Thames Street.

'Why the 'urry, missis?' Cutter asked, as he struggled to keep up with his companion.

'I have good reason, Lloyd, which I dare say is not beyond your powers of deduction.'

Cutter grinned. His powers of deduction were well in tune with those of his escort.

'Did you see anyone staring at me?' Jualth asked, having not dared look over her shoulder.

'Only the usual gents with an eye for a pretty—'

'*Lloyd!* That is not what I meant.'

Cutter smiled, enjoying his moment of cheek to the full. Eventually, having taken on board that the remark was also rather flattering, so did Jualth. 'No one else, missis, sure of it,' said Cutter to ease her worries.

Jualth's sense of guilt was set at a shamefully high level that morning. She wished, at all costs, to avoid bumping into the three women she had mistakenly lined up for the bridge master's fancy.

Once past Cannon Street Station, and at what she considered a safe distance, she allowed their pace to slacken. 'Did William have a word with you, Lloyd?' she asked with casual interest.

Cutter quickly grasped her meaning. 'He did, missis; with Jamba too. You can rely on us.'

Jualth smiled, having suffered nothing more than niggling doubts. 'No bribery needed, then?'

'No, missis, wouldn't 'ear of it.' Having said that, and despite his allegiance to his master's lady, a long night of reflection had not stopped Cutter considering the leverage he could gain from her predicament. 'Although—'

'*Lloyd* ...' Jualth's heckles rose, just in case she was being misled.

'It's the name you've given me, missis – does it 'ave to be Lloyd?'

'It does. It's distinguished, as I have said, and one day you will be too.'

'No one else calls me Lloyd.'

'Really!' Jualth thought about it. The lad was right, she could not recall one single occasion when another had used his new name. 'Leave it to me, Lloyd. That situation will soon be rectified.'

It was not the answer Cutter had wished to hear. Maybe he should have used his leverage more forcefully. 'Mrs Tuckle knows as well.'

'I know she does. I allowed her a peep into your master's bedroom this morning.'

'She might see things different to us, being that much older.'

Jualth's heckles rose again. The mere mention of the housekeeper's name seemed to set her off. 'Why should she, Lloyd? Is William not allowed a private life under his own roof? What gives that woman the right to interfere?'

Cutter edged away, widening the gap in the expectation of looming danger. 'I was only saying, missis.'

Jualth grunted and drew closer. She had not meant to take her frustration and disapproval out on someone for whom she *did* have a high regard.

'Mrs Tuckle and I have the same concern. William is well respected and neither of us would like to see that hard-earned reputation diminished or his chances of a good courtship ruined.'

'Can't see that happening, missis.'

'Which, Lloyd? Which can't you see happening?'

Cutter did not answer, but his expression was not difficult to interpret.

'It will not happen, Lloyd. Do not run away with any wild thoughts about last night. *Nothing* has changed.'

Cutter cast a glance over his shoulder, noticing another two, well-dressed gentlemen passing an admiring eye in the direction of his companion. He was not so certain.

A lesson followed their late return to the bridge and then, before mealtime, Jualth received an invitation to join William in his office.

'Am I supposed to be worried by this summons?' she asked, seating herself on the opposite side of the desk.

'Are you a tenant?'

'Sort of ... the non-paying kind.'

'Then you should be worried.'

'Still got no money.'

'But you have got a meeting to go to on Monday morning at nine o'clock sharp.'

Jualth held her breath as she hoped against hope that this was the meeting she had been waiting for. During the next few moments, the only sound to be heard was the mechanical, rhythmic click of the grandfather clock out in the hall.

'With someone very important I hope, William,' Jualth said eventually. He nodded his head in confirmation. Jualth slowly exhaled and smiled faintly. 'So now I know how to get things done,' she murmured. There was no confirmation on that point, just a dismissive grunt. 'Go on, then,' Jualth prompted urgently.

'You are to see the person overseeing your case, who in this instance happens to be the most important man working in the Customs and Excise service.'

'I'm honoured.' After a moment of reflection upon this apparent honour, her manner assumed a more circumspect stance. 'Why, William? Why do I merit a meeting with the top man?'

'Because procedure has been altered to keep the numbers in the know to a minimum.'

'That did not answer the "Why?"'

William refused to elaborate. 'Wait until the meeting, Jualth. All will become clear then.'

That was an easy request to make, less so to follow. The *why* still bothered her. It could not be down to William's standing alone.

'Will Mr Pennan be there?'

William nodded.

Jualth breathed in deeply. The time for a reunion with the very person she had travelled so far to see – the wretched Excise inspector – had at last been set. The interminable, patient wait was nearly over. William tapped his finger on the solid oak desk to attract Jualth's attention; he had additional news to impart.

'For this one occasion, Jualth, you will need suitable attire, which means …'

'Oh no, William, *please.*'

'Hat included,' he said firmly.

Jualth gasped. 'Not a hat. I'll agree to the morbid outfit but, please, not a hat.'

'No half measures, this meeting is too important. You *will* be wearing a hat. Drop into Hats & Boaters first thing tomorrow morning. They'll be expecting you.'

Although visibly distressed, Jualth submitted to her lack of choice. Help had arrived and with only Saturday and Sunday to survive, perhaps a sign of willingness was appropriate.

'Do I need to go properly dressed to choose a hat?'

'Just the jacket. Carry it if you like. The two must match.'

Jualth nodded. She would play along, create a good impression – at least to begin with – then go home. The home bit she liked, especially if she had something to take home with her. 'Do I need to prepare for this meeting, William?'

'No, Jualth, you will let me do the talking. Only answer questions that are put directly to you and tell no lies – they already know far too much about you for deceit.'

William and Jualth stared at one another, regressing into their former stubborn and interminable state of eye contact. William suddenly realised what he had asked – *tell no lies, speak only when spoken to*. When her reply came, he did not believe a word of it.

'Of course, William, as you think best. I shall follow your lead. That doesn't sound like *too* much to ask, does it?'

Chapter 63

At eight forty-five, Jualth, dressed in fashionable gloom from head to foot, was escorted across Old London Bridge, her hand wrapped around the arm of a tall, handsome escort.

A dark-brown jacket buttoned up to her chin covered her one concession to normality: an all-but-invisible white blouse with lace trim that peeped through at the wrists and collar. Gloves covered her hands and lower arms, and a ground-hugging skirt – which matched the jacket and bulged slightly at the rear – swept a clean trail in her wake. Elegantly perched upon her head, and with the desire that it should be blown into the river as they crossed central arch, was the dreaded and much-hated hat. And on her feet, crying out to every rodent that there was a new queen in town, were an extremely annoying pair of squeaky, black leather shoes.

'Why are we leaving so late, William?' Jualth demanded in a worried manner. 'We cannot afford to be late, you said so yourself, and there's a limit to how far I can walk in these unforgiving foot vices.'

The assurance that they had plenty of time did not settle her nerves. Cutter approached along with Nipper and wished his missis luck.

'Thank you, Lloyd, and as you picked most of what I am wearing, it had better impress.'

'It will do, missis, no doubt about it.'

'Real smart,' Nipper agreed.

The two Hawks watched approvingly as their master and his young lady funnelled elegantly through the arcade.

'A right handsome couple,' Cutter observed.

Nipper agreed, though he was slightly more circumspect with his own observation: 'But can you imagine taking orders from 'er as well?'

Cutter's proud countenance did not alter. 'Don't have to imagine, Nipper. Already knows.'

Having reached Lower Thames Street, Jualth and William were soon passing Billingsgate Market. Jualth tilted her hat, casting a long shadow over her face, and drew her diminutive figure closer to the broad, upright frame of her escort.

William tentatively cleared his throat, 'Hmm … what are you doing, Jualth?'

'I don't want Sid to see me in this. His heart isn't strong enough.'

They managed to pass the hall and its thinning traffic without detection and William supposed all obstacles to a normal walk had been adverted. He was mistaken. Jualth tugged on his arm and slowed – she had assumed the colourless complexion of her white lace cuffs.

'Now what?' he asked with waning patience.

'William, we're heading towards the Tower, the most heinous place in the whole of London. *Please* tell me you're not taking me to the Tower.'

William gritted his teeth and dragged her forward. 'If you could bring yourself to keep moving, otherwise we'll most assuredly be late.'

A hundred yards farther along, just before the road rose and bore around to the left, they stopped.

'This is it,' William announced.

'This is what?' Jualth asked, taken aback by their abrupt and premature halt.

William indicated to the right, where three steps led up to an open door sheltered beneath an unlit gas lamp and a stone carving of a coat of arms.

Jualth mouthed the words on the shield. 'HM Customs and Excise.' She was now even more dumbfounded. 'This … this is it?'

'It is, and you'll be glad to know we've arrived with time to spare.'

The colour flushed back into Jualth's face. 'You mean that enormous slab of faceless grey we can see from the other side of the river is … is *it*?'

William nodded, well-satisfied that he had concealed its identity from his companion – Cutter had never once brought Jualth east along Lower Thames Street.

'And you didn't think to …?'

William placed his hand on Jualth's back and applied sufficient force to gently nudge her forward. 'We can talk about this later.'

'You're damn right we can talk about this …' Jualth respectfully lowered her voice as they entered the open hallway. 'You mean Mr Cecil Pennan has been in this building all this time, a mere five-minute walk away and you haven't … *you haven't—*'

William cut her off, 'Later, Jualth. *I said, later.*'

Having made their presence known, they followed an official to the second floor and a large room overlooking the river.

'If you would care to take a seat around the table, sir, madam,' said the well-spoken official with the utmost courtesy, 'I shall inform Mr Tombs of your arrival.'

A large, well-polished oval table stretched the length of a highly impressive and daunting room.

'How many trees did they cut down to make that?' Jualth lamented as, in defiance of the official's request, she strolled towards one of three ceiling-high sash windows. A clock, perched on a tall Georgian mantelpiece, ticked loudly and monotonously above the quiet, occasional crackle of a frugally lit fireplace. And, from lofty positions on each wall, austere paintings of past but highly important government servants watched proceedings they could no longer personally preside over.

Jualth stared across the river to the Bridge House. Like herself, it was tiny in comparison to this intimidating building. But diminutive size or not, neither regarded themselves as insignificant and neither were prepared to sit obediently back and suffer a fate prescribed by others. She turned from the window and sniffed at the interior.

'Very nice; the top executioner certainly has an impressive office.'

'It's just a meeting room, Jualth. His office is twice the size.'

'I bet he's a small man, then; small, round, beady-eyed with bushy whiskers—'

Jualth's conjectures ended abruptly when the door opened and Mr Tombs, the Chairman of Commissioners in Her Majesty's Customs & Excise, entered. She watched closely from beneath the brim of her hat – her conjectures had been prophetically accurate. The commissioner was plump, if not rotund, below average height and with ridiculously bushy and greying sideburns.

The men greeted one another with a firm handshake. Jualth was introduced and, for the sake of civility, smiled thinly. They took up their seats with Mr Tombs at the end (back to the window), William to his side and then Jualth.

'We will be joined in a moment by Mr Pennan. Jacobs has gone to fetch him,' the commissioner informed them. 'He will bring the relevant file and the evidence he gathered on site.'

'Are you not already aware of what is on the file?' Jualth asked brusquely.

Mr Tombs peered over his spectacles at the source of the sudden interruption.

'Jualth, if you would care to let Mr Tombs conduct the meeting,' William gently prodded. 'You will have plenty of opportunity to comment as we progress.'

Jualth continued in the same defiant manner: 'Of course, William, I forgot, I'm supposed to only speak when—'

'Yes, Jualth, you are.' The bridge master's reply was quiet, but stern.

Jualth tapped her finger on the table, already feeling irritated by the proceedings. William was asking a lot if he expected her to sit back whilst the two men argued her fate.

'I am aware of the contents of your file, Mrs McTavish. We will be using it only for reference during our meeting. I have been informed by Mr Halar that you have come a long way to see us, and the Excise Service would like to convey its appreciation for the effort undertaken on your part to embark upon such an onerous journey. Discussing your case face to face should help us reach a speedier conclusion.'

'And such cooperation by Mrs McTavish will be considered in her favour when you make your judgement?' William tendered respectfully.

'Indeed, but it will not override any points of law that have been broken. The seriousness of the case cannot be alleviated by subsequent actions of compliance or regret.'

There was a knock at the door and Mr Pennan entered, holding a file to his chest in one hand and the neck of a bottle in the other.

'Ah, what we have been waiting for,' said Mr Tombs. Mr Pennan walked the length of the room and placed the evidence in front of his superior.

'Mr Pennan, this is Mr Halar, the bridge master of Old London Bridge, as I am sure you are aware and, of course, you have met the young lady sitting to his side.'

'Indeed,' said Mr Pennan courteously. 'Mrs McTavish, I hope you are well.'

'I am *not*, Mr Pennan.'

'Jualth!' William warned again, impatiently.

Mr Pennan took a seat at the table facing William, ready to assist with the documentation. Jualth fixed her icy glare on the man who had paid her community such an unwelcome visit. Even now she questioned the wisdom of letting him leave. The unpleasant sight of his tilted nose and flared nostrils was enough to divert her eyes back to the commissioner.

'Now then,' said Mr Tombs, 'the main issues we have to talk about are the running of an unlicensed distillery in the eastern Highlands of Scotland and the subsequent supply of a distilled malt, with an extremely high proof level, to the inn run by Mrs McTavish.'

Mr Pennan pushed the bottle forward, now labelled: 'Confiscated property of Matilda's Inn (proprietor – Jualth McTavish), by Mr C Pennan, officer in Her Majesty's Customs & Excise Service'.

Mr Tombs opened the file, extracted the summary sheets from the top and pushed it aside. A few interminable moments passed whilst he leafed through each individual page. The ticking of the clock and the crackle of the fire were soon joined by the restless tapping of Jualth's fingers.

'Mr Pennan's report is thorough and extensive, but to summarise the findings in as brief a form as possible ... an illegal distillery has been operating within your community for a considerable period of time. The actual number of years is so vast, the specific period is not relevant. We can barely extend our investigation back to the commencement of its operations but, in terms of collecting back taxes, we can estimate a figure using the details of production gathered by Mr Pennan and a period of collection, the length of which we shall determine. It is noted that part of the production is taxed at another source under a different guise and however unorthodox its method of inclusion, we shall take this into account.'

'How many years are you going back?' Jualth asked without invitation.

William made to interrupt, but Mr Tombs waved his intervention aside – he was prepared to deal with the query.

'In our opinion, twenty years would be a reasonable period considering the seriousness of the case and the number of years involved.'

'That's practically my lifetime,' Jualth gasped. 'Can you do that?'

'The number of years is at our discretion,' Mr Tombs informed her factually, and then continued with his summation.

'In addition, some of the whisky has been bottled,' he indicated towards the example on the desk, 'and sold at Matilda's, a properly licensed inn run by Mrs McTavish. No tax of any kind has been accounted for on the sale of this whisky, which is again illegal. From Mr Pennan's report, we can assess the total production from the distillery, the number of casks that have been distributed to Brethna and calculate a balance which, we must assume, goes to only the one outlet, namely, Matilda's.'

Mr Tombs looked up at Jualth, an action calculated to express the gravity of his words. Jualth began to bore holes into the Chinese carpet with the heels of her brand-new leather shoes.

'Looking at the figures, Mrs McTavish, it is a substantial balance. It is our view that this act should be treated in the same way as the distillery, with twenty years' back taxes due on our estimate of your income.'

If the conclusion of the commissioner's summation could have been worse, Jualth would like to have known how. There seemed little point in acting out the role of the remorseful offender and compliantly holding her tongue. The situation could not deteriorate much more.

'And just supposing we had the money to pay any of this tax, what then?'

'The distillery would be allowed to conduct operations under license and the close scrutiny of the Excise Service. As part of our demands against the inn, however, you would naturally be barred from ever again holding a licence to act as the innkeeper. That responsibility would be relinquished and no member of your immediate family who has conspired in its running would be permitted to hold the license in your stead.'

'That means losing our home,' Jualth said angrily.

'If the inn is to remain where it is …' Mr Tombs answered without emotion.

'And Mr Pennan would no doubt be sent again to invade our privacy, just to make sure we are acting according to your rules.'

'Jualth!' said William, fearful that she was losing control.

Mr Tombs unwisely neglected his aide. 'If you want to put it that way – yes.'

'And if we don't have the money to pay you, what then?'

'Then proceedings will be considered against you as the proprietor of the inn and against the owners of the distillery.'

'The distillery is not owned by anyone, it belongs to the whole community; your file should tell you that. If you prosecute, you prosecute everyone and me twice over.'

'Only if you can't pay the back taxes,' said Mr Tombs.

'We can't, so tell me, what will be the outcome of a successful prosecution?'

Mr Tombs did not answer. What the young woman was referring to was not in his jurisdiction and he had no intention of passing a sentence on behalf of a different authority. 'That is the summation of our assessment on your community's distillery and your inn, and the possible proceedings that could arise from these findings. Do you have anything you would like to say?'

Some Gaelic phrases came to mind, her own summation of the proceedings so far, as well as the notion to declare outright war. All were briefly restrained.

'What about Brethna? What happens to Jack Vardy and his distillery?'

'Brethna is a different case that will be dealt with separately. The business arrangements between the two distilleries are included in both enquiries.'

'And the fire?' said Jualth.

Mr Tombs stopped, unable to follow what he considered to be a sudden departure from the matter under discussion. He did not comprehend the reason for its mention.

'The *fire*, Mr Tombs, the one at Brethna that immediately followed your inspector's visit and took the life of both my husband and niece. How does that fit into the issues we are discussing here?'

Mr Tombs looked towards his inspector, but invited no comment.

Mr Pennan glanced away, unhappy that the situation would make any words of sympathy seem cold and insufficient. It was not easy to maintain the persona of a distant, authoritative government official in the light of such human tragedy, especially after he had stood so close to the child whilst talking to her mother. But, in the presence of his superiors, and in a meeting when the rules were of paramount importance, this rigid separation had to be maintained.

'We are aware of the unfortunate incident and welcome this opportunity to pass on our condolences to yourself and your sister,' said Mr Tombs with a genuine air of compassion.

'Why don't you pass them onto my sister yourself?' said Jualth, directing her comments across the table to Mr Pennan. 'Why don't you retrace the footsteps of your *interesting diversion* and tell her how sorry you are that your visit resulted in her child's death. Then she might give you the benefit of her opinion on what is more important: your wretched license or her daughter's life.'

'*Jualth*, this is not helping,' said William, attempting to pacify emotions that were fast running out of control.

'*Well*, Mr Pennan, how does it feel to be so diligent in your job and so indifferent to human life?'

'What has our visit got to do with the fire?' Mr Tombs asked, requiring immediate clarification.

'*Fire equipment*, Mr Tombs. To control the spread of a fire you need fully functioning fire equipment. With a few seconds leeway my husband might have had the time needed to carry my niece out of that burning warehouse alive.'

'The fire equipment?' said Mr Pennan in puzzlement. Although sensitive to her loss, he was as confused as the commissioner as to its relevance in the enquiry.

'Aye, that's right, the fire equipment kept in that wee hut where you spent so much of your time prodding and poking about.'

'Mrs McTavish—'

'*No!*' Jualth shouted, jumping to her feet and banging the table. 'Not interested, Mr Pennan. Your job came first, and the life of my people and my community came second. As long as you did a good job and filed a commendable, rule-abiding report nothing else mattered to you and your bosses.'

'*Jualth, stop this!*' William said abruptly. 'If you do not stop this right now, this meeting is over.'

Jualth pushed away the arm that attempted to pull her back down to her seat.

'What else can happen in this meeting, William? Am I going to be told what a naughty girl I've been, the ridiculous sum of money that I owe and how many years I can expect to be locked up in prison because I can't pay?'

'*Jualth!*'

'No, William. I've heard all there is to hear. I now know where I stand, and I realise that these people don't care about destroying lives and communities. In this place, taxes are more precious and important than anything else.'

'*Sit down, Jualth.*'

'I'm going, William. I'm going back to Scotland, to my home, the place I should never have left. I'll await my fate there, amongst my own people and my own kind.'

'Wait a minute,' said William, doing his utmost to stop her from leaving.

'*Get off me, William*. I'll find my own way out.'

Jualth pulled away, giving the Excise inspector one last glare en route to banging the door behind her.

The three men sat in silence, permitting the echo and vibration circulating the room sufficient time to settle.

'Mr Pennan,' said Mr Tombs, in the aftermath of Jualth's explosive exit, 'I wonder if you might follow Mrs McTavish to ensure she has found her way to the front door.'

Mr Pennan motioned to rise.

'Oh … and there'll be no need for you to rejoin us. I shall retain the evidence from this point forward. Perhaps if you come to my office at two this afternoon. We can discuss matters further then.'

'As you wish, Sir. Mr Halar.'

William nodded infinitesimally and waited for the inspector to leave the room. His presence was not required whilst the abrupt ending to their meeting was reflected upon.

'A fiery, impetuous and forthright woman,' Mr Tombs concluded. 'Could she not have waited before launching into that tirade and blaming poor Mr Pennan for all the ills that have befallen her family?'

'I had hoped to avoid such a show,' William said regretfully. 'But I did warn you, Henry. I told you to proceed carefully.'

'I thought I did. Did I not allude to "possible proceedings"?'

'I think she had stopped listening by that time. A brief, *initial* mention of the existence of an alternative course forward would have helped. Jualth could see nothing but the prison walls closing in around her.'

'Which is a distinct possibility, more so now considering the manner of her exit.'

William concurred, his mood subdued by the mere thought.

Mr Tombs pushed aside the file and glanced over to a cabinet set against the wall. 'Ah, there they are.'

William looked across, first to the cabinet and then, as the commissioner turned his back, to the door. Guilt and a thousand worries flashed through his mind in that brief, unobserved moment. By the time the commissioner had returned and filled two glasses with a sample of the evidence, his fears lay concealed and undetected.

Mr Tombs held his glass aloft for scrutiny. On recognition of an old friend, the glasses came together in a soft chink and their contents were sipped. After the customary, involuntary intake of breath, the embers were allowed to glide out appreciatively between their lips.

'Two years is far too long to have waited,' said Mr Tombs with a satisfying sigh.

William reflected – two years had indeed passed since his late-night foray into the lounge at Matilda's and the pilfering of its bar stock. He had thought it an impossible mission and yet, with heart pounding, had managed to avoid detection and the much-feared need to explain an inexcusable act.

'One bottle was a considerable achievement, Henry. Any more and the hunting pack would have been after a trophy.'

Henry Tombs laughed and indulged himself in another gratifying sip. 'I've never tasted a malt quite like it, not even Samuel can find anything to match. And to think how long it has existed and been enjoyed in secrecy by just a few. Well, William, maybe it's time for others to share in that privilege.'

'You sound confident.'

'I am. Of course, it's up to you now, what you say to Mrs McTavish when you manage to find her will be of primary importance.'

Henry Tombs grinned and tilted his glass for another mouthful of sheer pleasure, so adding a ginger glint to his bushy, grey sideburns. 'Are you sure you can handle her, William? Perhaps if I came with you … The alternative course forward may still be better coming from me.'

If he had considered the commissioner capable of avoiding airborne missiles long enough to get the vital few words across, William would have grasped the offer gladly. Instead, he respectfully declined.

'It's a tough assignment, William. I wish you luck.'

'I said no harm would come to her and I intend to honour my word. When is your meeting?'

'Later this evening, in this very room. There will be only a handful of trusted staff in the building by that time; knowledge that it has taken place will not get out.' Henry Tombs emptied his glass with a flourish and a final gasp.

'I will need to know the outcome,' said William.

'Return tomorrow morning at the same time and you'll have your answer. In the meantime, be discreet. We are all under a code of secrecy.'

William understood and took his leave. His task back at the Bridge House was now far more critical than he had wished for. He could not afford to fail.

Chapter 64

Jualth stomped down the three steps onto Lower Thames Street smouldering with rage. In a mood fit to kill, she hurled her hat at the first passing automobile that had the misfortune to be in the wrong place at the wrong time. The subsequent hoot that followed a crazed bout of corrective steering received an equally strong riposte from her lungs. The jacket soon went the same way, a gift for a hackney-carriage driver to take home to his wife, whether it fitted or not.

By the time she had covered the short distance to Billingsgate Market, her hair flowed freely over her white blouse, her arms were minus their gloves and her uncomfortable shoes were in imminent danger of not making it much farther. Cries of her name that resonated from the hall swept over her head as quickly as she flew past. She was of the same mind as the traders – to pack up her wares and head on home.

When Cutter and Nipper felt the platform tremor, they wisely concealed themselves within adjacent shops until the quaking cobblestones resettled.

'No 'at,' Nipper observed, as they re-emerged to watch the rampaging figure scale central arch.

'Didn't suit 'er anyhows,' said Cutter. 'I should've been there to 'elp out.'

'Don't think the governor will be 'appy she's lost it, all the same.'

At the mention of their master, both turned sharply in the direction of Princes' Gate. What had she done with him?

To their relief, the bridge master followed ten minutes later, dismissing all questions and ordering an immediate return to their duties. By the time he arrived at the Bridge House, Jualth was dressed in white, her bags packed and impatient to leave. William disappeared into his study and poured himself a whisky.

Ten seconds later, Jualth burst in. 'William, I need money. I cannot get home without money.'

'That can be arranged. Take a seat.'

'No time to sit down, I have a train to catch.'

'*Take a seat, Jualth!* Sit down, calm down, have a drink!'

The red of Jualth's rage quickly returned to her cheeks. 'Do not shout at me, William! And I will not calm down—'

'*Jualth! Take. A. Seat.* I will not give you a farthing until you have heard me out.'

In a weak, penniless position and facing a determined opponent, Jualth had little option but to kick the chair, then the desk, growl in frustration and finally fall into the chair. 'One minute, William. I will give you *one* minute.'

William poured then handed her a whisky that, with due irreverence, was quickly dispatched. 'Och, I cannot wait to taste the proper stuff again. The moon has more warmth than this vile liquid.'

William took a seat on the opposite side of the desk. 'You should not have walked out like that or attacked Mr Pennan in the manner you did.'

'Believe me, that was not the manner in which I wished to attack him.'

'*Jualth*, setting up that meeting was not an easy task. You paid no respect to *me*, the *commissioner* or Mr Pennan by—'

'What was difficult about *that*, William? How difficult can it be to set up a meeting that tells me nothing other than what I had expected to hear? I'm going to prison, we're all going to prison, the whole lot of us, and when, and if, we ever come out, we'll have no home to go back to. I could have waited in Scotland to learn all that.'

'Jualth, that is not all you would have been told, *but* it is something that you had to be told first.'

'Why?'

'So the commissioner could satisfy himself that you realised the seriousness of your situation and how damned lucky you'd be if the Excise Service did not seek such a recourse from their findings.'

The volley of abuse suddenly screeched to a halt. William had at last grabbed her attention. The noticeable red in her cheeks drained to a pallid white.

'What?'

Recognising a partial victory in the ensuing silence, William stood up. He needed to mask his own tension and any lingering odour from his indulgence in the Custom House. 'Wait a minute. Let me get another drink first.'

'William!'

'It will give you time to realise that by storming out of that meeting, you neglected to hear a possible way out of your problem.'

Having refilled the glasses, he returned to his seat – care was still needed for the meeting to proceed as he wished. 'Are you prepared to listen now or is this one more occasion when your temper will gain the upper hand?'

Jualth said nothing. Sulkily, she sat back and permitted William the same icy stare she had reserved for Mr Pennan.

'Firstly, if you insist on returning to Scotland today, that will be it – no way out. What you heard from the commissioner will be the final, unalterable outcome.'

'Tell me why I'm staying, then.' Her cold response was understandable; Jualth believed she had been badly let down. It made the task of helping no easier.

'It's a possible way out that will depend upon one more meeting. I shall know the outcome of that tomorrow.'

'What's the way out?' Jualth asked, her manner unaltered.

'It's an agreement between three parties—'

Impulsively, Jualth interrupted, 'Us, the Excise and ... and who else, William?'

The bridge master took a deep and very irritated breath. 'Jualth, will you please let me explain before jumping in and speculating? The agreement will be between the Kvairen Distillery, the Brethna Distillery and one other.'

'The Excise,' said Jualth, ignoring his instruction.

William ground his teeth, exasperated, but determined to maintain control.

'It must be the Excise,' she insisted.

'I can't go into specifics, except to say the agreement requires one person to represent your interests, one person to represent the interests of the Brethna Distillery and a final person to represent the interests of the third party.'

'Why do we need Brethna to be included in this deal?'

'It's impossible to leave them out. They have knowledge of your whisky and the investigation into you and your distillery.'

'What about their own investigation?'

'It's covered in the agreement. Once it is signed, both investigations will be concluded.'

Jualth shook her head – she didn't believe it. No heroic knight, however noble, could rescue her that easily. Something was wrong, something she had yet to discover.

'And to get such an agreement, William, we will have to do *what* precisely?'

'Very little. Be prepared to supply your whisky unblended or in any way altered to the third party.'

William allowed a moment for contemplation. Jualth had not instinctively jumped in and refused the condition – that was an encouraging sign.

'Because of the secrecy of this transaction, no payment will be made to you and no paperwork, other than a contract, will be issued. The agreement can only work if all parties agree to total secrecy and do not delve where their curiosity would not be welcome.'

Jualth continued to shake her head in disbelief. 'What's going on here, William? What is Her Majesty – our omnipresent sovereign – and her Excise Service up to? If they are not the third party, why are they turning a blind eye to us wee Scottish lawbreakers?'

William took a mouthful of whisky – all he needed was Jualth's acceptance to the arrangement, not her understanding. The least he had to explain, the better for everyone.

'This is not a perfect solution, Jualth. You will be kept in the dark and will have to trust me and others to keep the agreement binding.'

Trust! The word induced a flicker of amusement – was that all? Have faith in an unknown person or persons, hidden somewhere in the maze of London streets. 'Maybe you, William … *maybe*, but no one else.' Her head did not stop moving. 'Are you sure you're telling me everything you're able to?'

William was resolute in his assertion and his delivery. He did not waver. 'I can tell you no more.'

'What about the name of the third party?' William refused to budge. 'All right, everything you can tell me *other* than the name of the third party.'

'Nothing, Jualth. If you do not agree to this arrangement, the help I can give you finishes here and Mr Tombs will have no option but to prosecute. It's up to you. If all goes well tomorrow, you must tell me if you wish to proceed.'

Jualth didn't much like the answers she had been given. There was little comfort in a lack of options and the need to rely on blind trust. It would be nice to know *who* she was trusting. Maybe with some Hawks of her own … 'How much whisky will you require?'

'A relatively small amount.'

'And what will happen to it?'

'Its consumption will go no farther than the third party.'

'Really,' Jualth muttered sceptically. It was hard to accept that she did not have the right to know the destination of her own whisky. It had always been her job to control its flow.

'These people must be very powerful, William. *You* must be.'

William shook his head. 'Influence maybe, but not power.' Institutions and the individuals that ran them had power. All he knew to be fallible in its misuse.

'How legal is this, William?'

'The agreement will bind all parties and provide what mutual protection it can afford.'

Jualth choked on an involuntary laugh – what sort of an answer was that? 'So, is it legal or merely protected by powerful people – powerful but dishonest people?' She did not expect an answer to that question and neither did she wait for one. 'And is that it, the enormity of this incident can be resolved in one simple, questionably legal document?'

'It sounds simple, Jualth, but it has been anything but simple to put together and, need I point out, this arrangement has a fair distance to run before it is fully agreed.'

'But effectively, our whisky, the very thing that has got us into trouble will, if everything goes well, provide the way out.' Although the agreement lacked her control, it seemed to deliver everything she had sought when she set out from Scotland. She and her community would be safe.

'If you'd have waited for Mr Tombs to explain, he might have provided a better explanation than I have managed.' Either that or, coming from an eminent Excise official, its credibility may have suffered even more.

Jualth stood up and sauntered over to the drinks cabinet. She brought over the bottle, sat back down, poured herself a glass and left the bottle on the desk. 'This might not be much, but it's all there is.' She downed two large mouthfuls to maximise its limited, calming effect. 'I almost wish I hadn't been so nasty to dear Mr Pennan.'

William grunted, choosing to maintain his outer sternness, but the inner tension in his muscles had eased – Jualth was towing the line. 'Your conduct was inappropriate.'

'No it wasn't. I told him what I believed to be true. I hate that man and I'm glad I had the opportunity to acquaint him with my loathing. Mr Rule-Abiding Almighty can live with it just like we, and our like, live with the damage he has done to our lives.'

William rose to defend the much-maligned inspector – he had an important role to play in the agreement that, due to blinkered vision, Jualth could not see. 'He was doing his job and doing it well. You should be thankful for his discretion.'

'*What?*'

'If the agreement goes ahead, you can rely upon Mr Pennan to keep quiet.'

'Really,' Jualth said derisively. She took another swig of whisky, swished it distastefully around her mouth and swallowed. The ensuing fit of choking was only partially due to its inferior taste. 'You mean I have to return to that place to sign this thing?'

It was the bridge master's turn to pick up the bottle and pour a glass that was immediately put to use. 'The lack of the necessary clothing now in your possession aside, I think all parties can be spared another of your lively visits to the Custom House.'

The trail of discarded garments on his return, and the culprit's minimal guilt, had not gone unnoticed. But, with Jualth's apparent acquiescence to the plan, all other matters vanished into insignificance.

'I can pick up the unsigned agreements without calling upon your presence. Any questions you have, I shall endeavour to answer.'

Jualth felt mightily relieved, perhaps too relieved for her own good. 'So I sign it here?'

William shook his head. 'You will take three copies home for the two Scottish parties to sign and place their seal of authenticity on them. The third party will do likewise upon the contract's return to London. A copy will then be dispatched to the Brethna Distillery and yourself.'

'I understood most of what you just said, William. The bit about the seal I did not. I don't have one.'

William thought for a moment – an agreement could not be completed without an official stamp. 'Does anyone have a seal?'

Jualth screwed up her face – there had never been a need.

'Then we will have to get one made up. The Brethna Distillery will have one, as it is a company, and the third party will have one. I will need a name for your seal.'

The request prompted nothing but confusion. 'A name? What name?' The distillery did not belong to her, it belonged to the whole community. 'Do we have to become a company?'

William shook his head; the idea was fraught with danger. 'Perhaps, due to the secrecy of the arrangement and your situation, filing information that is open to the public at Companies House would not be advisable.'

'Then what name, William? How do we represent the whole community and retain our secrecy?'

Jualth tapped her glass against the bottle, the embryo of an idea taking shape in her head. Unwittingly, the weak mixture had provided some benefit, after all.

'What about me, William? Why can't I be a party to the agreement on behalf of everyone else? The tenure of the inn belongs to me, as does that of the distillery in a way, and if this whole thing unravels, then it will only be me that gets into trouble. Whilst I'm alive, no one else in my community can be held accountable for this agreement.'

'What happens when you are gone?' William asked. 'The agreement will still be in your name and not that of the community.'

In that respect, Jualth was way ahead of her fellow conspirator. 'That's one way of making sure you're never forgotten.'

The full implication of Jualth's idea took a moment to register. Although not entirely sure he approved, he could not help but admire the lightning ingenuity of the woman. 'You can't name the community after yourself, Jualth!'

A large self-satisfied grin slowly crept across the young redhead's face – on the contrary, she could do as she pleased.

'*Jualth*, you can't—'

She laughed wickedly, for the first time that day feeling thoroughly pleased with herself. 'Watch me, William, *just* watch me. Put my name on that seal and be as discreet as you wish.' She stood up, about to depart.

'Where are you going?'

Jualth smiled. 'To see Albert. I need to cajole him into making an important adjustment to my plaque.'

She thought for a moment, her mood lightened by a conclusion she could never have foreseen after her melodramatic exit from the Custom House.

'Come to think of it, maybe cajoling will not be needed. After all, I'm only giving him what he asked for – a name.'

She wandered over to the door but stopped for one last departing word, just in case the bridge master was not the honest, trustworthy broker that he would have her believe.

'Oh, and by the way, William, tomorrow there will be one more Hawk on your bridge, one with her eyes firmly set upon its master. Just a friendly warning.'

She left the room, leaving William to reflect on the lack of thanks for his efforts. If she suspected anything, it was not obvious. He would, nevertheless, take her warning seriously. They were not out of the woods yet and much could still go wrong.

Chapter 65

On the murky grey morning that followed, Jualth adopted her accustomed position on Central Arch, her back to the thinning stream of City-bound commuters. It was a day when neither the passing traffic nor the sombre sight upstream tempted the slightest glance. All attention lay in the direction of Lower Thames Street and the fleeting appearances between the buildings of an upright, striding, eastbound figure.

'Good news, William, that's all I want to hear – return with nothing less.'

A wave of a hand from the steps outside Billingsgate Hall caught her eye. It was Sid, worried by her lack of response the previous day. His wave turned into a questioning thumbs up. Jualth raised a hand, enough to indicate her wellbeing and sufficient to allay his fears. He smiled, tapped this forelock in a small, but friendly salute and returned to his stall in much better cheer.

Cutter sidled up from the Southwark end; Jualth had not been herself the day before, at mealtime or on the bridge. It was unusual for her to prefer isolation and not seek company. He adopted his most spirited manner. 'How ye doin' today, missis? Better, now?'

Jualth looked around. Her voice was muted. 'That all depends upon your master, Lloyd. Let's wait to see what he brings back.'

That didn't sound too good. Cutter persevered with his exuberance. 'How's about a walk before 'e returns then? Plenty of places we 'aven't been to yet.' Jualth remained unresponsive. 'Or maybe the same places as before, the ones you like.'

Jualth reached out an arm, beckoning the young and persistent Hawk to her side – she did not want to appear too unfriendly. 'The future is uncertain, Lloyd. I cannot plan a solitary hour ahead, let alone half a day.'

Cutter nodded; that really did not sound too good at all. Her mood had taken a turn for the worse with the donning of the much-hated outfit the previous day, and the trip to the Custom House had only served to compound it further. He hoped that the consequences of his secretive errand to the Custom House on the first day of her arrival had not added to the dip in her spirits.

'Saw Sid earlier on, missis. 'e asked after you, said you stormed past yesterday without a word, sheddin' most of what you were wearin'. Think 'e's worried about you.' Him and everyone else, Cutter thought. ''E asked if you'd like to come back, spend a full morning with him and the lads. He said they'd all enjoy your company again.'

Jualth forced a grin; it was a nice sentiment even if a trip to the fish market no longer served a higher purpose. 'We'll see, Lloyd.'

Cutter sighed, noting the lack of enthusiasm in her voice and his failure to extract any uplift in her spirits. Uncertain what else to say, he assumed the role of the Hawk, looking around, assessing the immediate environment for threats.

'You missed your lesson yesterday, Lloyd, I'm sorry,' said Jualth, showing regret for having let him down. 'We'll make up for it today.'

'Will we, missis?'

'Yes, Lloyd, we will. And …' she added, 'I want to invite William along if you're willing. It's about time I collected on my wager. Do you feel up to it?'

Of course he felt up to it. He knew the importance of the dress, just as Jualth knew how much he wanted to prove himself worthy to his master. He smiled, but the reassuring look soon turned into a pensive frown.

Jualth sensed a problem. 'What is it, Lloyd?'

He began to shuffle uneasily. 'Well … I was just wondering, with you wanting to collect the outfit for your sister, does that mean you will soon be leaving?'

'It does, Lloyd. Regardless of whether it's good or bad news that William brings back, I shall be leaving very soon.'

The prospect of an imminent parting came as a much bigger blow than he had expected. In her short spell in London, she had become part of bridge life and, as a consequence, part of all their lives. Nevertheless, Cutter showed his support. 'Let's hope it's good news, Jualth.'

Jualth heard the sorrow in his voice and was again touched; she had grown very fond of the young man. The minor miracle that he had managed to remember her name was a bonus and hopefully a good omen. 'Mrs Tuckle might wish otherwise, but thanks anyway, Lloyd. It was a sweet thing to say.'

For the umpteenth time, Cutter grimaced – try as he had, he could not get used to his new name. Up until that point, Jualth had ignored his struggle.

'Why not come and visit me in the countryside, see where I live? You might like it or, better still, prefer it to your life here.'

'Don't think the master would let me, missis.'

'He would if I asked him. Think about it, Lloyd, let me know before I go. And as for your name, and that funny face you make every time you hear it … you'll keep it, won't you? Keep it for me?'

Cutter again shuffled uneasily; the battle was far from won and without help there seemed little chance of success.

'Oh well, I'll leave that to you to decide, but whatever decision you make, you will always be Lloyd to me.'

Cutter nodded, having taken on board the choice he had and her wishes. He again cast a studious eye over his territory and the well-dressed City folk.

'Best be about my business, missis. Far too many dodgy-lookin' characters out today to stand 'ere for too long. You know what to do if you need me.'

Jualth pursed her lips together and blew silently into the breeze as Cutter, saddened by the news that his watch would soon lack its central character, trundled off towards the chapel.

Before St Magnus had tolled a quarter past the hour, Jualth observed the westerly return of a very important messenger. Although keen to head him off, she stayed exactly where she was until the bridge master had settled on the balustrade and both, for some reason, were staring at the Tower of London.

'Well …?' she asked after five interminable seconds of silence. 'Am I to be a free woman or an imminent resident of *that* chamber of horrors?'

William took a few unnecessary seconds before finally relenting. 'Hopefully, a free woman. From this end, at least, the work is done.'

Jualth's outward stillness did not change as she breathed in and held her breath. When she finally exhaled, all the enormous, built-up tension ebbed away with it. Those were the words she had wanted to hear and the reason she had journeyed so far south. Her eyes left the Tower and settled upon her companion, a prelude to a gentle kiss on the side of the face.

'There, that's allowed, isn't it? And if you say no, I don't care. Thank you.' The thanks were acknowledged with a thin, but appreciative smile. 'I'm glad I came to London, William, and I'm glad you came to see us all that time ago. If you ever choose to visit again, we'll allow you back.'

The invitation was received with guarded enthusiasm. 'We'll see,' he said. 'There's plenty of time to consider such things.'

'No, there isn't,' Jualth refuted. 'Be complacent and time soon runs away and all the opportunities that go with it. Make your mind up now, William, before it's too late.'

The return of Jualth's spirit and her forceful advice was not enough to sway the bridge master. 'Thanks,' he said, 'but the answer remains the same.'

His reluctance to commit needed no more explanation than his refusal to allow her back into his bed after their one night of turbulent passion. His inbred sense of duty carried a life sentence for both parties.

'When will I get the agreement?' Jualth asked.

'In a couple of days, no more. It will be drafted without delay.'

'And the seal?'

'The same. I took pre-emptive measures yesterday.'

'I admire your confidence. So, I could be going home very soon?'

'You could,' William agreed before quietly adding, 'if that's what you want?'

Raising a question mark against her future plans took Jualth by surprise – was this the reason for his subdued mood since his return and his way of expressing his true feelings and wishes towards her? If so, there was little that she could do to help him. He knew she had to go back in the same way she knew he had to stay.

'London has been an experience, William, but there are things I cannot live without: clean, soot-free air for example and cross-country gallops through an unspoiled landscape. It would also be nice to have a sight of gleaming blue water as opposed to the dirty, grey-brown stew we see before us. I love your bridge and I'm proud of what you've done. I'm even quite fond of the people on and around it too, but it's in the wrong place, you know it is. I could never be happy in London, just like you could never be happy living anywhere else. What does your town and my home have in common?'

William didn't bother to argue; it was clear her mind was already halfway back to the Highlands.

Jualth turned her head away and allowed the breeze to caress her face. 'Can you hear them?' she whispered gently.

All William could hear was the usual noise of the city: the rumble of horse-drawn traffic, the chugging sound of boat engines and the occasional backfiring automobile. 'Hear what, Jualth?'

'Voices, William, voices from the past that look out for all us living souls of the present day. Seven hundred years of bridge history is a considerable amount of experience for the spirits to have gained. All you have to do is open yourself up and listen to what they say.'

'And that's what you do at Jade's Fall?'

'It is.'

'But why there? Why not the bay or on that large rock? What's so special about that small, rocky, fall of water?'

'I don't know that special is the right word, but it has a history and if something has a history it can speak to you.'

William glanced over his shoulder, just to make sure no one was listening. The mention of the spirits had rekindled his interest in the waterfall. He had a feeling its name resulted from no mere fairy tale, but a story that carried a particular resonance, quite possibly one that was not for an outsider's ear.

'If you want, I can tell you,' Jualth offered. 'I said I would and, if you're still interested, I'm prepared to keep my word.'

It was too late to back down now, his curiosity would not allow it. If necessary, William would curse his need to know later – in private. Facing east, with the breeze ruffling her white blouse, Jualth spoke as if talking to the river and its spirits as well as the bridge master.

'Many years ago, Jade lived on a smallholding in the eastern Highlands with her mother, scratching out enough to survive on but little more. They were poor though well respected, largely down to the position held by Jade's mother as the local witch.'

William fought hard to contain his astonishment. 'Sorry?'

Jualth smiled, enjoying his unease. 'Well, to some she was a witch. To others she was a pagan healer with an expertise in herbal medicine that she had passed on to her daughter.'

'Herbal medicine?'

'That's right, and well has it served us over the years.'

William nodded; somehow, he did not doubt it. He let the storyteller continue. She told him about Jade's friend Ruth and their secret place, a small waterfall where they could play in the water, climb on the rocks or just lie on the grass to chat about boys, children and their hopes for a better future.

When they grew up, their fortunes had differed, with Jade working as a barmaid at The Hidden Lodge (now called Matilda's) and Ruth (who was the landlord's niece and heir) already a young widow. Ruth lived in Lonistle with her baby daughter Isobel and Jamie, her brother-in-law.

'Jade got on well with the landlord, Tapper Joe, and eventually moved in to care for the old boy. She saw it as an opportunity and was prepared to marry him to provide her own heir. The age difference meant little; she was not marrying for love. Security meant more and, even with the best intent in the world, the union could hardly have lasted for long.'

'You make her sound cold. How can you know that?' William asked.

'Because we know Jade and, very shortly, so will you.'

Jualth then told of Tapper's premature demise, leaving his barmaid newly pregnant but unmarried. Ruth inherited the inn and took up residence, bringing Jamie – whom she was sweet on – with her. It was an unwitting ruse on Ruth's part that did not account for the demands of another woman. Jade, needing to conceal the true identity of her unborn child's father, quickly seducing and married Jamie, a young man yearning for manhood.

'Why are men so easily led?' William muttered.

'Because they all want to be loved and are vulnerable because of it. Women merely know how to be resourceful when the need arises. I see no harm in that.'

William grunted. That was something they would have to disagree on. He let it lie.

Taking up the story, Jualth told him how Ruth had received help and affection from Jade, so much so that she took as fate the news that her best friend had fallen in love with Jamie. Ruth was far too trusting and could never have comprehended Jade's betrayal.

This only confirmed William's assessment of the young woman. It did not bode well for the rest of the story, which appeared to be heading towards anything but a righteous end.

'Jade had a girl, a touch premature in the eyes of a canny few, and she continued to live at the inn. The daughters grew up as their mothers had, exploring the countryside and discovering the waterfall. It was here that, with Ruth and Jade's encouragement, they spent many days playing in their own special world. But, as you have seen for yourself, the waterfall is a place to treat with respect. Bear that in mind when you think of careless youngsters who used it as a playground.'

In the context of the story, William braced himself for what was to come.

'One day, Jade's little girl, Braid, came home in a shocking state, telling of a dreadful accident. Ruth and Jade took to their horses and when they arrived at the falls, they found the body of Ruth's child at the bottom. There were no witnesses apart from Jade's daughter and, as she was no more than a wee lass, nobody saw how Isobel's fall could have resulted from anything *but* an accident.'

William did not like the doubt Jualth posed. Why place a sinister slant on such a dreadful event? '*Was* it an accident?' he asked

'It might have been, but it also might not. From this distance who can tell? Let's just say there was room for doubt.'

'The reason being?'

'The reason *being* ... Jade's influence on her daughter.'

'Which, you know about?'

'Yes, William. Where I come from, we all know how a mother can influence a daughter.'

William regretted making the comment. As Jualth had put it to him at the waterfall, a couple of years previously, there were things he quite simply did not need to know.

'Whilst growing up,' Jualth continued, 'Jade had confided in her daughter that they were the rightful owners of the inn, and Ruth and her daughter Isobel had taken it from them. Now whether this resulted in Braid pushing her best friend to her death ...? To all accounts, she suffered no mental anguish from the tragedy and carried on as a happy playful child. Read into that what you may.'

The story was getting worse and worse, and William had a feeling they had just touched on its meaning. Jualth told him how Ruth had heavily depended upon Jade's support after her devastating loss and, with her encouragement, had often visited the falls to be closer to Isobel's spirit. It came as no surprise when she did not return one day. Her body had been found as close as makes no difference to the place where Isobel had lain. The assumption was that Ruth had jumped from the same position as the daughter had slipped.

'Jumped?' William asked, 'or pushed, if not literally, then by some other means?'

Jualth smiled, he seemed to have grasped the point. 'As before, Ruth's reliance on Jade meant there were no witnesses to say she died from anything other than her own grief.'

Even so, to the bridge master there was no doubt where the blame lay. 'But Jade still didn't inherit the inn.'

'No, it went to Jamie, Ruth's next of kin.'

'And so the resourceful scheming did not end there,' said William.

Jualth smiled again, the bridge master was proving a good listener. She then told of Jamie's growing suspicions. Braid in no way resembled him and, although he did not believe it possible that his wife had slept with Tapper Joe, the thought festered every time he clamped eyes on his supposed daughter. He took to drink, and Jade made sure he had plenty pushed his way. His premature death – thrown from his horse – came as no surprise.

'Any witnesses?' William asked.

'None … as before.'

William nodded; he should have known and perhaps he did.

'Jade played out the role of the bereaved widow and received solace from her community.'

'And no one doubted Jamie's death was an accident?'

Jualth shrugged. 'So the story goes. But the long and short of it is that Jade had achieved the very thing she had sought since donning the barmaid's apron. She had what she wanted and if the locals wished to continue enjoying Kvairen whisky, it was in their interest not to care how she got it.'

If Jade had not been such a deplorable, unsympathetic figure, William might have found that comment amusing. 'How far has the herbal medicine bit been passed down in your community?'

'To the present day. Lily knows far more than I do; you should have asked her whilst you had the chance.'

'And it had no part in this story?'

'I expect it did, but who's to say.'

William grunted; it was just a passing thought and, upon reflection, he was rather glad that he had not asked at the time.

'There's one last thing, William.'

'And what's that?'

'Out of respect to the landlords – up to and including Tapper Joe – Jade took on their surname. And from that day forth, the family name of the proprietor has never changed.'

William nodded; that much he had expected. Jade McTavish, matriarch to Jualth and all landladies in-between. How alike were they? It was a worrisome thought.

'You did ask, William,' said Jualth sensing his disquiet.

'I did; I have no one to blame but myself. Having said that, a tale loosely based on the truth that did not show your ancestors in quite such a savage light would have sufficed.'

Jualth disagreed. 'You asked because you wanted a better understanding of my family and its position at the centre of our community. Distorting the truth would not have achieved that.'

That was true, but William had not expected the truth as told. Most families covered up their unsavoury history, letting it die in the mire of the distant past. Jualth was the embodiment of the complete opposite, and her willingness to tell was not without reason.

'No one crosses us if they have any sense, William. We are very unforgiving. Finding a place where we belonged was only achieved through much suffering. We will not give it up easily.'

'Ruth didn't cross you.'

'In a way she did, though of course, she wasn't to know.' Jualth paused a moment before adding, 'When you think about it, it's really rather sad.'

The sympathetic afterthought suggested that it was quite possibly the first time Jualth had spared such a thought for Ruth. He wondered if her family's other victims had suffered the same callous disregard.

'But what about Jade's Fall? Why was it named after Jade and not Ruth or Ruth's daughter?'

'Because it helped to fulfil her dreams. A family and a home, in short, a better life.'

'And the spirits?'

'Are there to guide whomever they deem a friend. That includes you.' Jualth smiled, noticing the disquieting effect she had wished to see. 'This isn't a happy tale, William, but there you have it. Just remember, you were told in confidence.'

As with everything else that involved a certain isolated community, little travelled beyond its borders.

'So, William, in future if you need to know anything, come here to this spot, ask your question and let the spirits talk to you. It works for me – Lily too.'

'I'll bear it in mind.'

'Don't just bear it in mind, give it a go. That was half the reason for telling you the story. I'm part of your history; when you come here you can talk to me, ask me questions, as I do of you at Jade's Fall.'

William had not realised. It touched him to know he had not been forgotten during his absence – far from it.

'Romantic, aren't I?' said Jualth. 'Good job my dear husband never knew.'

Having finished on a note that had moved the recipient, Jualth decided it time to mention her reward. 'I will be departing shortly and I want that dress you promised Lily. You can come to Lloyd's lesson this afternoon to see how much he's improved under my guidance.'

'That won't be necessary.'

'Yes, it will,' Jualth insisted. 'Lloyd wants the chance to impress. He deserves that after so much effort.'

Ignoring the young Hawk's efforts had not been William's intention. He wanted Lily to have the dress regardless of any debt owed. William had much to thank Cutter for, not least for finding Jualth in the first place and then keeping her occupied. And he hoped his gratitude to the lad would not end there.

'I shall be happy to come to his lesson,' he agreed, 'but first I would like to make a suggestion that involves Cutter.'

'Why not call him Lloyd? Cutter will do him no favours when he leaves you.'

'Has he taken to the name?'

'Perhaps if you helped me.' William looked doubtful. 'Well think about it, but make sure you do something.'

William could not commit himself to such a promise. Instead, he returned to his suggestion. 'I want you to have company on your journey back to Scotland and, although Cutter may only be a boy, he will be more than adequate insurance for your safety.'

'Why not come with me yourself, William?'

William felt another tug of the emotions; the reasons were complicated, more so now. Even a trip north that was intended to last for no longer than the duration of the journey might turn into something more permanent. He needed to be in London for his bridge and, although she did not know it, for Jualth as well. 'You know I can't.'

'Do I? One day your bridge will survive without you, it will have no choice.'

'When the time comes, I will make sure it is left in good hands.'

It was not the first time she believed William had chosen the bridge ahead of her and, although she understood, it still hurt. However, providing Cutter as an escort was a touching sentiment, even if she had managed the journey south without the need for a protective guard. 'Lloyd will have to do, then. It will give me a chance to show him the world beyond London town. Shall I tell him?'

William shook his head. He was keen to perform the task himself.

'You never know, I might keep him if he wants to stay.'

'You can have him for a week and no more. And do not initiate him in your whisky whilst he is with you.'

'I was much younger …'

'Jualth!'

She laughed freely, just as she had done in Scotland in his company. 'Okay, I'll look after him, just like a big sister. It will be fun showing him the wonders he's missing. You never know, maybe I'll succeed with him where I have failed with you.' She gave him a teasing look. 'In fact, I think I'll enjoy the challenge.'

Chapter 66

Jualth managed to purchase Lily's dress in Silk 'n' Lace Street without calling upon Cutter's fashion expertise, though his ability to carry all the wares when they were ready did come in handy. With William's permission, she also bought garments for her daughter and grandmother, so impressed was he by the advance in her pupil's reading and writing. Proud would have been a more apt description, but perhaps competitive jealousy rcined in the urge to make such a feeling known.

A trip to her favourite park had preceded the liberal spending of the bridge master's money, but only because it took them past Frostfair Art College. On this occasion, Cutter succumbed to the pressure and allowed Jualth to drag him inside. Much to her delight, when the time arrived to leave, the same force was needed to drag him out.

The Highland Fires did not receive another visit. Jualth rightly surmised a continued smarting by the proprietor for the financial loss incurred on her previous visit. Samuel's blood pressure needed more time to recuperate.

The agreement arrived early the following morning. In the study, its contents received close scrutiny. Jualth had little to say; all that was required to fulfil her part of the bargain were a few bottles of whisky on request. How could she refuse such an agreement if it left her community the right to an indefinite existence without fear of official interference? Cutter took the agreement straight back and by the evening three copies of the full contract rested in Jualth's baggage.

Dinner that evening involved all of William's staff, including Albert and Three-Fingers White, the Bridge Carpenter. The latter had presented William with a paperweight depicting the Chapel, Central Arch and Nonesuch House to replace the priceless artefact damaged in the heat of passion. He had also carved a replica for Jualth as a reminder of her time in London.

Albert had finished the plaque, been awarded a huge kiss and a warm hug, and further encouraged to retire to the countryside. William would provide directions if he chose to take up an invitation to visit her home.

Mrs Tuckle received apologises for a poor appetite – except on the two occasions when the menu had included fish – and, in return, Mrs Tuckle asked after the arrangements for her homeward journey: firstly, to make sure nothing had been overlooked and, secondly, for the sheer joy of hearing (for the umpteenth time) that their guest was leaving.

Finally, commendations for spying were imparted upon each of the Hawks – who took turns to patrol the bridge – along with thanks for the care they had shown.

When the next morning came, Mrs Tuckle even accompanied Jualth as far as the front door but, unsurprisingly, did not linger once their guest had crossed the threshold. Jualth said her farewells to Albert and Three-Fingers White, who stood waiting by the side gate to wish her a safe journey.

'I feel almost sad,' said Jualth as, accompanied by William, she commenced her last walk across the bridge. 'If all goes well, I'll never see any of this again.'

'There's every reason to suppose it will,' William assured her.

A three-strong party of Hawks stood waiting at the edge of the Southwark arcade.

'Never been able to get farther than this point without Jamba knowing,' said Jualth, smiling warmly.

'The quietest footsteps I've ever had to listen out for, Miss Jualth; as if you were walkin' on air.'

Jamba received the first hug, affection that followed for Stretch and Nipper on their final parting.

'Seen much of Josephine, Emma or Polly since our informal evening?' Jualth asked with a hint of mischief, as they walked through the first arcade.

'Lucy, I've seen a lot of Lucy,' William answered in kind. 'Now we're on first-name terms, it seems impolite not to enquire into the progress of her reading and writing.'

'She's too young, William,' Jualth said in all seriousness. 'Please tell me you won't wait for Lucy to grow up.'

To her chagrin, Jualth received no assurances. William was too busy glancing around to make sure she had not been overheard. 'Looking forward to seeing your daughter?' he asked.

'I am desperate to see everyone: Jessica, Grandma, Lily ...' Jualth sighed almost painfully. 'Dear Lily, I wonder how she is? Another week and I swear she would have come looking for me. I seem to recall an intention to write, but ...' Her brow furrowed as she struggled to recollect. 'Something must have happened to distract me.'

'Remember to pass on my regards to all your family and friends,' said William, choosing to skip past that particular distraction.

'I will pass on your love, William, especially to Lily. She needs all that is on offer.'

William nodded; regards did seem overly formal.

They reached the top of Central Arch and Jualth, for the last time looked east, towards Tower Bridge, the Tower of London and, finally, the large colonnaded grey building. The deep blue of her eyes grew cooler: the institution within still held her fate in its hands. A building with fonder memories stood closer by – Billingsgate fish market, still busy at that early hour.

'I did the best I could with their fish,' said Jualth, in a defeated tone, 'but there's nothing like a Scottish freshwater salmon.'

Both smiled. *Freshwater* hardly went close to describing her true meaning. She took one last, lingering look, waved to Albert and Three-Fingers White, who had remained outside the Bridge House, then tugged on William's arm. Standing outside the arcade's last building at the City end was an extremely smart, good-looking lad waiting by his bag.

'Lloyd, I could not have asked for a more dashing escort.'

Cutter could not have put it better. 'Nothing but the best for you, missis.'

'Where did you get those clothes?'

'I took him shopping yesterday,' said William. 'All in all, I've spent rather a lot on clothes these past few weeks and without managing to furnish one garment for myself.'

'I know what you mean, William, the pleasure is in the giving, though for me, I must admit, it's in the receiving.' She laughed and let go of her escort. 'Right, one last stop and then it's onto the horse and cart.'

'It's called a buggy,' said William, as she moved away.

'Whatever, anything but the smoky Underground. I wonder how many people suffocate in those tunnels each day?'

It was a passing thought; Jualth was already heading down the steps towards St Magnus, leaving William and Cutter waiting at the top. Once inside, she sat in the same pew as on her first visit and waited for Anthony to join her.

'So you did not need my counsel after all,' said the priest as he sat alongside.

'Crisis averted, Anthony.' She crossed her fingers to indicate that the dense surrounding woods had thinned but not vanished.

'In which case, I will not get to hear about the troubles that brought you so far. I would have welcomed the chance to help.'

'Thanks for the thought but, from now on, it's down to my own priest and he pretty much knows everything already.'

Anthony nodded. 'Sounds like he has an interesting parish.'

If only the priest knew the half of it. Jualth felt relieved that the need for solace had not involved another. A warm scrap of paper appeared from somewhere within her clothing and was handed over.

'An address to write to in Brethna, Anthony. You'll keep me informed, won't you? I want to know what happens to William *and* to Lloyd. I shouldn't like to lose contact completely.'

'I'll write and, as promised, will not let them know, though why you cannot write to them directly ...?'

'It has to be this way, please don't ask me to explain.'

The priest conceded; it was not the time to go against her wishes.

'I'd better go, I have a train to catch and they're waiting for me. I thought about riding the whole way, but I'm desperate to get back the quickest way possible.'

'Have a safe journey, Jualth, and I hope your troubles are soon resolved.'

'So do I, Anthony.' Jualth embraced the priest and left the church to rejoin the party patiently waiting on the bridge platform.

'Okay, William, Lloyd, all done. I'm ready to go.'

'What about Sid?' William asked.

'Did you not hear me creep down the stairs first thing this morning?' Jualth asked. 'As it was my last day, Jamba switched allegiance and as for Lloyd … conspicuous by his absence.'

William looked at Cutter, who shrugged his shoulders. 'Getting a good night's sleep, Guv, as ordered.'

'And stop sniffing, William. You can smell nothing but the sweet scent of the country upon me.'

They jumped into the waiting buggy and commenced their ascent of Fish Street Hill. As they passed the towering Monument, Jualth turned for her last glimpse of Old London Bridge and the church by its side. She knew she would never see either again. They slipped over the crest of the hill and the river was gone. An overland journey to King's Cross railway station lay ahead.

They arrived in good time to catch the imperious black monster that stood puffing steam by the side of the platform. William dealt with the bags, stacking them onto overhead racks inside their carriage. He called down, noticing both passengers had remained outside.

'Do you need a hand up?'

Jualth tapped her companion on the shoulder. 'You first, Lloyd. I'll join you after I've had a word with William.'

'Take good care of her, Lloyd,' said William, giving him a farewell pat on the back as he stepped down.

With a curious glance back for his master's choice of name, Cutter climbed into the carriage, then made sure he had selected the best seats.

'Well, William, that's the second time we've met without prior warning. Do you think there'll be a third time?'

Much to his regret, he did not. 'If I do not see you again, I shall know you are safe.'

Pedestrians laden with bags shuffled past, passengers and helpers who thought nothing of the young couple – possibly a husband and wife – in the throes of a tearful farewell.

'You're not going to kiss me, are you?' said Jualth, having stood expectantly for long enough.

'It's a public place ...'

'Aye it is, William, and it's also the last opportunity you may ever get.' She bridged the small gap between them and reached up to impart a soft kiss on his lips. She stood back, the touchpaper lit. 'That ain't going last me.' She closed in again, reached up and gripped tightly. This time the kiss was long and heartfelt, neither caring for the public indiscretion.

Jualth staggered back, surprised by the passion and fierceness of his embrace. 'Whoa, William!' she gasped breathlessly. 'I'll certainly remember that.'

They stood motionless, capturing a lasting image in their final seconds together.

'Look after yourself, Jualth.'

'I will and I'll send Lloyd back no less pure than he is today.'

'And with the agreement signed. I'll handle the rest.'

Jualth wanted to show her appreciation again. She resisted, settling for a softly spoken word of gratitude. 'Thanks again, William. If this doesn't work out, I won't blame you. You did everything you could.'

They shared a final lingering stare, then Jualth stepped into the carriage and William closed the door behind her.

'You have a few minutes before the train moves out,' he said through the open window.

'Take care,' Jualth whispered, knowing he would not stay to watch the train depart.

William stepped back, his eyes still on her. With only her memory to look forward to, he broke the tie and, without another glance, strode into the distance.

Chapter 67

Jualth cast a concerned look to her side. Perched uncomfortably upon the most docile mare the stable-hand could find, her companion sat drained of colour and, for five whole minutes, bereft of the will to even moan. 'How are you now, Lloyd?' she enquired tentatively. 'Got used to sitting on top of the "snortin' beast"?'

The pale-looking youth summoned up what little energy he had left to answer, 'Don't think I'm gunna be sick again, if that's what you mean, missis. Don't think it's possible.'

'You looked unwell when you got off the train. Blame the iron monster instead of the "snortin' beast".'

Thanks to Jualth's patient encouragement, Cutter had eventually forsaken his tight grip around the horse's neck for a more conventional upright posture. Sadly, he had yet to master any rhythmic empathy with the mare, so restricting their progress to a gentle stroll.

'Is there much farther to go, missis?'

'Not in distance, Lloyd, but, at this pace, a considerable amount in time. How about trying another jog?'

Cutter shook his head; the mere mention turned his stomach. He suggested an alternative course of action. 'Can I get off and walk again, missis?'

'*Lloyd!*'

'Just for a few minutes. Get some blood circulating in my behind again. It damn near feels like it's died.'

Jualth groaned – horse riding was apparently not second nature to city dwellers south of the border. 'This is the last time, Lloyd. At some point we *must* make haste.'

She jumped down to help her unhappy novice dismount. Once again she found herself walking alongside her supposed protector. She looked at him curiously as his nose began to twitch and his teeth to strangely gnash. On previous occasions when he had felt sick he had just thrown up, there had been no preamble. 'What are you doing?' she asked.

Cutter raised his face slightly to the sky and breathed in. 'It's this air, missis. Never tasted anything like it. Takes some getting used to.'

'After what you've had to breathe in all your life that doesn't surprise me. That said, it's not the best time of the year to visit the countryside with autumn upon us. I'll invite you back in the spring when the McTavish girls cast their colourful spells of rebirth.'

'Never took you for a witch, missis.'

'A kindly one but with a supply of nasty spells up my sleeve for the deserving. You can mention that to everyone when you get back.'

Cutter stopped his strange facial expressions and stared about him. He saw nothing but a landscape full of fields, trees and distant hills. 'Where is everyone?' he asked. 'Does no one else live up here?'

'That's another thing you'll have to get used to. The only crowds you're likely to see will be those drinking in the locals, and the only similarity you'll find with the town is that the roads go all over the place. I wonder if they'll ever think to hire a sober worker?'

'How did the master manage to find you? There's no telling where we're 'eadin'?'

'A map will get you to Brethna but not my home. With one notable and unwelcome exception, only friends and those born and bred in our community know the way.'

It was all new to Cutter – a park with no boundaries and a wilderness with no buildings. 'Scary,' he muttered.

Jualth smiled. She had felt the same way only a few weeks before when everything about her was also new and unfamiliar.

'You could be the only person alive out here,' said Cutter. 'No 'ouses, no people, no 'elp on 'and when needed.'

'What do you need help for?'

Cutter shrugged. 'Highwaymen.'

Jualth groaned again – Cutter was already proving a challenge. 'So, your first impressions of the countryside are mixed. The horses make you sick, the air doesn't contain enough soot for your taste buds, you're worried about being attacked by roadside bandits and, if it wasn't for me, you'd be running back to the railway track.'

Cutter nodded.

'*Townies!*' Jualth despaired. Why was she bothering?

Darkness had descended by the time the foot-weary travellers arrived in Brethna. They tied the horses to the railings under the sign of the Whisky Makers' Arms.

'A quiet evening,' Jualth observed. 'Perhaps the village is still in mourning.'

She hesitated on the doorstep; it was little more than a month since Brethna had lost one of its sons – her husband. She should have been in mourning herself and yet …

She pushed open the door. Gus sat at the bar, the palm of his hand supporting his chin whilst he gazed into oblivion. An extremely underworked landlord looked up to gaze upon his fifth and sixth customers of the evening.

'Hello, Gus, fancy meeting you here,' Jualth said cheerily.

Despite a gathering of only four sleepy locals, the unusual hush that descended seemed deafening. Jualth stared from face to face – their astonishment could not have been greater if her dead husband had walked into the inn instead.

'Say something, Gus. Anyone!'

Gus slipped off his seat and straightened his creaking back. 'The missing woman,' he declared in a ghostly whisper.

Jualth shrank – if only she had remembered to write.

'Folks in these parts were beginning to wonder if they'd ever see you again,' said Gus, in a more earnest tone. 'You'd better get off home first thing in the morning before your family go stark raving crazy.'

Jualth decided to accept the admonishment, feeling perhaps that it was well deserved. Cutter stared uneasily between them – it had so far proved a less than friendly welcome. Jualth put her arm around him, so adding to his discomfort.

'This is Lloyd, Gus, a dear friend who looked after me on foreign soil and once had the good fortune to save my life. Likewise, he's been my protector on my journey home.'

'He looks very pale,' Gus said gravely. 'Are you feeling unwell, lad?'

'First time on a train,' said Jualth on his behalf.

'And an 'orse,' said Cutter, just to prove he was capable of speaking up for himself.

'Aye, well just as long as it isn't one of those city sicknesses,' said Gus in all seriousness.

'*Gus*,' Jualth said sternly. The landlord had not moved from the bar or changed his manner of address since ordering her to return home in the morning. 'I appreciate the concern for Lloyd and the worry caused by the length of my absence, but are you or are you not pleased to see me?'

In the shock of discovering Jualth to still be alive, Gus realised he had overlooked the customary pleasantries that befitted the arrival of an absent friend. All that quickly changed. A flicker of a smile turned into a full welcome. He lifted the hatch and, together with his sparse patronage, greeted the tired travellers warmly.

The horses and bags were taken care of, rooms allocated, and hot water provided. When Jualth and Cutter returned to the bar suitably refreshed, Craig had swelled the numbers to seven.

'How was the great city?' Craig asked once they had settled.

'Good in parts, horrible in most others. The good parts were the people and, as you can see, I've brought one of the best home with me. Do you like him?'

'C'mon, missis, stop muckin' about,' said Cutter, shuffling with embarrassment in the gaze of unknown faces.

'And I'm proud of how he's adapted to the countryside, even if it did take longer than expected to make a horseman out of him.'

'Any chance of a rest tomorrow? I ache all over,' Cutter said with innocent optimism.

'No, Lloyd, trust me, tomorrow you will be fine.'

'You'll be straight off in the morning then?' said Craig.

'After I've seen Frazer's mother. I should show my face.'

'You won't find her at home,' Gus said hesitantly. There was something ominous in the way he delivered the news and then fired a quick glance at Craig.

'There's nothing wrong, is there?' Jualth asked.

'Nothing wrong in the sense that she is ill or worse,' said Craig.

'So why have you got me worried?'

Gus braved the responsibility to pass on the news. 'Lily took Martha home when she departed with Jessica. She didn't like to leave her behind.'

As they had feared, Jualth did not greet the news warmly. 'And she's still there?'

Gus nodded.

'It mightn't be permanent,' Craig said, a scenario that did nothing to lift Jualth's spirits.

'You're damn right there, Craig. Whatever ideas Martha has, and however much sympathy I feel for Frazer's loss, my mother-in-law is not living under the same roof as me.'

Cutter, who had convinced Gus that he was old enough to sit at the bar or, more likely, sit where Gus could keep an eye on the shifty-looking urchin, listened intently whilst supping a soft drink. 'Frazer was your husband, missis? You've never said his name before.'

'Not something I choose to talk about, Lloyd, though I should have mentioned his name to you. How is Lily, Gus? I take it you've heard from her.'

'Daniel has paid a visit more than once. Needless to say, she's found your absence difficult, especially with no word and …'

With a deeply felt pang of guilt, Jualth completed the landlord's sentence. 'And … without Harriet. She must be missing her terribly. I shouldn't have stayed away so long.'

'But you did and I expect with good reason,' said Gus. He had not pushed the point but, like Craig, he was more than interested to hear the news. Only a life-and-death battle would have kept Jualth from her home.

'There is hope, Gus. Nothing is certain, but we do have hope. I shall pop in to see Jack Vardy before I leave tomorrow. I need to arrange a board meeting.'

Craig glanced cautiously at Gus. Despite the sleepy appearance outside, life in Brethna had not stood still in her absence. 'Jualth, there's something else you should know. The old warehouse ...'

'What about it?'

'It's umm ... gone, cleared away. They've already dug foundations for a new stone building. It's quite a bit larger.'

Jualth looked aghast. 'What! Could they not have waited for the ashes to cool before they scraped my husband into a heap and dumped him on some godforsaken wasteland! Are the dead given no time to rest?'

'Did seem a bit premature,' Craig admitted.

'But that's Jack Vardy for you,' said Gus, 'a good head for business, but sometimes ...' He paused, not wishing to sound too unfair to the most important person in the village. 'Well, let's just say the human side gets overlooked.'

'Perhaps that's his way of thinking about the human side,' Craig said thoughtfully. 'Looking to the future; creating a sense of security for the rest of us.'

Jualth found the speed puzzling; it was almost as if the plans to replace the old warehouse had already existed. 'A much larger, stone building,' she whispered.

'What about it?' said Gus.

'He must've been very confident of surviving the inspection to have committed the distillery to such a large expense. That ramshackle, old warehouse would hardly have warranted a huge insurance payout.'

'Best to be optimistic for all our sakes,' said Craig.

'That's some optimism and some gall to turn a misfortune into such a quick business opportunity.'

Gus attempted to deflect the conversation away from the distillery boss. All knew about the ill-feeling between the two but neither he nor Craig wished to malign a man that held the respect of the entire community. 'A temporary replacement for Arthur came last week. Arthur's putting him up.'

'Let's hope it *is* temporary. If we manage to get through this, he shouldn't be the only one to suffer. Does he ever drop in?'

'Rarely. He was always more popular with you two girls than anyone else.'

Cutter tugged at Jualth's arm. 'Any chance of some grub, missis? I'm starvin'.'

Food was the last thing on Jualth's mind after a day of babysitting an invalid. 'Are you sure, Lloyd? I want to get home double-quick tomorrow and I can't have you being sick every five minutes.'

'Got nothin' but a big hole inside me. Got to have somethin', missis.'

Jualth found it impossible to deny the imploring, innocent face. 'Gus, any chance?'

Gus looked dubious. 'You sure you're all right, lad? No fever?'

Cutter shook his head.

'What about coughing fits or a rash?'

'Gus, believe me, Lloyd does not have the plague,' Jualth assured him. 'It's the equivalent of sea sickness, nothing more.'

Gus looked no happier. The last thing he needed was to run an errand in the small hours to fetch the doctor. 'All right,' he muttered, 'I'll see what can be found.' The landlord made to move towards the kitchen. 'How about yourself, Jualth?'

'Not for me, Gus. All I want is news of the comings and goings whilst I've been away. So don't be long, I've got a feeling there's a lot of catching up to do.'

Chapter 68

Early in the morning, Jualth and Cutter led their horses up the winding lane to the distillery. The chimneys and kilns were smoking, signs of an inner life not matched by any discernible activity outside. A makeshift workshop now stood next to the stables, but the absence of one of its workers did not encourage Jualth to wander up to greet those that remained.

Nobody met them at the gates. They wandered in and stopped at the edge of the foundation work, close to where Jualth had last seen her husband alive. His shouts had started her frantic dash down the office stairs.

'Big space, missis,' Cutter said quietly.

'It was a big fire, Lloyd, and soon there'll be nothing to remind us that it ever took place.'

Only the scorched and blackened ground around the perimeter showed signs of the fire, but when the flora again flourished and new buildings stood on the network of trenches, no visible reminders of that fateful day would remain.

'Things always get rebuilt, Jualth. It's 'appened to our bridge countless times.'

The bridge, the warehouse – they had a lot in common. Both had seen fire and suffered tragedy as a result.

'You'll remember what I said?' Jualth asked.

Cutter nodded. 'No mention of the fire to Lily unless she mentions it first. I won't forget.'

Jualth glanced around to the office building. A dark shape that made no attempt to conceal itself was visible in the first-floor window. All the time they had been standing there, she had felt the razor-sharp stare of the distillery boss on her back.

'It's time I did what I came here to do, Lloyd. Do you mind staying with the horses whilst I go inside? I shouldn't be long.'

At the gates, they momentarily parted.

'I'm expected, Samantha,' Jualth called out to the secretary on entering the office lobby. She made straight for the stairs. After the briefest of taps, she pushed open the impressive oak door and found Jack Vardy in front of his desk, a glass of whisky ready for his visitor.

Their last meeting in his office had been anything but pleasant. It had marked what she had thought to be the end of a long-standing business relationship. Bitterness lingered – Jualth did not forgive quickly.

'Hello, Jack.'

'Jualth … welcome back.' He gestured to the desk. 'As you can see, I knew you were coming.'

The atmosphere in the room could not have been more false – Jualth did not feel he was pleased to see her at all. She shut the door and sat in the chair held out for her. 'This meeting will be short, Jack. I need to finish the remainder of my journey in great haste.'

They watched each other closely as Jack moved around the desk to his chair. 'It's been almost a month, a long time away from your family and friends,' he said, as if to score a disapproving point. 'How was London?'

'Interesting.'

'In what way interesting?'

'In many ways, Jack, but as far as you and I are concerned, in one way in particular.'

Jack waited patiently; they both knew the business with the Excise was his only interest. 'Did you manage to achieve anything whilst you were there?'

'Maybe, Jack – I hope so. It rather depends on others now.'

Jack looked faintly annoyed. He was not in the mood for games. 'Others?'

'You, Jack. You and your board of directors.' Jualth handed him a copy of the agreement.

'What's this?'

Jualth's voice did not waver in answering. 'It's a contract between three parties: you and your distillery, me and mine and someone in London.'

Jack looked cautiously from the agreement to its young bearer. Jualth noted the disappearance of the false smile. This was business and Jack Vardy treated business in the only way he knew how. 'What sort of a contract?'

'The type that extracts both of us from our present predicament. Not only will it get the Excise people off our backs, but it will also allow the relationship between Brethna and Kvairen to continue. It will be as if the inspection never took place. The only visible scar left by their intrusion into our lives will be the one you saw me standing by just now.'

Jualth paused to make sure the distillery boss had his eye on her and not the contract. 'I see you have swept away my husband's ashes, Jack. Are you sure you gave them sufficient time to cool?'

Jack resented the need to defend his actions; the ashes could not remain a shrine to mourning indefinitely. 'It did none of us any good to be reminded of that terrible day. What we lost in the fire needs replacing and it is better done sooner rather than later in my opinion'

'The foundations have already been dug,' said Jualth, to score her own point of disapproval.

'And the rebuilding will shortly commence. My job is to look after this business on behalf of its employees and customers, and if the measures I've taken seem hasty in your eyes, I'm sorry, but there it is. I can no more change what happened on that day than you can. So, this agreement …'

The defence was as cold as the action. It seemed that business had indeed made him impervious to human feelings.

'Not now, Jack. I shall give you time to study it first. If you have any questions, ask me at the meeting; I'd like to call one for Wednesday afternoon. Assuming we are of a similar mind, we can sign the agreement straight away and then discuss our future.'

Jack rested the document on the desk and smoothed his hand over the cover. 'So be it. I shall make sure all directors are present and fully informed.'

Jualth motioned to leave.

'Would you care to drink your whisky first? Guard against the morning chill.'

'I'm well wrapped up, thank you, Jack.' She again made to leave.

'You have someone with you, Jualth, a young man,' Jack said hastily.

Jualth responded curtly, 'A friend from London, nothing more.' He could die of curiosity for all she cared. What he did not know could not hurt her. 'Till Wednesday.'

Jack courteously stood up as Jualth left the room and found her own way to the front door.

'All done, missis?' Cutter asked when they were reunited.

'All done, Lloyd, and all very business-like; our meetings used to be much warmer.' A distant capitalist had replaced the father figure of her youth. The loss was a sadness, but one Jualth would soon get over.

'Do you think he'll sign it?' Cutter asked.

'Let's hope so. I felt a lot more confident in London. I shall return to find out after he's had plenty of time to mull it over. Jack likes to think things through very carefully.'

Heading back to the gates, they passed the tightly closed Excise hut. Whoever sat inside, did not wish to make their acquaintance.

'Feeling better this morning, Lloyd?' Jualth asked, as she helped him onto his horse.

'Like my old self, missis.'

'Glad to hear it; we should make good time then.'

After a short distance, they turned off the track and began to trot cross-country. Jack turned away from the window and looked down at the agreement in his hand, an unwelcome twist he had not anticipated. He returned to his seat and, with Jualth's untouched whisky put to use, picked up the document. As he read, he could only marvel at the young woman's resourcefulness.

Chapter 69

'Well done, Lloyd, half a day's riding without being sick once,' said Jualth, as she slipped down from her horse. 'Must have been the train's fault after all.' To her delight, she watched the young man dismount unaided. 'We'll make a master horseman out of you yet,' she declared.

'Can turn my 'and to anythin', missis,' Cutter boasted, with renewed confidence. He looked about, searching for the unseen. 'Where is it then?'

'Where's …?' Jualth caught his gist. 'You mean, where's my home? Hidden, Lloyd. Once we've put the horses in the paddock, I'll show you.'

Minutes later, having walked down a short, tree-lined path, Jualth and Cutter stood in a patron-free beer garden at the front of the inn. 'There you go, Lloyd, my home and, as you can see, no one is here to greet me. Fair to say, my return is unexpected.'

Cutter viewed the deserted garden and then gazed at the inn and the sign hanging from the first-floor wall. 'Mat … Mat-il-da's. Matilda's?' He looked puzzled. 'Come again, missis?'

'My mother, Lloyd. She was Scottish by ancestry and spirit, though not by birth.'

The front door opened with enough force to wrench it from its hinges and Lily, dressed in phantom white, flew out. The impact of their greeting was enough to make Cutter wince as, locked in an impassioned embrace of blurred monotone, each attempted to squeeze the life out of the other. Then, in a sudden fit of rage, Lily pushed her sister away.

'Have you forgotten how to write? Have you not heard of telegrams or *pigeon* post?' Tears began to well up in her eyes. She wanted to yell, yell and yell some more, but could do nothing more than grab her sister and hold on tight and long.

Jualth gently stroked her sister's newly grown mane of hair. 'Back to your old self, I see, Lily.'

'Not one word,' Lily growled in a broken voice. 'You could have been dead these last few weeks for all I knew.' She wiped the tears from her eyes, then blinked to clear her vision, her chin still resting on her sister's shoulder. 'Jualth?'

'Yes, dear.'

There was a small pause whilst Lily focused. 'Who am I looking at?'

'That's Lloyd, dear.'

Cutter shook his head and quietly mouthed the name he steadfastly wished to hold on to.

Lily stared closely, in the same manner as her sister, as if searching for the person inside. 'Hello, Lloyd Cutter,' she said, repeating what she presumed to be his full title. 'I like your name.'

Jualth let go and swivelled around. 'I like it too ... "Lloyd Cutter".'

Cutter thought about protesting, but he was on unfamiliar territory and in the company of not one but two, very similar-looking redheads.

'How about a compromise, Lloyd? It's the best offer you'll get from me.'

Commonsense told him to agree, after all, no one would know once he returned to London. 'Seeing as the master also called me Lloyd yesterday ...' he said, trying to appear as grudging as possible.

'Well done, Lloyd,' said Jualth, feeling thoroughly pleased with Cutter's apparent acceptance. 'I'm proud of you and, if you hadn't already realised, this is Lily, my sister.'

'Nice to meet you, missis.'

'Missis! My name's Lily, not missis.'

Jualth heaved a disconsolate sigh. 'The struggle I've had, you wouldn't believe.' She looked down upon her outnumbered companion. '*Well*, you can't call us both "missis", so how about trying our real names ... Lloyd Cutter?'

Jualth received the same welcoming embraces from Edith and Jessica, both of whom she had missed dearly, and took the overexuberant pats and squeezes from locals in the spirit she hoped they were intended. They found a room for Cutter – which was very much to his liking – then sat him down in the kitchen, where Edith struggled to satisfy a healthy appetite.

After the initial fuss had waned, Lily dragged Jualth into the sanctuary of their back garden and introduced her to a new landmark. 'A gift to me from the men at the distillery,' she said, showing off her new bench. 'Took me ages to decide on the right spot for the perfect view.'

Jualth was suitably impressed. She released Jessica from a prolonged bout of hugging and sat down on the bench next to Lily. Velana shimmered in the early afternoon sun, the broken light playing with the outlines of birds as they skimmed over the surface. It was a dearly missed sight.

'How are you coping?' Jualth asked her sister softly.

Lily smiled bravely. 'Jessica has helped. I've needed a baby to hold on to.'

'Then hang on to her as much as you like. When did a McTavish girl ever turn her back on too much attention?'

As if preordained, Jualth's daughter took a tumble on the grass. Her bottom lip quivered as she studied the damage done to her knee. The quiver quickly turned into a steely resolve.

'She's always bumping into things,' Jualth said sadly.

'Aye, we've noticed.'

'You can thank Frazer for that. Why open a door when you're strong enough to walk through it?'

Lily smiled; with Jessica around, the silent but manly Frazer would never be forgotten.

'Gus told me some disturbing news whilst I was in Brethna.'

Lily looked anxious, wondering what on earth else could have happened.

'Martha.'

'Martha!' Lily sighed. 'You mean … is that all?'

'That's plenty, Lily. Where is she? What have you done with the woman?'

'Absolutely nothing, there was no need.' It was Jualth's turn to look anxious. 'She's with Ned. He's taken a fancy to your mother-in-law.'

'What?!'

Lily laughed, not quite as of old, but a determined effort nevertheless that was good to hear. 'Seriously, when we brought Martha back, he was a tower of strength, so much so that she's taken up residence in his cottage. She isn't even staying with us.'

Ned, had he known it, had managed to cross a forbidden path and was in deep trouble with the landlady. 'What did he want to do that for? She may never go home.'

'They are of the same age,' Lily said unhelpfully, 'and Ned likes a woman nearby to chat to, especially when there is *no potential threat involved*, as he puts it.'

'The cheek of the man,' said Jualth. He enjoyed the 'potential threat' as far as she was concerned. 'You don't think those two …?' Lily shrugged – the possibility existed. 'I will have to speak to Ned and, failing that, tell Martha some terrible things about him.'

In that quarter, Jualth had plenty of leeway available to her. Little was known about Ned before his travels landed him in Brethna with nothing more than a small bag and a fishing rod. As fortune had it, the night he chose to stay at the Whisky Makers' Arms coincided with a visit by their mother. During that evening, a long one by all accounts, Matilda took a shine to her 'eloquent Irish rogue' and any confessions about a sinister past went no farther than her ears. She judged him trustworthy and made him an offer, the type that men could never refuse. And ever since that day, he had helped behind the bar of their inn, a loveable if enigmatic rascal.

Jualth imparted the second piece of disturbing news from Brethna, just in case others had thought it wise not to mention it. 'You know they've cleared the site. The warehouse, workshop and fire hut, they've all gone.'

Lily nodded. 'Daniel told me. He's been out this way several times with Jack's permission, so he says, but I know it's off his own back. He had no reason to come all this way other than as a friend.'

She recalled the morning of her return when Daniel had made the cart as comfortable as he could for his injured passenger. 'I collected some ashes before we left – filled two pots. One I gave to Martha, the other I kept. When I felt up to it, I rowed into the middle of Velana and spread the ashes over the water. It helped knowing that both mother and daughter are nearby. The next time I swim across those waters, I'll be in good company.'

Lily wiped a tear from her cheek, one to follow the many thousand that had flowed since the fire. 'I wonder if these will ever stop.'

For the second time in twenty-four hours, Jualth felt a pang of guilt. Her mourning had ceased on her arrival in London – there had been no choice – but it was unsettling how easily she had accomplished the feat. 'What about Nathan, have you seen him?'

'Once. We sat out front and talked. We haven't done that for ages. I'm sure he felt her loss as much as I did, though he barely saw Harriet often enough to recognise her.'

'Will it make a difference to the pair of you?'

Lily shook her head. As far as Nathan was concerned, there was little point in being anything but a realist. 'It's been too long; we've become strangers. He hasn't returned since.'

'But he will, Lily, you know he will.'

Lily chose to watch Jessica playing on the lawn with a patched-up rag doll rather than dwell on a life of separation from her whisky-dependent husband.

'Jessica's missed Harriet. She's tried to say her name and searched here and there for her. It's only this last week that Harriet's memory has begun to fade, and Jessica's resigned herself to getting on without her help. I wish forgetting could be that easy for the rest of us.'

Jualth put her arm around her sister and kissed the side of her head – there was no use in pretending that the pain would ever go away. 'What did you think of the clothes William bought you?' she asked.

Lily made an effort to perk up – gifts of such quality were a rarity. 'He can buy me as many of those as he likes. That skirt and blouse are beautifully made *and* my favourite colour. They're almost too good to wear.'

'Glad you like them. I had to work very hard on your behalf.'

Lily looked at her sister suspiciously.

'Lloyd will provide the evidence at a later date.'

Lily waited patiently – she required a better explanation than that.

'Okay, I helped him with his reading and writing, so you can thank him as much as me. He's a bright pupil and I'm proud of his progress.'

Lily glanced over her shoulder. The distant sound of chatter could only mean the young man's continued entrenchment at the kitchen table. 'Who is Lloyd? *What* is Lloyd? Why have you brought him here? You needed no escort home.'

Lily's suspicions were already growing and with barely a word spoken about Jualth's trip south.

'First and foremost, he's a friend who more than anyone made my stay in London bearable. William is a sort of guardian to him and three other boys. Each works on the bridge and in return gets a basic education and a start in life. William is the helping hand to a better future.'

'The Good Samaritan,' Lily said thoughtfully. 'I hope he's not making up for some past evil he has committed.'

'Now, now, Lily. William is an honourable, warm-hearted man with a mission to help where there is genuine need, so let's not have a go at him so soon on my return.'

Lily did not argue the point, but neither did she acknowledge it to be true. A warm heart and a mission to help were subjective and not given to all. 'How did you find the honourable William? By swimming against the tide of severed heads till you found their source?'

Jualth frowned, though not in respect of Lily's cynicism or the thought of decapitation. 'The river, Lily, you should have seen it. It made the doctor's medicinal broth look appetising.'

'I'll try to remember that next time I choose his ahead of mine. Now go on, tell me how you found him.'

'By tortuous means. London town can be an unfriendly place to an innocent traveller and, if it wasn't for Lloyd coming to my rescue, I might not have made it.'

Lily grunted but did not comment – how fortunate one of William's boys should have stumbled upon her sister. 'What was the bridge like?'

'Far better than William led us to believe. It's the best part of London and one of the few places you can breathe anything closely resembling fresh air. I chose it as a suitable place to introduce William to his, and *our*, spirits.'

Despite all protestations to the contrary that could mean only one thing – Jualth had her doubts. Why else inform the gallant Sir Galahad about the unsavoury and vengeful side of the McTavish character. 'You mentioned Jade?'

'I had to.'

'And his reaction?'

'He is neither stupid nor slow. He got the message. I left a few days later.'

'Wise move, sister dear. Allow our William plenty of space to reconsider his silent ways.'

'Lily!' Jualth warned again.

Lily flapped her hands, a small gesture of irritation to counter her sister's lack of suspicion. 'Was he shocked to see you when you suddenly appeared on his doorstep?'

Jualth thought for a moment – it was a good question. 'It's difficult to tell with him. He has a stillness that defies interpretation.'

'But if anyone can it's us, unless, of course, we're in some way blinded.'

'*Lily!*'

Lily sighed, but resisted the urge to press the issue further. It was not the time to fight. 'Tell me how he has helped us, then,' she asked quietly.

How not whether. Jualth appreciated the faith and found Lily's mistrust of William all the more galling because of it. Perhaps that was why she had waited a full hour before bothering to ask about the outcome of Jualth's visit.

'He took me to the Custom House, a huge ugly stone building that stands just across the river from the Bridge House. Two minutes and you're outside the front door.'

'Fancy that,' said Lily. The amazing coincidence did nothing to lessen her mistrust. She raised her hand and pressed it gently against her red skin. 'And did you see *that* man again?' Jualth nodded. 'Please tell me you killed him.'

'I was tempted.'

'Only tempted?'

'I let him know how we felt. If he has a conscience, he will now, for ever and a day, lack for a restful berth.'

'Those people do not have a conscience. Their blood is black like their deeds and it feeds on us. What did you do?'

'I lost my cool and stormed out. The punishment for our supposed guilt was untenable.'

Lily remembered a similar action of her own and the hugely regrettable consequences that had followed. She hoped regret would not result from Jualth's action. 'And yet William has helped us.'

'He stayed on after I departed.'

'He was in the meeting?'

'He arranged it. It was only natural that he should attend.'

Lily again stewed over William's involvement. She kept listening.

'He informed me of a possible agreement that involved the supply of our whisky – just a few bottles – to an unknown party on demand. In return, we stay as we are and no one bothers us again.'

Lily's sixth sense had told her to prepare for an answer that was little to her liking. She had not counted on a solution where the word *suspicious* barely summed it up.

'Jualth, we've been running an illegal distillery for centuries. We have not paid one farthing in tax and, under this deal, we will receive the Excise's blessing to continue. *And* all we have to do is supply a few bottles of whisky to … to a *mystery* person?'

Jualth knew how improbable it sounded; she barely believed it herself. Its credibility suffered all the more when repeated out loud. 'Lily, I know this appears too easy, but I've got the agreements. All we need is my signature, Jack Vardy's, and this other person in London.'

Lily began to shake her head, the soreness causing discomfort each time she stretched her skin. 'That is a ridiculous agreement, Jualth. Nothing can be resolved that easily. Have you any idea who this other party is? And what has Jack got to do with it? Why should our future lie in his hands?'

'Because we supplied Kvairen whisky for blending under the strict instruction that it was used for no other purpose. It was an unwritten condition of our choosing – to protect us. Now, we're informing Jack that we wish to break our own rule. There's a fair chance he will not be happy.'

Lily huffed. Who cared whether the loathsome Brethna boss was happy when the survival of her community was at stake. 'Has he seen the agreement?'

'I left a copy with him. We'll discuss it at a meeting on Wednesday. If he agrees, we shall sign there and then, and Lloyd will take the agreement back to London.'

Lily suddenly understood the real reason for Jualth's shadow – an errand boy for William. Whichever way she looked, others had control over their destiny. 'Who is the other party?' she asked again. 'Are you sure it isn't William?'

'William is our friend and quite possibly the only one. He would not betray us.'

Admittedly, she had noted a tension in his manner that was not evident whilst he was their guest, but that could all be explained. The responsibility of managing one of London's most famous landmarks was considerable. Add that to the troubles she had brought with her and who wouldn't have shown signs of strain?

'I trust him, Lily. He said he would do us no harm and I believed him then and I believe him now.'

'And if he turns out to be the other party or a part of it?'

'If he does, he does; we will never know. As long as we have a home and a community with no official interference, that's all I care about.'

Lily shook her head again as she struggled to believe the unbelievable.

Jualth began to despair. 'Lily, are you in any way comforted by this solution to our troubles? What is the alternative – letting the cold, grey, all-but-dead Excise people take all this from us? I don't understand the agreement any more than you do, but it exists, we have an option, so let's take it.'

Lily fell silent, not wishing to diminish the efforts made by her sister. In truth, she was anything but comforted by finding herself in the controlling hands of others, none of whom she trusted. She forced a fleeting but troubled smile.

'I'm not getting at you, Jualth. What you did was very brave and no one else could have done it, but I remain worried. Our destiny lies with people who have all the power in the world over us; that's more than enough to make me worry, even after your agreement is signed.'

Both women suddenly flinched. Without warning, Cutter had appeared at the side of the bench.

'Lloyd, I didn't hear you come out,' Jualth said hurriedly.

'Finished my grub, missis. There's some waiting inside for you if you're 'ungry.'

Jualth tried to disguise her guilt as she wondered how much he had overheard about his master. 'Later, Lloyd. I'll give you your lesson first.'

Cutter's face dropped. He started to rub his back. 'Couldn't we skip it today, Jualth? I'm damn near tired out from all that riding. How about a gentle stroll around your lake instead?'

'It's called a *loch*, Lloyd, unless you're looking to get yourself lynched and, as for your lesson, why stop when we're doing so well together?'

'I'll show you around the loch,' Lily said smartly. 'I know more about it than Jualth. In return you can tell me about London. There's a lot I wish to learn.'

Jualth bit her tongue, choosing the same course as Lily had earlier on. She had been away too long to launch into an immediate and heated argument. But if Lily persisted in her doubts about William, sooner or later, daggers would be drawn.

Chapter 70

On her first full day back, Jualth took Cutter riding, his emerging mastery in the saddle only going to show that he was a born countryman at heart. His references to the huge number of horses in the town were understandably ignored – the skill needed to overcome London's chaotic roads hardly compared with that of an undulating Highland landscape.

On the following day, Lily was permitted custody of the young Hawk. Keen to make good on her offer, she escorted him down to Velana and along the southern shore. 'There's a bay just ahead of us where I used to take my daughter swimming. She loved to play in the shallow water. Do you swim, Lloyd?'

Cutter screwed up his face. 'Nah, never. 'Ates the water. I keeps well away.'

Such a statement was paramount to sacrilege to Lily and her kin. She demanded an explanation.

''Cause I comes from London where the water's as dirty as a chimney's black, missis. It carries all sorts of diseases, always 'as done. Don't even likes the rain much. Before the master took me in, getting caught in the rain could leave you wet for days, especially in winter. Kids I grew up with got fevers from the damp and never recovered. Best plays safe and keep dry, that's what I say.'

Cutter's grounds for disliking the water were almost heartbreaking to listen to. Lily understood, but it was not an opinion she could share. 'Water reminds you of death because you associate it with disease and sickness … well, through swimming it reminds me of life, of freedom and empowerment. It meant the same to my mother and would have done to my daughter given the chance. You know what happened to both of them?'

'Jualth told me. Said not to speak of it unless …'

'Unless … unless I did first, I see. Sadly, ignoring their existence does not lessen the pain. I shall remember them both and you may speak of either at any time.'

She pointed across Velana to its northern shore. 'You see that rock over there, the big one jutting out into the water?' Cutter nodded. 'That's where your master chose to do his fishing when he stayed with us. He sat there for days on end with nothing but Ned's rod and a slack line for company. He didn't prove himself to be an accomplished angler.'

Cutter looked surprised. 'Unlike 'im, missis, he's normally good at things. He wouldn't have sat there that length of time if there were no point to it.'

'But there was a point to it, Lloyd. He's a bit of a thinker, your master, and quite happy to take time figuring through his problems.'

'Probably thinking about the bridge. There was a lot going on back then.'

'I'm sure he was, but he had plenty of other things to occupy his mind whilst he was here.'

'Like what, missis?'

Lily put her hand on Cutter's shoulder to stop him moving forward – she wanted his full attention. 'I thought you might be able to tell me that.'

Cutter did not follow. 'How should I know what else he was thinking about, miss—?'

Lily cut off his plea of innocence: 'How did you know my sister was coming to London, Lloyd?'

'I-I didn't, missis.'

The slight hesitation was enough to confirm what Lily already knew. 'I don't believe you, Lloyd. I don't believe in heroic knights arriving miraculously out of the smog to save a lone damsel in distress. You knew she was coming and the only person who could have told you was the guy who spent his day *thinking* on that rock. Lloyd, I know you're hiding something and we both know you can't hide it for ever, so why not tell me?'

'I'm not lying, misses, 'onest. That day she came I had no idea she'd be there.'

'But …?'

Cutter squirmed uncomfortably. His eyes darted across Velana rather than focus on his interrogator.

'I will get it out of you, Lloyd, and I'm prepared to sit you down in front of my sister to do so. You either tell me now or we head back up to Matilda's to find Jualth.'

Cutter did not welcome the prospect of confessing in front of a person whose respect and trust he valued. His situation was not an easy one.

'All right, but you mustn't tell 'er or anyone else. If word got back to the governor, I'd be in right trouble.'

Lily yielded no ground; she would be the arbiter of any compromise. 'Go on,' she said.

'He told us to look out for a woman dressed in white with long red 'air, but he said it a long time ago, longs before she actually turned up.'

'How long?'

'A good six months.'

'That long?!' Six months made no sense one way or the other, not in terms of William's visit or that of the Excise officer.

'He told all the 'awks to keep an eye open, not just me,' Cutter pleaded.

Lily wanted more. 'What else did he say?'

'He told us she was a Scot and that 'er likely purpose in London was to find 'im. We had to make sure she did.'

'And he told you six months before she turned up?'

'Maybe nine, can't really remember now. Could have been longer.'

'Now I'm even more confused!' Lily exclaimed. 'I'm not sure that makes any sense at all; that's far too long.'

The confusion did not lie solely with Lily. 'Too long for what, missis?'

'*Just* too long, Lloyd.'

Considering the brusqueness of her answer, Cutter did not push further. He was more worried what Lily would do now she knew. 'Are you going to tell Jualth?'

Lily relented, but not by much. 'For the moment I shall keep this to myself. As you're off after Wednesday's meeting, I'll let you escape first. But before we draw this confession to a close, one last thing: how did my sister get on with your master during her *lengthy* stay?'

Cutter managed to answer without hesitating, though he did lose most of his colour. 'Well they had their run-ins, Lily.'

'Lily! You suddenly remembered my name, Lloyd.' She shook her head and tutted, knowing there was more to her sister's 'lengthy stay' with William than she was being told. 'Oh dear, Lloyd, that was a mistake; you should have kept calling me missis. Tell me what happened after their "run-ins"?'

'They made up … sort of.'

'By shaking hands?'

The colour flushed back into Cutter's cheeks. He couldn't hold her gaze.

Lily groaned in despair. What did it all mean? Had the man her sister should have married blinded her judgement. 'We will not mention this, Lloyd, is that agreed?'

'Whatever you say, Lily.' Having seen one redhead lose her temper on a regular basis, Cutter was in no doubt that this one was just as bad and quite possibly worse.

'All right, Lloyd, anything else you wish to tell me before we finish?'

Cutter most definitely had nothing else to say. He had already said far more than he wished.

'Let's walk then and we can talk about you instead. I want to know what your life was like before you met Master William, and when you didn't have a home. Your experience might prove invaluable.'

Chapter 71

When Wednesday came, Jualth and Cutter set off early, reaching Brethna by midday. Leaving her companion at the gates, Jualth nipped into the office and arranged for the meeting to take place as soon as the directors could be gathered.

'We'll take the horses up to the stables, give them a short rest, Lloyd. If you could look after them whilst I'm in with Jack? It shouldn't take long, then we can start for the railway track.'

By the time Jualth had returned to the office, all were present in the boardroom: Jack Vardy in his usual place at the head of the table; his two managers, James Gravid and Lewis Cravett, to either flank; Daniel opposite Jualth's seat and Samantha at the far end ready to take the minutes.

'All right,' said Jack, formally starting proceedings once Jualth had sat down, 'this is a meeting called by Jualth McTavish to discuss one item: a contract she has procured from her recent visit to London concerning the supply and distribution of Kvairen whisky. Everybody has had a chance to see the contract in the past few days; it's a relatively simple document between three parties: the Brethna Distillery, Jualth as representative of her community and a third party who chooses to be represented by a certain "Fareland Nominees". The arrangement is for the Kvairen Distillery to supply this unknown person or entity with an unspecified but limited amount of whisky in its original single-malt form for no consideration. For this to happen, the Brethna distillery must overlook the infringement to the implied business rights that presently exist between the two distilleries. And, in addition,' Jack Vardy looked directly at Jualth, 'I think there is something not covered in this contract that you wish to add.'

All eyes turned towards the broker of the contract. 'Yes, Jack, there is. In exchange for agreeing to this arrangement, the Excise Service will waive all repercussions resulting from its recent inspections of the Brethna and Kvairen distilleries. Presumably, the file will be lost and signs put up to prohibit entry into our wee Scottish hamlets.'

'Quite an extraordinary agreement to have returned with, Jualth,' said Jack. 'There is no denying the commendation that should be attached to your resourcefulness but, at the same time, we do marvel at how it was achieved.'

'In what way, Jack?'

'In that we do not know how you managed to obtain it and why the Excise Service would agree to such a deal. I have spoken to a solicitor. He was equally perplexed and, more importantly, dubious as to its legality.'

Jualth could barely believe Jack had discussed a highly sensitive arrangement with an outsider. That was no way to keep it a secret. 'I hope he has your full confidence, this solicitor?'

'He has a duty of confidentiality. It is not in his interest to be careless with privileged information. As far as I can see, the exercise of this *waiver* by the Excise Service will result in a wilful neglect of their official duties and make them party to a dishonest act.'

'That's up to them. I, for one, do not choose to understand their reasoning. What I do choose to understand is that when we sign this document, it will become a binding contract between the three of us, with the blessing of the Excise.'

Jack Vardy was not convinced; relying on ignorance was complacent at best, foolhardy at worst. 'You might not care to understand the reasoning behind the apparent willingness of the Excise Service to ignore its legal responsibilities, but I am not, and accepting what you've so far said regarding the apparent lack of consequences is not enough. We have nothing in writing from them and we're unlikely to get it, as I presume they want no official trail leading back to their doorstep. So, our knowledge concerning their complicity in this arrangement is coming from your lips and nowhere else. Jualth, what precisely did they say to make you believe they will no longer proceed with their prosecutions if we sign this agreement?'

Jualth hesitated – she had not expected to recount the sordid details of her unpleasant encounter in the Custom House. 'That was their meaning. I don't know the exact words used, just that the investigations will end once the agreements are signed.'

'What do you mean when you say, "You do not know the exact words"?' James Gravid interrupted, taking the initiative ahead of his chairman.

'Does that matter?'

'I think it does,' said Jack. 'You were *at* the meeting?'

'Of course, most of it.'

'Most?' said Jack, searching for clarification.

Jualth had hoped for a cursory explanation of the background to the deal. The revelation of her early departure from the Custom House was an irritation. 'I had to leave before the end. William Halar, the Master of Old London Bridge, whom you all know, represented me during the remainder of the meeting. I think we can rely upon a person of his standing to relay a message in its correct form.'

Jack Vardy sat back and started to tap the desk with the heel of his fountain pen. The uncomfortable body language of his two managers clearly showed a shared unease. Jualth cast a puzzled glance to Daniel who shrugged – the cartman had no knowledge of any prior discussions between the managers.

'No one is questioning the integrity of Mr Halar,' Jack assured the representative of the Kvairen Distillery, 'but this unwritten part of the agreement would have carried more credibility if you had been present when it was negotiated.'

'You're not asking me to go all the way back and ask Mr Tombs to repeat himself, just so you will take my word?'

'We would, Jualth, if we thought the agreement was one we could sign. However—'

Jualth cut in sharply. The indication that he was about to withhold his signature sent her heart plummeting into the pit of her stomach. 'What do you mean, "*If* you thought it was one you could sign"?'

Jack threw his pen on the desk and leant forward. 'Jualth, the complicity of the Excise Service is just one matter we have a problem with; we also know nothing about the person this nominee represents. Beyond your word, what evidence do we have to make this agreement credible? If we had an assurance backed by the rule of law, matters might be different.'

'Mighten they?' said Jualth, struggling to understand the opposition she was facing. The agreement was in everybody's interest, so why the resistance? What was Jack playing at? 'If you get that assurance, will the other party still be a stumbling block or is there some other reason that I have yet to hear, which is stopping you from signing?'

Jack Vardy stared at his young adversary, making her wait. Jualth knew something else was coming but had no idea what. In an awkward silence, the distillery boss's cohorts shifted uneasily. Jualth glanced at Daniel for help but he, like her, occupied the same uninformed wilderness.

'Well, Jack, what else do you wish to tell me? And please, for my sake if not yours, make it good, cause one hell of a lot is riding on this agreement.'

Jack took a sip from a glass of water, unprepared to let anyone but himself dictate the pace or manner of the meeting. He knew what he wanted for his distillery, as did his managers, and it did not coincide with the wishes of Jualth or any unknown party.

'I have an alternative plan to this agreement that I would like you to consider. You will remember at our previous meeting you asked for ideas – *any ideas* – that could help. Well, at the time there was nothing on the table to present as a viable alternative.'

'But now there is and you're telling me it's better than this agreement.' The belated unveiling of an apparent rescue package could not have been less welcome.

Jack held up a hand. 'Please, Jualth, hear me out. I have spoken to the shareholders I represent and to Lewis and James in their capacity as shareholders and we have all agreed that it would be in both our interests if *we*, the Brethna Distillery, make a bid for *you*, the Kvairen Distillery. I know it is a big step and you will have to—'

'*A what?*' Jualth started to yell. 'You want to—'

'*Jualth*,' said Jack, raising his deep baritone voice to silence her impulsive rejection, 'let me finish before you make your mind up that we're all against you. If I am right, you left that meeting in London because of your temper and you regretted it later. So just hang on and listen to what I have to say!'

Jualth dug her nails into the table's surface, knowing to her cost and embarrassment the consequences of not listening, a fault often witnessed by a man who had known her since birth. Seething, she sat still, staring defiantly at an opportunist who wished to justify his inexhaustible self-interest.

'Bearing in mind you have no accounts, the shareholders of the Brethna Distillery are prepared to pay you and your community a price based on our knowledge of your production, plus a generous premium, in exchange for full control of your distillery and its stock of whisky. The necessary measures will then be taken to have a license put in place to provide a legal foundation for subsequent supplies to the public.'

'But what about the Excise people? Are you forgetting they'll prosecute without this agreement? What good is all that money if it doesn't cover our taxes, and what good does it do me if I cannot run my inn? You'll have to raise additional funds yourself to pay for your own back taxes and that's on top of the cost of that new, *larger* stone warehouse. How do you know you can raise the money to buy us out? At our last meeting all you could think about was saving your own skin and you were mighty worried about that.'

'We have the finance, Jualth,' Jack assured her. 'We will not be making an offer for the Kvairen Distillery based on a false premise.'

'But how, Jack? Where is the money coming …?'

Jualth stopped abruptly, as a sudden realisation dawned – the Excise investigation had become a smokescreen for an opportunist's plot that should have occurred to her whilst still in London. What was it Mr Tombs had said during her brief presence in the Custom House? That the taxes on the whisky supplied to the Brethna Distillery had already been paid. However unconventional the arrangement between the two distilleries, Brethna had paid the tax due when its supply of Kvairen whisky left the bonded warehouse and the Excise Service would 'take it into account'.

So, Brethna could look forward to a slap on the wrist and a small but insignificant penalty, but not the punitive punishment and financial hardship that would drive her local distillery workers out of a job and her family from Matilda's. Armed with that realisation, she could have figured out the rest the moment she had clamped eyes on the scale of Brethna's rebuilding work.

'You've got backers, Jack. You're not in this alone. The Brethna Distillery could not put a realistic offer together to tempt us by itself. Who are they, Jack? Who are they, Lewis, James? Where are you getting your finance from?'

Lewis and James stared down at the table; they were prepared to let their boss explain away their betrayal.

'A consortium, Jualth, that can be identified as a whole but not by its individual members.'

The element of the unknown sounded remarkably familiar. 'Just like our third party, Jack, whose anonymity you so strongly objected to not two minutes ago. We can trust one but not the other?'

'I know the consortium and I am sufficiently qualified to assess their credibility. They in turn are likewise qualified to back my judgement. If you wish to say any more—'

'You've done a deal,' Jualth whispered. 'You don't need this agreement, do you? Your mess with the Excise is already sorted.'

An awkward silence ensued; Jualth had a much firmer grasp on his underhand dealings than the Brethna boss wished to divulge. 'We have spoken to the necessary officials in London and agreed a settlement and that, as I was about to say, we can also discuss at our next full meeting.'

'Oh, no we couldn't, Jack, 'cause our distillery is not for sale, to you or anyone else.'

'You can decide that, Jualth?' Jack said sharply.

'Of course I—'

'Since when did the Kvairen Distillery belong to you?'

Jack's callous but accurate observation struck the desired nerve. Jualth could not decide for others, however much she thought they would follow her lead. In the break in conversation, her seething turned to loathing – she could not answer the question as she wished. Jack took it upon himself to ram the point home.

'That isn't your decision to make alone, you have a duty to talk to your community and to let me do the same. Only then, and on a collective basis, can you decide.'

'They'll do as I say.'

'I don't think so, not if it's the only option left open. Do you think they'll watch you go to prison if a means to prevent it exists? Think about it, Jualth. One way or another you are going to lose your distillery. You have a choice: to see it in the hands of people you know or to see it seized by the Excise and either sold to the highest bidder or closed for good.'

'I would prefer to see your signature on this agreement, so it can stay in *our* hands. If you have already sorted out your mess with the Excise people, why can you not sign it? There's nothing here that stops you from agreeing to settle.'

'We prefer the route that we know to be legal,' Jack retorted.

'Even if it leaves us with insufficient money to pay our taxes, or would that compromise a good business opportunity?'

'We don't know if that will be the case.'

'But it might be and you could live with the suffering it would cause?'

The distillery boss did not yield. The basis for suffering did not lie at his doorstep, and which self-respecting businessman would let slip a gilt-edged chance to own a priceless asset? It was only the long-standing personal relationship that stained the transaction with a degree of discomfort.

'We will help you as much as we can.'

'*Jack!*'

'*No, Jualth*; that is our offer. Give yourself time to think about it. Talk to your sister, your grandmother, those at the distillery; have a meeting of the whole community and let me speak to them as well. Then come back here next week with your decision.'

Jualth raised her hands to her ears, attempting to blot our words she did not wish to hear. 'I've heard enough of this, Jack. I called this meeting to have an agreement signed that could save us all.' She prodded the papers lying on the table. 'I want this agreement signed, that's why I'm here.'

Jack nodded and gestured towards the agreement. 'As you say, Jualth, that's what this meeting is about, so let's put it to the vote. Those who wish to accept the agreement raise your hands.'

Jualth looked around the table. The hands belonging to the purchase and sales managers stayed on the table. Jack did not flinch. Jualth turned to Daniel, her last hope for support. Regardless of its futility, he raised his hand. Jualth raised hers.

'And those against?'

Lewis, James and Jack raised their hands in unhesitating unison. 'The decision of the board is to reject the agreement by three votes to two, and that, I think, concludes the one item of business on today's agenda. Jualth: midday Saturday, on the distillery premises – do you agree to my visit?'

It was not a solution she could easily accept and every sinew in her being yelled out for a blanket refusal. She despised Jack Vardy for the manner in which he had conducted himself, his callous dismissal of the agreement and his manipulation of her vulnerability for cold-blooded gain. But even in that moment of utter hatred, she knew she had no choice other than to allow his visit. There were many more livings at stake than those residing at Matilda's. She nodded curtly. Jack acknowledged in kind.

'Thank you. I hope to see you there. Right, the next meeting will be in a week's time at … say, two o'clock. I hope you will join us, Jualth.'

Jack, Lewis, James and Samantha rose from the table and walked out, leaving Jualth and Daniel alone. Footsteps noisily reverberated on the stairs before disappearing into a room below where the door closed firmly upon words that were not for the ears of an outsider.

Jualth sat motionless, too stunned to comprehend the scale of her defeat – the intention to sign had never existed. Her actions had merely provoked a further attack from another source against herself and her community.

Daniel poured a glass of water and pushed it across the table. 'Have a drink, lass. Get rid of that lump in your throat.'

Jualth needed a drink, a strong one from a very large bottle. She made do with the water. 'Thanks, Daniel … thanks for your support. That was brave of you to vote against your boss.'

'I reckon it's what the workers would have wanted and I represent their interests, not the management's.'

Unlike his hardened boss, he could not look at the distraught young woman without feeling compassion. Gathered in the bar of The Hidden Lodge all those years ago, he had been on hand to hear and celebrate her first scream. Little did the newborn know on entering the world of the innate misdemeanours that existed within her community. Her inheritance – to contend with crimes she had never instigated – now appeared a heavy and insurmountable burden.

'What now, Daniel?' Jualth whispered. 'What am I to do? I thought our troubles were over, our future assured but, oh no, Jack has decreed they should be extended and added to.' She sipped her water as Daniel rose and walked around the table to sit by her side. 'I wish my mother was here, she'd have known how to deal with Jack Vardy. He'd never have got the better of her.'

'Come on, lass, it's no good hanging around here. Go back home, talk to Lily and Edith. You need to be with them.'

Jualth had every intention of following his advice, but not straight away – she had a duty to perform on behalf of a distant acquaintance. 'I have to put a young man on a train first and send him home to London without these useless scraps of paper. I cannot see myself returning till tomorrow morning.'

Daniel gathered together the abandoned documents. 'Look after them all the same. You never know.'

They parted outside the office door and Jualth walked up to join Cutter at the stables. Her expression left little room for doubt about the meeting's outcome.

'No good, missis?'

'No, Lloyd, no good at all.'

They saddled up and, as they rode west out of Brethna, Cutter heard the full sorry story.

By the railway track, with the puffing beast drawing alongside, and despite the failure to win her approval of Jack Vardy and his board, Jualth's hug made sure Cutter knew she was saying farewell to a dear friend.

'Perhaps I should stay, till you picks up a bit, missis? The Governor will understand.'

'I promised William I'd send you home and I intend to keep that promise. I hope this won't be the last time we meet, Lloyd. Wherever I am, whatever I am doing, you'll always be welcome.'

Cutter smiled and made an oath to himself that this would not be their last meeting.

'Look after yourself, Lloyd, and do something with your life – make me proud.'

'It's not right what's 'appened, missis. I 'ate leavin' you when you're down like this.'

'I'll get over it and I'll come back fighting. Tell your master that things have not worked out and thank him for trying. It's not his fault that we have failed. Now give me a kiss and one last hug, then we'll get you settled on the train.'

Cutter did as he was told and soon the train took him out of sight, leaving Jualth alone and bereft of outside help. Her trip south had ultimately revealed the hopelessness of her cause. Too many hostile forces had left her with nowhere to turn.

Chapter 72

Jualth returned to Brethna under the cover of darkness. A long soak in a steaming tub washed away the grime and accumulated aches and pains gathered from a long day on horseback – if only her sense of fast-approaching depression could be so easily vanished.

In the bar, Gus and Craig made sure she knew she had friends in the village if not with Jack Vardy and his management team.

'He was a human being in my mother's day,' Jualth lamented. 'Now what is he? A ruthless, cold-blooded, all-powerful tyrant, that's what.'

'He owed a lot to your mother,' Gus recalled. Matilda had preceded her daughters as a regular guest at the Whisky Makers' Arms, and had spent many long nights talking about all matters of concern with the landlord. The passage of time had not lessened the memory or the deep sense of loss. 'It was Matilda's influence that secured him a place on the board and helped him succeed Horace Hobbs as distillery boss on the old boy's retirement. Others with longer service and more experience were expected to get the nod but, with Matilda's help, somehow they got overlooked.'

'Bad move, *Mother*,' Jualth groaned angrily, for some reason directing her comments to her glass of whisky.

All three sat draped over the bar cradling a Brethna Burn, the bottle left uncorked to the side. It was the nearest they could get to Kvairen whisky.

'And, to think, she could have married that man,' Jualth grumbled on. Tongues had certainly wagged at the time, but no one had ever dared to broach the subject directly with either.

'Their friendship was a close one,' Gus said thoughtfully, 'but as for getting married ...?' He shook his head; he couldn't see it. 'Too many admirers, your mother, and Jack knew it. Being tied to one man went against the grain. Matilda liked attention and she had plenty of it.'

The two men shared a smile, knowing that both mother and daughters were very much alike.

'He always was a career man, our Jack,' Gus went on, 'and it has to be said, a well-respected one. The works have expanded greatly under his leadership with many new jobs created. How he found time to marry with the hours he puts in ...?'

Jualth found reason to voice another grievance: 'But he did, Gus, and very soon after my mother died. I hope it was because he needed emotional comfort.'

The truth, as all knew, lay in another type of comfort. 'It helps to be a well-connected woman from a wealthy background, especially when that wealth includes a large holding in the place you manage,' said Craig, summing up the collective thought.

'Jack looks at every situation in terms of personal gain,' said Jualth, drawing the only conclusion possible. 'I wonder if it has made him a happy man?'

'Aye, I wonder,' said Gus. 'Have you ever been invited to his home, lass?'

'Never, and an invitation is now unlikely and would not be well received if it came. There's no warmth left in our relationship.'

Gus picked up the bottle and topped up the glasses of the gloomy gathering – it was the only medicine available to ensure a half-decent night's sleep.

'What will you do?' Craig asked the dejected young woman.

'I have little choice. I must speak to the others back home. The decision is not mine alone.'

'But if it was?' Gus asked.

Jualth did not hesitate in condemning a place she truly loved. 'I'd burn everything we have rather than let Jack Vardy or anyone else own it. However, and as you may know, I'm rather an emotional person and my impulses are not always best acted upon.'

Many would live to regret such an action, but Gus did not put the deed past her. 'What about Velana? Destroy one and you destroy the other.'

'It will be destroyed anyway. Once the distillery is wrenched from our hands, we lose everything that goes with it.' Morosely, she put her refill to good use. This was as serious as it got and there was no use in pretending otherwise.

When Jualth arrived home, she did not need to tell Lily or Edith how she had fared with the Brethna Board; that was self-evident from her subdued nature. The deflated traveller disclosed the sorry details of a wasted journey and a fractious meeting, then spent the remainder of a quiet afternoon in the company of her daughter.

In the evening, the Elders congregated at the far end of the lounge for a briefing of the previous day's events. It did not make for a happy tale. Thomas left for his tied cottage the moment the meeting finished – he would shoulder the responsibility of informing the workers. A couple of the Elders followed, entrusted with spreading the word farther afield and gauging opinion. Father Donald moved to another part of the lounge to converse with fellow patrons, leaving Jualth alone with her sister, grandmother and a bottle of Kvairen.

'It does me no good to see you like this,' Edith said with great concern. 'You haven't raised a smile, let alone your voice, since you returned.

Where's that seething anger you're so infamous for? Where's the hot, lightning temper?'

'And if I rediscovered those things, Grandma, what then? Who can I use them on and for what end? When I handed Jack the agreement and saw his lukewarm response, I convinced myself there was nothing to worry about. I raised everybody's hopes and I returned home empty-handed.'

The whole experience had clearly been a massive drain on Jualth's emotions and, although sympathetic, Edith could not let her wallow in self-pity. As Matilda's landlady, she held a position in their community that demanded a show of leadership in difficult times.

Edith picked up the bottle and filled her glass. 'Have a drink, a *proper* one.'

Jualth required no encouragement to drown her sorrows. She performed the task swiftly, returning the glass to the table minus most of its contents.

'Feel its fire?' Edith asked, having watched carefully. 'The whisky has lost none of its power, none of its desire to burn a hole in the back of any wee human's throat. It needs you to be the same. We all need you to be the same.'

Jualth remained dejected, unable to raise the strength to respond. She had journeyed to face the mighty and powerful in search of an answer – what more could she do?

Edith glanced across at Lily; perhaps a younger person could succeed where the experience and wisdom of an Elder could not. Someone had to lift her spirits. 'I think I'll leave you two alone for a wee while. I need to find Father Donald for a quiet word before he departs.'

Lily waited, disinclined to say anything whilst her sister chose to look down and fiddle with her glass. She opened the collar of her blouse and began to scratch her neck, so exposing the red slow-healing burns that scarred her body.

Bitterness surfaced across the table at the sight of those wounds – Jualth did not need reminding. Diverting her eyes, she began to remonstrate with her sister, '*Lily*, I've tried and I've tried and I've tried, and I'm tired of trying.'

'We're all tired, Jualth. Four weeks of wondering whether my sister was alive or dead was, believe me, tiring. But with Grandma, Jessica, Ned, Father Donald and our friends, I struggled through and I did it because I knew all of them needed me. You told me as much before you left. And now, more importantly as you're back, they need you.'

'But what is there left to try? What else can we do?'

'That's not the point. Even if we cannot do a thing, we have no right to act as if we have accepted defeat. You are the landlady to this inn; you cannot be seen to give up. If you do, Jack will get the decision he wants.

Jualth, we are both daughters of Matilda and one of us needs to show our fire. It should be you, but it *will* be one of us.'

Lily was still brimming with anger for everything that had happened – Jualth could see it in her eyes. If she did not fight, Lily would leap into the breach without a moment's hesitation.

'Can you stand up to Jack?' Jualth asked.

Lily audibly hissed at the sound of his name. 'If it's the last thing I ever do, I will stop that man taking control of our distillery! He has betrayed us and he has betrayed our mother. The arrangement with Brethna suited Jack – he saw profit in our dealings and possible control through marriage. That opportunity went by the bye when Ma drowned, so the plan changed and he bided away the weeks, months and years until another opportunity came knocking at his door. That's all he wanted, Jualth. He has never been a friend to us, he was never a friend to Ma, just an ambitious greedy man with his eye on a pot of gold. And now he's the thickness of one of his grey whiskers from fulfilling his ambition.'

Farther along, a table emptied, its occupiers heading for the exit. Edith at last found herself alone with Father Donald and in a position to have that word.

'I'd love to know the identity of his backers,' Lily murmured, attempting to incite life into the waning spirit of her sister. 'What kind of people would put money into a business under investigation and then stick by when it's found guilty of complicity? Any ideas, *Jualth*?'

Jualth felt a flicker of resentment course through her veins; she did not appreciate the insinuation. 'No, Lily, *none,* and if you're implying what I think you are, *drop it*. I do not wish to start fighting over an argument that will get us nowhere.'

'Jualth, if we can find a way to get at Jack Vardy, we *are* getting somewhere.'

'But we can't get at him and we can't stop him unless we're prepared to destroy our own distillery! We can hate him all we like, for all the good it will do, but can you see Jack caring one jot, unless we can … can ...?' Jualth tailed off, suddenly lost in thought.

Lily watched her sister closely, wondering if a spark had just lit inside. 'What is it, Jualth? Unless we can … what?'

'It's not much, Lily, but Jack Vardy is bright enough to pause and take stock.'

Lily waited as Jualth ruminated over some inner idea. She lost patience. '*Jualth*, he needs to stop *because* …?'

'Because … he knows about Jade's Fall, Ma made a special point of telling him. Perhaps she had her doubts and told the story to make him wary.'

'And that would worry a hard-headed businessman like Jack Vardy?'

'Yes,' said Jualth without hesitation, 'because the story is based on real people and we descend from those people. It would make anybody wary if they truly knew the lengths we go to, to get what we want and that the name McTavish and vengeance go hand in hand.'

Glass chinked under the bar counter as Edith emerged with a bottle of Kvairen for the departing priest. Having overheard her granddaughters, she cast a quick eye towards them knowing that their knowledge of the McTavish clan's darker side barely scratched the surface. Another time would suit for such tales; for the moment, the requirements of the priest took precedence. A busy time listening to the views of his parishioners lay ahead.

'Okay, so it won't be much, but what exactly are you aiming to do?'

'This weekend, at his insistence, Jack will visit the distillery to speak directly to the workers and our community.'

'So-o, what of it?'

'Can you remember when he last paid us a visit?' Lily shrugged – it wasn't in recent memory. 'Well, when he comes to speak to the men, I'm sure he'll want to inspect the works.'

'And we will allow it?'

'Yes, Lily, because an inspection will remind him of Jade's Fall and its meaning.' Jualth had lost her sister. 'Stay here, I've got something to show you.'

Jualth swept away and briefly disappeared upstairs. When she returned, she carried in her arms a memento of her time in London. 'I forgot how heavy this thing was,' she puffed, placing it in front of Lily. 'Take a look.'

Lily peeled back the cloth to reveal Albert's beautifully carved masterpiece. 'Jualth, where did you get this?'

'I had it specially commissioned. Lloyd helped with the design and Albert, the one remaining blacksmith in the employment of Old London Bridge, applied his great skill to make it.'

Lily tilted the surface to better inspect the detail. Suitably impressed, she agreed it was no ordinary plaque. 'Albert is definitely someone I'd like to meet. I can but imagine how difficult it was to create this.'

'One day I hope you will meet him; he has an open invitation to visit us. Some of the commissions in his workshop are incredible.'

Jualth felt a tinge of discomfort as her sister began to studiously rotate the plaque. Lily's teeth began to gently tap as the concentration needed to study grew into a much longer period of inspection.

'Jualth, the words around the edge … I think I know what you're trying to say …'

'But I haven't quite mastered the spelling.'

Lily balked at the understatement. 'Jualth, your Gaelic is dreadful. If I didn't know you were cursing vengeance on our enemies, your inscription would make no sense to me at all. I hope you spared Albert a translation.'

'Albert was far too sweet to worry with its meaning. I should not like him to think badly of us.'

Lily turned the plaque one way and then another, a look of puzzlement growing on her face as she fiddled with it. 'Jualth?'

'Yes, Lily?'

'Why is your name, or rather the letters of your name, scattered over the plaque?'

'It was a last-minute addition and we had to put the letters where we could fit them without ruining its appearance.'

Lily remained confused – the spelling of a name usually had an order. 'But why is it there? And why last minute?'

Not wishing to incite further discontent, Jualth had deliberately held the plaque back to avoid such awkward questions. But with the agreement no longer on the table, perhaps her bright but self-indulgent idea no longer mattered, even if the explanation still held a degree of embarrassment.

'Because the contract I had hoped would see us through our troubles required a name to represent all who had an interest in the distillery – to my way of thinking the whole community. I chose a name with a unique quality to protect everyone from potential comeback. That's why my name is on the plaque.'

Jualth paused; understanding of her laudable motive appeared to be absent from her sister's expression. 'Lily, surely one person shouldering the blame is better than a whole community. And, let's face it, I could hardly return home to have the idea sanctioned, then nip back to London and give the go ahead.'

Judging by Lily's lack of agreement, she begged to differ. 'So, let me get this right, if Jack had agreed to sign that piece of paper you brought back with you, the name that would represent our community would be … We'd be living in …' Lily could not bring herself to utter her sister's name. Her nerve was too galling. Help came from an unexpected quarter.

'Jualth,' the barman enunciated. 'Jualth,' he repeated, not calling towards the landlady, but rather throwing the name into the air to see if it landed comfortably upon their tiny hamlet. The barman's intervention gave Lily the opportunity to vent some of her growing anger.

'*Ned*, are you eavesdropping again? I've told you before …'

Ned put his hand on his heart and started to plead his innocence. 'I just wandered along to see what you were looking at, that's all.'

'And how long ago did that wander take place?'

Ned thought deeply. 'Umm ... I sort of followed Jualth along the bar when she came back down. I'm surprised you hadn't noticed me.'

'So you heard *all* of our conversation, Ned?' Jualth asked.

'About Albert, and your dreadful spelling ... yep, got all that.'

'And is there any chance of you keeping it to yourself?'

Ned rubbed the stubble on his chin, weighing up the ins and outs of a nigh on impossible task. He tutted, 'Well, let's see now. Do I not have a duty as barman to keep the clientele fully informed on all matters affecting our community?'

'You could very quickly become an ex-barman,' Jualth warned, 'and that's before I get banned from running the inn.'

The threat, added to the many multitudes dished out over his long period of service, received scant regard. Ned knew he was a permanent fixture – the bullying merely added ambience to the bar.

'Hold back on the name bit till Jack Vardy has gone, then do what you must,' Jualth relented. 'We can't have people siding with the enemy due to any misunderstandings.'

Ned murmured his agreement and gave his assurance that he would try his very best.

'Perhaps you'd like to find something more useful to do,' Lily suggested. 'Later on, we can have a quiet word about my sister and consider some sort of recompense, something along the lines of what she did for Lloyd. I have a leaning towards Mildred.'

Ned chirped and promised to give it some serious thought. He set off the way he had come, continuing to toss the present name of the landlady into the air and receiving strange glances for his trouble from Edith and the few remaining locals.

Lily refocused on the plaque and its inscription. 'Okay, Jualth, this will only be a meaningful way of getting at Jack if he knows about it. Do you intend to make a presentation when he visits on Saturday?'

'No, Lily, I intend to hang it where he can see it.'

'And when he does and *attempts* to read the inscription, that, and the small waterfall, will remind him of our mother and her telling of Jade's Fall.'

'Should be quite a surprise,' said Jualth, already savouring the moment.

'He might regret helping us with our Gaelic.'

'The more he regrets, the better.'

'But it won't put him off buying the distillery,' said Lily.

'*But* it will make him think about the people he's dealing with, and that's a start.'

Lily smiled; she was glad to see Jualth had remembered what the McTavish name stood for. 'Where shall we hang it?'

'In the centre corridor above the storeroom steps. Touch our whisky at your peril, Jack Vardy.'

Pleased with her idea, Jualth refilled her glass and felt the fire burning in her throat. 'I shall be surprisingly pleasant to Jack on Saturday; that will unnerve him. I will make sure he sees everything that he could possibly wish to see, plus the delights of an added extra.'

Lily noted with satisfaction the spark that had rekindled in her sister's eye – the plaque had served a useful purpose on two counts. 'I shall not join you unless you wish to witness a murder,' she said.

Jualth smiled; life was indeed returning to her veins. 'You know, Lily, the plaque wasn't the only thing I brought back from London. I have another surprise and the feeling that you're going to like it just as much as I do. I've a mind to hang it up on the side wall here, so everyone sitting at the bar can see it. It deserves the best gallery possible.'

Chapter 73

On Saturday afternoon, with only the odd elderly local to serve, Matilda's required nothing more than a bored barman to man the bar. Martha had helpfully abducted Jessica for a session of storytelling in Ned's cottage and Jualth had long since departed for the gathering at the distillery.

With two crackling fires providing warmth on a cool autumn's day, Edith and Lily sat in perfectly positioned ringside seats.

'Shameless! Absolutely shameless!' Edith muttered.

Lily's lips curled. She could not but admire her sister's audacity: 'Aye, Grandma, but a finely drafted masterpiece of a "shameless" model, all the same.'

'That's not the point, dear. She's stark naked, showing herself off and clearly enjoying every second. It's one thing to be confident, it's quite another to walk into a room full of strangers and offer to shed every stitch of clothing covering your modesty.'

Lily nodded thoughtfully. 'That is very confident,' she admitted. 'I wonder if I …?'

'I hope not, dear. I'd like to think that a leaning towards humility exists in at least one of my granddaughters.'

Lily laughed and patted her disgruntled grandmother on the thigh. 'It exists in us both, Grandma; we just don't let it hinder us.' She inspected the signature in the bottom right-hand corner of the picture. 'I wonder who Collette is?'

'A bright student with a perceptive eye and an excellent grasp of anatomy,' Edith answered. 'She'll do very well for herself, especially with such willing help provided.'

'We could have a very valuable original, just what we need at a time like this.'

'I'm all for selling it,' Edith muttered. 'Not even your mother would have gone to such lengths to flaunt herself in front of the locals, and that's accounting for her vanity.'

Lily chuckled. 'Competing with Ma would have been fun.'

'I dare say, and kept the place buzzing as well, not that it hasn't been an interesting place with just the two of you.'

Talk of Matilda always evoked memories of that fateful night when she did not return from her evening swim. With lanterns lit, Lily had led one of two search parties that had scoured the shores until, as daylight dawned, they had discovered her mother's body amongst the reeds. How a strong swimmer with full knowledge of Velana's dangers had met her death was a mystery never likely to receive a satisfactory explanation.

'I still miss her, Grandma.'

'As many do with biding memories of her brief time with us. She left nobody untouched, particularly my brazenly adventurous granddaughters. I think we have Matilda to blame for that far more than my Matthew.'

Lily's father did not evoke such memories. The young woman had been little more than a toddler when a gastric problem had spelled his early demise.

Edith sighed and a bout of tutting soon followed. 'I don't know, for all its artistic merit, it's not the sort of picture to display in a public bar. If she's that proud of her body, what's wrong with her bedroom? I mean, just look at the number of glasses Ned has dropped since she hung it up.'

Lily laughed. 'If he starts dropping bottles, we'll take it down. The odd glass we can afford, especially in the light of our dramatic upturn in trade these past few days.' She laughed again. 'You know, Grandma, it is tempting.'

'It might be, but I'm afraid you'll find no one from these parts who can light a candle to that young artist's talent. I'd give it a miss, if I were you, and claim the higher, dignified ground.'

The sound of a faint whimper had Lily glancing over her shoulder. 'Ned, you're staring again. How many times do I have to tell you?'

Ned, in earshot as usual, was resting on the bar forming his own opinion of Jualth's picture. 'I can't help it. It won't leave my eyes alone.'

'Try standing at the other end.'

'It can still see me down there.'

'Well, try anyway. It would be nice to have the occasional conversation without you listening in.'

Ned vehemently protested, 'But there's nothing happening at the other end.'

'Or this end, Ned. Now go – *go on.*'

Ned stuck his nose in the air and reluctantly did as ordered, assuming the same spellbound pose as before.

'You can't blame him,' said Edith. 'You can't blame any of the men.'

'But I can have a lot of fun,' Lily said mercilessly.

Edith turned her head to look out of the window and expressed a thought that occupied the mind of all those waiting in Matilda's, 'I wonder how she's getting on.'

Lily had a ready answer: 'Knowing Jualth, giving the second most-hated man in the world a dose of his own medicine. Perhaps I should have gone along to give Jack my opinion as well, just in case he doubted our unity.'

'Jualth will have all the unity she needs. She's regathered her spirit and that's enough to keep the men on our side for the time being.'

Lily grunted in disdain at the injustice at what was happening. It was almost too hard to believe. In fact, everything that had happened in the past few weeks was almost too hard to believe. 'Why, Grandma? Why did this threat have to rear its ugly head now?'

It was a question everyone wanted an answer to, Edith more so than any. Why that moment in time should be different to any other remained an unsolved mystery. 'I'm at a loss, as are we all, but I have not given up hope and neither must you.'

'I won't, Grandma. There's no way I'll let Jack Vardy prevail.'

Lily swivelled irritably around and called to the barman, offering him an early reprieve if he delivered two whiskies. They swiftly appeared and, as Lily sipped her Kvairen, she grunted out her frustration. 'I'm glad Ma never married Jack. I couldn't bear the thought of an evil stepfather.'

'Not evil, just a man who doesn't deserve our trust. Your mother was clever, she got what she wanted. The arrangement with the Brethna Distillery has allowed our community to survive and flourish with the inn at its centre. But Jack's proved to be a rather manipulative, selfish man that uses his friends for his own ill-gotten gain. I should have known and perhaps Matilda did and, for that reason, held back on marriage.'

Lily thought about Edith's description of Jack: *a user of friends for his own ill-gotten gain.* It reminded her of someone else – a proud man with responsibilities who could play a patient game to get what he wanted.

'He may not be the only man to have wandered into our midst and taken us in, Grandma. Are you not that tiny bit suspicious that a certain gentleman from London has done the same?'

'William?' Edith asked cautiously. 'You do not trust William?'

'Should I? Is our whisky not a prize asset to someone who knows its supply is restricted? With the agreement signed, the only change around here would be a few bottles travelling south, and more than likely to him and his co-conspirators. Alternatively, the agreement could all be a cover, something that never had a chance of working, as Jack pointed out. In that case the Brethna Distillery, and its *backers*, end up with everything.'

'Lily—' Edith said, attempting unsuccessfully to interrupt.

'When William sought us out, he found what he wanted and, on his return to London, devised plans with far more powerful people than Jack could ever reach. He did leave here alone, remember, Jualth was not permitted to ride with him. It could have all started that day, with the one man she trusts knocking on Jack Vardy's office door.'

It was possible but still only conjecture. Somebody was acting against their interests and Edith preferred to concentrate on the enemy closer to home. 'I'd hate to say you were right, dear, so I will not. Whilst Jualth's judgement lies with William, so must our trust.'

'But she's too close to him, Grandma. They were close before Jualth married and within a week of Frazer's death, they were back together.'

'Like I say, I'm accusing William of nothing. Jualth's not one to be easily taken in, even if strong feelings do exist between the two of them. As with Matilda, the inn and our community all come before any relationship and if that were not the case, Jualth would have left for London the first time she met William.'

'That might have worked out better, having someone there to watch our backs.' Lily brooded, she did not trust William and had hoped for her grandmother's support. She tried another quarter. 'What do you think, Ned?'

The barman sprung into life, delighted to have received an invitation to enter the conversation. 'Well,' he said thoughtfully, his eyes glued to the life drawing of the landlady, 'if you were to decide to have your picture drawn, I wouldn't mind having a go myself.'

It was not the answer Lily had expected. She growled and ordered the impudent scoundrel back to the farthest reaches of the bar.

Chapter 74

Later that afternoon, Jualth paid an earlier than expected visit to her mother-in-law. She was actually searching for a haven from the outside world after the gathering at the distillery and a couple of hours enduring Martha's non-stop chatter seemed a small price to pay. Only when Martha began to hint how welcome she and Jessica would be in her house back in Brethna, if they found themselves without a home, did Jualth decide enough was enough.

When she returned to the inn with her daughter, Jualth spurned the bar for the kitchen and then, later, a bedtime story for Jessica. Only after that did she venture into the lounge. It was, as expected, a solemn place with small groups of unhappy faces mulling over a single inauspicious topic. Even with Kvairen whisky flowing freely the mood had barely lifted.

'Welcome to the wake,' said Lily who, along with Ned, stood slumped over the bar and more than a little concerned by the lack of communication between themselves and the patrons. If anything, the gathering seemed determined to avoid the slightest eye contact – a worrying omen.

Jualth lifted the hatch and adopted the same pose. The quiet, inaudible murmurings provided the most depressing atmosphere she had ever witnessed in Matilda's. 'Has it been like this since they arrived?'

Lily nodded. 'I shall do the rounds again shortly, refill a few glasses, but I'm not holding out for any great change.'

Ned uttered a plaintive whine, deeply distressed by the whole, sorry state of affairs. 'What a way to go. We'll be giving away free bottles as parting gifts next.' There was no professional pride in dispensing whisky without charge.

Jualth empathised with her patrons and poured her own glassful, a prelude to many intended encores. 'It's their whisky, Ned. They shouldn't have to pay Jack Vardy for what already belongs to them.'

'They should not,' said Lily in heartfelt agreement. The less they left for Jack Vardy the better. 'Did he ask to come back to the inn?'

'The question did not arise, nor the need to tell him that his presence would lack for a welcome. After all but measuring up, he and his two lapdogs rode straight back to Brethna.'

'How thoughtful of them,' Lily said acerbically, praying for a fatal mishap as the light faded. 'And what was your view of Jack's performance?'

Jualth recalled the big man's confident and nonchalant manner. Perched on a crate to add stature to his authority, he played the role of the dependable managing director, the father figure that could and would take care of his workers and all those with an interest in the Kvairen Distillery.

'He was very impressive, Lily, he always is. He talked about a union between two great distilleries and praised Kvairen as the greatest whisky in the world.'

'And that needed saying, did it?' Ned asked cynically.

'No, but hearing it directly from someone who's well respected, if not liked, never got in the way of a favourable opinion. He talked about modernising the plant, creating more jobs and providing better wages than are presently paid.'

'With what he pays us, that would not be difficult,' Lily said bitterly. Jack Vardy's refusal to sanction an increase in their prices could all have featured in his long-term master plan. It was possible – more than possible – and a further source for immense irritation.

'I'll do it,' said Ned. His lack of movement for an implied action had both girls looking bemused.

'Do what, Ned?' Lily asked.

'The rounds,' he muttered painfully. With as much dignity as he could muster, he straightened, picked up a bottle, lifted the hatch and started towards the first group of depressives. Jualth and Lily watched closely, trying to glean a response to their generosity – no one so much as glanced in their direction to acknowledge the gesture. The worrying lack of communication continued.

'How did they react to Jack's benevolent words?' Lily asked.

'None of them are stupid. He received no warm applause for his eloquent speech, but that doesn't mean the men wouldn't like the extra money, however much they dislike the process by which they get it.'

'Did no one speak out, tell him his offer and presence were unwelcome?'

'No, Lily. Everyone listened in virtual silence, feeling perhaps that honesty with a prospective new employer and guardian of their interest, was probably not the best idea. Can you blame them?'

Lily muttered a curse and watched as Ned continued to dole out the whisky; even Father Donald appeared to be in the doldrums. The will to hold out seemed more uncertain than ever. They waited in silence until Ned had returned to his slumped position on the bar.

'Well, what did they have to say for themselves?' Lily asked. 'Have they given up or are they still with us?'

Ned shook his sorry head. 'If I'm any judge, they want to be with you and they'd like things to stay as they are with you girls here, but they're just not quite sure how that's going to happen.'

'They could *still* be with us if they can summon up the resolve to do what's right.'

Ned looked quizzical – he did not share the sisters' ruthless streak when it came to indulging in extreme courses of action.

'Light a flame and move on,' Lily whispered in his ear.

'Oh!' he said. Such a drastic action had indeed never occurred to him. 'That would be some fire.'

'The best ever and, at the same time, the worst ever,' said Jualth. 'Imagine a whole community abandoning its home and leaving the best malt that ever blessed this land as nothing more than a burnt-out and forgotten relic.'

'Imagine,' said Ned, not enjoying the imagery at all. 'And when the fish returned, what then?'

'They'd probably stay and some of their cousins might reappear as well,' said Lily, discovering a chink of light in an otherwise uniformly grey future. 'Think, Ned, normal fish in Velana and all fighting to be the first to dangle from the end of that rod of yours.'

Jualth's sudden laugh startled several locals. She held up her glass and assured all that it was the whisky's doing and no shame would fall upon them if they cared to follow suit.

'Have you ever been fishing, Ned?' Jualth asked out of casual curiosity. She could recall others using his rod, but never him.

'On and off,' Ned confessed, 'but not in recent years.'

'So why have you kept your rod?' Lily asked.

A mischievous smirk that would have done Lily proud brought life to his tired face. 'To lend to our guests, of course, the ones that ask if fishing is permitted. It has given me many happy hours of amusement watching them toil.'

Jualth laughed again and rewarded her barman with a peck on the cheek. 'He's worth fighting for as well, don't you think, Lily?'

'Be lost without him,' Lily agreed, though her meaning was not quite as flattering as it first seemed; Ned provided an extremely useful target for her Gaelic curses.

Ned perked up even more, basking in the sudden warmth of endearment. 'Well,' he confessed, 'that's pretty much what Martha said to me.' It was a careless remark that he immediately regretted.

'What?' the sisters said as one.

'I said …'

'Yes, I heard what you said, Ned, and it worried me greatly,' said Jualth. 'It's beginning to sound like my mother-in-law is angling for an indefinite stay.'

Ned stuttered, rocked by the sudden and unexpected reversal in admiration. He sipped his whisky, straightened his back and pluckily set about defending his guest: 'I can't tell her to leave and I wouldn't want to. She has many wonderful qualities.'

'Such as?' Jualth demanded.

'Such as ...' Ned swallowed, thinking hard, '... her recollections of Brethna for one. The idea of writing them down and dedicating them to her son's memory has crossed her mind.'

Jualth and Lily glanced at one another, stunned by the woman's audacity. 'She had better be careful what she writes then,' said Jualth, 'otherwise her memories will not see the light of day, whether dedicated to my late husband or not.'

'Someone will need to keep a close eye on her,' said Lily, staring menacingly at Ned to test where his loyalties lay.

'Mind,' said Jualth – having laid down the law she now decided to think more deeply – 'if we're not here it barely matters. There's no point in keeping secrets if we have nothing to protect.'

'Jualth, you're straying into the bleak deserted wasteland again. Come back before you end up like this morbid lot. And, Ned, make it clear to Martha that she'll have to pass our censorship before anyone else sees her book. We cannot have her revealing everything she can remember.

'I'll have a word with her,' said Ned.

'So will I,' said Jualth grimly.

Ned noticed the arrival of a new customer and backed away to serve him. With an eye on the barman, the sisters resettled and turned their thoughts back to the afternoon's event.

'Did the impressive Jack notice our plaque?' Lily asked.

'I made sure he did. He had a good long stare and made a point of praising the craftsman. He then moved on.'

'No reaction?'

'No outward reaction, but the message hit home, I know it did. It will provide sustenance to chew over on his return journey.'

'And what about the agreement?'

'I informed him that I still have it in my possession and that its existence, if not the details, was now open knowledge. He quietly ignored me.'

Lily grunted; the man appeared unwilling to revisit a battleground he assumed he had already conquered.

'I'll remind him all the same at our next meeting,' said Jualth.

'Do that and let him know I'm thinking about him and always will be.'

Lily pushed herself away from the bar. 'Time we moved amongst the brooding masses and instilled life into waning morals. I shall take the far end where, for some reason, the fascination for your picture remains.'

'And I shall bless this end with a further instalment of how my masterpiece came into being.'

They lifted the hatch and set to work, aiming to raise spirits and dispel the overhanging cloud of gloom.

Chapter 75

Outside the wind gathered strength, gusting autumn's organic debris into a chaotic airborne dance. The night did not offer a friendly passage for those wishing to travel and only those sufficiently warmed by the whisky and log fires felt able to depart. It was, then, with some surprise that a sudden draft fed its way through the hall and into the lounge as, with one swift movement, the front door opened and closed.

Jualth, who was handing empties over the bar to Ned, stared in the direction of the hall, waiting for the visitor to reveal himself from behind the small partition. Slowly and hesitantly he emerged, hat and riding crop in hand, a dark cloak falling from his shoulders to below his waist.

Jualth's eyes widened, then narrowed with disdain. Ned glanced to the far end to see if anyone else had noticed the new arrival's presence. Panic festered not far beneath the surface as his eyes flicked between Lily and the visitor. If there was one person above all others who was not welcome at Matilda's, it was fair to say that this person had just walked in.

'Good evening, Mrs McTavish,' said the windswept Excise officer with as much dignity as his bedraggled appearance would allow.

Jualth's reply was anything but cordial. Her voice seethed with anger but did not rise above a whisper. 'What the hell are you doing here? How dare you … how dare you walk back into my inn.'

'Mrs McTavish, if I could just explain—'

His pained efforts to reason with the landlady got no further. A glass smashed at the far end of the bar, not by an accidental slip of the hand, but an intentional assault upon the wall. The moment Ned feared had arrived and he was heading with great haste through the hatchway, hell-bent on preventing a murder. Jualth temporarily abandoned her own display of loathing and leapt in front of Lily to help Ned and Father Donald stop a screaming, raging, fire-breathing redhead from getting her hands on Mr Cecil Pennan.

'Let me go!' Lily yelled, 'I want to kill him, *let-me-kill-him!*'

Lily's struggled to free herself – her hatred and desire for vengeance ran deep. 'He killed my daughter, that man!' Lily screamed, spitting venom with saliva. '*What* is he doing here? *Why* has he come back?'

Jualth managed to wrestle Lily to the ground with Ned holding onto one arm, Father Donald the other and her lying on top facing the cause of all the trouble.

'I don't know, Lily,' she said, fighting to catch her breath, 'but he had better have a damn good reason if he thinks I'm going to hold you at bay for long.'

The sound of crying started on the floor above.

'Oh great,' Jualth fumed, glancing to the ceiling. '*Grandma.*'

'It's okay, dear. I'm on my way.' Edith stepped around the grounded group and, without the slightest attempt to acknowledge their visitor, passed through the archway.

Jualth indicated towards one of the tables. 'Thomas, *anyone*, do you think you could clear the table nearest the door and put the glasses on the bar?' The request was quickly complied with, so providing a surface free of potential weapons.

'Mr Pennan,' she said, still breathing heavily, 'get rid of your cloak and take the seat with the hall to your back.'

The Excise officer did as instructed.

Jualth then addressed her sister, 'Right, Lily, we're about to get up. We shall then sit opposite that man and, before you feel the need to inflict any more damage on either him or us, I want you to listen to what he has to say. Have you got that?'

Lily's chest heaved from the spent exertion of her struggle, but her mind remained set on murder.

'*Lily*, before we get up, I need an answer. If you don't give me an answer, we'll be listening to that man's explanation where we are ... on the floor.' Lily remained silent, her eyes fixed on the visitor. '*Lily, say something!*'

Her sister's mouth twitched, but remained resolutely shut. The best she could do was a tiny, grudging nod that provided an answer if no softening of her manner.

Jualth emitted a pained groan. 'Right, that will have to do. Ned, I shall get up first and take over on your arm. Father Donald, if you wouldn't mind holding onto yours, I'd like you to sit on the other side of Lily at the table.'

'I don't need either of you to hold onto me,' her sister said tersely.

'Fine, then once we're seated, and you've proved you can be trusted, we'll let go. Ned ... are you ready to move?' He nodded nervously. 'Right, on the count of three.'

They carried out the manoeuvre with the utmost caution and Lily soon found herself sitting opposite Mr Pennan, penned in between two minders. Everybody else stood staring down upon the unwelcome guest.

Ned cleared his throat. 'Perhaps if we gave them room,' he suggested, holding out his arms to usher the angry mob away.

'If you wouldn't mind,' Jualth said to aid her barman. 'I'll speak to you all in a minute. Thomas, if you'd like to stay on hand at the bar with Ned.'

Reluctantly, the locals moved away, murmuring their own judgments for desired retribution on the visitor.

'You're still holding my arm, Jualth,' Lily informed her sister without deviating her eyes from her intended victim.

Jualth let go but remained alert to the slightest movement. 'Over to you, Mr Pennan, and if you could be quick about it.'

'I shall be as brief as I can, Mrs McTavish.'

'Get on with it then and, for your sake, the explanation for your return better have nothing to do with the results of your inspection.'

'That's not the reason for my visit.'

'Then what is?' Lily whispered with unremitting hostility.

'To t-tell …'

Mr Pennan stuttered. He never stuttered. He put it down to a quickening heartbeat brought about by his fight against the elements. He put his hand to his mouth, coughed and tried again. 'To tell you something that perhaps you do not know and to revisit a comment you directed at me in London, Mrs McTavish.'

Jualth couldn't imagine which comment he meant. 'Let's start with what we do not know,' she suggested.

Mr Pennan had not expected a warm welcome on his reappearance, but he had expected a degree of civility. He now found himself trapped between the hostile elements of a Scottish night and the barely contained wrath of the landlady and her sister. The only thing he had on his side was his steadfast belief in his mission.

'I'v-I've come to explain what initiated my inspection of your distillery,' he said slowly, unable to conceal a quiver in his voice.

'Was it not your observations at the Brethna Distillery?' Jualth interrupted.

'No, Mrs McTavish. I knew of you before leaving London and arriving in Brethna.'

For the first time, Lily released Mr Pennan from her vice-like glare and glanced at Jualth. Both sisters feared what was coming next.

Jualth assumed a cold menace of her own. 'I might not believe what you are about to say, Mr Pennan, so you be very careful how you tell me.'

'It is not what you think, Mrs McTavish, you have no need to cast any blame in the direction of London. The Brethna Distillery itself called us in. The arrangement between them and you was brought to our attention by its general manager.'

A moment of stony silence passed as all in earshot found the revelation all but untenable.

'No way!' Jualth retorted. 'Not even Jack Vardy would do that.'

'You're making this up,' Lily snarled, angered that such a suggestion could be true. 'Why would someone deliberately inform on themselves?'

The disbelief in this revelation was at least one thing that the Excise officer *had* anticipated. 'I admit, it is not standard practice and it is the first time I have come across such a circumstance. Normally, I would not be able to discuss this with you, but I have been authorised by my superiors to do so.'

'How good of them,' Jualth muttered through gritted teeth.

'The reason why I shall mention presently.'

'Now is a good time,' Lily hissed.

The Excise officer halted. The intimidating undertone lacing each interruption did not aid the delivery of a speech he had carefully rehearsed many times during his long journey north.

'Go on, Mr Pennan,' Jualth nudged. 'I want to hear all there is to know about Jack Vardy.'

Father Donald offered the Excise officer a faint smile, Mr Pennan's only encouragement from the one man capable of defending him if the explanation proved insufficient.

'The apparent reason given by the Brethna Distillery for calling us in was to bring our attention to an unlawful act that they were involved in but did not wish to remain a party to.'

Jualth continued to struggle. 'But that's putting themselves in trouble.'

'That is correct, Mrs McTavish. Once I received my orders, I had to do a full inspection and report my findings in the accustomed manner. However …'

Mr Pennan took a quick breath in a determined effort to re-establish authority to his voice. 'I have since been made aware of a short visit to London undertaken by Mr Vardy where the connection between your two distilleries was discussed and an understanding on liability reached between the Brethna Distillery and my office. This understanding would only be exacerbated if my work provided additional findings.'

Despite initial reluctance, the actions of Jack Vardy seemed plausible – his capacity for scheming knew no bounds.

'So he already knew the punishment he would face,' said Lily, though her comment was not strictly directed at the Excise officer. 'He sat at that meeting making out the roof was about fall in when, unbeknown to us, his betrayal merited nothing more than a smack on the wrist and an undetectable amount of guilt.'

'Meeting?' said Mr Pennan.

'Held on the day of the fire,' said Jualth. 'The fire occurred only minutes after Mr Vardy declined to help us.'

Lily maintained her hostile manner towards the man from the Custom House – he was still far from off the hook. 'Why have *you* come to tell us this? Who sent you?'

Mr Pennan diverted his eyes towards the bar, to the uncompromising expressions of the two men who stood there. If he could have seen beyond the three bodies sitting opposite, to the remainder of the inn's occupants, he would have discovered no better. The priest remained his only apparent protector.

'I was invited into a meeting on Friday morning in which Mr Tombs and Mr Halar were both present.'

'William!' said Jualth. 'He was there?'

'Yes, Mrs McTavish. I was informed of an agreement that had been negotiated by the Excise Service on your behalf and notified of an impediment that had arisen to obstruct it.'

'Brethna's desire for an acquisition,' said Jualth, translating his words into English. She held up her hand to stop Mr Pennan continuing. 'Let me get this straight: they sent you all the way up here to tell us who was responsible for the upheaval your visit has caused our community.'

'How does that help us?' Lily said sharply. 'It doesn't change anything apart from raising our hatred levels for yet another man. With no signed agreement, you will still prosecute.'

Edith quietly returned and hovered near the archway where her granddaughters could see her. Jessica was now asleep, a condition she wished to maintain.

'That isn't the only news I've brought from London,' the Excise officer continued. 'There was another reason that made me return and face *this* reception.'

Mr Pennan opened his hands in a gesture designed to extract a degree of sympathy. It did not succeed. Unfriendly faces stared back in a silence broken only by the crackle of two log fires. Although all recognised his bravery, he had so far said nothing that would rescue them from the plight he had been so instrumental in bringing about.

'We're listening, Mr Pennan,' Lily said coldly.

The Excise officer reverted back to his rehearsed story. 'As I alluded to previously, you said something to me in London, Mrs McTavish, which I did not have an opportunity to respond to.'

'The fire,' said Jualth.

Lily stirred, eliciting an involuntary movement from Father Donald and her sister. 'It's all right,' she said quietly. 'Just getting myself comfortable.'

Father Donald and Jualth glanced at one another. They relaxed, but only marginally.

'Indeed,' Mr Pennan continued. 'You intimated that I had in some way been responsible for the fire equipment not working, which, if it had, could have prevented the fire from taking hold so rapidly.'

'And given us the chance to get my daughter out of the warehouse before it exploded,' Lily added, to aid Mr Pennan's discomfort. It worked. He looked away, finding the strain of the moment as difficult as those around him.

'Yes, Mrs McTavish, that is the point I wish to address. The powers inherent to my inspection allow me to go wherever I chose to check all functions of the distillery. The fire equipment kept at Brethna was not in an operational state *before* I inspected it. I brought that to the attention of Mr Vardy prior to leaving Brethna to come here. It is part of a distillery's duty, and the residing Excise official, to make sure the equipment is in working order and is regularly checked. My understanding is that nothing was done to rectify the situation in the few days before the fire.'

Mr Pennan's efforts to deflect the blame only resulted in charging the atmosphere further – he had just succeeded in attacked a dear friend.

'Don't go blaming Arthur,' Lily remonstrated. 'We only have your word that it wasn't working properly. No one else has mentioned there was a problem with the equipment, only that you spent a considerable amount of time in the fire hut.'

'Well, maybe if you asked them directly, *and* in confidence, they'd have more to say.'

'What do you mean?' Jualth demanded, deeply disturbed by Mr Pennan's insinuation.

'The fire equipment was not the only problem that I found.'

Lily moved again, agitating the reflexes of her minders. Revealing problems that she did not wish to believe was causing torment. As on previous occasions in the past few weeks, she wanted to blame Mr Cecil Pennan and no one else for everything that had happened.

'Go on, we're still listening,' said Jualth, once Lily had resettled.

'Brethna produces excellent products and runs the main distillery and blending process to the highest of standards. But its spending on peripheral maintenance and on tasks not directly connected to the production of whisky is poor – very poor.'

The next part of Mr Pennan's explanation threatened to be the hardest yet. He glanced at Jualth and her sister and was thankful for the third person at the table and, however hostile, the two bystanders to the side.

'One of my items of concern was directed towards the manufacture of the whisky casks.'

Jualth inhaled sharply. 'Be very, very careful, Mr Pennan. My husband helped to make those casks and he died in the fire along with my niece.'

'I know that, Mrs McTavish but, nevertheless, I have to inform you that some of the casks were not well made.'

Jualth looked at Mr Pennan. Her countenance froze into the same fearsome mask as worn by her sister.

'What was wrong with the way they were made?' Father Donald asked softly, in an effort to nudge forward a conversation that had reached an alarming halt. His intervention also served to remind the two women of his presence.

'The staves had been incorrectly cut, Father Donald.'

'What are you trying to blame my husband for?' Jualth said, raising her voice.

'I'm not blaming your husband, Mrs McTavish, I can assure you. The making of the casks at the Brethna Distillery is a matter for management and most were made correctly. Any change in the manufacture process came as a direct instruction from them. Your husband made casks as he was taught, in a traditional method. I had occasion to watch him do it. He knew how to make a sound cask.'

Mr Pennan noticed a slight change in expression and atmosphere. Although his audience continued to listen intently, he had said something to ward them off. If he could have conjured up an image of Daniel and his cart laden with casks from the Kvairen Distillery, as all others around the table were doing, he would have understood the significance of his remarks.

'The casks I am referring to were put together in such a way that the grain of the oak panels was cut in the wrong direction. When this happens the wood does not properly seal.'

Lily and Jualth stirred; they shared pensive glances with Edith and those at the bar. The Excise officer's explanation had taken a nasty turn.

'We have a few casks like that ourselves; Brethna makes them for us,' said Jualth in a more conciliatory tone.

'And they hold the same danger for you as they held for Brethna. The reason the fire took hold so quickly was because the ground had been soaked in the highly flammable liquid contained in those casks. The moment a flame touched the ground, nothing could have stopped the consequences, not even fully functioning fire equipment. Add to that the poorly maintained roof and door of the warehouse …'

'You don't need to say any more,' said Lily, who was now staring coldly into the distance, contemplating the consequences of the intentional defect in the oak casks. Instead of being stored in the Kvairen warehouse for the sole purpose of feeding Velana's feeder stream, it appeared some may mistakenly have been sent back to Brethna.

'But I do,' Mr Pennan almost implored. He needed to know he had convinced the sisters and everyone in listening range where the blame lay. Little did he realise just how far that blame stretched. 'Bad maintenance and poor storage were the reasons that the fire took hold with such speed. What happened could have been prevented.'

Jualth put up her hands to stop the Excise officer; she had heard enough. She experienced the same chill as her sister and for the same reason. She glanced to her side. Lily merely shook her head and continued to stare into the distance. Jualth followed the gaze of Father Donald to Edith and then Ned and Thomas. All of them appeared to have aged ten years.

'Okay, Mr Pennan, I think I understand all of that and, much as I do not like it, I'm in no mind to question its truth. However, I do need to know why you have come *in person* to deliver this message. Is this a matter of conscience or orders?'

The Excise officer did not appreciate the limited choices and, although he understood the underlying reasons for their inhospitable welcome, he had hoped by now for a sign of gratitude directed towards his endeavours. He persisted, nevertheless. 'I was asked and I agreed to come. I was given full authority to report these findings at the next meeting held in Brethna.'

'Why so helpful?' Lily asked, questioning his motives.

'I am representing the interests of my office who have not been pleased by the recent developments. My understanding is that the outcome they most favour is for the signing of the agreement made by Mrs McTavish whilst in London. We would be reluctant to pursue any other course.'

Lily groaned and shut her eyes. She leant back and pitched her face towards the ceiling. 'I think I'm dreaming and I cannot decide whether it's a good dream or a very, *very* bad one.'

'And I don't know if any of this will help,' said Jualth. 'We can blame Jack Vardy all we want, but that's a long way from getting our agreement signed or understanding *why* you are doing this, Mr Pennan.'

Their suspicions remained, but what could they do except grasp every helping hand that stretched out towards them? Control did not lie with them – it never had.

'The inspection was unavoidable after we were called in,' Mr Pennan explained. 'We had no alternative but to investigate. I was not informed of the prior arrangement between my employers and the Brethna Distillery and I had no knowledge of your subsequent agreement to avoid prosecution. This agreement is one I've never come across, though in the case of the prior arrangement, leniency is normally granted for cooperation with the Excise Service.'

The extent of Jack Vardy's deceit remained staggering, but perhaps his cunning would end up being his downfall once the Kvairen Distillery workers were acquainted with *all* the facts?

'Were you told anything else before you returned to us, like what we're supposed to do with all this new information?' Jualth asked.

'All that is needed is for you to attend the next meeting and ask for your agreement to be reconsidered. I will return to Brethna and ask to attend the meeting as a representative of my employers.'

'So we vote again, and with Jack Vardy and his two yes men, we lose again.'

'Jack shares the blame for the death of my daughter,' said Lily, breaking her silence. She was resigned to letting the Excise officer live. Someone else could die in his place.

'Leave the meeting to me, Lily. You stay here with Jessica and Grandma.'

'I want him to pay!'

'I know, Lily, so do I, but another demonstration of your temper will achieve nothing.'

'Will anything?'

Lily needed retribution. Their own responsibility in Harriet's death was an admission neither wished to make.

'Did you not pass Jack Vardy and his party on the way here?' Thomas asked the Exciseman from his position at the bar.

'I passed no one and I did not linger in Brethna, Mr Brown.'

Jualth was not surprised their paths had not crossed. 'Mr Pennan would have kept to the lanes, Thomas. He knows no other way. Jack will have ridden cross-country to get back in the shortest time possible.'

'Does that mean you've been travelling all day, Mr Pennan?' Father Donald asked.

'Since I disembarked from the train, early this morning.'

'You need a room,' Jualth stated, an informative if not friendly remark, to let him know he could spend the night under her roof.

'I'll do it,' said Lily. She motioned for her sister to move, but Jualth remained seated, staring at her sister's unhappy face. Lily virtually pleaded to be released. 'I need something to do, Jualth. I do not want to sit here any longer.'

Father Donald nodded and Jualth moved aside. Lily swiftly disappeared through the archway. Her concerned grandmother followed.

'Your horse, Mr Pennan?' Jualth enquired.

'I left it at the stables.'

Jualth turned to her barman. 'Ned, can you take care of it?'

Ned sighed. 'Now, why did I know you'd ask …?' He caught a glimpse of Jualth's uncompromising glare and wisely decided to change tac. 'I'll get my coat,' he said gruffly.

When Ned departed for the stables, Thomas moved in beside the landlady. For the first time, Jualth showed a small degree of respect, if not warmth, to the Excise officer's effort.

'You were very brave to have come back to see us, Mr Pennan. You're not the most popular person to have stepped inside this inn; you'll understand why a second visit is a considerable strain on our instincts to show hospitality.'

In his job, the Excise officer needed no reminders. He expected respect but nothing more. 'My inspections do not normally require a speedy return to the site,' he replied.

'But you had your orders,' said Jualth, intimating that he was nothing more than an obedient lackey.

'In light of the death of your husband and your sister's daughter, I wanted to come.'

Jualth heaved a sigh at the human side of a government official. She still did not wish to give Mr Pennan credit for having feelings.

'Come now, Jualth,' Father Donald interrupted. 'Mr Pennan is no different to anyone else and has the same right to express his sadness for our loss. You should not judge him in any other way.'

The priest was a person Jualth did respect. She moved on, but did nothing to make Mr Pennan feel at ease – she just could not bring herself to be pleasant.

'Do you not find all this a bit strange, Mr Pennan? You are a man who knows and lives by rules. It is your job to implement them, but here we are aiding others to bend and break them for unlawful gain. Surely that is against your conscience and the principles of your office?'

The Excise officer had a stark warning: 'The rules might yet apply, Mrs McTavish. My department have expressed their preference to resolve this matter; it is not something they can implement themselves. And to answer your question, I do my job. It is not my position to find issue with decisions that are made with many more facts than I have at my disposal.'

'But as you are aware that the rules are being *bent,* do you not feel like questioning those in a higher position?'

'This is an unusual situation, Mrs McTavish.'

'Isn't it just, Mr Pennan.'

'And Mr Tombs and Mr Halar are well-respected men. The thinking and reasoning behind this arrangement I trust to be sound.'

Jualth didn't believe a word of it, but she understood the reason behind the carefully chosen words. 'And what about you, Mr Pennan? Will you conveniently forget about your scathing reports on our two distilleries?'

'I am kept busy, Mrs McTavish. I do not have time to dwell once reassigned. When Mr Tombs picked up your case, all decisions on the course of action, and my future involvement, fell under his jurisdiction.'

Thank God for lackeys, and such obedient, unquestioning, ambitious ones like Mr Pennan. If anyone knew how to get on in his chosen profession, surely it was the inspector sitting opposite.

'I'm glad to hear it, though I wish there was hope for you in a world where people question rules and feel they are an unnecessary intrusion into civilised existence.'

'I think we've all learnt this evening that abiding by rules can have considerable merit and save many from unforeseen, consequential heartache,' said Father Donald. There was a limit as to how much he would let Jualth get away with. Everybody occasionally needed reining in.

Lily returned to the table via the bar door. 'My grandmother is preparing some food for you, Mr Pennan. You're in the same room as last time, *if* you can remember the way.'

'Could I have some hot water?'

'Already there. Your meal will follow shortly.'

'Thank you, Mrs McTavish.' He took the hint and courteously withdrew from a cool display of unhappy faces.

Lily sat opposite her sister in the Excise officer's vacated seat. '*Jack Vardy!* Are you seriously telling me to leave him alone?'

'Yes, Lily, I am. My husband died because of him, as well.'

'*Jualth!*'

'*Lily!* Sort it out in your mind; this is not the time for vengeance. Now grab a bottle – we have a lot of patient people brooding over Jack Vardy's offer who require urgent updating. The sooner we sort them out, the better for everyone.'

Chapter 76

'Where is he?' Edith asked, her patience having long since reached the dregs of the barrel. Sitting opposite Jualth at the kitchen table sipping coffee, her mood was as overcast as the morning sky. The tempest of the previous night had abated down to a light, swaying of trees.

'A good question, *Grandmother*. His horse is in the stables but he's not in his room, the lounge, the garden ... In fact, there's been no single sighting of that man since he regained the right to live. *And*, if he is snooping around on behalf of his Excise bosses again, then he's doing a wonderful job of undermining all the good work—'

Edith interrupted, if only to display her own, more controlled, displeasure. 'They cannot change what the system has turned them into. He's an inspector under instruction who cannot function without guidance. If his orders were to close us down yesterday, he would have done so.'

Jualth smouldered in outrage at the very thought. 'We should thank our lucky stars for the orders he was given then! Lily could have done anything to him last night if she'd managed to get hold of him.'

Edith did not doubt it having witnessed the primeval instincts of her granddaughters, where action preceded thought far too often. She had worked hard to rid them of their aggressive tendencies but with little success.

Jualth reached out to her side and rocked her quietly snoozing daughter in her cradle with a touch more energy than was strictly necessary. It was an action more likely to rouse Jessica than soothe her rest.

'Poor, dear Lily,' said Edith with a long drawn-out sigh. 'One day she has a mind to kill one person, the next that person is reprieved and she wants to kill another.'

Jualth stopped fidgeting with the cradle and instead drummed the table top with her fingers. After their guest had departed to his room the previous evening, Jualth, Lily and Edith had sat amongst their patrons to discuss the underhand ways of their supposed saviour. Ill-feeling and condemnation had been rife and support for the takeover quickly crumbled as a consequence. All present agreed to follow the landlady's lead and accept the fate that followed, though the subdued manner in which they backed her only emphasised the communal sense of guilt – no one was blameless for their recent loss.

'We're in there, aren't we, Grandma, in there with Jack?'

Edith breathed in sharply as if reacting to a low blow that had hit its mark.

'Not all our casks leaked,' Jualth continued, 'just a few, the ones put aside for us to feed Velana. The Brethna Distillery either mixed up its barrels and used them for their own whisky or … or we mixed them up with our delivery and sent Brethna casks that leaked. How Lily will cope with that possibility ...?'

'She has her ways and killing Jack Vardy seems high on the list,' said Edith. 'She will not accept the blame is ours whilst responsibility for poor upkeep can be laid at Jack's door.'

Jualth was of a mind to agree with Lily's preferred form of retribution, wishful thinking she knew, but why not savour the thought? Her daughter's cradle suffered a renewed bout of uneven rocking; Jessica grumbled but managed to stay asleep. 'Och, I wish I knew the whereabouts of that piteous man. What is he doing, Grandma? Where is he?'

Disbelief and mistrust prevailed. Mr Pennan was an Excise officer; if he could not be cajoled – as in the case of Arthur – he was a danger, so why this mission to deliver eleventh-hour aid?

'Lily told me Mr Pennan mentioned William last night?' said Edith.

'Aye, in his very correct English manner. His boss summoned him into a meeting where William was present. Why Lily cannot see he's fighting our cause …?'

'Her doubts are not without grounds, and it is wise for all of us to remain wary. After all, none of us – with the possible exception of your mother – foresaw Jack Vardy's willingness or ability to deceive.'

'I've got to meet him again on Wednesday,' Jualth bemoaned. 'It won't be a pleasant reunion but at least I now know Jack Vardy's a businessman and nothing more. I'll treat him as he treats me and work hard to keep my cool. At least that's one positive lesson I've learnt from my trip to London.'

Jualth sighed deeply, yearning for the presence of her absent mother and the counsel she would have provided. 'If only Ma were here, Grandma. I'd love to see her sitting opposite Jack Vardy, making the traitor explain himself. She'd have been his match.'

'And so will you, dear, so will you.'

Jessica began to stir, at last succumbing to her mother's overzealous rocking. 'Thanks again for looking after my wee bundle of joy last night. When this wretched business has passed, and provided I still have my freedom, I shall endeavour to resume where I left off – pre-fire.'

Jualth lifted her daughter out of the cot and, leaving Edith at the kitchen table, wandered into the garden. In the distance, in self-imposed isolation, they spotted a preoccupied Lily sitting on the grassy bank of the northern shore sketching.

'There you are,' Jualth whispered. 'I wondered where you'd got to.' She was not, however, referring to her sister, but to a certain missing Excise officer who had just appeared from underneath the canopy of shoreline trees.

Alarmingly, he had seen Lily and turned in her direction. Jualth tutted her disapproval, settled on the bench and watched closely.

When Lily noticed him, she shut her sketchbook and stood up, determined to walk away from unwanted company. Her enmity persisted and Mr Pennan remained a potential target, even with her anger redirected. She lingered, fighting the impulse for blatant ill manners. It was a fight liable to fail.

'Mrs McTavish, good morning.' The Excise officer's voice had regained the assertiveness that denoted a man of standing.

'Mr Pennan,' Lily replied in restrained acknowledgement. 'Yet again we bump into one another at the edge of my loch when, on this occasion, I and all others had expected a thoughtful and definitive dawn exit. But, oh no, how silly of us, we forgot you were a true-blue Excise man who cannot resist the opportunity to prowl and forage. Do you ever switch off, Mr Pennan?'

Lily did not let him answer, she was ill-disposed towards the excuses and justifications made by the powers-that-be. 'No, of course you don't, last night was an apparition, a mere blip. Now you can revert back to your very own officious, rule-abiding self again.'

Mr Pennan hesitated, startled that the aggression towards him remained so vehement. 'Mrs McTavish ...' he started. Even a few well-meaning words were difficult.

Lily provided unsympathetic encouragement. 'Yes, Mr Pennan, you were about to say?'

The Excise officer appeared to lose heart. His expression visibly fell, making Lily wonder if she had overdone her bitterness. 'Mrs McTavish, I just wanted to say how sad I was to learn about the death of your daughter.'

Lily looked away, stunned to have received sympathy from a man she barely regarded as having a heart and whom she had wished dead up until only a few hours before. Her attitude towards him had probably made him express his sentiments with considerably more emotion than intended.

'I did not get the opportunity yesterday evening to express my condolences. I hope you will accept them now.'

Lily stepped back and half-turned, warding off any further words. 'All right, Mr Pennan, that's enough.'

'But ...'

'*Enough*, Mr Pennan. Let's just leave it there, shall we? You're sorry and so am I – we all are.'

Mr Pennan heeded her wishes. He had surprised himself with his show of sincerity. His sympathy towards the bereaved mother had felt very personal.

'So ... as you've just come from the north, I presume you've been up to the distillery this morning? Why the visit? There's no one up there today and, without further supplies from Brethna, when the current run is finished that will be that for this year – maybe for ever.'

Mr Pennan needed no reminders of their predicament or the person they blamed. 'I needed to see if anything had changed. Assuming production is still a long-term proposition, Mrs McTavish, there are certain safety measures you need to be made aware of.'

Lily's guard instantly rose – the loathsome man just could not stop interfering! 'Such as, Mr Pennan?'

'The doors, Mrs McTavish.'

'What about them?'

'They are never locked. It is possible for all and sundry to walk in at any time without first gaining permission.'

'Up until recently, no unwelcome visitor has ever felt the need "to walk in" without permission. And what is the point of bolting the doors to keep out someone who possesses an unrepentant right of entry like yourself?'

On another occasion, the Excise officer would have been more inclined to stand his ground, but the circumstances here were complicated and he did not wish to widen the gulf between the two of them. On the contrary, he had hoped to narrow it.

'Perhaps it would be better to leave the recommendations until you receive my report but, please, take note of them, they are very important and could prevent a future fire. As the warehouse storing your whisky is attached to the rest of the distillery, a fire would be far more destructive than at Brethna.'

Lily clenched her teeth; she, Jualth, Edith … everyone knew about the dangers, but no one cared for a deep and lengthy lecture on the matter, especially after Brethna.

'And what about your report to Jack Vardy, Mr Pennan? What will you say to him when you sit down to deliver your findings?'

'I shall highlight the fault that did exist – the lack of attention and state of disrepair to the ancillary building – and express what I expect to happen in the future. I will then notify the management that the conclusion of their inspection will depend upon the outcome of the meeting to be held on Wednesday, which I will ask to attend.'

Mr Pennan took a moment to reflect on what he had just said. Though the action went against his training and the principles that guided his character, it did fit in with his orders and these rules took precedence over his understanding and individual judgement.

For her part, Lily was thankful he could not see far enough to include the Kvairen Distillery in his condemnation. The danger of such an insight when he presented his findings to Jack Vardy could end up doing them more harm than good.

'I want that agreement signed, Mr Pennan. Just give them your report and leave. In fact, leave altogether, go back to London and don't wait until Wednesday's meeting. Let them work out the possible consequences for themselves without your assistance. I don't want you to doubt us by anything they might say. Jack Vardy is a very clever man.'

Mr Pennan also did not wish to doubt her, though he clearly understood little of the reason behind her fears.

'I will be wary, Mrs McTavish.'

'Good, then I will believe you are on our side when you speak to them. After that, you can go back to being your old self if you so choose unless, of course, this experience has in some way changed you.'

Mr Pennan looked away. He had aspired a long time to reach the position in society he thought a respectable gentleman should seek. But his trip north, into a close-knit community dominated by the family that ran the inn, had touched his emotions in a way he had not expected or could explain considering their run-ins. In the process, the McTavish women had subtly opened his eyes to other, possibly more important, aspects of a feminine nature. 'It is beautiful here,' he said after a long pause. 'I wish I had more time to look around and study the habitat.'

'Wrong time of year for that unless you like to see it withering away, Mr Pennan. When are you leaving?'

'Tomorrow. As I will be unable to arrange a meeting today, I thought I'd take the chance to explore and relax in this breathtaking landscape.

'Wonderful,' Lily muttered under her breath. What did it take to make someone realise they were not welcome?

'I see you have your book with you again, Mrs McTavish. What have you drawn this morning?'

Lily held the book close to her chest as if to protect it from a schoolmaster's intrusion. Irritatingly, Mr Pennan waited, expecting an answer to his earnest question. With the enthusiasm of an uncooperative pupil Lily relented, but only as a means to an end. With his curiosity satisfied, the schoolmaster might then leave her alone – for good.

'It's a project I have set myself, Mr Pennan. I draw the local habitat to capture its early growth, when it is in flower and as it starts to die back. It keeps me busy throughout the seasons.'

'Do reference books not provide—'

'I am my own reference book, Mr Pennan. I've learnt what I can from local sources, the rest I assume I am discovering for the first time.'

Had Mr Pennan known it, she was actually right. Velana was a unique habitat in a part of the Highlands few had discovered, fewer still who had an eye for the flora. 'One day, when time permits, I would like to do something similar,' said the Excise inspector.

'Then make time whilst you have it, Mr Pennan. I've never met anyone who could tell me when "one day" actually happens. For most, I don't believe it ever arrives. Drag yourself away from your work in case something unexpected prevents you from ever doing what you most want to.'

Cecil Pennan bowed his head, taking the sage advice on board. 'Well, Mrs McTavish, I won't take up any more of your time. I shall continue my walk.'

Lily watched the Excise officer as he stepped back onto the path. She wanted him to go, to leave her alone, but she also felt a reluctant tinge of sympathy for a man who rarely experienced human kindness in his pursuit to do what was right. She didn't like him but no longer hated him; if anything, she felt frustration that the one person to show any interest in the plants and animals of the loch had to be so different. A mixture of guilt and self-interest added to her frustration – they needed the Excise officer on their side until Wednesday at the very least. She relaxed her grip on the book.

'Mr Pennan, before you go, let me show you what I have drawn.' She sat down and waited for him to return. Hesitantly, and at a formally correct distance, Mr Pennan joined her on the grassy bank.

Lily edged closer. 'No need to worry, Mr Pennan, it is safe. Do as I ask on Tuesday and promise never to return wearing your official hat, and you'll have no future reason to fear my wrath.'

Chapter 77

'Well, Mother, what do you think?' Lil asked.

'That our daughter is playing a clever game. The man is obviously infatuated by her ...'

'That's down to us,' said Jade, glancing at Tily.

'... and, if he wants to come back, he knows what he must do to earn the privilege. If he succeeds in his task and decides to return, our daughter can then break it to him in any manner she so chooses that he is not welcome.'

'Tut-tut, Matriarch, that is not very nice,' said Tily.

'Cold and cruel, is that what we have become?' Jade asked by way of reprimanding her grandmother. 'If the man helps us, does he not deserve a reward? Making it so obvious he has been used will not endear him to us.'

'We have no further use for him, so what does it matter?' the matriarch asked.

'What is wrong with having a well-positioned friend to call upon when needed?' Lil asked, for once more inclined to agree with daughter than mother.

'Like Jack Vardy, you mean?'

'At one time he was a friend,' said Tily.

'One that ultimately betrayed us. We can do without that type of friendship. All we want is to be left alone.'

'We do, Matriarch, but sadly, life is no longer that simple. Threats from determined people like Jack are not so easily dealt with.'

'Yet you managed, Tily dear, didn't you? Jack did not get the better of you.'

Eyes turned to Matilda who, as a mortal, had struck up a close business and personal relationship with the Brethna Distillery boss. The bond had spawned the covert arrangement between the two distilleries.

'That is more Edith's doing than mine, though she might not be aware of it,' said Matilda, knowing that she was at last confessing a long-kept secret.

'What do you mean?' the matriarch asked.

'That you should thank her as much as me. We hardly had the closest of relationships and you all know why – some people will never accept an outsider.'

'It is wise for the Elders to always be on their guard,' Lil said, stating what should have been obvious.

'Something they did with commendable determination.'

'Come now, Tily,' said Lil. 'Not so bitter. The community has always come first – Jade will tell you that.'

'Us, our community – it amounts to the same thing,' said Jade scathingly, being more open about the spirits motivation. 'If we fight for one we fight for the other, so why try to be noble about our self-interest?'

'You still haven't forgiving us, have you dear?' said Lil.

'And you have never shown any remorse for what you did.'

'What we did, dear. Don't forget your part.'

'Girls, please, another time,' said the matriarch firmly. 'Tily, what on earth has Edith got to do with it?'

'Nothing directly but, through me, absolutely everything. I learnt from Edith that the best way to deal with outsiders was to treat them as she treated me – with caution.'

Matilda was a McTavish girl by marriage only. She had been born in Australia, but her roots were in Scotland, a country she came to live in as a teenager after both parents had died. It was then, whilst on a walking holiday with her uncle, that she had discovered The Hidden Lodge.

'In some ways, I'm responsible for what Jack has done,' Tily confessed candidly.

'How do you mean, dear?'

'The community needed money to survive – it was obvious even to Edith that the costs of maintaining the distillery and running the inn were not being met by the income that slid across the bar. So I took it upon myself to approach our friends on the Brethna Distillery board for help. None was forthcoming. Although they admired our stand, breaking the rules was not something they wished to emulate.'

'Cowards,' Lil proclaimed to the general agreement of the spirits.

'After the meeting, I retired to the Whisky Makers' Arms and, whilst I was confiding my troubles to Gus, Jack walked in. He was the youngest member of the distillery board and had been present when I put forward my proposal. We soon struck up a close friendship.'

'Which, considering you were married to Matthew, was very naughty,' said the matriarch. 'The priest was not at all pleased.'

'Well that makes a change,' Lil said sardonically.

'And I should have felt guilty about it, I know, but I didn't. Jack was intelligent, amusing and ambitious and, most important of all, he was on my side.

'So we helped one another. Through his introductions, I got to know influential people closely related to the distillery and, with his hard work and my charm, Jack found himself with the top job when it became vacant. In return, we got our arrangement with Brethna and the extra income that we needed.

'Well worth upsetting a priest over. Well done, dear,' said Lil.

'I must admit, I was pleased with myself. I'd achieved something that no one else had even thought about doing. With some that meant a lot and I felt more included as a result. Edith and the rest of the Elders even commended me for my efforts, but I sensed a resentment too. I soon realised that Edith would not like me whatever I did.'

'You two are going to get along so well when her time comes to join us,' Jade tutted.

'I doubt she expects to see you with us,' said Lil.

'Then it will be a pleasant surprise for her, won't it?' said the matriarch. 'Now, Tily, you had better tell everyone what happened next.'

'Jack's ambition, that's what. With my help, he had quickly risen to the top, but he wanted more. He had wanted me but, at the time, I was still married to Matthew. When he died due to his own stupid indulgence in the whisky ...'

'Quite,' Jade agreed.

'... I presumed he would act upon his intention, but for some reason he held back. I didn't realise till much later just how far his cunning stretched. His plan had always been to get his hands on our distillery and, to that extent, I was a means to an end. But I was not the landlady and did not have sufficient influence or power in our community for him to achieve his aspiration.

'So he lost interest in me and chose a different route, through a woman of social importance with an inheritance that gave him what he wanted. I had known her well, she was the daughter of one of his introductions and had become a good friend of mine.'

'Had he asked for your help before he abandoned you?' Jade asked.

'He had, but with Edith's attitude towards me, there was little I could do.'

'And if the circumstances had been different?'

Tily shrugged. 'The man was compelling. I think I could have resisted his advances for the sake of the community, but who's to say? As things turned out, I managed to get tangled up in the reeds before he announced his engagement to my dear friend. I never got around to telling the elders about Jack's ambition.'

'You could have told us,' said the matriarch.

'And what would you have done? Killed him?' Jade asked savagely.

'We have our ways.'

'Bad ways, Matriarch.'

'Which could have jeopardized our arrangement,' said Tily. 'Another man in charge may not have liked what was going on.'

The matriarch grunted, not at all taken by Tily's secrecy. 'In which case you are right, Matilda, Edith did save us, and you are responsible for what has since transpired.'

'That's a bit harsh, Mother,' said Lil. 'This situation would have happened at some time. Nothing Tily could have done would have stopped it.'

'Perhaps, but we are more resourceful when it comes to our interest.'

'Don't presume we are all with you in that respect,' said Jade. 'It's a mistake I would not like you to make.'

The matriarch sensed dissent amongst her daughters that she did not like. Nevertheless, she would do what she had to. 'Are you one of us?' she asked Tily, for the first time casting doubt on her inclusion.

Tily nodded. 'Yes, Matriarch, and, by being honest with you, I hope I have proved it.'

'Delayed honesty. That hardly counts, my dear. I will need you to put right what you failed to do during your lifetime if you want me to believe you.'

Tily nodded. 'I will travel with the Excise officer when he leaves and reacquaint myself with old friends.'

'Do that. When you return, and depending upon how you get on, we will talk again.'

'About?' Jade asked.

'Our adopted daughter's right to be considered one of us. The priest may decide it is time to allow her soul to rest.'

Jade shook her head. 'No, Matriarch. You and the priest will not make that decision. It is for Tily to decide, as it is for the rest of us. Do not interfere, I'm warning you. If you want me on your side, you will leave her alone.'

Chapter 78

'If there is enough light, I shall return this evening, otherwise you'll see me tomorrow,' said Jualth as she sat astride her horse outside the stables early on Wednesday morning. A party of well-wishers was there to see her leave.

Edith advised caution: 'Do not rush back on our account, dear. We can wait an extra day to see you home safely.'

'Just make sure you return with the agreement signed,' said Lily, 'otherwise tomorrow I shall be riding to Brethna myself.'

Jualth was on the trail of Mr Pennan who had left a couple of days previously. Lily had ridden the first couple of miles with him, ignoring his assertion that he now knew the route very well – an irksome fact that pleased no one and one she did not need to hear. What Lily did need, however, was to see him leave and to do so with one last abiding memory of his visit – the scars she openly displayed upon both neck and arms.

Jualth tightened the reins and called out one last word, 'Ned, look after this lot whilst I'm away. I'll hold you responsible if anything happens to them.'

Ned smiled and held up a hand to wave her off. Nothing would happen but, for someone who was considered to be part of the family, he would watch over them all the same.

The day was dry and overcast, perfect weather for a speedy journey, and Jualth reached Brethna in record time. At the distillery gates she stopped but did not dismount. It was a brief act designed to announce her arrival – a prelude to the duel that would soon follow. She steered her horse away and headed for the inn.

After freshening up, she lingered for an unrushed dram of courage in the company of the landlord. Much to her consternation, rumour had been rife since the re-emergence of the inspector on already vanquished land.

'I hope Mr Pennan has kept a diplomatic silence since his return, Gus.'

'Barely said a word. He was a very quiet guest.'

Jualth noted the use of the past tense. 'Was? As in …?'

'He paid his bill and left this morning, first thing. Should be well on his way to London by now.'

'But … but I thought …' Jualth could not believe it. The Excise officer had said he would attend the meeting and yet … 'Why did he leave, Gus?'

Gus held out his hands. 'He never mentioned a reason. His plan was always to leave this morning.'

As with Lily, who had not cared to pass on the blunt request she had made to the Excise officer, Jualth had not welcomed the idea of his presence – he might have seen things that troubled his innate sense of duty and changed allegiance again. But she had expected his presence and it was odd for him to say one thing and then do another. 'Did you see him after he delivered his report?'

'Only briefly. He was out most of the evening.'

'Out where?'

Gus shrugged. 'Maybe a stroll. He said he was partial to that sort of thing.'

'Nobody strolls in the dark, Gus, not in this climate. And if he went to see Arthur, why did he not stay with him again?'

'Perhaps because he did not stay with him on his first visit.'

That was news to Jualth, as it had been to everybody else in Brethna until Mr Pennan himself had revealed the actual lodgings he had stayed at. In the light of recent revelations, being a guest of Jack Vardy made perfect sense, as did the lack of an invitation on his second visit.

'I shall drop in to see Arthur after the meeting, find out how he's faring. Maybe we will yet see him back in his little hut.'

The landlord made no effort to rally to the suspended Excise officer's cause. Jualth looked at him curiously – someone had to occupy that hut, so why not a known and trusted individual? 'Tell me, Gus, what's the mood in Brethna? Are you for the merger or are you willing to show support for a beleaguered friend?'

Jualth had hit upon a sensitive issue; the backing she had presumed she could rely on appeared wanting.

'Jack is the person who pulls the strings around here and most of the folks hereabouts owe him their livelihoods. They trust him, and they trust his business judgement.'

Jualth could not help but feel disappointed by the landlord's answer. Despite the years of friendship and mutual benefit, Brethna's self-interest came first. Later on, she might be more understanding, but for the moment it just strengthened her resolve to fight for her own self-interest. She finished the whisky and bade Gus farewell, accepting the good luck offered as well intentioned if not wholehearted.

Jualth walked up the hill to the distillery where the smell of burnt ash still tainted the air. The effort of management to remove the offensive evidence would never wipe away the terrible memories of all those affected. The wounds ran deep, now more so than ever as guilt ran alongside blame.

At the gates, the door to the tiny hut was closed, so concealing the presence of the unknown figure inside. Jualth felt no compulsion to introduce herself or, on seeing the reconstruction work, to delay her entrance into the offices of administration.

Samantha directed her to the boardroom where she found Daniel waiting alone. His greeting was warm. As they sat in their accustomed positions, on opposite sides of the table, Jualth knew that his was the only friendly face she was likely to see for the duration of the ensuing meeting.

'You made good speed,' said Daniel.

Jualth was unsure whether he was commending her riding skills or warning her to slow down in future. 'Good speed for a good reason. Matters need resolving and the sooner the better.'

She was glad of a quiet moment with the cartman; they had some urgent catching up to do. 'Daniel, Jack had a meeting with Mr Pennan yesterday. Were you invited?'

'As a member of the board, Mr Vardy deemed it appropriate to include me. It was an interesting meeting.'

'In what way?'

Daniel quickly relayed the news: 'Well, to begin with, little was said by the board. James and Lewis were quiet throughout—'

'They always are, they're the boss's men and act accordingly. How about Jack? Mr Pennan should have mentioned in his report a certain trip to London that Jack made and the subject of poor maintenance at this distillery.'

'He did,' Daniel confirmed.

'And Jack's reaction?'

'Defensive. I could see these were matters he had not previously discussed with his fellow managers. Mr Pennan's words were unexpected and not well received.'

Jualth felt a certain sense of satisfaction at the thought of Jack Vardy's discomfort. 'What else did Mr Pennan say?'

'Apart from stating his findings and that he had visited you, little else. He was aware of our meeting today and thought that his report should be a topic for consideration between all members of the board. His superiors in London would then wait to hear from us. And after saying that, he rose sharply and left, allowing no time for discussion.'

Mr Pennan's behaviour continued to surprise. He was normally so courteous, aloft admittedly and partial to control, but always courteous.

Footsteps sounded in the corridor heading towards the boardroom. Jack Vardy entered followed by his underlings. James Gravid and Lewis Cravett took up their accustomed positions as did Samantha at the end of the table.

'I see everybody is here, so let's get going straight away,' said Jack, dispensing with any formal welcomes. 'This meeting was called a week ago to enable Jualth, in the interim, to discuss with her community the proposal made by the Brethna Distillery to purchase the Kvairen Distillery. In that time, members of the board have travelled to the Kvairen Distillery, spoken to its workers and to members of the community and been permitted a tour of the premises. We should like to take this opportunity to record in the minutes our thanks for such access.'

Jack looked at the representative of the Kvairen Distillery for the first time since entering the room, offering neither a word of greeting nor a sign of the friendship that had once existed between them.

'Well, Jualth, a week has passed and you have now returned. This indicates to me that you have had sufficient time to consider our proposal. The board would therefore be pleased to hear your response.'

His wish to gloss over the findings in the Excise officer's report and direct the meeting to matters that concerned only him was expected, but contrary to what Jualth had in mind. As all eyes focused on her, she slowly turned her head from side to side – this was one meeting where Jack Vardy would not dictate proceedings purely to his liking.

'A week *has* passed, Jack, and, in that time, events have rather overtaken your proposal. My mandate from my community today is to ask the board to reconsider the agreement put before it last week in response to those events.'

Jack put up his hand, determined to hold his ground. 'No, I am sorry, Jualth, that is not the purpose of this meeting—'

'I think Jualth should be allowed to finish what she is saying,' said Daniel, taking the unusual step of interrupting the chairman. The intervention elicited a sharp movement of heads and an even sharper rebuke – the chairman had no intention of letting the workers' representative or anyone else usurp his authority.

'Thank you for that *uninvited* contribution, Daniel—'

'I'm with Daniel on this point,' said James Gravid, creating a precedent that surprised everybody at the table.

'James …' Jack started, only to see his sales manager turn his head towards Jualth.

Although stunned by the sudden show of support, Jualth seized the opportunity to continue before the chairman could again intervene.

'Thank you, James, Daniel. I would like it recorded *in* the minutes that the board was not aware of the full facts when it voted and made its decision last week. At that time, I was not conscious of an agreement between the Brethna Distillery and the Excise Service that limited the potential liability suffered here as a reward for inviting Mr Pennan to inspect both our distilleries. Not a nice thing to do, Jack, especially when you consult no one before acting, not even your fellow managers.'

A sufficient pause followed the rebuke, enough to heighten the distillery boss's discomfort. Jack glowered, his skin turning crimson with his growing anger and embarrassment. He did not appreciate a public reminder of his underhand dealings.

'In the light of Mr Pennan's findings,' Jualth continued, 'none of us were aware, with the possible exception of you, Jack, that poor maintenance at this plant could have contributed to the fire that resulted in the deaths of two people. As a direct result of these findings, the agreed liability is likely to be re-examined by the Excise service, leaving Brethna's financial position in an uncertain, if not precarious, situation. That might in turn affect the willingness of backers to invest in your proposed enterprise. Would you agree with that, Daniel, James, Lewis?'

'Your comments are noted, Jualth—' Jack begun.

'More than noted I think, Jack,' said James, again interrupting when not invited or expected. 'The possible consequences of heavy penalties and the legal costs, if a prosecution for wilful negligence is pursued, are serious matters. If the insurance company – which has already paid a considerable sum in good faith – and the Excise Service reconsider their positions, the consequences could seriously undermine the financial strength of this company.'

James Gravid's comments caused considerable consternation amongst the other board members and complete astonishment to Jualth. She cleared her throat to regather the attention of those around the table.

'So, gentlemen, if your arrangement with the Excise Service was the unstated reason for not signing the agreement last week, then that reason is now nullified. Not only are you, Jack, responsible for the poor maintenance of the Brethna Distillery, you are also responsible to Lily and myself for the death of our loved ones.'

Jack glared at Jualth, who stared resolutely back. He looked fit to explode, unable to defend against the falsehood in Jualth's accusation as she lay blame solely upon him and his distillery. The casks in his warehouse may well have come from the Kvairen Distillery, but how could he prove it if the records showed the whisky to be a product of Brethna?

'You are a director as well,' Jack countered.

'I know I am, Jack, and if you can find any evidence in your precious minutes that I had anything to do with the running of your distillery, I will willingly go down with you. Failing *that*, how can you deny that the responsibility does not lie with you first and foremost?'

With the unexpected backing of the sales manager, Jualth took care not to alienate his support, even if, to a lesser degree, he shared in the board's alleged mismanagement.

'I'm giving you another chance, Jack. I'm giving the board another chance to enter an agreement that will allow the Brethna and Kvairen distilleries to continue trading as before and without further liability. And unless anyone has anything else to say, I would like to take a vote on it now, without delay.'

Jack looked around the table, to assess the level of support that remained on his side. Nobody had objected to Jualth's proposal.

'All right, Jualth, we might as well get this out of the way. Those in favour of the agreement for operations to continue between Brethna and Kvairen unchanged, and for a supply of unaltered Kvairen malt to go to an unknown third party, raise your hand.'

Jualth and Daniel raised their hands without hesitation. Heads now swung to James, who had his eyes fixed upon the table where the index finger of his right hand beat a regular rhythm upon the varnished wood. He looked up, not at his boss, but the purchase manager sitting opposite. Slowly, he lifted his arm to indicate his support for the motion.

Jack Vardy's countenance did not alter. Not one muscle twitched with emotion. After James Gravid's intervention, the likely outcome of the vote came as no shock.

'For the record, those against the motion.' He raised his hand, as did the purchase manager, his one remaining ally. 'It is therefore the decision of the board to ratify the agreement. Have you recorded that, Samantha?'

The secretary indicated that she had.

Jack Vardy leant forward as all eyes focused on him. Jualth knew there was something coming – Jack would not give in that easily. He stared at each person in turn before settling upon the one irritant doing all that she could to undermine the plans he had painstakingly taken years to prepare. Jualth stared back – neither were prepared to show the slightest sign of weakness.

'So, that is the decision of the board,' Jack stated, as if he was casting shame upon each of its members. 'But on an issue of this importance, which could have long-term implications for the company, I think it right to call a meeting of *all* shareholders to see if they are in agreement with the way the board deems fit to run this company. I therefore propose—'

'If I could just break in there, Jack, before you make a proposal to call the shareholders together,' James said quickly. 'I've got something with me that I think you should read first.'

James pulled out two envelopes from the inner breast-pocket of his jacket and handed one to the chairman.

'This is a letter from the shareholders you represent, Jack. They have full knowledge of these proceedings and would like their support for the agreement Jualth made in London to be made known. If you were to add their shares to the ones owned by those that have already voted today, there would be no change to the decision made by the board.'

Jack eyed the letter and then his sales manager. A supposedly loyal employee had clearly been acting behind his back. Such treachery came as a considerable shock to someone who had ruled unchallenged for nigh on twenty years. He tore open the letter and read its contents. It only confirmed the message his sales manager had already communicated. The name and signature at the bottom he knew to be genuine.

He felt the stabbing pain of cold steel in his back, inserted by those he had most trusted. The situation was serious: the possibility of a manslaughter charge for negligent maintenance of the plant was very real. The evidence from the Excise Service would be damning and, yet, it had so far withheld this information from the relevant authorities. That in itself was an extraordinary failing on the part of a public body. Powerful forces lay behind this omission but who were they and why were they conspiring against him?

Jack considered his own strengths. He had powerful friends also and if he could convince the other shareholders that culpability for the fire lay with the irresponsible actions of those to the east, then maybe he could turn them back in his favour. He was by no means ready to concede.

'How did you manage to get this letter written and signed?' he growled angrily at James Gravid. 'I do not accept that when I have spoken to all the shareholders …' He flapped the piece of paper in the air. 'That they'll be of the same opinion expressed in this letter. The composition of this Board will change James, and then this agreement—'

The sales manager handed Jack the second letter, refusing to cower in the face of his attack. He did not reveal its contents, merely watched and waited as Jack opened, then read. In the momentary silence that ensued, Jack did not move – nobody moved. The spell was only broken when a sudden, uncontrollable rage swept across the chairman's face. With his eyes bulging and the veins protruding on his forehead, he screwed up the paper, flung it on the table and stormed out.

Those that remained listened to the footsteps in the corridor and the slamming of his office door. There was a brief exchange of glances before eyes turned to the screwed-up piece of paper lying on the table between Jualth and Daniel. Lewis held out his hand, gesturing to Daniel to pass it over. Daniel obliged. Once read, an already stunned purchase manager went paler still and the paper slipped from his grasp and fell onto the floor. He glanced at James and then away, needing time to comprehend the message. No one tried to stop him when he stood up and made a dignified exit to the stairs leading to the rooms below.

Daniel glanced around at the remaining board members. 'Does that mean the meeting is over?'

'Not quite,' said James, 'we still have a sufficient number present for the meeting to continue and, if we are in agreement, I shall assume the role of chairman.'

For someone who had never sought to express a view beyond his remit, James Gravid's presumption to take control and lead was as surprising as it was swift.

'You seem to be the one person who knows what's going on, so by all means,' said Jualth.

Daniel nodded. He had no objection.

'Samantha, I wonder if you would note the change in attendance and then leave us for a moment?' James requested. 'I shall call you back when we recommence distillery business.'

Samantha did as instructed, closing the door on her way out.

Jualth glanced at Daniel who looked as perplexed as she did. She fixed her gaze upon the acting chairman. 'Well, in your own words, please.'

James looked at each of them in turn, quietly satisfied that events had gone as he had anticipated. In his early forties, and still with a full mane of hair, James Gravid had designs on making his elevation to chairman a permanent one. For that, he would require the support of the board.

'Please forgive the lack of warning. I need to explain, I know. It's the how that is the difficult part.'

'Why not start with Mr Pennan,' Jualth suggested.

James nodded. 'First, I think I should say that I've not gone out of my way to instigate what's just happened. It rather fell upon me and left me with little option but to carry it through. As you know, Mr Pennan presented his report yesterday. It came as a shock to us all, as did his abrupt departure. Jack asked me to follow him to make sure he found his way to the front gate and nowhere else. To my surprise, Mr Pennan asked to meet me outside the inn that evening. He didn't say why and it was only later, when we rode out of the village, that he revealed his purpose.'

'To visit the major shareholders,' Daniel said quietly.

'The trusting parents of dear, hard done by, Mrs Vardy,' Jualth added, knowing they were one of the main reasons Jack had held on to his power for so long.

'Indeed,' said James Gravid. 'Mr Pennan had wished to disclose certain information and acquire their opinions. However, on arrival, we found the need for disclosure unnecessary. Full knowledge of proceedings at Board level had already reached their ears and further additional facts too.'

'Not from Jack, I bet,' said Jualth. James confirmed her supposition. To Jualth, it meant one thing: word, by some unknown hand, had arrived from London. If only she knew who that hand belonged to.

James Gravid pressed on, 'Mr and Mrs Garvey – the parents of Mrs Vardy – were very forceful in passing on their opinions to me. Important issues that required their agreement had failed to reach their ears, either formally or informally. The fact that Jack had not said a word, just seemed to exacerbate another grievance they nurtured: his commitment to the distillery at the expense of his obligations to them, their daughter and grandchildren. For their part, they had offered unwavering support and financial backing to expand the works. In return, they had a sound investment but, after an initial show of attachment, little else.'

'In other words, they suddenly woke up to the fact that they were being used,' said Jualth. 'I'd like to meet them some day. We have much in common.'

'They expressed a similar desire to meet you. Mr Pennan spoke very highly of yourself and your sister.'

'He did what?' Jualth looked astonished. Shocks were coming thick and fast.

'The Garveys attended the service in the field a few weeks back; you probably don't remember them. They did offer their condolences at the end.'

'I don't remember much of that day, James, but I will make a note to seek them out. Now tell me about the letters. I have an inkling of the contents in the second but tell me all the same.'

James held back, preferring to deal with each letter in turn.

'The first instructed me to vote on their behalf to ratify the agreement. They were not without their misgivings – the lack of the other party's identity is as troublesome to them as it is to us – but they judged it preferable to the uncertainty that would otherwise surround the company's finances.

'The second refers to the matters I mentioned earlier resulting from Mr Pennan's investigation and the consequences of the fire. Ignoring the problem with the casks, your niece got into the warehouse because of the plant's poor maintenance and, if this became public, it would reflect very badly upon the distillery. In fact, it could cripple it and our community.'

'None of us want this to be made public, James. I'm sure Mr Pennan said many things to the two of us that will not feature in his final report.' Mr Pennan might be overlooking the rule book, but his superiors had the final say and, in obeying them, he was proving that he was as ambitious as the man sitting next to Daniel. 'You were saying, James.'

'That the second letter stated the Garveys' intention to call a meeting of all the shareholders with a resolution to remove the managing director from his position. With their votes counting against him, Jack would have lost control and found his continued presence at the distillery untenable.'

Daniel felt a tinge of sympathy for his departing boss, having neither the apparent ambition of James Gravid nor Jualth's desire for vengeance. They had worked together for many years. 'That must have been quite a shock for him, and perhaps a cruel one having spent his life building up this place.'

'It was either him or me, Daniel, and I'd have lost a damn sight more,' said Jualth, adamant that the right sacrificial lamb had perished.

'Even so, the distillery has been his life's work and he won't be happy to have lost it.'

'There's nothing he can do,' James assured him. 'He has no choice but to move on.'

'He's lost this battle, but there may be others, James, that's what Daniel is saying. It wouldn't be wise to expect Jack to leave quietly.'

A door opened and then slammed shut as heavy, deliberate footsteps pounded along the corridor and thundered down the stairs and out of the building.

'Goodbye, Jack,' Jualth whispered. 'Hopefully we will never meet again.' As the rumble of his noisy departure subsided, an afterthought threatened to deflate her moment of victory. 'Do you think he's cleared his desk, James?'

James understood the reason for the sudden panic. He was able to reassure her. 'All the documents that Jack or Arthur possessed that linked our two distilleries were confiscated by Mr Pennan. That includes everything in his desk and the minutes of these meetings. Using them against us would only have served to devalue his own shareholding.'

'And if he chooses to sell it?' Daniel asked.

'He must offer his shares to existing members first. He'll be sure to get the best price in return for a written condition that will govern his behaviour once they're sold.'

Jualth and Daniel admired the confidence of the sales manager. They did not share it. With or without powerful allies, Jack Vardy was not the type to submit to control.

'What now?' Daniel asked, resuming his role as workers' representative. 'Without Jack, who will run the distillery?'

'The best course of action is to set up a meeting of the shareholders,' James informed him. 'They should be updated and involved in the decision-making process. Assuming Jack will resign of his own accord, a new general manager needs to be appointed.'

'Will you put your name forward?' Jualth asked, with more than a passing interest. The future of the Brethna Distillery had just reached a watershed and, with it, its relationship with her own. The basis on which they were to continue was now of prime importance.

James answered without hesitation, 'Yes, I will.'

Jualth had her answer and, if this was the man she now had to deal with, so be it. However nondescript, he, like Mr Pennan, had eventually come to her aid. 'In that case, you will need support James,' she said, dangling her own shareholding in front of his nose. 'So, tell me, the business between our two distilleries, are you in favour of it continuing?'

Again, James did not hesitate. 'It's a good arrangement that has served us both well and without any looming Excise problems, we can all relax and look forward to a long, untroubled future.'

Jualth remained unsure; her faith and ability to trust business partners had taken a severe knock. He said the right things, or tried to, but Jualth did not intend being taken for a second ride, not by this man or any other.

'I agree with most of what you just said, James …'

'But … you still have a problem?'

'Aye, James, I do. Kvairen could do with a revision in our terms of business. We want more money.'

A slow smile crept across the face of James Gravid and then, amazingly, almost a chuckle. It seemed that his first act as general manager, if the position came his way, would be to favour another distillery at the expense of his own.

'Your request does not come as a surprise. Knowing Jack, I expect trade was weighted heavily in our favour.'

'I would not go that far, James. I do have some experience in business. *And* it was a little more than a request.'

James Gravid nodded, the smile still evident. 'I shall take the matter very seriously and can assure you that a revision in terms will be honoured if I am in a position to do so. I value your business, Jualth.'

As opening gambits went, Jualth felt entirely satisfied with this one. She even managed a smile of her own though a handshake, she later thought, would have served better, especially with a witness present.

'What about Arthur?' Daniel asked. Although not a worker he represented, Arthur was not badly thought of by the cartman, despite the unpopular position he held. With little personal gain for himself, all had benefitted from his tenure in the small Excise hut.

'That's not a decision for me or anyone else in the distillery, Daniel. I hope he won't suffer more than he has done so far and I'm sure a word can be sent to Mr Pennan underlining that we have no objection to his continued presence. The relationship between Brethna and Kvairen is a major reason for keeping him on.'

That was good news and a hopeful sign to pass on to Arthur when Jualth saw him later on. 'What about the agreement, James? I have all three copies with me; can they be signed now or does the shareholders' meeting have to take place first?'

'The motion has been passed by the board, so it can be signed.'

'And what about getting them to London?'

'Leave that to me. I can take care of all these matters and forward your copy on its return.' He pushed his chair back and stood up. 'First though, I have to find the company seal and then Lewis and Samantha. Both should be present.'

James left the boardroom leaving Jualth and Daniel as they had started. It was a moment to savour – Jualth had her agreement and had succeeded in ousting the man who had betrayed her. To her eyes, the meeting could not have gone better.

'You know, Daniel, I thought the world had ended last week and, if it wasn't for Mr Pennan, I'd still be of the same frame of mind.'

It was the most absurd statement Jualth had ever made. She was thanking an Excise officer for saving her life, a man she had utterly loathed for what she saw as a callous pursuit of duty. His transformation into saviour was still a difficult notion to grasp but, as she had what she wanted, grasp it she would.

'So, Daniel, when are you coming to see us again? What we thought to be our last batch will be ready for collection by the weekend.'

'Next Tuesday then, provided I get the go ahead from the new boss.'

'And we need our supplies replenished. Remind me to be very nice to James.'

They heard footsteps gathering in the hallway and then ascending the stairs.

'The signing party approaches,' said Jualth, the tension she had felt from the first moment Mr Pennan had entered Matilda's at last lifting. She sighed and then smiled. 'Daniel, I think we're almost there.'

Chapter 79

In relaxed mood, Jualth spent the evening attached to the bar of the Whisky Makers' Arms, where her company consisted of many agreeable admirers of old. Not all words were expressed in her favour, which to a degree she understood – Jack Vardy had been the distillery boss for much, if not all, of their working lives. His absence was bound to cause anxiety but, as she put it, if the distillery was truly well run, then there should be few problems when his successor took over. On top of that, they had the company of Lily and herself to look forward to indefinitely. This latter argument won the day, keeping spirits elevated for an extended session.

Earlier on, Jualth had visited Arthur and was pleased to find out that Mr Pennan had all but guaranteed his reinstatement. It had depended on one factor he had not been at liberty to divulge at the time. Jualth happily passed on the news that no hindrance to his reappointment now existed and, very shortly, he would be back in his little hut.

When she returned to Matilda's the next day, her fully restored smile was enough to tell the reception committee that all had gone well. Free whisky again circulated amongst the patrons, all of whom concluded that they would rather have assembled a Celtic army than succumbed to an invading force. Thomas went as far as to say that he had already designed their battle tartan and now felt a keen sense of disappointment that he could not wear it in the field.

Whilst Edith and Father Donald sat together in a corner of the lounge, where they could witness the proceedings in relative safety, Jualth and Lily found themselves slumped over the bar once more. A peaceful lull had fallen, a temporary respite before further re-enactments of imaginary battles.

'Just shows you, doesn't it,' Lily sighed.

'How quickly things can change?'

'How you should never take your family for granted. I never thought for one minute they would turn against Jack.'

'I don't know what I expected,' said Jualth, 'but definitely not aid from James Gravid. I had prepared myself to take on Jack and, in the light of the Excise report, force another vote. Faced with overwhelming opposition he should have backed down but, being the man that he is, his pride got in the way of his intelligence.'

All men had weaknesses and that included the former boss of the Brethna Distillery. 'Jack acted as if he had complete power over an empire where he lacked a controlling interest,' said Lily. 'He's paying the price for his vanity.'

It was almost sad to see the end of such a strong opponent, but not sad enough for either woman to feel much sympathy. He had shown none to them.

'Pity we can't afford to buy his shares,' Jualth sighed despondently. 'Perhaps I should write to William and ask for more money.'

'You will do no such thing,' Lily said sharply. She abhorred the idea but for totally the wrong reason. 'If you can't write to me you're certainly not writing to him. Besides, what if he finds out you can't spell?'

'I won't be writing in Gaelic, Lily.'

'Leave it to me. If there's any writing to do, I shall do it.'

'What do you want to write to him for?'

'I can think of a few things to say and as you're unlikely to write to Lloyd, regardless of good intentions, you're lucky you have me as a sister.'

Jualth put her arm around Lily and gave her a squeeze. 'You can be my secretary if you like. I shall dictate, you can scribe in your impeccable handwriting and then I can apply my seal.' The more Jualth thought about it, the more she liked the idea.

'Jualth!'

The women looked around. A certain someone farther up the bar had, in the guise of an erudite classical actor, just launched the landlady's name towards the rafters.

'Ned, this isn't the time,' said Jualth through gritted teeth, as the barman approached.

'Ah,' said Ned, raising his finger as if to make a point of order, 'but surely this is very much the time. With the agreement signed, are we not, and will we not for time immemorial be living in the Highland wilderness of *Jualth*?!'

Lily was even less amused by the barman's untimely observation. She found the whole issue highly vexing. 'Ned, keep your voice down,' she urged. 'There is no need to make the details in the agreement more widely known than is necessary. What would folks think if they got to hear?'

The question ushered a ponderous silence behind the bar, providing ample opportunity for Lily's vexed state to worsen.

'Ned, please tell me you haven't …' Lily stopped as Ned glanced knowingly at Jualth and casually wandered back the way he had come.

Lily turned on her sister – the signs of guilt were unmistakeable. '*Jualth* … not you?'

Her sister pleaded her defence, 'I didn't mean to, Lily, but I thought it only right that one or two leading members of our community should be made aware of the finer details. It's an official document, after all, and you know how powerless I am when it comes to officialdom.'

The owner of the sharpest ears anywhere in the Highlands chuckled. 'Well, there's a thing,' said Ned, 'I never thought to hear Martha being called a leading member of the community. She'll be thrilled to know it.'

Lily's jaw dropped. 'Jualth! You told your mother-in-law!'

'She got it out of me,' Jualth lied, having led a gullible listener to the very point where the naming of the community just casually slipped into the conversation. Jualth had rather taken to the idea and if that English queen could rename the whole of London after herself, then why couldn't she, in a far more modest manner, do the same with her tiny part of the Highlands?

'Jualth.'

'Yes, Lily.'

'No, Jualth, not Jualth … *Jualth!*' Her erudition did not match that of Ned's – the bile in her throat would not allow it. 'No, Jualth, it's your name and Ma christened *you*, not the community. We don't even know what the word stands for. It could mean anything.'

'It's got to be something nice otherwise why give it to me? And I, for one, like it, so you and Ned will just have to get used to it unless, of course, you want to tear up the agreement.'

Lily turned to Ned, scouting for support. Self-preservation told the barman to stay well clear – siding with one spelled trouble whichever option he took. However, on this special night, he went against his instincts and chose to live dangerously. 'I had to get used to it once; I dare say I can get used to it again.'

'There, if Ned's happy …'

'He didn't say that,' Lily snapped. 'He said he'll get used to it, just as we all will. Now wait here.'

'Wait …? What do you mean? Where are you going?'

'To the end of the bar for a quiet word with Ned.' The barman straightened – he had not expected such speedy retribution. Lily had second thoughts, at least as far as her sister was concerned. 'In fact, you can go to the other end where we cannot be overheard.'

With Lily gripped by one of her sudden mood swings, and Jualth the feeling that she was responsible, the landlady acquiesced – Ned would obligingly reveal all secrets later, when pressed.

'Can you believe my sister?' Lily moaned to the barman. She looked at Jualth who belligerently stared back from her exiled position.

Ned nodded. 'Uh-huh.'

'All right, so can I, but it still takes a nerve. How many people do you think know?'

Ned glanced around the lounge. 'Just that lot.'

Lily seethed with rage. 'What do you mean? How can they know, and I don't know that they know?'

Ned thought carefully, just to make sure he understood the question. 'I think it could be something to do with the way you threw that glass against the wall the other evening and then what you tried to do afterwards.'

Suggesting to Lily that the locals had a strong regard for her temper was, as Ned knew, a shrewd move – Lily enjoyed her reputation.

'So what have they been saying, then?' she asked.

'They also think that your sister has a nerve.'

'Good.'

'But they could also get used to it.'

Lily sighed. Sadly, she was not the only one with a fearsome reputation. 'Great! Why are people so submissive, Ned?'

Ned rubbed the stubble on his chin, feigning deep thought, the type that really tested Lily's patience. 'Maybe it's something to do with respect.'

'For Jualth?'

'Jualth for one, your mother for another.'

'What's Ma got to do with it?'

'You mentioned the reason yourself, just now. The name came from her, not your sister, and you know how people feel about Matilda.'

That explanation, again shrewdly made, helped but only a little; her sister still had one heck of a nerve. 'Why couldn't it be named after me?' said Lily, posing a bizarre question.

'*Lily!*' said Ned, not even attempting an erudite pronunciation.

'All right, it's a ridiculous name for a small community, I agree. Something else, then. Think of something else.'

Ned duly put on his thinking cap; Jualth had set out her store and her competitive sister on a quest to join her. Lily would only be happy when she too possessed something eternal. 'Umm, let's see now,' he said, preparing to run through the limited options, 'the inn is named after your mother, as is that large rock you dive from when swimming. Finlay Bay was named after one of the guys that dug it and who subsequently won the mass brawl to see whose name would be attached to it.'

'And we've only got his word that he won. Most were too drunk to remember why they were even fighting.'

'The loch is named after Velana, which leaves practically nothing, unless you care to have your name attached to the stables?'

'Who was she?' said Lily, appearing to trawl through centuries of folklore for a meaningful clue.

'Who was who?' Ned asked.

'Velana. There's no story attached to her; she never lived in these parts.'

'But she was a special person to one of the most revered priests who ever *did* live amongst us.'

Lily revered the priest as well, but not the unknown Velana. Did not a true kin of their native soil deserve some reward for the pain she had endured? 'That was centuries ago, Ned, and I reckon it was falsely attributed.'

'No, it wasn't.'

'Why wasn't it?'

'Why?' Ned tried to think of a reason. He was very attached to a name that conjured up the long, dark-haired figure of a lightly shrouded, beautiful Italian goddess. 'Look at it this way, what if, in a few centuries time, somebody felt the same need to rechristen a loch named after you. Those who bestowed the original name would not look kindly on their descendants.'

Lily's unreceptive glare said exactly what she thought about Ned's opinion and reasoning. It was evident that, for the sake of peace, the much-loved Velana would soon become the next person to disappear into the Highland mist.

'Finished your quiet word, Lily, dear?' Jualth asked when her sister strolled back along the bar. 'Care to let on?'

Lily did not.

'I will find out, you know I will.'

Quietly satisfied, the dial of Lily's mood swings once more flicked around to the amenable side. Whilst Ned found consolation in Jualth's life drawing, the two girls started to plot the tack that their future relationship with the Brethna Distillery would follow.

'James Gravid – can we trust him?' Lily asked.

'Our options are limited to say the least. He has a wife and kids who he likes to see, so I gather, which when balanced with his duties should be enough to satisfy his aspirations. Daniel and Arthur will watch him closely until we know him and his intentions better.'

'To avoid any misunderstandings and the fate of his predecessor, I think he should know from the start that we are not the sort of people who take kindly to being crossed.'

'I think he knows that already, Lily, and the fact that none of us really understand the reason for our reprieve should make him even more wary. There are forces at work here that none of us are privy to with the possible exception of those two over there.'

Jualth and Lily stared across the lounge to their grandmother and Father Donald. Neither could put their finger on it, but something was odd about their behaviour. They knew something, both of them.

'By the way,' said Jualth, 'before Mr Pennan left, and with the proviso all went well, I told him he could visit us again if he cared to expand his passion for the countryside.'

Lily looked aghast. 'Why did you do that?'

'Because he deserved an invitation.'

Lily for the life of her could not see why. 'I think what he put right went a very small way towards what he put wrong. There was no need to offer a reward.'

'No?'

'*No!*'

Jualth was not so sure. Even with the traumatic association, she felt Lily was not as opposed to the Excise officer's company as she made out. Her sharpness towards him was as much a fight against her own feelings as against what he stood for.

'I thought you had mellowed. He does share your interest, and he's the only one that does.'

'But he's still an arrogant taxman and an English one at that.'

'Oh, he is most definitely, but even so, I was never totally convinced by the reason for his return. Why should he, of all people, take the task upon himself and defy every principle that glued his rule-abiding body together? The man that returned was a different person to the one who had previously left.'

Lily found the inference extremely disturbing. 'I hope I'm not following your line of thought, Jualth.'

'He *is* a man and even the arrogant and very strange can be attracted by one of Scotland's finest, although, admittedly, he did not know at the time that the favoured one wished to kill him.'

Lily cleared her throat, hoping to jog Jualth's memory in the process. 'Are you forgetting I am a married woman, Jualth? The highly principled Mr Pennan is hardly likely to travel to Scotland in pursuit of a skirt that is already taken.'

'We're all entitled to have lives, even him. And as for you, I think it's about time you forgot Nathan. A miracle recovery will not happen.'

Lily could not disagree. With an abundance of spirit, but no husband and no child, what was she to do? Spend the rest of her life feeling sorry for herself? That wasn't her and never would be. She felt a sudden urge for the outdoors.

'I feel like a walk, Jualth. There are a couple of spirits I wish to talk to in my loch. Are you coming?'

Jualth glanced over to Ned. 'Will you be all right on your own?'

'Always at my best when on my own,' the barman answered brazenly.

'Really! Are you saying we're not needed?'

'I would never be so bold,' said Ned with continued light-hearted insolence. That said, his nagging landlady and sister could, with his blessing, vanish into Velana's mist.

And so they did, leaving by the side door and heading down a familiar track to a strangely unique loch that, to their way of thinking, had just survived its biggest threat yet.

Chapter 80

As the echo of the hour faded into the aether of the night, Henry Tombs and William Halar continued to wait for their long overdue guest. Three documents, plus pen and ink, rested on the boardroom table with a bottle of whisky and a tray of glasses to the side. In the fireplace, a fire crackled, sending fumes billowing up the chimney into the heavy, oppressive, chill air that blanketed London. It was the only sound in the Custom House that, apart from the presence of a trusted, skeleton staff, stood empty and in darkness.

A hansom cab rattled to a halt outside the main entrance and two figures, bedecked in beavers and long flowing cloaks, disembarked. Without a sideways glance, they ascended the three stone steps and disappeared unchallenged into the building. The cab driver pulled back the lever to secure the wheels, climbed down from his seat and warily scoured the hill to the east. No one had followed. To the west, Lower Thames Street trailed away past Billingsgate into the distance haze. The frugal light cast by gas lamps was sufficient to confirm an absence of life. Their discovery seemed unlikely.

He walked forward to check the bridle straps on each horse, then beat his leather-clad hands together in the cold, musky, smoke-burnt air. Looking up, a light moved on the second floor and three shadows passed by the landing window. He wrapped his arms across his chest and commenced a cautious circuit of the carriage, the only movement in the ghostly stillness of the deserted street.

A small tap on the door preceded the entrance of Mr Pennan escorting the two visitors. Mr Tombs and Mr Halar rose to greet them. Handshakes were exchanged, cloaks removed and hung, and a seat taken by each around the end of the table.

'Thank you, Mr Pennan. If you could wait outside, we will not be long,' Mr Tombs instructed his member of staff.

Mr Pennan withdrew leaving the four men to their business. The documents were handed to one of the gentlemen who grunted his approval for a moment that had taken longer to transpire than anticipated. He then passed the documents over to his companion who picked up the pen, dipped it in the ink, and signed each in turn. His seal sunk a round impression into the paper to the side of his signature, so completing the triumvirate of parties to apply their commitment to the contract.

'Mr Halar, would you care to do the honours?' Mr Tombs said, motioning towards the bottle. William picked up the unlabelled whisky and poured four glasses, handing one to Mr Tombs and to each of their guests.

'To the successful completion of a troublesome agreement,' said one of the gentlemen. The glasses were raised and a few satisfying moments allowed to pass. 'I'd like to say it's been a long time, but that would be a lie and for a man in my position that would never do.'

The man laughed, mocking his own inappropriate comment. 'I can see you are mystified by my remark, Mr Halar, and so you should be, but rather than explain myself, I shall allow Mr Tombs to reveal the intricacies behind my involvement once I have departed.'

'If I have your full permission, sir,' said Mr Tombs.

'You do, Henry.' He raised his glass. 'I wonder if we should drink to a certain Mr Vardy who, after a *taxing* few weeks, has inadvertently managed to bring greater order to our shameful lives. I must say, I do admire his ambition in wanting to own this most special of special whiskies. If only he could have appreciated the danger he was putting us in.'

The gentleman indulged in a satisfying gasp and looked at William. 'Still troubled, Mr Halar? Good, the slightest sign of you understanding my preamble would worry me greatly. You have acted honourably throughout, more so than me. Through necessity, all aspects of this matter have undergone close scrutiny, which includes its participants, I'm afraid. That's right, I know the reason for your actions and, for what it's worth, I thoroughly approve. I hope you will forgive the intrusion.'

The gentleman smiled and gestured to Mr Tombs. 'All will be explained, William, and soon. You have worked hard these past two years and gained admiration for your reliable counsel, though few, if any, have been privy to the purpose behind those efforts. Indeed, when you quietly allowed me to sample this very brand knowing, as you did, my leaning towards fine malt whisky, you could never have known that I had already tasted this gift from heaven. And, if I might observe, your expression now indicates my supposition to be true.'

William did not interrupt. Voicing his shock, outrage or any other emotion was of little use at this time.

'I was worried, very worried,' the gentleman continued, 'and it was only after speaking to Henry that my fears were allayed. I then understood you better, and in particular your complete reluctance to divulge anything further regarding its source. I wonder, did you not think it strange that I did not pursue you to name the distillery, or at very least, the supplier?'

'My efforts were to create an awareness and an interest whilst alluding to its scarcity. By not divulging the itinerary of my visit to Scotland, I had hoped to dissuade active pursuit.'

The gentleman laughed, impressed by the depth of the bridge master's loyalty. 'So you were playing with me, as I with you, two games that ended up with two winners and a loser who knew nothing of the rules that guided us.' He turned his head towards the commissioner. 'You will keep a close eye on Mr Vardy for me, Henry?'

'We will not lose sight of him, sir, rest assured. After a short period of reflection, we expect to see him back in the whisky business.'

'Where he belongs,' their guest decreed. 'Mr Vardy is a fascinating and first-rate businessman. He achieved considerable things at Brethna and I, for one, have no fears for his future.'

He raised his glass and sipped his whisky, his pleasure unconcealed. Those around the table respectfully followed his lead, remaining quiet and attentive. The gentleman laughed again and raised the document from the table to cast his eye over the signatures.

'Jualth – what an intriguing name. Where did it come from, I wonder?' He tutted, his admiration laced with a touch of sadness. 'But, if this agreement was challenged in court, it wouldn't stand a prayer. It has no legal standing whatsoever and, in law, the place doesn't exist, even if the young lady does.'

He glanced at both Henry Tombs and William Halar, unable to suppress a glowing esteem. 'Mind, I consider myself very fortunate to have witnessed her victory over Samuel, albeit from my darkened corner of the Highland Fires. She certainly knows her whisky and Samuel has yet to recover from the disgrace of his financial loss.'

'Samuel will survive,' said Mr Tombs, showing little sympathy. 'I dare say there's no more profitable establishment in the whole of London than that laudable whisky den.'

In contrast to their guest's light tone, William retained his serious demeanour. He neither understood the reason for the high level of importance attached to this matter, nor welcomed the covert scrutiny both he and Jualth had unknowingly suffered. Inferring that the documents in front of them were meaningless confounded him further. He sought clarification. 'Sir, if the agreement is not legal, what significance or binding value does it have?'

It was an understandable question if, as it appeared, it did not guarantee the future. 'Its value exists in what it has already achieved, William, as Henry will no doubt tell you. Beyond that, there is little I can or should need to say. As long as our Scottish friends believe they are safe, which I believe to be your primary purpose, and I get a guaranteed supply of their whisky charge free, how can anyone argue that this is not a worthy deal? Our Scottish friends have what they want and the country has its occupant prime minister at his best and, with the finest malt in existence, how can he be anything else?'

The gentleman smiled and held out his glass. 'If you wouldn't mind, William?'

Obligingly, William refilled his glass.

'Obviously, the risk is all mine whilst I remain in office, but who would suspect the highest public servant in the land of receiving unlicensed whisky? I hold a position beyond reproach, where integrity is not questioned and the duty to serve outweighs all private needs. I wonder why people are so trusting and where that perception comes from?'

It was a hypothetical observation with no discussion required.

'To a degree, it's true of course, and as long as the general public are informed on a need-to-know basis, why should we worry about minor transgressions? After all, are we not doing what everybody else does in their defiant battle against fiscal rules. We are not guilty of a crime but a blessing, for allowing future holders of my office to benefit from a great legacy.

'Indeed we are,' said Mr Tombs, approving of the tainted morals that also secured his own small, personal gain. 'Let's hope that our future leaders are not hindered or overscrupulous in their thanks.'

'Well, if they are lacking in gratitude, there are other considerations that should keep them in check, embarrassment to our noble office for one. The risk in this arrangement is minimal and only goes to add a rakish edge to our lives. As long as we can continue to trust each other, I foresee no problem.'

There were to be no worries on that account. The commissioner had handled the case with great care – he knew who he could trust in his department. 'Mr Pennan is a very loyal servant. His silence is assured.'

'Good, I like a servant who knows how the system works. Have you anything in line for him, Henry?'

'We will be discussing his future in the next few weeks.'

The gentleman laughed and sipped his whisky, delighted by the irony of everything: his government made the rules for the common man, knowing full well every effort would be made to bend, twist and break them in the pursuit of individual self-interest. Was he not acting in the exact same way, manipulating the system from the inside to make his life that little bit better?

'You did the country proud with your fight to retain London's most important landmark, William. I only wish I had held a higher office at the time to facilitate real and substantial help.'

'Your help would have been appreciated, sir.'

'You deserve this payback, that's the very least the country and your friends can do, though I can't see precisely how you benefit from the arrangement, apart from the odd bottle you can be certain I will direct your way.'

William put up his hand. 'I think that I should decline such reward—'

'I'm sure you do, William, but I shall personally overrule your reluctance. Henry has no such reservation and you have the same taste for whisky as we do. You will not be denied. I take it arrangements are in place for not troubling our friends in Scotland again, Henry?'

'Indeed, sir.'

'Good, then beyond the people in this room there'll be no additional sharing of Kvairen Whisky. The secret will be ours and stay ours until we hand it down to our lucky successors.' With a satisfying gasp, he finished off his whisky.

'I fear it is time to return to the ministerial office, lest search parties are dispatched. We have our copy of the agreement, which we shall conceal well. The remaining two I shall leave for you to deal with, Henry. I trust the recipients will, likewise, conceal them well.'

'We'll make sure they do,' said Mr Tombs.

'Good. I will take my leave then, gentlemen, and await, with great anticipation, my first *official* delivery.'

He chuckled again as the men rose from their seats, shook hands and, with the two visitors re-cloaked, were guided by Mr Pennan to the front entrance.

The two remaining members of the meeting returned to their seats. Henry Tombs poured his friend a final whisky to mark the end of a successful evening and a lengthy saga. 'An interesting meeting,' he ventured to suggest, noting William Halar's inclination to agree. 'But, unsurprisingly, you are still troubled and require further clarification.'

'If you wouldn't mind, Henry,' William said stiffly. 'Up until this evening, I had presumed that glass of whisky I gave to you and to our guest, a couple of years back, was the first time either of you had tasted Kvairen. That assumption now appears misplaced.' As the meeting had progressed, he had felt more and more like a very small, unwitting pawn on a grandmaster's chessboard.

'Some had a lot to lose if news spread beyond the close confines of those already in the know. The knowledge had to be guarded, hence you were kept in the dark.'

Although a prominent public figure with high integrity, the lack of confidence shown towards him, and the surveillance upon his person, again indicated a matter of great importance. He hoped for a better understanding.

'When young Mrs McTavish turned up and then you turned up, everything changed, William. The truth is, we already knew about that tiny, hidden enclave in the Scottish Highlands. Exactly how it came to our attention in the first place, I don't really know. Let's just say it happened a long time ago and, for the same reasons that brought about the very arrangement we have put pen to paper to this evening. When Mr Vardy called us in, he threatened a situation that our departed guest was keen to maintain. The boss of the Brethna Distillery became a significant problem but, with this agreement and the help of the young woman, we have managed to restore matters to their former state.'

William felt for the first time an inkling of sympathy for Jack Vardy. He also had suffered the questionable pleasure of being a small pawn in a bigger game. 'How did the whisky find its way to London?' he asked, peering into his glass.

Henry Tombs smiled, wondering if his companion had actually worked it out and was merely seeking confirmation. 'Through the cloaked hand of the Church, William, how else?'

William nodded – the close confines of those in the know seemed to engulf every revered and trusted institution in the land. He recalled an incident he had witnessed in Scotland, the sudden departure of a stranger in the company of Father Donald by the graveyard. Perhaps he should have pursued the priest for an explanation, but why suspect the Church in such an unlikely conspiracy?

'I can only assume that, whatever happened all that time ago to prompt this arrangement, it possessed the same motives as you have demonstrated – to protect a small community and its whisky from outsiders. You may have a better understanding of the why, having been there.'

William understood his own motives but nothing more. If anything had happened in the past and the knowledge handed down, then their confidence again did not stretch to cover him. 'I take it the Church will no longer have a role to play in this deception?'

'I should imagine their involvement will remain concealed and, in time, be forgotten. As the community does not know of the part it has played, there seems little point in revealing it now.'

'Someone must know.'

Henry Tombs shrugged. Perhaps they did, but he offered no confirmation.

'So when I invited you to my office to update you on the reconstruction of my bridge, you already knew.'

'As I have said, William, my predecessor passed the knowledge onto me and only me. I must take care to do the same. You should understand the dangers by now of involving another. You, yourself, were taking a considerable risk by implying there was an unlicensed distillery out there.'

The decision to do so had not been an easy one, nor living with the subsequent doubt of having done so. 'I found it hard to believe you did not already know, but instead of concluding that you actually did, I assumed it was only a matter of time, with or without my help. Having stated my interest, I hoped to be privy to any subsequent move.'

'We offered them no threat, William, and we knew they offered no threat to us. Unfortunately, the same could not be said for the other distillery, hence our inspector's visit. We needed to know the risk to our supply of whisky if we brought the Kvairen Distillery into line and, judging by Mr Pennan's appraisal of young Jualth McTavish and her community, that risk was high. Your connection then became very important to us.'

It should have been the other way around – the battle of the individual against the rules laid down by state institutions, not the institution's desire to help the individual defy those that governed them.

'So an option for me to remain detached did not exist?' said William. 'If I had not sent my Hawk to set up a meeting …'

'I would have come to you,' Henry Tombs confirmed. 'Your contact with Mrs McTavish was vital. We did not hesitate once we knew you were on our side.'

William almost smiled, and then tried to laugh. He could do neither; the deception had a bitter twist. 'All those hours, Henry, hours upon hours of getting to know people through my connections with the bridge. And all with one purpose.'

William picked up his whisky, his mind retreating back two years to his first kiss with Jualth under the trees by Jade's Fall. How he had wanted to kiss her back.

'And now I discover that a far more powerful hand, with its own vested interest, had already been looking out for those people and my time could have been spent … there was no need for me …'

William stopped. The regret in his voice barely reflected the pain he felt. He had played a vital role, so Henry had told him yet, somehow, he doubted his significance. Without him, the powerful hand would have found another way to maintain its vested interest. The commissioner's words that followed, although meant well, only exacerbated his pain.

'But you did give your time, William, and we all know why; I saw the reason for myself when she came to my office as did our friend whilst in the Highland Fires. You saw a threat of prison to that young lady and you would have done anything to prevent it, even if it meant taking her abroad and never returning. I wonder if she knows how lucky she is to have you as a friend?'

It was a sobering thought on which to end the evening.

Chapter 81

On Sunday morning, Jualth and Lily left Matilda's for the adrenalin rush of an early-morning gallop. Glades and forest trails were tackled with equal vigour as two battle-hardened competitors embraced a contest to match the hazards of their encounter with the Excise Service. With victory tales concocted, embellished and retold each evening, life in the community stood little chance of returning to normal until Daniel and a cart laden with supplies arrived from Brethna.

Jade's Fall received a visit and the spirits of the departed were consulted. All seemed content and vowed to look out for every living soul that similarly looked out for them.

Returning via the northern hills, they met up with Velana's feeder stream and followed its winding course until they reached the Kvairen Distillery. It sat void of activity, the wooden waterwheel motionless against the stone wall as it waited for the grinding of grist to recommence.

'As impressive as any sight I saw in London,' said Jualth. 'Putting a flame to her would have been a great shame.'

'Aye, but if you hadn't, I would. This is our distillery – we built it and we own it.' No outsider would ever benefit from spoils unfairly gained from them.

They rode across the stream, around the storage annex and into the empty courtyard, where the unexpected sight of the workshop door swaying in the breeze caused both to pull up.

Jualth struggled for an explanation – there were no other horses in sight. 'Someone must be inside,' she said.

'But nothing's going on in there!'

'Perhaps Thomas walked up from his cottage,' Jualth suggested.

They dismounted, tied their horses to the hitching post and rushed into the workshop only to find it empty. The wide central corridor that ran the length of the two adjoining buildings was no different. They stood still and listened. Apart from the familiar whistle – the passage of air blowing through the wooden end panels – there was no sound, only an eerie, unaccustomed silence.

Jualth called out, 'Thomas, is that you?'

The cry went unanswered. Lily scurried down the stairs into the storage annex, whilst Jualth headed for the doors lining the corridor.

Lily quickly returned. 'No one there, Jualth, it's deserted.'

Jualth swung around. 'Someone must have forgotten …' She stopped in midsentence, her eyes fixed on the wall above her sister's head.

Lily turned to look, backing several paces along the corridor as she did so. 'It's gone, Jualth! Your plaque … it's gone!' Each stared in bewilderment at the empty space. 'Why would anyone ...?'

Stunned by its disappearance, Jualth glanced around, hoping to lay her eyes upon the missing object. 'No one should have taken it down without first asking me,' she said. Her stomach suddenly churned in a fit of anguish. 'Unless … unless they had no intention of asking me.'

Lily stared at her sister as an obvious culprit and bearer of grudges came to mind. 'You don't think Jack …?'

Jualth flew into a fit of rage. 'Yes, Lily, I do. A once close friend is making sure we never forget him.'

Lily twisted the heel of her boot angrily into the floorboards. 'How dare he! People should know when they are beaten and quietly stop breathing. He's stolen our curse, Jualth. That wretched man has stolen our warning to those that cross us.'

It was a petulant act that, in Jualth's opinion, was beneath her former adversary. 'Why didn't he just set fire to the place? Taking the plaque is maddening, but there's far worse he could have done, like incinerating a distillery that does not exist. That's the way to put pay to a curse.'

'And it's also a way to upset our unknown friends in London. Whatever his motive, he had the intelligence not to incur their displeasure.'

'I want it back, Lily. I want it there, above the entrance where it's meant to be.'

Jualth growled, infuriated by the theft. What was he trying to do, make them feel vulnerable by removing a symbol of protection? That was petty. How could he ever consider her small community that superstitious? But if not that, what else? Would he allow others to see the plaque so they could put the letters together and form a word that could lead to their discovery? If so, perhaps they were still in danger and maybe the addition of her name had been a very selfish and silly mistake. 'Were you thinking of writing to William soon?' she asked her sister.

Lily looked quizzical.

'If you were, you might care to mention the unlawful removal of Albert's plaque and ask him to keep his eyes open. I'm sure Jack has a purpose in mind. It could turn up anywhere.'

Lily thought it unlikely. Having committed the crime, Jack was hardly likely to facilitate its return. 'We will never see it again, Jualth, with or without William's help. It's gone for good.'

'No, Lily, not for good; the spirits will not allow a permanent loss. One day they'll help us find it and when they do, one of our girls will place it back on the wall where it belongs.'

2003

'Go on then, Janie. You have a prophecy to fulfil, so get up the ladder and do as Jualth told you.'

The order came from Sally McTavish, who stood holding the plaque for her daughter – the current innkeeper of Matilda's.

'Shouldn't it be you doing this, Ma?' Janie asked. The honour of performing the task suddenly seemed daunting.

'It should be Annie, she's the one who found it.'

Janie's eyes flicked to the small group that had assembled for the ceremony, as if searching for her older sister. The company included Tommy and Jim – the retired distillery boss and his successor – Janet her grandmother, and Grandma Mary, the oldest generation of her family.

'But she isn't here, so up you go,' said Sally. Janie needed no further prompting and stepped onto the ladder.

'I never thought to see the day,' said Grandma Mary, as she watched Janie's short ascent. She had waited longer than any living resident in Jualth to witness its return.

'Nor me,' Janet whispered with equal reverence. 'It's a shame Annie chose to leave for London instead of staying to witness it.'

Sally brushed away the flaps of the cloth that covered the plaque and held up the heavy, metal object for Janie to grab with both hands.

'Is that straight?' Janie called down, after placing it on the hook.

'Get your head out the way and I'll tell you,' said Sally.

Janie obliged.

'Round to the right,' said Sally, motioning with her hands in a clockwise direction. 'Aye, that's about it. Come down and have a look.'

Janie quickly stepped down and stood back with the others to admire Albert's beautifully crafted masterpiece. The story of its appropriation had, at last, come full circle with its recovery.

'Welcome home,' said Grandma Mary on behalf of everyone. The plaque showing Jade's Fall – with its misspelt message of vengeance – once again hung from its rightful place, cautioning all who wandered in of the consequences of betrayal.

'Perhaps you boys can do something to fix it securely,' said Janet.

'Leave that to me,' said Jim. 'If anyone has a mind to steal it again, they'll have a need to take the wall with them, as well.'

'Did anyone remember to bring a bottle with them?' Sally asked. It was a surprising oversight considering the occasion.

'I'd prefer not to disturb those maturing in the warehouse,' said Jim.

'In which case, everyone is coming back to Matilda's,' Sally ordered. Having recently bequeathed the role of landlady to her youngest daughter, it would take a while to stop treating the inn as her own.

With the ceremony concluded, its participants slowly filed out through the workshop and into the courtyard. Only Janie loitered to stare up at what to her had always been an empty space.

'There you go, Jualth, and you too, Lily. It's not just a tale any more, we actually have it back.'

She picked out the letters scattered over the plaque's surface and reflected on the woman who had bestowed her name upon their community. An impish smile crept across her face, 'I wonder …' she whispered. She recalled the picture of Jualth that now hung in Grandma Mary's cottage. In that alone, she had the answer she needed – the new landlady and her distant ancestor were very much alike. The horn of Sally's car sounded in the courtyard and Janie dragged herself away from the passageway and the Kvairen premises, locking the door as she went.

1896

'Anything else you want to tell William in my letter?' Lily enquired.

Jualth looked at her sister suspiciously, wondering why she had asked. 'You can tell him how much I miss Mrs Tuckle, if you like.'

'That's not what I meant, Jualth, and you know it. You have other news – I know you do. I'm just not sure whether you wish to tell William, that's all.'

Jualth was taken aback at the speed her sister had uncovered her secret. 'You know?'

Lily stared back but did not answer; it was for her sister to tell.

Jualth lowered her eyes, put her hand to her midriff and rubbed it gently. The act served to confirm Lily's suspicion.

'Sure Frazer had nothing to do with it?'

Jualth shook her head. 'No, Lily, this one belongs to William.'

Lily feared as much. 'Jualth, what have you done? You may not have been wearing black, but you were still in mourning.'

Jualth shrugged but made no attempt to excuse her actions.

'What about Martha? She has a right to know.'

'William and Frazer are not dissimilar in looks or size,' Jualth started.

'No, Jualth, don't even think about concealing the child's true parentage. Martha will hear from your lips or mine.'

The early shoots of Jualth's plan to explain the birth of her second child had just hit a major stumbling block. A battle against Jack Vardy was one thing, against her sister, quite another.

'You're sure the child belongs to William?' Lily asked again.

'No doubt at all,' said Jualth. 'I would not have minded Frazer being the father, but he isn't. I'm carrying William's child and I'm proud to do so. But as for telling Martha …'

'Jualth!'

'*No, Lily*, this is not something I'll allow her to put in her little book. I must think of William and his position. If we jeopardise that, we jeopardise us. I'm not ashamed of what I've done and if people guess, *they guess*, but they'll receive no confirmation from me.'

Secretly, Lily could not have been more delighted that another child would soon be screaming its head off in Matilda's. But she had serious reservations about her sister's reasoning.

'And William?' Lily asked again. 'Do I tell him or not?'

Jualth had already decided; she had no intention of concealing the matter from him. 'Put it in your letter. He has a right to know and tell him when his daughter is old enough to understand, and can be trusted, she will know the identity of her real father.'

'Are you trying to drag him away from London?'

Jualth shook her head. 'Quite the opposite. He now has even more reason to look after our interests from afar. I will not see William again. He has made his choice, we both know it.'

Lily agreed, but only to a point, doubting the willpower of any man to stay away from a daughter spawned by a union with her sister. She did not rule out the possibility of some sort of future meeting. 'I thought William had betrayed us and you were too close to see it,' she admitted openly. 'Did you not think it yourself? You must have had your doubts.'

'No, Lily ... *none*. You remember me telling you of the time we kissed at Jade's Fall? Well, just before our embrace, the tale of our whisky cropped up. I did not realise it then, only when in London, but those few words were the reason he left me. If we had been licensed and legal, he would have stayed, I'm sure of it. He left to look after us, all of us, not just me and not just the whisky.'

The explanation made some sense, but Lily could still not banish all her doubts. 'Did he take the bottle?' she asked cautiously.

'With a purpose, Lily, and not for his sole use.'

'Are you sure? What's in this arrangement for him if not our whisky?'

'I hope he will get our whisky, the odd bottle, but as I have already mentioned, he did this for us and not himself.'

Lily narrowed the list down. 'For you, Jualth, not us.'

Jualth did not much care for her sister's scepticism. 'All right, have it your own way. Maybe he did just do it for me, in which case, perhaps I should reward him by taking his child to London and becoming an honourable housewife.'

'You will not go and live in London,' Lily said firmly. 'For one, you hate the dirty, smelly town and for two, I refuse to be left alone. Except for Grandma, and she won't be around for ever, you and Jessica are all I've got. You're going nowhere.'

Jualth smiled; she loved it when her sister reminded her of the closeness of their bond. 'It's a maybe that will never happen. One day, I'd like to think one of my girls will sit in William's office, as I did, and feel she belongs. But it will not be me. William is gone for good.'

The whistle of the wind breathing Highland life into and through the distillery brought the subject of William and his chapter in their lives to an end. It was time to move on. Jualth peered up at the empty space.

'To the devil with Jack Vardy and wherever he's taken our plaque. We have all that we want and he, our enemy, is a beaten man.'

'Aye, Jualth, and if the devil cares to cause us any more trouble, we'll remind him of Jade and deal with him in the same way.'

Jualth laughed; the comment, although made in jest, somehow rang a fearsome truth. 'You know, Lily, sometimes I think we are not the nicest of people.'

'Whoever said we were? But I can live with it – can you?'

To protect her family and her community, Jualth could live with it. Neither was likely to ever change. 'Shall we go?' Jualth asked, feeling the urge to recommence her duel through the glades.

'Aye, why not?' said Lily.

They backtracked through the workshop and into the courtyard, shutting the door behind them. In the stillness, the only noise that lingered was that of the breeze blowing through the timbers and the fading sound of horses galloping into the distance.

2003

Annie stood on the central arch of Old London Bridge, facing east. It wasn't a view that entirely pleased her, in fact much of it made her very angry. But Annie McTavish had a way of changing things she did not much care for, warning signs she had aptly demonstrated on her election to the post of bridge master.

Six McTavish generations since Jualth had passed, but only one Halar since William, and Wil – William's son and Annie's predecessor – had already travelled to the far reaches of the Scottish Highlands to catch up on a hundred years of family history.

'Good luck, Wil, enjoy your retirement,' Annie whispered into the autumn breeze. Her family connection had never been openly revealed – her relatives had a habit of keeping important matters to themselves until the very last moment. A call home on her return to London had confirmed what had taken three years of living in the city to work out for herself. It was only then that she fully understood the urge that had compelled her to desert her home and live down South for good.

In Annie McTavish, Old London Bridge now had a new master, a descendant from the briefest of liaisons between two proud, determined people, who cared deeply for their respective communities and histories. It was now Annie and Janie's charge to carry forward the fight against the threats posed by an encroaching, ruthless, modern world. It was a task in which neither intended to fail.

Author's Note

The first committee to discuss the amalgamation of the Customs service with the Excise service took place in 1862–63 (*Something to Declare* by Graham Smith, 1980), but amalgamation did not take place until 1909. At that time, staff from the Excise moved from Somerset House to the Custom House in Lower Thames Street. However, for the purpose of this novel, as the main storyline is set over a decade prior to this date, I have slightly deviated from the actual timeline in my portrayal of the fictional Excise Service. To minimise confusion, rather than refer to the Inland Revenue (of which the Excise department was a part) or the Customs service, I have simply made reference to the Excise Service and aspects of it throughout the book.

I also wanted to write a story that included a historical and well-known London feature that sadly no longer exists. Although there is a functional road today, London Bridge has been remembered and reimagined in one of its phases when buildings ran from the southern to the northern banks of the Thames. *Old London Bridge* by Patricia Pierce (2001) was an excellent reference book in this respect.

Printed in Great Britain
by Amazon